Vivienne Kelly was born and educated in Melbourne, where she now lives. She has worked in university administration, and has a PhD from Monash University on myth and history in Australia. *Cooee*, her first novel, was shortlisted for the *Age* Book of the Year in 2008. 'Passion Fruit' was included in *Best Australian Short Stories*, and 'The Third Child' won the *Australian Women's Weekly* short-story competition. *The Starlings* is Vivienne Kelly's latest novel.

For RJWS

Cooee

Vivienne Kelly

TEXT PUBLISHING MELBOURNE AUSTRALIA

textpublishing.com.au

The Text Publishing Company
Swann House
22 William Street
Melbourne Victoria 3000
Australia

First published in 2008 by Scribe Publications
This edition published in 2017 by The Text Publishing Company

Cover design by Sandy Cull, gogoGingko
Cover images from Shutterstock
Page design by Jessica Horrocks
Typeset by J&M Typesetting

Printed and bound in Australia by Griffin Press, an accredited ISO/NZS 1401:2004 Environmental Management System printer

National Library of Australia Cataloguing-in-Publication entry
Creator: Kelly, Vivienne, author.
Title: Cooee/by Vivienne Kelly.
ISBN: 9781925498066 (paperback)
ISBN: 9781925410426 (ebook)
Subjects: Interpersonal relations—Fiction. Families—Fiction. Domestic fiction, Australian.

Part One

Who am I? It's a good question, when all's said and done. It's something I often ponder. To Sophie I am Gandie. To Kate I am Mum—a nice, normal name, which absolutely fits, given that Kate is such a nice, normal person. To Dominic (who repudiates relationships filial or maternal, doubtless for his own good reasons) I am Isabel. His partner Paula doesn't call me anything at all. To my sister Zoë, for reasons relating to a childhood joke long since forgotten, Minky. (Interestingly, I never had a name for Zoë. She was just Zoë.) My oldest friend and professional partner Beatrice calls me Izzie. I detest the name, but she's always done it.

To Max I was Belle. Belle, Bella, ma belle.

The hapless Gavin calls me Millie. This is because he has constructed and sportively elaborated an acronym for Mother-In-Law. When I say that this is one of Gavin's better jokes you will have some idea of his general standard. And Liam of course knows me as Gandie, because that's what his sister calls me.

What's a name, anyway? (Others have said this before me, I know.) It's a handle, for our acquaintances and relatives to use in their dealings with us. It's a handle that frequently tells us more about the people using it than ourselves.

I don't have a name for myself. Do any of us? Do we

create names for ourselves, to add to our comfort or security or confidence or simply for a welcome clarification of one's role in a complex and bewildering world? I don't. I change, as chameleons are supposed to do (although I never really believe that's true: it seems one of the unlikelier myths, like pelicans piercing their breasts for blood—so implausible when you think of it, given the shape of a pelican's beak—or phoenixes being reborn from their own ashes); I change depending on who I am with, who is conversing with me, seducing me, launching the current demand at me. Sophie draws my sweetness, Kate my anger, Dominic my yearning.

Yet it seems to me I must somehow—mustn't I?—be more than the sum of the parts I play. I don't believe anybody profoundly knows me—least of all my granddaughter Sophie, who loves me best, and to whom in curious ways I feel closest.

But there's nobody now who takes in the whole inchoate lump of me, who understands the messy ins and outs, who gets past the particular stereotype he or she has constructed to deal with the tricky thing—the problematic and demanding thing—that the relationship with me seems always to turn into.

The acerbic mother, the resentful daughter, the thorny little sister, the distant wife, the passionate lover, the indulgent grandmother. How we all rely on these paradigms to navigate ourselves through the maze of communicating with people, of relating to our relations!

I've created stereotypes of my own, of course, for them. Kate is the dutiful daughter; Dominic the edgy, prickly, whimsical son; Zoë the irritating authoritative big sister. It's a matter of expectation—especially, I suspect, where one's children are concerned.

When those small explosive bundles of babies burst into our lives, each is freighted with its burden of parental expectations.

I expected my children to be good children; I expected to love them; I expected them to love me. I wouldn't have been surprised, oddly, by major reversals: I wouldn't have been amazed to find a bit of hatred in the mix, because hatred is passion, almost a part of fierce loving. What I didn't expect were the minor blemishes, the trivial flies in the ointment. I didn't expect to be annoyed by them, to find that they produced inconsequential but perpetually discordant notes in the harmonies I was trying blindly to build into my life, the music I was trying to live.

You would die for your children. You would kill for your children. I thought it would be like that, and it was. Even when you don't like them much, you'd still die for them. It's such a big, sweeping emotion, you expect it to carry everything before it like a vast thundering avalanche, and instead it gets tripped up and subverted by pebbles, branches, bits and pieces aggravatingly strewn across the course of every day.

Children are the centre of one's emotional existence, the fuel for all one's hopes, the source of one's most profound joys; they are also bothersome and inconvenient and exasperating. This is the ambiguity no one is prepared for before actually becoming a parent; it is also the tiresome truth not enough people admit to after becoming one.

But my grandchild slid into my world without beforehand arousing my expectations, and I was therefore unprepared for her. When Kate put her into my arms with that fey and timorous smile of hers that always infuriates me even as it moves me, I had not anticipated the great surge of passion that flooded my body.

I gazed into Sophie's pale squashed face with its eyes closed into slits and its black eyelash silk forming a short fine crescent on either cheek. I started to tremble and I was afraid I would drop her. I sat down, abruptly, and admired this tiny, new person.

I tried to stop the tears from rising. I glanced up, and saw Kate's face, which was now apprehensive, fearful.

Why must she always want my approval? I wondered, vexed with her for not looking proud and triumphant, as a woman should look who had produced such a miracle.

'Do you like her?' asked Kate.

'Don't be silly,' I said. 'How could I not like her? I adore her.'

'She is gorgeous, isn't she?' As if Kate needed to be reassured, I thought; as if she had to be told her own daughter was beautiful. Where were her wits?

'She's very gorgeous,' I said, steadily, still trying to deal with all this starry blood that was flushing through me, scouring my veins, thumping behind my eyes. 'Very beautiful.'

Kate leant back on the pillow and closed her eyes, as if vindicated.

It is an interesting question, this one of grandchildren. I think one of the reasons they tug at us so is that we have lost the bounce we had as parents: we are older and tireder and less elastic; we sag more, emotionally. We have lost our brightness. We have disappointed the people we love; they have disappointed us. The new child is the opportunity for a new relationship; it offers the chance of being a new person, one who is still bright, who does not disappoint.

I have tried never to disappoint Sophie. As she nibbled her way into my heart with her pearly little teeth, I did not need to try to love. But I have tried to be loveable. I have consciously tried to attach her to me, tried to beckon and fascinate and hold her, in ways I never tried with my own children—or perhaps was not capable of, with them.

Perhaps I give in to her too much. There was a curious incident when she was five or so. We had been shopping, and it turned out that what she wanted most in the world was a string of lilac beads. It was a small-enough thing, and I had no idea Kate would disapprove. Truly, I did not.

When we returned, the child with her sparkling trophy (I have to admit, they were dreadful, tawdry things, but she was only young after all) strung around her neck, Kate pulled me up sharp.

'I don't allow her to have jewellery.'

'For heaven's sake, Kate. It's a string of beads.'

'I don't think little girls should wear such things. You never let me wear them.' Suddenly Kate's eyes are brimming with tears; she is screaming at me. 'Why didn't you let *me* have them? If it's only a string of beads, why wasn't *I* allowed to have them?'

This is a grown woman, weeping for something that happened—or didn't—twenty years ago. This is typical of Kate: the big emotional storm over sheer trivia, the accusatory tears, the sudden tornado that blows up in an instant out of nowhere and disappears as rapidly.

'Kate,' I snap. Sophie is looking on, curious, interested, ready to be upset because her mother is upset. 'Kate, get hold of yourself, for goodness' sake.' I indicate with a jerk of my head what she already knows, that the child is there, that the child will be distressed at any moment. How ungovernable she is, with these swift storms! Has she really never grown up past this stage of simmering indignant adolescence?

I never did learn how to manage Kate. Zoë used to take me to task over her. Once, I remember, when Kate was I suppose fourteen or so and had done something silly, I spoke sharply to her and she fled.

'Why do you treat her like that?' says Zoë, speaking sharply herself, as she usually did. To me, anyway.

'Like what?'

'Why do you flick at her like that, all sarcastic?' 'Because I love her.' Isn't it obvious?

'It's cruel.'

I roll my eyes. *Cruel?* I think. *Moi?* This is Zoë speaking, my sister, she who bit painfully at my heels all through my childhood and adolescence, she who constantly berated and criticised and attacked and punished. And, suddenly, *I* am the cruel one?

'Why don't you do it to Dominic, then?' she asks, accusingly.

Because I love him. What other answer is there? Because I love him, my dark, remote Dominic, who refuses ever to permit a diminutive form of his name. He has always scowled when called Dom, Dommy, Nic, Nicky; once we even tried Domenico: to himself he is always and only Dominic. *He* knows what his name is and who he is.

My Dominic, my changeling son, who as a baby used wide-eyed to pump my breasts, gazing at me distrustfully. 'Where did you come from?' I'd ask him. 'Not from me, I'm certain. Someone swapped you, didn't they?' His steady stare agreed.

We love in different ways. Different people demand from us different love, different hopes, different agonies.

One of the surprising things about Dominic was that in some ways he was so much what I had hoped for, what I had even expected, albeit nervously. As dark as Kate was fair, as mercurial as she was placid, elfin where she was bovine. Physically and temperamentally, he was all I'd imagined; and as he grew older it became clear that his intelligence was as lucid and ranging as I'd assumed it would be. But the closeness I had also imagined, the intimacy and transparency that was to have existed between us: this never eventuated.

I suppose there were occasions on which Dominic as a toddler raised his chubby arms to me and did or said something that made me feel he loved and needed me. Offhand, I can't bring such occasions to mind. Always, he regarded me dispassionately and from a distance: across a playground, a table, a breast. Never a loving child, he has grown into an unloving adult.

It is astonishing, in fact, that I care for him as I do: so much of love is a response, an answering involuntary warmth to the warmth projected. It mirrors that warmth: no, not just mirrors it, reflects and expands it. Dominic has never tried to attract me, never tried to radiate this warmth, this tenderness, kindliness, that ought to exist between us, not only on my side.

But without the most minimal offering of affection from Dominic, finding itself treated with this entire absence of tenderness, my love simply becomes more stubborn: it digs itself in like some spiky leather-leaved plant whose only object is survival. It feeds off itself, since there is nothing else to sustain it.

Sophie is a loving child. Sweet-natured and gentle. It's a problem, really: how will she ever defend herself in a hostile world? So far she has met kindness at every turn—but, as we all know, that won't last.

Sometimes I think Kate ought to try to toughen her up a bit—so she'll be a more competent person than her mother, apart from anything else. But she says she hasn't the heart, and I understand that. I say *Humph*, and cast my eyes upward, and drum my fingers, and tell Kate she's a fool; but I see what she means.

When the child comes to me (which she does, after school, Monday to Thursday, four o'clock prompt); when she slopes in the door with her wide, shy smile, her clear green eyes and her ready hug and kiss for Gandie, I melt, too. I look forward to seeing her, and I'm sorry when she leaves. Even when I love people dearly (and I am a loving person; I am not a cold person), I am usually at least a little relieved when they leave, when we part. Such a strain, sometimes, supporting relationships, maintaining conversations. Sophie's not a strain.

She's taken to asking me about days past, about when I was a young woman, about when her own mother was a child. I found this hard, at first. Kate was an unremarkable child by any standards, after all, and her childhood was undistinguished: I found it difficult to reach back through the tangle of memory, to pluck bright stories from the long-ago. But once I started, I found I could manage. For a twelve-year-old she is quite mature, I think. Kate would not at that age have been able to grasp some of the concepts her daughter easily handles. She startled me when she first began to ask questions.

'Gandie, you used to be married to Grandpa Steve, didn't you?'

I can see her, lolling against the kitchen table, her slim, tanned legs inelegantly splayed, white socks rucked about her ankles. It disconcerts me, this question: it comes like a mild bomb out of the blue, all kinds of straying tracer bullets to follow in its wake. I've never spoken to Sophie about Steve—why would I?—but somehow I've always assumed she understood the relationship.

We both turn up regularly for the big occasions—birthdays, school concerts and the like. It was difficult at first: we would eye each other suspiciously across the room, speak together only stiffly, draw a sigh of relief when we could withdraw from each other. I did, anyway, and I assume it was the same for him. As these things do, it has become easier over time.

We even sometimes go to each other's houses for a family event, although I think that is stretching the tape: how friendly can divorced couples ever be, after all? How can we step smoothly to meet each other over the mess of the past, the mangled trust, the dead dreams?

We have surfed together on a surging sea of bile and bitterness, leaving in our single wake a foul detritus, a jetsam of anger and shame and guilt and betrayal. It is obscene, really obscene, to expect us to maintain civilities. Still, we do it, for Sophie's sake. At least, that's why I do it, and I assume it's the same for him. And for Liam, of course: we do it for him, too.

'You don't mind me asking, Gandie?' says Sophie, taking a bite of her apple and regarding me with slight anxiety.

'No, no,' I say, heartily, lying through my teeth. 'Of course I don't mind, sweetheart.' I do, of course. I mind terribly. She's fond of Steve: I don't want anyone filling her head with a lot of rubbish about the divorce, about how I behaved. 'Yes, we were married.'

'And then you stopped being married,' observes Sophie, cheerfully.

'Yes. Yes, we did.'

'Why, Gandie?' Ah, why?

'Well, honeybunch,' I say. 'It was all a long time ago, you know.'

'How long?'

I pause to think. I make more of a meal of it than I need to, as I count over my fingers, to try to give myself a bit of a buffer, a few moments to think, to make sure I don't blurt out something wrong. Steve and I separated when Kate was fifteen. Three years older than Sophie is now. Kate had Sophie when she was twenty.

What an easy sum it is.

'Seventeen years,' I say, brightly. 'Good heavens, Sophie, seventeen years! What a long time that is. More than your life.'

Sophie absorbs this.

'But why?' she says. 'Whose fault was it?'

'Sophie, honey, people sometimes decide not to keep on living together. There's nothing wrong about it; it needn't be anyone's fault. Grandpa Steve and I just decided not to keep on living together. It was all perfectly friendly.'

I mouth these barefaced lies in a kindly voice, watching my granddaughter's face. I don't blame her for looking dissatisfied. Why do we try to protect our children in this hopeless way?

When they are little, we put them to bed with the hot, rank breath of the wolf, slavering down the front of Granny's night-gown; we torment them with stories of children whose parents desert them in thorny, hostile woods, of children whose parents force them into the world on murderous quests, of children who do battle with ogres, who are imprisoned alone forever in dank stone towers or pierced by glass shards or abused by vindictive stepmothers, children who go to bed in their flowerlike innocence and unexpectedly fall asleep for a hundred years, waking to find the world still cruel but differently so.

And we expect them to sleep soundly. *Don't let the bedbugs bite*, we say, tapping their downy plump cheeks lightly as we leave them to the dark solitude of the bedroom. And then, when they are only a little older, we cannot find it in ourselves to tell them the plain truth, to admit that a marriage went badly wrong, that people lied and shouted and hated.

'And then you married Max,' she states, bending to pat the old dog Borrow, who has a penchant for apples and licks the sweet juice from her fingers.

12

I rearrange my features to try to produce an impression of offhandedness, of undisturbed good humour.

'Yes,' I say. 'I married Max.' Well, near enough. 'Gandie, you look so cross.'

'No, no, sweetheart.' I stretch my lips to show how unconcerned I am.

'You sure you don't mind me asking you about it?' 'Heavens, no. It's just—sweetheart, Sophie love—it's such a long time ago, and I don't know—I mean—why are you suddenly talking about these things?'

'Mum told me about it,' says Sophie, apparently losing interest and showing me what genuine unconcern looks like as she mooches off to glance at the newspaper, which is lying on the kitchen bench.

I will give Kate hell the next time I see her, I think, the old fury my daughter can always generate stirring deep and cold and snakelike inside me.

But then I think, later, she is twelve, after all, my Sophie. She will be adolescent, soon: to all intents and purposes, is already. She is of an age to take an interest in these things.

I suddenly wonder whether her periods have begun. Surely Kate would have told me? But I have noticed her little breast-buds under her white school T-shirts. A sliver of fear pricks my heart. It is at this point that your children start to change, to regard you with alien and uncommunicative eyes. It is when puberty kicks in, when hormones perk up, when the blistering new juices of life start to sizzle. *Hello*, you say. *Hello? It's me here. It is I, your loving mother. I haven't changed.* But they have.

I dread the day this happens to my Sophie, the day when she ceases to run to me with the fierce pressure of her kisses and her sharp, squeezing hugs. I dread her being caught up in the pitiless impassive tides of womanhood, the impersonal coercive rhythms, the bleeding and the desire and the pain.

We ought to have some kind of ritual to welcome our daughters into their maturity, into the sisterhood. There ought to be a ceremony, a thumbed cross of blood on the forehead, the musty perfume of incense, prophecies from the crones. Picking up a box of tampons from the supermarket shelf doesn't rate.

Not that the sisterhood is up to much, though. On the whole, taken by and large, really one would sooner not be part of it.

The next time I was alone with Kate I mentioned Sophie's new interest in Max. I didn't shout; I wasn't heated. I was quite mild about it, and there was no need for her to look sideways at me in that infuriating kicked-puppy way she has.

'Sophie talked to me about Max,' I say.

She glances at me, drops her eyes. 'Yes?' she says, politely.

'You've been talking to her about Max.'

'She asked me.'

'She wouldn't have asked if she hadn't had some encouragement.'

'Sophie's quick to pick things up. She doesn't need encouragement.'

'She must have had some.'

'Mum,' says Kate, with a conspicuous effort at patience that irritates me. 'Mum, Max will come back one day. What are we meant to say to Sophie? Here's Max: he used to be married to Gandie, but we've never talked about him; we've never told you about him. What will she think then? Max was a fact in our lives, Mum. Is a fact. I know you and I don't speak of him, but there he is, just the same. And a fact in Sophie's life, too. We can't hide him. We can't pretend he never existed.'

'He won't come back.'

'I think he will,' says Kate, still not looking at me. Why will she never look at me when we speak? She never meets my eyes.

'Have her periods started?' I ask, abruptly.

Kate is startled. 'Sophie?'

'Who else?'

'Not yet.'

'She's twelve.'

'I know how old my daughter is, Mum.'

'Well, then. I only wondered.'

'Any day, I'd say. She's growing up fast.'

'I can see that,' I snap. Why does she always state the obvious in those dulcet explanatory tones? She drops her eyes again, ducks her head in that exasperating way she has.

'Mum, she is growing up. What I mean is, she's started to be interested in different things.'

'Do you mean sex?'

'Not really sex, no. Well, not that she's let on to me. But weddings, and babies, and that sort of thing. She's asked me lots about when I was little. When was I born, what happened, what sorts of toys did I have. That sort of thing.'

It's true. It isn't long before Sophie nobbles me about Kate as a baby.

'Mum was your first baby, wasn't she, Gandie?'

'Yes, honey.'

'Were you very excited?' 'Well, of course.'

'Did you have a nursery all ready for her?'

'I certainly did,' I say, brightly.

15

'And toys and things?'

'Yep.'

'Cuddly toys?'

'You bet.'

'Mum says her favourite toy was a blue bunny called Thumper.'

I think I do remember a moth-eaten ugly old rabbit. Kate used to take it everywhere with her and fall into despair when she lost it, which happened frequently. It drove me mad.

'Mum says Thumper was blue because you really wanted a boy and you got all blue things. Mum says you didn't really want a daughter.'

Sophie is munching a walnut brownie (I make them especially for her) and her enunciation is a little unclear, but there is no doubt she has just said this. She has presented it to me without animus, without any accusatory quality to the statement, in a matter-of-fact tone. It distresses me: it isn't true; and I've certainly never given Kate any reason to think it is.

'That's not the way it was,' I say. 'Of course I wanted your mum.'

'She says you didn't. Mum says you only ever wanted boys. Mum says you weren't happy till you had Dominic.'

'Well, darling, Mum's wrong.'

'Okay. But why did you have all blue things?'

'I didn't have all blue things. I had lots of different coloured things. In those days you didn't know what sex your baby was going to be, so I had some blue things and some pink.'

'And some yellow?'

'Probably.'

'And some white?'

'I suppose so. Sophie, it was a long time ago and I can't possibly remember what colour things I bought for your mum.'

'Okay. That's cool, Gandie.' She is pacific as ever once her stubbornness has borne fruit.

Why does Kate tell her these things? Why does she do it? Is it to get back at me, to awaken old guilts, old sadnesses? It wasn't my fault, anyway. And I never talked about it with her, so how can she be so sure she knows anyway?

Why is it a woman's fault, if she expects one sort of baby and another eventuates? Disappointment isn't a feeling you ask for, and it isn't something you can control. And I got over it pretty damn quick. I couldn't help it; I couldn't help feeling the thud when the bundle of hopes was dropped down the chute, the loss when someone who was confidently expected to turn up decided not to. I still remember it so well.

I am lying there in a sweat of pure relief, trying to understand that the pain, the racking pain, has gone, that my flesh is no longer bursting and I am not split in two up the middle after all, that I am still alive, that it is over, over, over. I am drifting, rather: I am just conscious enough for a sleepy voice in the back of my mind to be wondering if they gave me only pethidine—and, if they did, wow, what great stuff pethidine turns out to be.

I am aware that Steve is somewhat in awe of me, of what I have just accomplished, more or less single-handed. He is sitting beside me with his head down, overcome with emotion, stroking my hand. Normally I don't like this sort of contact from him, but right at the moment the stroking, which it seems to me betokens respect and admiration and wonderment, is perfectly appropriate and in fact rather soothing.

And I hear a voice—a woman's voice—saying: 'A lovely little girl!' And this is odd, because the voice sounds like the doctor's

17

voice, and here is the doctor's head swimming moonlike in the air above me, and she is smiling and nodding. 'A girl,' she repeats. But surely I am the only woman in the room to have just given birth, and therefore surely the only baby in the room is mine? I glance sideways, to see if perhaps there is another bed beside me. There is not.

And a baby is being placed on me, on my breasts, and the doctor is still smiling and nodding and repeating: 'A girl, a lovely little girl.'

A girl? A girl? How can it be a girl?

The baby makes an angry, snuffling sound and moves its head. It is almost the colour of beetroot—a dark, bright, pink-purple colour, and it is slick with some sort of grease. What have they smeared on it, for Christ's sake?

'Hold your baby, dear,' says the midwife, bustling around and helping me move one of my limp arms up around the creature. 'It's a dear little girl. You put your arms around her and give her a cuddle, now.'

A *girl*.

Where is my patrician Leo, my cub, my small king, he of Steve's blue eyes and my crisp, dark curls (so unnecessary on me, so attractive on him)? Where is the QC with a taste for Mozart and Tolstoy, the neurosurgeon with the exquisite collection of minor Heidelberg artists? What happened to the first Australian Prime Minister to be also a poet, a musician, a philosopher? Where is he, this son of mine with his rueful smile and his charming manner and his sensitive fingers? My cellist, my Nobel Prize winner, my Test cricket captain? My Wimbledon champion, my Astronomer Royal? My dark chevalier? Where is my son, who over the last few months has become realer than real to me, brighter than bright, my companion and saviour and pride and triumph? Goddamn it, where has Leo *gone*?

Wherever it is, it's not here. He's padded off on his ghostly paws to some celestial jungle, some vine-draped lonely clearing where he lifts up his head and roars in the moonlight, piteous and small and solitary. He's there for good: he's never coming back. And here's this peculiar, misshapen creature, this girl, glistening purple-crimson under the labour-ward lights, making off-putting nos while it tries to crawl beetlelike up my body.

It wasn't my fault. Emotions are not amenable to schooling. We cannot pretend to feel something we do not feel. I mean, to ourselves. Of course we can pretend whatever we like to the world, and if we're clever enough the world is deceived. I deceived the world, I think.

Once, early on, I started to explain to my mother how I felt about my first-born, but her clear gaze was so horrified that I stopped. She told me I was tired, I didn't know what I was saying, everything would be all right. And I suppose it was, in a manner of speaking.

I've read a lot about that kind of thing since then. These days, people would be sympathetic and call me a victim of post-parturition stress disorder or some such thing, and I'd get lots of counselling and support. But it wasn't like that, then. You loved your child; you struggled on. Count your blessings, people said.

And of course I did love Kate, and so forth. I do love her. But it was hard. I've never been able to forget how hard it was.

I waited five years before deciding to have Dominic: I was so terrified he would be another girl, another blond, chubby, docile little girl who played with dolls and sat around amiably and enjoyed fiddling with frilly doll-sized clothes. The son I had expected Kate to be still dawdled in the shadows of my imagination, witty and satirical, elegant and sleek and quick, my dark

19

prince, my soul's companion. So long as I delayed his birth, the safer he was from the ravages of reality.

Well, I got him. As soon as I saw him, I knew I'd got him. Dominic slid out of me with a minimum of fuss: he glanced around him, took stock of his new world, and determined his course. A baby of remarkable self-possession and clarity of vision; a child who knew what he wanted.

'He's not a cuddly baby, is he?' said the infant-welfare sister one day, thoughtfully. She picked Dominic off the scales, gave him a hug. He resisted, pushing against her. Dominic always resisted.

'I thought all babies were supposed to be cuddly,' I said.

'Good heavens, no.'

'My first was cuddly. My first wanted to be cuddled all the damn time.'

'Mmmm.' She glanced at me sidelong.

'I thought I was doing something wrong. With this one, I mean.'

'No,' she said, decisively. I still bless that woman when I think of her. I can't remember her name, but I loved her: I loved her for telling me Dominic's hostility wasn't my fault, that his unloving-ness was not to be laid at my door.

She had a square jaw, steady eyes, large hands, a no-nonsense look about her. 'No, see how he pushes away from me. He doesn't like it: he doesn't want to be held. All babies are different. They're just people, you know. We forget that. It's so obvious, but we forget it. Babies are just small people. Not all people are cuddly. I shouldn't think you're a cuddly person, are you?'

'No,' I said, reluctantly, wondering why she asserted this with such confidence.

'Well, then. It doesn't mean he's not affectionate. He just

20

doesn't like close physical contact. Not at this stage of his life, anyway.'

Such a relief! I had spent the first few months of Dominic's life being pushed away from him. I spent the next several years of Dominic's life in the same manner, but at least I knew now it was nothing to worry about. Satirical, composed, distant, critical, even disdainful, he resisted intimacy from infancy.

He used to remind me of that bit in *Twelfth Night* where Olivia is rhapsodising about Cesario/Viola: '*O, what a deal of scorn looks beautiful / In the contempt and anger of his lip!*' (I know that bit because I once played Olivia in a school production. I wanted to be Viola, and wear emerald satin capri pants, but it was Olivia or nothing.)

From the age of approximately three (which I believe was when he decided he was too old to hold my hand), Dominic did a great curled lip. It's the look aspired to by those surly male models in fashion magazines: it came naturally to him. And she was right, that large-handed infant-welfare lady: it didn't mean he was unaffectionate. He was a fervent child, but selectively fervent: he didn't bestow his love on just anyone, in the indiscriminate way Kate had.

Sophie is a cross between them, I suppose. Less obsessively fastidious than Dominic, more judicious than Kate. Readier with her embraces than her uncle, not as clingy as her mother. 'Love you, Gandie', Sophie will say, hugging me goodbye with her rapid firm touch. 'I love you too, sweetness,' I will say, but she's so quick, I'm often saying it to an empty room, a closing door.

The next time Sophie asked me about what she so insouciantly calls the olden days, I was ready for her. She wanted to know about our wedding, mine and Steve's. She'd want to know about my second wedding, too, one of these days, I knew, but sufficient unto the day and so on.

I'd gone through the old case under the bed and I'd pulled out the wedding album. I don't know why I have it and Steve doesn't, but that's how it is. I'd even spent a bit of time going through it on my own, turning the pages with amazement, with sorrow.

There Steve and I are, captured forever with imprudent smiles on our faces, foolish hopes in our hearts. We stand awkwardly, trying to follow the photographer's directions, both too self-conscious, too young, lacking in composure or the sense of the theatrical that permeates good photographs of big occasions, landmarks, milestones in one's life. I remember him telling Steve to stand on an angle, his feet just so: Steve simply couldn't manage it. His feet were like clown's feet, flopping over the ground in awkward dispositions. He turned too far, anxiously, then not far enough, shuffling, his face splitting into his daft grin.

I remember it as a black day, a disastrous day, the day of my greatest mistake. Yet we all look as happy-go-lucky as kids on a picnic. No prevision dulled our spirits; no disquiet fingered us with its bleak chill touch.

We look so innocent: that's what I can't quite fathom. I don't mean sexually innocent: Steve and I had slept together—not often, but a few times. I suppose there was a political and moral dimension to our innocence. We simply had no idea that such good intentions might take one on so shadowy and truncated a route, no idea of the sharp, mashing teeth of the traps that would jump from the dark corners of the path to cripple our feet and confuse our confident, stupid steps.

But Sophie is pleased with the photographs, and with the

album itself, still in reasonably good condition, its ivory satiny cover not much discoloured, the photographs themselves still miraculously crisp and glossy behind their protective tissue. I suspect she is amused by certain details—my hair, for instance, starched and curled like some extravagant origami project, and the bridesmaids' dresses. These things date, after all. But she is satisfied with my dress, which was classic and elegant. Stylish, that was the word my mother used of it. At least I avoided the meringue syndrome.

'You were so slim, Gandie,' she says, reverently. 'And so beautiful.'

What she actually means is, I was so young. I am not plump even now, when slender has metamorphosed into bony and slight given way to lean; but I was svelte then, and lissom, and young. And, yes, beautiful, damn it. I am nearly as impressed as Sophie is by my willowy waist, my high breasts, my graceful arms.

She wants to know who everybody in the photos is: she recognises Zoë as bridesmaid, and my mother, and Steve's parents. It takes ages, as we go through it all: she wants to know what the cake was made of, and what sort of shoes I wore, and what the menu was. The menu? No, I can't for the life of me remember the menu. Didn't I keep a copy? No, I didn't. Or, if I did, it's long since gone, vanished down the obliterating slippery slide of discarded keepsakes.

The honeymoon? Well, yes, a week in Tasmania: not an inspired choice in June (so cold, the air so perishing cold in your lungs), but cheap and I suppose picturesque. We were keen on bushwalking (or at any rate Steve was and I pretended to be so), and went tramping around Cradle Mountain. I guess we enjoyed it.

The first night together? Yes, a city hotel. That part is fairly clear in my mind. I had not stayed before in such five- star splendour: the heart-shaped pink soaps, the flowers and chilled champagne thoughtfully ordered by Steve. It was all ravishing, and I was brimful of the novel delectable nature of my world as I undressed and showered and arranged the new white lacy nightie over my shoulders, tweaking it down to make it more revealing.

How strange it is to remember happiness when one has come since to realise its cause was so superficial, so mistaken. Memory is like layers, needing to be peeled off: finally you have done with the endless stripping, the painstaking unwrapping and recon-structing; finally you arrive at the kernel and see how pathetic and wizened it was, really, after all.

Not that making love was a source of great contentment, even in those days. I was already familiar with Steve's style in bed: the dog, the baker, the jackhammer. First he pawed me, hesi-tantly, like a dog who's desperate for approval. Then he became excited and started to knead my sparse flesh, as if he thought I was made of dough and would eventually rise if he expended enough energy. And then he lost all control: I'm sure I don't need to describe the jackhammer phase to you. But I knew nothing else, at that stage. And it's like poverty: if it's all you've known, you don't miss wealth.

I had hazy notions of climax and pleasure, but I thought these would occur at some distance into the marriage, when we knew more about each other's bodies, when we had fairly launched ourselves on the broad surge of marriage and togetherness, when presumably a more sophisticated lovemaking would supersede these first crude experiments, when…when…when.

But the worst came later. Although we had made love, we had never actually spent a night together. We had never, literally, slept together. I had envisaged a period of lying in each other's arms,

24

whispering, murmuring, touching, sharing secrets, exchanging our sleepy, contented impressions of the wedding, me falling asleep on Steve's wide warm chest, within his strong embrace. But after Steve had penetrated me and obtained his staccato climactic peak, he patted my stomach benignly, muttered something bleary, and hunched himself over, falling asleep within a minute.

I lay there, disconcerted and trying not to feel deserted. It had been a big day, of course; and when he had got his speech over and done with he'd knocked back a few wines, and I was sure there was every excuse for fatigue; but I had expected something a little more conversational, a little more…well, attentive. Courteous. Some demonstration of consideration, of husbandly care.

And then, just as I started to succumb to the warmth and the wine and the tiredness, and drift into sleep myself, a great sound exhaled itself into the room. I jumped in fright.

It was a bubbling, cascading, raw sound: a sound of turgid, rumbling rhythms and insistent plosive beats, a gaseous, volcanic, assertive, cavernous noise. It terrified me. There was something subterranean about it, yet we were on the twentieth floor of a city hotel. It rolled and roiled around the room: it echoed into the corners and bounced aggressively off the walls and the ceiling. I sat upright and stared around the bedroom in consternation and fear: Steve was snoring.

I slept very little that night. I shook his shoulder, but he only grunted. I lay next to him, gazing into the dark, absorbing the blubbering, grunting tide as it rose and fell, rhythmically, without cessation, without interruption. I suppose I dropped off at around five or six in the morning, and small wonder if I was hazy at breakfast.

We had it delivered to the room: all part of the Lovebird

Special Steve had paid for. A smart, diminutive waiter with a bald head and a long, black apron set up the table with a damask cloth and lots of really quite good silver. I had taken some toast and was helping myself to marmalade when Steve leant over the table and clasped my hand, immobilising it just as I was about to tip the spoon onto the side of my plate.

'I can't believe how lucky I am,' he whispered.

'Um,' I said, watching the marmalade drip onto the white damask. 'Honey, just let me—'

'I can't believe you chose me. I can't believe you said yes. You're my darling, my sweetheart, my lovely one. I'm the proudest man in the world, Isabel.'

Don't misunderstand me: it's pleasant to be adored. I'm no different from anybody: I can take a lot of adoration. But I'd had maybe two hours of sleep and I wasn't at my best and I didn't want to drip marmalade on the crisp white tablecloth. I tried to keep the twang out of my voice, but it was hard.

'Steve, love, just let go of my hand, would you.'

He looked absurdly stricken. He dropped my wrist as if it had burnt him. He goggled, slightly.

'You don't regret it?' he asked, tense, desperate. 'You don't regret marrying me?'

'No, of course not. I haven't had much sleep, that's all.'

'You do look tired,' he said, fondly. I had seen myself in the mirror earlier that morning and I could attest to this. It was an understatement and I should have been more grateful than I was. 'Maybe you were wound up, nervous? It was a big day, wasn't it, lovely? I was tired; I bet you were, too.'

'Well, yes, I was tired. But I couldn't sleep. I couldn't sleep at all.'

'Were you worried?' he asked, taking my hand again and

pawing it.

'Steve, are you aware that you snore?'

'Well, yes, of course. All men snore, lovely. Women get used to it.'

I didn't like being called lovely all the time. I was starting to hope he wasn't going to make a habit of it. And all men didn't snore: I was sure of that.

'Well, isn't there anything you can do about it?'

'Do?'

'I don't know. A mask, or a clothes peg, or an operation, something. There must be something you can do. Steve, I can't sleep through that noise. I can't sleep. I haven't slept. I won't sleep. What can you do?' I could hear my voice, thin and high and rising to hysteria.

He looked concerned, but not enough. 'Lovely, all men snore. You talk to my mum. My dad snores. All men snore. Didn't you realise that?'

I didn't see that it followed, quite like that. But he was right. Not about all men snoring (Max didn't), but about getting used to it. I got used to it. I did learn to sleep through it—for the most part, anyway. Steve was so convinced that it was his bounden right to snore that he managed to convince me, not through argument but simply by smiling fondly and ignoring anything I said to the contrary.

'It's so sad, Gandie,' says Sophie, eventually, closing the album and solemnly regarding it lying in her lap.

I am a little nonplussed. Sad? She's been twittering on about how lovely it all is. Bridesmaids, and cake, and champagne, and all the associated fairy floss: I'm quite disconcerted by the rosy glow with which she surrounds it all. And suddenly we're sad?

'Sad that you're not still together, I mean,' she explains.

Well, I don't know. It seems to me an extremely good thing that we're not still together. Wasn't seventeen years of snoring enough?

And then again, I think, perhaps it's not fair to brush off seventeen years of marriage so abruptly, so flintily. It wasn't all bad. There were good times, especially at the start. Sex improved. Well, a bit, anyway. It's too easy, after a divorce, to slam into the ex: I've heard otherwise apparently nice women say the most appalling things about their exes, whipping themselves up into frenzies of hatred.

It's such a temptation, to make out it was always bad, that none of it was your fault, that you were always trapped somewhere you didn't want to be. Something in me always wants, meanly, to play devil's advocate. *Yes,* I want to say, *but you didn't think that at the time, did you? I saw you, giggling and holding hands. I was at your wedding. I saw how it was between you, then. So don't pretend, now.*

No, it wasn't all bad, though sometimes it suits me to pretend it was. I remember happy times. The wedding night was a disaster, but at least it had the advantage of making what followed seem a distinct improvement. For at least a year or two we travelled a mostly enjoyable learning curve, discovering curiously and, on the whole, happily how to live together.

I look back on the early photographs. We're picnicking; we're at the beach; we're at the playground or blowing out birthday candles or having a barbecue or fooling around in the backyard. Some of it was good. I was a sweeter, richer, funnier person then. I could be charming, and perhaps even loveable: my soul had more cushiony places, fewer prickles and spikes. Steve adored me, anyway, and I enjoyed being adored.

And I was fond of him, I admit, in the way that one becomes fond of a large and good-tempered dog—maybe a St Bernard, now that I think of it. If I hadn't fallen in love with Max, I probably would have finished up in the same crematorium niche as Steve, and not often thought of myself as desperately unhappy on the way through life. It's just that once you've discovered paradise you don't want to stay married to a St Bernard.

I don't know how to explain any of this to Sophie. Still, I suppose it's good that she will talk to me with this kind of frankness, this utterly translucent degree of openness. I try to be even-handed, as a grandmother, of course I do; but it's hard, sometimes. It doesn't always work, trying to spread yourself evenly.

And it makes a difference that Sophie is a girl, that she will be a woman, like me. It's much harder to talk to a small boy: he doesn't want to be like his grandmother when he grows up. Nor should he, of course: I'm not suggesting that Liam has to make a role model of me in order to communicate with me. But it's different, with women: we have common ground on which to pitch our tent and chat. I've explained this to Kate, to make sure she doesn't think I always favour Sophie.

Thinking about these things puts me in mind of Liam's fourth birthday. I remember it well. If Liam was turning four, Sophie must have been nine.

I was careful to turn up on time and with a good present: Kate had started to hint to me once or twice, in that tentative oblique way she has, that I appeared at times to be in danger of neglecting Liam. What she means, of course, is that I indulge

Sophie. I'm aware that it's a danger, but, as I say, I *am* aware of the dangers of partiality, and take care not to be trapped by it.

Liam was a pudgy dumpling of a child: he did a lot of sitting and smiling—radiantly, I grant you, but not very intelligently. He's very like his mother used to be. He is a sweet-natured child, I suppose, but has none of his sister's swift, dark charm, nor her quick, astute glance. He is all Kate: the sandy curls, the pink cheeks, the blue eyes, the slightly glassy stare.

Insipid. It has to be said. Sweet but insipid.

We divide comically into the dark and the fair, Steve and me and our offspring. We used to joke about it: he would refer to my genes as the devil's side of the family, and to his as the angels'. He is stocky and fair and blonde: so are Kate and Liam. I am slight and olive-skinned and dark, and so is Dominic. And Sophie, of course.

The luckless Gavin is a kind of pale fudgey brown, and long and gangling: his genes don't appear to be particularly insistent.

So I was careful, as I say. On time, a big present. I felt in my bones it was going to be a bad day when Gavin opened the door with a glass of beer in his hand, a cardboard pirate hat on his head, and a silly grin on his face.

'Millie!' he guffaws. 'My favourite mother-in-law.'

It puts my teeth on edge. But I see Kate and Liam hovering in the background, so I kneel and stretch out my arms to the child.

'Come to Gandie, sweet,' I cry. 'Come give Gandie a hug.' But he clings to Kate's leg. She nudges him gently forward. 'Give Gandie a hug, Liam. Gandie's come for your birthday party.'

'Look!' I call, holding up the brightly wrapped present, covered all over with balloons and Sesame Street characters. Inside there is a toy fire station with lots of fire engines and hoses and so forth. I don't know what boys like, really; but this seems to fit the bill. 'Something for a little boy! Something for a little boy who's turning four!'

But Liam is not persuadable. I get up, feeling a bit of a fool, dusting my knees down and straightening my skirt.

'Sorry, Mum. He's very shy, sometimes.'

'I'm his grandmother,' I say, perfectly reasonably. 'What is there to be shy about?'

'Well, Mum, just because you're his grandmother it doesn't make you less...er...'

'Less what?'

'Well, daunting, I suppose.'

'It might indeed make you more so,' says Dominic, glinting darkly from a corner of the room.

I catch a supercilious expression—quickly veiled—from his girlfriend of the time. Dominic was never without a girl-friend, even as a teenager; and by now he would have been in his mid-twenties. What was her name? Bec. I never liked her.

Steve is in the background, as usual, looking at the floor, as usual. The face of the hapless Gavin is over Steve's shoulder, bobbing away in the kitchen, looking worried. Zoë has on her disapproving expression and is bringing out a tray of some-thing to eat; and Zoë's awful husband, Henry, is sitting next to Dominic and staring at the ceiling.

Hey, hey, the gang's all here.

Dominic and I glare at each other. I pick up the present from the floor and deposit it on the table. Liam starts to cry. I pick up the present from the table and hand it to Liam. He runs away, sobbing.

'You need to tone it down a bit, Isabel,' says Dominic, evilly. 'The poor child's confused: he's not used to such human warmth from you. It's like being exposed to a blast furnace when you've always had a two-bar radiator.'

Dominic has missed his vocation. He's a lawyer. He should be writing one of those dreadful bitchy gossip columns in a women's magazine.

I glance around, half waiting for someone to remonstrate. A light reprimand would have been acceptable. Just for someone to say: *Oh, come on, Dominic.* But nobody says anything.

From these not very auspicious beginnings you would say the day has to improve. This is not the case. We sit around and manufacture noises of the kind we imagine a non-dysfunctional family might generate under similar circumstances. I sip tea and think longingly of a stiff brandy and a cigarette. The brandy I can manage later on, when I blessedly return home; but I haven't smoked for years and seldom miss it, these days.

A chocolate birthday cake is produced, iced in Kate's habitual lopsided inexpert manner. The song is sung. Liam tries to blow out his four candles but succeeds only in showering spit over the bedaubed icing.

Sophie, always such a good big sister, helps him with the candles and then with taking around plates of crumbly slices. I pick at mine, leaving the icing. Liam eventually plucks up enough courage to open my present and it transpires that the identical object is already in his possession.

Well. How was I to know?

We limp along. Bec looks patronising; Dominic loses no chance to launch his poisonous little arrows into my quivering flesh. Kate gets pink and flustered. Steve sits silently and looks as if he wishes he were a million miles away. I'm sure I don't blame him: I do, too.

The hapless Gavin drinks slightly too much beer (Gavin is one of those men who assumes that at these occasions men require alcohol where women are permitted only non-spirituous beverages) and becomes hearty and talkative. Not that I can remember anything he says. At one stage Sophie whispers in Liam's ear and they leave the room together.

When they return, Kate, who has been watching for this, says anxiously: 'Liam has a surprise for you, Gandie. Sophie's been coaching him. Now, Liam!'

Liam stands foolishly in the centre of the room and regards the carpet with fascination. After some minutes of this he is persuaded to say, in a half-whisper: 'Gandie, Gandie. Sugar, sugar.'

I realise what it is. Sophie has taught him—well, tried to teach him—the little nonsense rhyme she and I made up, long ago, when she was around Liam's age.

Gandie, Gandie, sugar candy
Legs all twisted, bent and bandy
Make sure she's all fine and dandy
Put her to bed with Andy Pandy
Tuck her in with a swig of brandy.

We used to chortle it together with disproportionate pleasure. It was one of the lovely things about Sophie, from when she was very tiny: the huge joy she was able to derive and communicate. She adored this silly rhyme.

Liam cannot see the point of it, and looks around in patent anguish when he has twice failed to get through the first line correctly. I try to be helpful and prompt him gently: he starts to cry again.

When I leave, Kate says to me, worriedly: 'I'm so sorry about Liam, Mum. He is very shy. It's just a phase.'

I'm tired, and my head has started to throb with that particular kind of vibration behind the eyes that so often presages a migraine. And I'm hurt by the whole thing anyway. I'm really hurt. I'm the child's grandmother: I'm there to be loved, aren't I?

So I probably snap at her more than I mean to. I say something about manners, I think, and four-year-olds not being too young to acquire such things. And then I'm surprised when, for once, she snaps back at me.

'If only you showed him a little warmth, Mum. If only you gave him half the warmth you give Sophie.'

I'm rather pleased. For once, she has the gumption to bite back. I scowl at her, just to show she hasn't got me bluffed, and I leave. I blunder home to all the large silent confusions of my life. I'll ring her in a day or two, and make peace. Probably she'll ring first, I think.

I can't remember, now, who rang whom. We always do make peace, though.

But she's wrong. I'm not a cold person.

The business of the rhymes is interesting. Sophie was herself not much older than Liam when she made up that rhyme. With a little help, I admit: still, it was her impetus.

The children in our family have always done this: made up rhymes. Zoë and I used to hurl them at each other as abuse. *Dizzy Izzy, in a tizzy! Doughy Zoë, gone to Moe! Stinky Minky!* Mainly pretty meaningless, I suppose, but they were a game we played—in many different versions, in many different places—on and off right through our childhood. I'm not saying they were great poetry, or even minor poetry, but it can't have done our verbal skills any harm.

I still remember how stunned I was when Dominic, aged three (am I exaggerating?), cocked his head at me over his messy breakfast toast and chortled: *'Funny honey, gone all runny!'* It was as if he knew he was participating in an old family tradition. And there was no way he could have known about it.

I'd never done it with Kate: she was a stolid and unimaginative child and had no interest in wordplay. I rang Zoë to tell her about Dominic and his honey, and we dissolved together in a rare sisterly exhibition of tears and laughter.

I still, sometimes, find myself haunted by doggerel. The words slide sideways into my mind and shift themselves into pulse and cadence and won't go away.

I'm not a cold person.

Sophie's interests are expanding. The other day she said: 'You used to be an architect, didn't you, Gandie?'

'Used to be?' I say, meaning to make a joke of it but perhaps letting it come out more sharply than it should. 'What is this "used to be"? Are you putting your old Gandie on the scrapheap already?'

'Well, but I mean you used to do it all the time, didn't you? Not just a couple of days a week.'

'Yes, honey.'

'Why?'

'Why? A girl has to do something.'

'Yes, but I mean why did you choose to do that? Why did you decide to be an architect?'

'I thought I'd like it, I suppose.'

'And did you?'

'Yes. Very much.'

'Then why? What did you like so much about it?'

She is persistent, Sophie, in this new phase of hers: I am learning this. She will not be shrugged off. I try to explain it to her. It's all ancient history: it's hard to bring it back. It had something to do with the constructing of new things, the excitement of generation, the buzz of creativity. Something, too (let's be honest), to do with sheer randomness, a friend's father, an architect himself, suggesting it to me only half seriously. I might never have thought of it for myself, but his suggestion somehow took root and prospered.

And the drawing, the discipline of it, the precision. I had always wanted to be an artist. I try to describe it to her, this urge to produce wonderful oil paintings, watercolours, even sculptures, to see things nobody else could see, to *show* that you could see things nobody else could see. I didn't have the talent. It always seemed to me that I had the first part of it: I could see. But I couldn't translate the seeing.

As an architect, however, I could learn to draw: I could do the technical side of things. I might not be able to paint glorious portraits or landscapes, but I could learn perspective, and precision. I could draw little, round shrubs, symmetrical obedient shapes, tiny detail penned in with meticulous care.

Even now, I don't use computers much for my sketches. I can do, of course, if I have to. But I choose not to, most of the time; I choose to draw. And I always try to do a watercolour for each project. I love doing the watercolours.

'That's one of yours, on the wall, isn't it?'

It is.

'That was your house, wasn't it, Gandie? You built it, didn't you?'

'I designed it, honey, and I lived in it.'

'With Max?'

'Yes, with Max.'

'What was the house called? It had a funny name, didn't it?'

'Rain. It was called Rain.'

'Why did you call it that?'

'I can't remember now.'

Sophie goes over and inspects the sketch. It's still there, framed, on the wall. God knows I never want to see Rain again as long as I live, but I can't bear to throw out my painting of it, when it had no history. It was so new, so fresh, it hadn't even been built, didn't exist except in my plans and my dreams and my mind's eye. It shimmered for me then.

'It's pretty,' she says, thoughtfully, as if she isn't quite sure. 'There's people in it, Gandie. Look, there's these two people, holding hands, looking at the house, over at the side. Are they you and Max?'

'No,' I lie. 'They're just two people. I always put people in my sketches. It makes it more fun.'

'This one looks like you. Look, she's short and thin, and she's got dark curly hair.'

I baulk, but silently, at 'short and thin': I had petite and lissom in mind.

'It's a coincidence, honey.'

'The man's tall. Was Max tall?'

'I suppose so. But those aren't us; they're not Max and me.'

'Who are they then?'

She doesn't believe me, of course. I'm not sure myself why I'm lying.

She examines the picture minutely, running her finger over it. It'll leave a mark on the glass, but I don't say anything. She's thinking.

'You always have funny names for things, Gandie. A house called Rain. A dog called Borrow.'

'Well, you know about Borrow.'

'I know. You used to share him with Mum. You used to borrow him, and she'd borrow him back.'

The dog raises his grizzled old Labrador head and looks at us. He knows he's being discussed.

'And it was Max who gave him to you? To you and Mum?'

Dear Christ, the child is relentless!

'Yes, honey, it was Max.'

She thinks, and then flashes one of her blinding smiles at me. *'Gandie wears the cloak of Zorro, in a house called Rain with a dog named Borrow.'*

I smile. It's an effort, but I do smile. But she's not focusing on me: she's working on another little flash of creativity. It comes and she smiles again. *'Lives in a house, for nothing it lacks, with a dog called Borrow and a man called Max.'*

For the rest of the day, into the evening, into bed, the knocking rhythms pursue me, but they're not Sophie's rhymes. They're my rhymes. I don't know where they come from but I know they're mine. Doleful and thudding, like a muffled hammer, they hum in my head: *Lived and loved in pain and sorrow, in a house named Rain with a dog named Borrow. Lived and loved, pain and sorrow, house named Rain, dog named Borrow.*

Perhaps I am going mad.

But madness takes its time, evidently, to sneak up on one. I know this from the past. There are the dark times, the times of spiralling down inside the vast slow cyclone, its walls black and unyielding, slipping, slipping all the time, knowing you're slipping, not able to do anything about it. I've got a bit of slipping still to do, I think, before I reach the stage of irretrievable lunacy.

The endless questioning about the past didn't stop there.

Kate swore to me that she wasn't encouraging it. 'She's twelve,' Kate kept saying, placidly. 'She's growing up. She's taking an interest in all these sorts of things. If you try to shut her up she'll just think you're keeping things from her, Mum.'

Well, aren't I?

The next assault concerns not my wedding but Kate's.

'Well, honey,' I say. 'You should ask your mum about that. She's got a whole album: you must have seen it.'

Sophie knows this, but it turns out that what she's after isn't the formal statement, the embossed frontispiece, the endorsed public announcement.

'I like your photos of Mum's wedding better, Gandie. They're not so stiff and posed. Everyone looks happier in them.'

There's an irony. The photos in my album were taken by Max, who loved taking photos and had a gift for it. He was good at so many things. This was in pre-digital days, of course; and Max's camera (like everything else Max owned) was absolute top quality, state of the art. I can't remember what it was—German, I think. Leica? Whatever. All sorts of special lenses, but he never made a fuss of it: he would sneak up on you and take it before you realised, and then he'd grin at you, and maybe wink, and move on to his next victim.

The photographs Max took at Kate's wedding were terrific: I remember when they came back from the developers and I leant over his shoulder as he sorted through them. He was pleased with them; Kate and I were delighted. Sophie has good taste, as always. They have a quickness and vibrancy—and, sometimes, a wit—quite lacking in the official version, in which Kate and

Gavin, both self-conscious and gauche anyway, look even more so as the professional carefully poses them, tries to make them appear happy, as they stare at their feet or glance wild-eyed at each other, as if to say: *My God, what have I done?* Which, to be fair, is not what either of them was thinking. At least, I don't believe so.

So we get out the album and flip through. At least, since Max took most of them, I am spared having to look at him for the most part. There are a few of him. There's one I took, of him with his arm around Kate, who is looking up at him adoringly. There are a couple of him and me together, me in the fine silky little number I bought specially for the occasion, mother of the bride, floaty soft pink and dark sepia, high strappy heels; Max divinely handsome in his monkey suit. Most men these days have to go and hire a dinner suit for these occasions: Steve certainly did. Max owned his own, beautifully cut. I can't remember now who took these of us together, who grasped Max's camera and lined us both up through the delicate hairline sights. We look awfully happy.

Sophie lingers on them. 'It's a pretty dress,' she says.

'Yes.'

'It looks soft as.'

'It was.'

'Have you still got it?'

'I don't think so. It was twelve years ago, darling.'

She draws a breath and I can see she is working up to something.

'Do you miss Max a lot, Gandie?'

'Yes, honey. Of course I miss him.'

'When will he come back, do you think?'

'I don't know that he will.'

'Did you ever report him?'

'Report him?' I repeat, confused. What would I have reported him for, I am wondering.

'As a missing person.'

'Oh. No. No, I never did that.'

'But he was missing, wasn't he? Is missing.'

'I suppose so. In a way.'

'You don't mind me asking?'

Why can't I just say: *Sophie, Sophie darling, don't talk to me about Max. I do mind, I can't bear it, for Christ's sake stop it.*

'No, of course not.'

Sophie looks at the photo again, traces around the edge of it with her slender, honey-brown finger. Sophie's like me: fine-boned, olive-skinned; she's got a tan all year round. She doesn't appreciate it yet, but she will, when she finds what a saving it is on pantyhose.

'He must come back one day,' she says. 'He must come back to you, Gandie.'

To my appalled horror I feel tears rising to my eyes. I turn the page and see a spread of Kate and Gavin fooling around with the cake, Gavin brandishing the knife in mock threat.

Sophie giggles. 'Dad's such a clown.' Well, that's certainly true.

When the children were small I would go in from time to time, in the evenings, to check on them—as all parents do, I suppose. Kate would always be asleep, curled up, rosy and boringly angelic. Dominic was frequently awake, ramrod-straight in the bed, his wide eyes glinting darkly.

'Why aren't you asleep, honey?' I'd sit down on the side of

the bed. Sometimes, if I dared (as I've said, Dominic never liked being touched), I would run my hands through his thick dark hair.

'Can't.'

'Are you trying?'

'The more you try, the less it happens.'

That's true. Insomniac from way back, I know this.

'Have you been playing word games?' I know this is one of the things he does, when he can't sleep.

'Boring.'

'Are you worried about anything?'

'No.'

Eventually I would give up and leave, patting him in what was meant to be a consoling, maternal way. I'd peek in later, on my way to bed. Sometimes, even then, he'd be awake.

I never knew what he was thinking, though. Not then; not now. I talked to Zoë about it; I asked her advice. This was a rare step, for me: the trouble with asking advice from Zoë was that she gave it. Then she followed it up, to see if you'd done what she'd told you. It wasn't worth the trouble, asking Zoë what she thought about anything: you knew you would be liable to her swift persecutions, her rampant assaults.

But I suppose I must have approached her when I was feeling yielding or unconfident, forgetting that the aura of sisterhood was more attractive than the actual experience. Anyway, she was a teacher: she was supposed to understand child psychology. I remember she raised her eyebrows at me.

'*You* worry about things, don't you, Minky?'

'Some things.'

'Some things, yes: that's what I mean.'

'Of course I do. Everybody worries about some things.'

'Well. Children worry, too.'

'He's three, Zoë.'

'The world is a worrying place, when you're three.'

'How do you know?'

'Use your brains.'

Well, that was Zoë all over. Use your brains, little sister. Don't get me to work it out for you.

It's always been edgy, my relationship with Zoë. I don't know that I would call it dysfunctional, entirely. I don't know enough about what sisterly relationships are usually like to be able to make that judgement. I am five years younger than Zoë, and she's never let me forget it. I think when I was born she regarded me as a little-sister present, straight from the stork to her, my parents incidental to the transaction.

My character, my clothes, my moral development, my diet: Zoë studied them all earnestly, and never fell short of her duty when she felt good advice was required. Her shadow, murky and persistent and I suppose well meaning, leans over my childhood: wherever I was, whatever I did, Zoë was there to help things along. There were good parts to this, of course: when I started school, for instance, it was comfortable to know Zoë was around to give Chinese burns to anyone who teased me; Zoë was there to look after me if I was ill, if I fell over in the playground, if I forgot my lunch.

It was less comfortable, as we grew up, to find Zoë had read my diary (she gave me marks for it), vetoed potential boyfriends (when they rang, she told them I wasn't home), and insisted on monitoring the sorts of bras I bought. Whenever I complained she always said she did it for my own good, because she loved me.

She said the same thing, many years later, when I complained about her girlhood interventions. She did them because she loved me. I didn't disbelieve her. That was precisely the trouble with Zoë: she did things because she loved you. They were awful things, but she did love you, loved you according to her lights and with a total absence of imagination.

It would have been far easier to cope with her if she had acted out of malice. Contrary to what many people think, it isn't malice or evil that causes most of the world's problems: it's stupidity—it's people thinking they know best and not seeing how disastrously wrong they are.

As I've said, we used to make up rhymes when were young, but Zoë's frequently had an admonitory flavour. I've never used rhyming as a means of instruction or inculcation with Sophie: it's a matter of having fun, of having a giggle and encouraging her to play games with language. It's a skill she already has and it'll never do her any harm. Kate is perpetually astounded by it and shakes her head. 'She's so *clever*,' she says to me, in wonderment. 'Just like Dominic. He could always do that, too, couldn't he?'

Once, when Sophie and I were doing some cooking together, she chanted this to me:

Great chefs are contumacious,
Disputatious and pugnacious
In kitchens that are spacious
They make soups that are audacious,
And salads all herbaceous.
Their desserts are ostentatious
And their pancakes farinaceous.

44

'Did she truly make it up on her own?' Kate asked later.

'Yes, of course.'

'You didn't help with any of it? Even the farinaceous bit?'

'It started with the farinaceous bit. She discovered that it was a word that had to do with flour, and she just took it from there.'

'Amazing,' murmured Kate. 'Amazing.'

One of the things Sophie has achieved by the very fact of her existence is to inject a little normality into her extended family. Split as we are by old histories, replete with enmities matured like ripened cheese, we gather at family occasions with an inbuilt propensity to eyeball each other across the room as if battlelines were about to be declared.

Sophie overcomes these divisions; she traverses the sharp and jagged crevices in our family landscape; she presents to us an image of ourselves as harmonious and ordinary. A regular family, a commonplace and unremarkable group of related people who don't bicker and simmer, who don't harbour fetid suspicions or implacable hostilities about each other. It isn't a bit true, of course: we're so lost in our dysfunction, so crabbed and twisted by it, that we'll never emerge from it. It's like an indelible dye: it's imbued the fibre and substance of our relationships with its telltale stain.

So we're a dysfunctional family: but then again, what's dysfunction? Show me a functional family and I'll show you a pack of poseurs and fibbers. Our dysfunction is at any rate remedied, if not completely repaired, by Sophie: it's partly why she's so important, so necessary.

When she was eight or so, Dominic's passion for old cars was just starting: Sophie was scornful. He came around to Kate's one time to show off his latest purchase when I was there (clearly, he didn't know I was or he would have chosen another time), and

Sophie poked fun at him. How did it go again, the nonsense rhyme she made up on the spot?

> Dominic, bominic, tinsel and stars,
> Spends all his money on silly old cars,
> Drives down the street in his burgundy Jag,
> Bominic, Dominic, Oh! what a dag!

And Dominic—proud, prickly, difficult Dominic—laughed and hugged her. Somehow Sophie could get away with all kinds of things I never could, where Dominic was concerned. I don't know how seriously close he's ever allowed her to get; but he certainly lowers the barricades for her.

I presume he lowers them for Paula, too. I wonder what he's told her—what he tells her—about me, I mean. I see her eyes resting on me sometimes with that kind of prissy speculative look she gets, and I wonder what he's shared with her, what she knows, what she guesses.

I wonder what he knows, too.

'What about your wedding, Gandie?' said Sophie to me one day, as I knew she would. 'I mean, your other wedding. Your wedding to Max.'

Ah. What about it? Well, it's a good question. I won't tell her how good. I'd anticipated the approach and I'm ready for her this time: I bring out the measly handful of photographs (they're not in an album: I never got around to doing that) and she studies them earnestly.

'Why did you get married on a beach?'

'Max decided to,' I say.

'Didn't you want to?'

'I didn't mind.'

'Was it sunset?'

'Yes.'

'Was it very romantic?'

'Yes.' I realise this must sound bald, but it's hard to enthuse.

'Where are all your guests, Gandie? Didn't they come to the beach?'

'We didn't have guests. Only witnesses. Two witnesses.'

'A wedding with no guests?' She is incredulous.

'We sort of eloped, honey.' She isn't impressed, I can tell.

'But didn't your mum come? Or Mum, or Dominic? Or Aunt Zoë?'

Hard to explain, especially from this distance: it's like something that happened to me in another life. Well, it is, really.

I could always tell her the truth, that Aunt Zoë (Zoë's her great-aunt, of course, but she always calls her Aunt) and my mother (if she'd still been alive, which she wasn't) would have stoned Max to death and eaten his liver sooner than come to our wedding. It doesn't seem worth it, though.

'Who took the photos, then?'

'One of the witnesses.'

'But why?'

'It's just the way it was, honey.'

Sophie studies one of the photographs closely, wrinkling the smooth skin around her eyes as she strains to see more clearly.

'Max is awfully handsome, isn't he, Gandie?'

Oh, yes. Max was handsome. Max was only *the* most attractive man I'd ever laid eyes on. How many women get to make their marriage vows to the most attractive man they've ever seen, I wonder, bleakly. Cross Cary Grant with Sean Connery; add a dash of Robert Redford. (I'm aware that these names betray my age.) Shake together.

People turned to look at Max. They took one look at him and they were ready to be seduced by him. Except for my family, of course. Other people fell about for Max: they lay on their back and waggled their paws in the air. It wasn't just that he was so good-looking. He had slathers of charm. Pots of it. Vats of it.

'Yes, honey,' I say. 'Max was very handsome.'

'But he's probably still alive, isn't he? He wasn't very old, was he, when he went away? Won't he come back?'

'He won't come back, honey.'

Sophie looks as if she's going to cry.

'But, Gandie, he can't be dead. He's not dead. You don't think he's dead, do you?'

I find I can't answer, and turn to the photographs instead. But it doesn't work. Sophie can't understand why I haven't mounted these shots in a satin-bound album, why I keep them in an old envelope. She wants them carefully arranged and lovingly displayed, and even offers to do it all for me. But I can't bear it, suddenly; I can't bear the way she's pawing the photos, the questions she's asking, the way she assumes I'm going to want to talk about all of this.

I cut her off sharply, and I go into the kitchen to make myself a cup of coffee with my trembling hands and my loneliness and my desolation. Sophie doesn't follow me. She's a tactful child: she can tell she's overstepped some line she didn't know existed. When she says goodbye to me she gives me a fiercer hug than usual.

'Poor Gandie,' she mumbles into my neck. 'Poor Gandie.'

I am poor Gandie, too. The episode upsets me and I spend the next day or so dangerously close to tears. It doesn't do, to stir all this up. Borrow senses my distress and shoves his damp muzzle into my hand, making those high-pitched staccato noises that are his way of saying: *Never mind*.

Strangely enough, however, the memories Sophie's interest awakens aren't so much of Max as of my mother's opposition to him. She was dying at the time: it gave her pronouncements an unfair and entirely spurious moral authority. Dying but not yet bedridden, as she was by the end: I remember her, engulfed by my father's old recliner chair, clasping and unclasping her tiny hands that always reminded me of the paws of some small and ineffectual animal: a rabbit, perhaps, or a guinea pig.

I hadn't left Steve yet, but I knew I was going to. I'd brought Max to meet her the previous day, and now I'd dropped in to gloat, to savour her capitulation to his glamour.

To my astonishment, she had failed to succumb. At once suave and earnest, unfailingly courteous, sober and gentle and intelligent, he had sat with her for over an hour, but she was unmoved by him.

'I don't like him,' she says, her hands starting their nervous wringing. She is looking down: she won't meet my eyes.

'Sorry?' I am completely taken aback.

I knew Zoë didn't like Max, but I put that down to jealousy and to the puritanical elder-sister streak that had so frequently during our lives snuffed out the small flickering flames that had given me pleasure.

'I don't like him. He's a con man, Isabel. I think he's a con man.'

'You've been listening to Zoë,' I say, contemptuously.

'What if I have? She's got sensible things to say. Why

49

shouldn't I listen to her?'

'She doesn't see straight on this.' *As on so much else*, I feel like adding.

'It's not Zoë that isn't seeing straight.'

'Mum,' I say. 'Mum, I can't believe this. He's a gorgeous man, a lovely man. Can't you see how kind and thoughtful he is?' And how sexy, I wanted to say—how ravishingly, gloriously sexy. 'Can't you see how we love each other?'

She shakes her head. 'Zoë says he's very rich,' she offers, peeking at me suspiciously.

'What's that got to do with it? It's not his money I'm in love with.'

'No, Isabel: I know that, darling. I'm not accusing you of being mercenary. But where did he get his money from?'

'He's an investor,' I say. 'He's an investor, an entrepreneur.' I don't at this stage have a clue where Max's money comes from, but I don't want to admit it to her. He could have blown up the Mint, for all I know or care. It doesn't matter.

The recliner creaks slightly as my mother rocks. As she becomes more agitated, she rocks faster. 'I don't know what's got into you, Isabel. You've got a lovely husband, lovely children. You've got everything a woman could possibly want. Career, money, security. And you're throwing it all away on this—this—mountebank.'

She releases the archaic word with a mouselike squeak. I say nothing. I am ridiculously disappointed.

'I'm glad your father isn't still alive,' she says, almost vengefully. 'He would be so upset. He loved you so much, Isabel. He was so proud of you.'

I think this is below the belt, and say so. My mother shrugs, weakly, peevishly. I know the cancer is causing her excruciating pain: the oncologist has told Zoë and me that she can't survive more than a year. I know this fact on its own should lead me to treat her kindly, but I am filled with anger at the unfairness of it all, and I say, more shortly than I mean to, that her opinion of Max is in any case quite immaterial, since he is in effect the summation and pinnacle of my heart's desire, all I have ever wanted in life, and nothing will change this.

I probably don't put this argument as well as I could; and inside me some small voice to which I am not listening tells me it isn't a convincing argument anyway. I am, however, by now irretrievably committed and, no matter how little I intend to wound my mother, I find myself launched on a tirade about the general unreasonableness of my family and the degree to which it has (especially Zoë) always conspired to ruin my life.

My mother may be a shrunken and vulnerable old woman, but she is stung by my remarks and retaliates with remarks of her own. From this point the outcome is predictable, and five minutes later I am slamming out of the house, leaving my dying mother weeping.

Zoë rings me that night (when I am in the middle of a stand-up battle with Steve) and bitterly rebukes me for my selfishness and cruelty.

'I couldn't help it,' I say. 'I can't help it if nobody likes what I'm doing, if nobody likes the new direction my life is taking. I can't help it if you don't try to enter into my feelings, if you don't try to sympathise with me and support me.'

'I've never done anything but support you,' snaps Zoë.

This is so manifestly and thoroughly untrue that I cannot think of any way to respond. Zoë misinterprets my silence as shamed acquiescence and, ill-advisedly, continues, in what she considers a softened tone.

'Minky, dear, you must think harder about all this. You're

51

throwing your life away for nothing more than an infatuation. Think of Steve and the children. Think of all you've achieved together. You're not thinking of other people's lives, Minky.'

'Nobody's thinking of my life,' I reply, right on the cusp between screaming and sobbing. 'You're all talking as if I've engineered this whole thing. It's not my fault. I can't help it, that this has happened to me.'

'That's what you've always said,' says Zoë. '*I can't help it. It's not my fault.*' She modifies her voice to produce a self-pitying whimper with which she intends to parody me. 'It's what you've always said. Nothing's ever your fault. You know what I think? I think it's time you grew up.'

I slam the phone down.

None of it is edifying. Even I can tell that. But to me my fate seems so inescapable. I cannot begin to understand why nobody likes this glorious man who has entered my life and so thoroughly transformed it; but, since they don't like him and are therefore unable to sympathise with my feelings, they leave me no choice. I was prepared to meet them halfway, to explain and elaborate and perhaps even (to some minuscule extent) compromise. But it's their fault: they won't meet me, so I'm left with no option.

Why can't they see it? It's as if they view the world—or me, anyway—from behind the wobbling curtain of a giant heat-haze, and the vibrations through which they gaze, discontentedly squinting and peering, distort their vision. And the more they gaze, the worse it gets, and the more mistaken they are. I'm the only one with clear vision.

The next time I see my mother, we more or less make up. But she's still brimming with disapproval, and I'm still full of love (though not for her) and despair, and we are each profoundly dissatisfied with the other.

And, suddenly, everyone's on *Steve's* side. Nobody, so far as I can tell, cares about *me*, about what I might have had to put up with in this marriage, about the blanknesses and gaps that have grown and stretched into cavernous black holes during the seventeen years of our alleged connubial bliss. Nobody is even interested in hearing my point of view.

Dominic, certainly, has never been interested. Locked in his dark, elegant shell, double-insulated against the insistent disharmonies of life, as remote from me as if he lived in the Himalayas, Dominic doesn't care. He never has.

With every meeting a skirmish, each of us caught in increasingly plastic rules of engagement where nothing, really, is off-limits any more, we meet in a kind of no-man's-land from which all mother–son tetherings have been ruthlessly stripped. Not by me, I might add. I don't know how it came to this. We meet; he has a go at me; I have a go back. What am I meant to do when he's so consistently aggressive? Ignore him? Curl up and whimper?

I certainly won't give up on him. One day, I'm sure he'll return to me. Well, approach me might be more accurate: he hasn't ever been near enough to me to return, precisely. But I really tried with Dominic. We had lunch one day. I suggested that he meet me at Southbank. He works in the city, so it wasn't far to ask him to come. When I rang to invite him, he hesitated. I suppose he was simply surprised, which was not an unreasonable response. I hadn't ever made a request like this before; but it was shortly after I'd had a brief exchange with him—at some family occasion, I suppose—during which I had thought I'd detected in his eyes, in his voice, in his expression, some sentiment not totally alien to, let us say, mild affection. It seemed worth a try.

'It's all right,' I said, trying to make it sound bantering rather than testy. 'I don't have nefarious designs.'

He gave a small cough that might have started as a laugh. Or might not. 'No, I'm sure you don't. It's only that it's a busy week, and I'm just not sure...'

'Make it next week, then,' I offered. 'It's not urgent.'

He seemed to debate with himself over this. I pictured him, pencil poised over diary. Except, of course, that he probably does all this kind of thing on computer, or palm pilot.

'No,' he said, finally. 'No, let's make it this week, then.'

I'm always very proud of Dominic, when I'm with him publicly. He's so spruce, so damn good-looking. I always think, well, even if I was a bad wife to Steve (not that I admit that, not on balance anyway), I gave him this glorious son.

It's interesting, the categories we invent for ourselves. Bad wife, good wife. Good mother, bad mother. When I married Steve, I intended to be a good wife. It was an explicit resolution I made. When I had the children, I promised myself quite passionately that I would be a good mother. I was determined in this endeavour. I'm still not sure where it all went wrong, at what point these naïve aspirations started to trip each other up.

Good mother, bad mother.

Dominic is six minutes late, but I forgive him as I see him striding across the restaurant. I see women watching him, as he approaches me. One woman—just a girl, really, with blonde shoulder-length hair, in a rather pretty purple shirt—turns to look at the person with whom Dominic is lunching.

I've gone to trouble, of course. I'm wearing a black pant suit with a biscuity-coloured shirt and an expensive silk scarf with a kind of butterscotch and cream pattern of leaves on it. Whatever Dominic thinks of me, I don't want him to think I'm daggy. It's important to me that he doesn't mind being seen with me, even if he minds being *with* me. The purple- shirted blonde decides I'm hardly competition and transfers her attention back to Dominic.

We don't kiss, of course. We never do. He nods, warily. I try to beam. He looks alarmed. I modify my expression.

I suppose I have imagined this as a leisurely and perhaps anecdotal lunch, both of us relaxing over a good wine, the river sparkling outside the restaurant's windows on this cool, sunny afternoon. It has seemed to me entirely possible, in this atmosphere, that all kinds of boundaries might be crossed, all kinds of fences knocked flying. In fact, as soon as Dominic sits down he glances at his watch.

'Sorry I'm late,' he says, but cursorily, as though he doesn't really mean it. 'It's a hell of a week. There's a lot happening.'

'We could have made it some other time,' I say, trying not to sound vexed. 'I told you, it wasn't urgent. We could have made it next week.'

He runs his hand through his hair. 'The thing is, Isabel, there's always a lot happening. It's quite hard to plan ahead. It seemed better to do it straightaway.'

The waiter looms and distributes menus. I study mine, and pass the wine list to him.

'Oh no,' says Dominic, as though shocked by the mere suggestion that he might imbibe an alcoholic beverage. 'I'll just have a mineral water, thanks. You have a wine, if you'd like: they do it by the glass here.'

'You don't want even a glass?'

'No, honestly. I've got to work this afternoon, you know.'

'Well, yes, but just one glass…'

Dominic is shaking his head, and I break off. If he doesn't want a drink, he doesn't want a drink, and naturally I'm not going to heckle him about it. But it's a bit of a shame, because it makes me feel that if I have a glass of wine I'm somehow dissipated (bad mother), and, because I'm nervous, I want a glass of wine. It'll settle me down.

I try not to look disappointed, and study the list of trendy little entrées and mains. Dominic pushes the menu away almost immediately. The waiter materialises at his side. What's his secret? I can't usually get hold of a waiter within fifteen minutes minimum.

'I'll go for the pasta of the day,' says Dominic. 'Isabel?'

I haven't actually made up my mind, but I say I'll have the same, entrée size.

'Have a glass of the house white,' says Dominic. 'It's good.' He doesn't even give his order for a drink, but a mineral water turns up almost instantly, along with my wine. He notices my slight surprise.

'They know me here,' he explains. 'They know what I always have.'

When I asked him to come to lunch, I also asked him for the name of a restaurant he'd like to go to. I meant it more as a special occasion, a treat, if you like, rather than just turning up somewhere he usually goes anyway. But he clearly hasn't seen it like this, and I can't help feeling hurt.

'Well,' he says, sitting back. 'Hello, Isabel.'

'Hello.'

'Anything in particular on your mind?'

'Should there be?'

'It's not usual, is it, our getting together as cosily as this?'

'No. No, it's not, but perhaps we ought to do it more often.'

'Ought we?'

'Dominic, what's happened to us?' I ask, a bit desperately.

I hadn't meant to do this, to jump into deep waters. All I'd meant to do was build a little bridge, maybe, the beginnings of a little bridge. But he's given me an opening: that cool 'ought we?' is a genuine opportunity, despite its chilly tone, and I'm not likely to get a better one.

And I'm so nervous: perhaps my judgement's off-kilter. Maybe this chink is something he's deliberately giving me; maybe it represents a sliver of opportunity that he positively wants me to grasp.

'What's happened to us, when we can't even be civil to each other any more? It usen't to be like this.'

He sips his mineral water, studies it, says nothing.

'Please. Couldn't we just try? Really, I don't want that much. Only...only to be able to be friends again.'

'Again?' says Dominic, with just that whippy little inflection at which he is so expert.

'Ah, Dominic,' I say. 'We were friends, weren't we?'

'I don't recall. Were we?'

'I don't understand. Dominic, I know I left home when you were still quite young...'

'I was ten,' says Dominic, flatly. 'I'd say ten was very young, not just quite young. Wouldn't you?'

Oh, Christ, I'm right in it now. I plough on.

'Yes, all right, ten is very young. I know it is. Dominic, things don't always work out the way we want them. I didn't mean it to happen the way it did. I didn't mean to leave you. I wanted to take you with me, remember?'

'Yes, but then you left.'

'Well, you wouldn't come.'

'You wouldn't stay.'

'Why should I have stayed?' I'm starting to get angry, and desperate.

'I was ten. That's why you should have stayed. I was ten. We go around in circles, don't we?'

'But that was years and years ago. You've grown up. I'm on my own now. Am I always and eternally to be defined by you as the mother who left you? Is that going to be my permanent status, forever? I mean, can't we move on from that?'

'Well. It isn't a definition I came up with, you know. It was what happened, not what I invented. To borrow that phrase you're so fond of, it wasn't my fault. You did leave me. You self-selected, as it were. I had nothing to do with it, except to have to cope with it.'

'Why do you hate me so?' I cry at Dominic, alarmed even as I speak by the keening note of my voice, the wretched and unpleasant nasal sob that catches at it. He gives me that narrow-eyed look I know and abhor.

'I don't hate you, Isabel. I just don't like you very much.'

The people at the tables near us aren't staring at us; they're averting their eyes, which is somehow worse. The waiter magically appears between us with two plates of pasta, and it occurs to me in a strange disjointed way that this is a strategy I've never before cottoned on to—if you want immediate service in a restaurant, cause an uncomfortable scene. The waiter makes much show of grinding black pepper and parmesan; we preserve a sullen silence until he retreats.

'Can't we start again?' I ask, trying to sound humble, not whiney.

'I don't think so,' says Dominic, stabbing at his pasta.

'Why not?' I'm speaking more quietly now, anxious not to embarrass him.

'I don't know how.'

And there we leave it. I am too shaken to try any further. I can see I'm going to get nowhere. We finish our pasta in silence, to the clear relief of the neighbouring tables. It's a farce. He glances again at his watch, mutters something, gets to his feet. I offer to pay. He shakes his head, settles the bill. Off he goes, back to the demanding world where there's so much to do and no mother to make a nuisance of herself.

This wasn't how I'd imagined it. When he was a child, I mean, or for that matter before he was born. I'd always thought of our being friends, easy with each other, casual and witty, unde-monstrative perhaps but affectionate, sharing an understated empathy, an unarticulated but deep mutual trust. I'd sketched out a number of scenarios, in the torpid moments of pregnancy, before I even knew him; and then again later, when he was a baby, mistrustful and opaque. I'd bowl to him in the backyard. I'd take him to galleries, to Mozart concerts, to poetry readings. We'd play chess together, and when he grew up we'd sip chilled pale wine on summer evenings. We'd discuss philosophies, scien-tific theories, whatever. Our relationship would rest on shared pleasures, shared opinions, mutual appreciation. And love, of course.

Kate and Steve were, needless to say, absent from these touching scenes.

But, the relationship never worked, never meshed. It was worse, far worse, after the marriage broke up, but it was never the way I'd planned it, never the harmonious rapport I'd envisaged. Zoë would say this was my fault, of course. Zoë would say I got it wrong with both children.

Once, she visited when Dominic was little. He was still crawling: he must have been around twelve months, I suppose.

Kate was six: that I do remember. She took a doll from him and his roar was passionate. I rebuked her. I wasn't savage; I wasn't mean: there was no need for her to burst into tears.

'She's very good with him, isn't she?' Zoë said, her voice just lifting towards that spiky tone it has so often when she addresses me.

I disapprove of discussing children in their presence. It leads to unpleasant precocity. I shrugged and nodded as non-committally as I could. At this stage Kate was whining loudly and showing little sign of being good, so far as I could see.

'It's my special doll, Mummy,' she wailed.

'It's her special doll,' said Zoë, regarding me meaningfully.

'She shouldn't have left it where he could reach it.'

'Oh, have a heart, Isabel.'

'For God's sake,' I snapped. Kate ran howling into her bedroom, clutching the damn doll. Dominic, sensing conflict, sobbed more loudly.

'You're hopeless,' snarled Zoë. This is her idea of sisterly support. 'You've got no idea, have you?'

'What's that supposed to mean?'

'You favour him. All the time. It's always: "Kate, don't do this. Kate, don't do that."'

'Zoë, she's six. He's a baby.'

'You need to watch it. You're making some big mistakes.'

'Oh, come on.'

'I mean it, Minky. You're so hard on her, and of course she gets upset. She is good with him. There aren't many six-year-olds who'd be as careful, as gentle. She's a dear little girl, and you're going to cause huge problems for her if you keep on going this way. You'll cause problems for him, too, you mark my words.'

'You've got so much experience, I suppose,' I said, meanly.

'I may not have kids of my own, but I do have experience with kids in the classroom. I spend every day with kids. Anyway, you don't need experience to see the mistakes you're making. It's just a matter of common sense.'

This is a good example of Zoë's tact and sensitivity. In any case, she was demonstrably wrong. Kate has no problems that I'm aware of—or none, anyway, that are caused by me. She had a perfectly happy childhood. She appears to me, in spite of everything, to be a perfectly happy adult. And if Dominic hates me because I was too kind to him when he was a baby—well, what kind of sense does that make?

I kept thinking the relationship would improve. I gave up work for Dominic, so I could spend more time with him. It was harder, anyway, to work when I had two small children at home. I've heard other women say this, too: it's three times as hard with two children as with one. But he always fought me, even as a baby, even as a toddler. He fell over once and I cuddled him, crooned to him, savouring the moment, because he so seldom let me do this. 'Poor Dominic,' I murmured, rocking him. He exploded in fury and struck my face. 'I'm *not* poor,' he screamed. 'I'm *not poor.*'

Well. What can you do?

This is one reason I so much appreciate Sophie's company, Sophie's unconditional love. I sometimes think Sophie and Max are the only two people who have ever really cared about me, who have truly loved me.

Yet I always feel, with pricking resentment, that I'm worthier of love than people seem to think. If only they could see me as I really am, if only Dominic could get past the protective spines I raise against him, if he could only lower the guns he mounts against me, if only we could meet in some pure space unhindered by our family, our history, our expectations of ourselves and each other, I'm sure he'd like me.

I'm a likeable person: I know I am. I'm a warm and loving person. *I love you, Dominic!* Sometimes I think I ought to scream it at him, every time I see him, just to drive the point home, to make him notice me, listen to me, listen to what I want to force into that sleek, obdurate head of his.

I know women who are entirely unremarkable but who nevertheless manage to retain cordial relations with their children, their sons. Of course we all adopt party manners for the world's scrutiny, and I imagine there are rough patches in such relationships, dropped stitches, torn pages, dark, vicious corners of psyches that never see the light of day or face exposure to outside observation. Still, such people manage to maintain a reasonable façade.

I'm quite positive most sons aren't as savage to their mothers as Dominic is to me; most sons don't chip away at their mothers' fragile veneers with anything matching Dominic's deadly ruthlessness. I can't, however, adequately measure or comprehend their success against my failure. I can't see *why* they've managed what should surely be a relatively simple manoeuvre, when I so conspicuously haven't. What is it about bringing up children, after all? What makes it so difficult?

I started off with intentions and resolutions as good as the next person's. I taught them manners, correct behaviour, consideration for others. I talked to them; I played with them; I didn't abuse them; I didn't take drugs; I didn't hit them; I tried not to shout at them. I know I split up the family, but it wasn't them I had to get away from: it was Steve, and I've always made that distinction clear.

I don't understand where it went wrong, at what particular

point Dominic decided to limit his communications to sneer mode, why he woke up one day and perceived my maternal limitations with such devastating clarity.

These women I know who are successful mothers—who at any rate seem to be successful mothers—there's nothing so special about any of them. Intelligence doesn't appear to be a prerequisite, nor does talent, nor (let's face it) good looks. They've just bumbled along, the same as all of us. I once said to a woman I knew how lucky she was to have such happy and successful children, and she fixed me with a dirty look and said: 'Luck, Isabel, had nothing to do with it.'

Well, luck always has something to do with it, in my book. If you can put in so much effort and still fail, luck has a lot to do with it.

Sometimes I fantasise about the kinds of circumstances that might enlighten Dominic about the value of a mother's love. Well, not any mother. Me. Some rescue I could effect, some unfortunate condition he finds himself trapped by (imprisonment, perhaps, for some shameful crime?) in which I waft back into the mainstream of Dominic's life trailing forgiveness and compassion. *Gosh, Mum, where would I be without you?* whispers a white-faced Dominic, as I gently raise him on my arm and spoon homemade beef tea between his unresisting lips.

Or perhaps we're hostages together (unlikely, this, I do recognise that element of the hypothesis), and I intercept the shot that's meant for him. Or then again, perhaps I'm simply dying, slowly and rather picturesquely (and let us hope painlessly), and Dominic in imagining his future without me is brought to his senses. *Gosh, Mum, what will I do without you?* whispers a white-faced Dominic, reaching to grasp my fragile hand as he sits beside the bed repenting of his former brutality.

And then there's the final scenario, the funeral one. That's where I'm in my coffin (adorned simply, due to my distaste for ostentation—perhaps only with a single crimson long- stemmed rose) and Dominic, still white-faced, is at the microphone, or in the pulpit, or wherever, choking over the revelation of his long-hidden adoration of me. Ah, the poignancy!

For obvious reasons, this particular scenario isn't one I treat myself to except when I'm truly depressed, but on certain occasions it does afford a kind of odd, luxurious enjoyment. In many ways it's a scene I find more immediately attractive than contemplation of either of my weddings, or for that matter anyone else's.

Strange, how we circle around these milestone occasions. We eventually decide they were of significantly less importance than we'd thought at the time (what did it matter whether I married Steve or not, after all, in retrospect?), but still we open the albums, still we dream over the pictures, wondering. Mind you, I've done it only because Sophie has egged me on, but once she's awakened my interest I find I'll spend longer than is sensible poring, and remembering trivia the detail of which had lain slumbering in the farthest recesses of my mind for (for instance) thirty years.

Sophie in her recent pursuit of family weddings has shown little interest in Zoë's, but I suppose that's natural: I'm her grandmother, after all. Zoë's more distant, just a great-aunt. In those days it mattered more, getting married: it was the thing young girls had rammed down their throats, the thing they were taught to regard as the very apex of aspiration, the miraculous consummation of our lives. Zoë and I were lucky that our parents judged we ought to have careers, too, or at least the option of careers: many parents didn't think like that.

And Zoë's five years older than I am (the same distance, coincidentally, as there is between Kate and Dominic, and between Sophie and Liam: the women of our family all seem to wait five years before the progenitive urge returns). But it meant a lot, then, that Zoë was five years older and yet I was married first.

I was aware of the superiority it conferred on me, and I was not above taking advantage of it, either, after all the years of bullying and condescension. She did not marry until two years after I did, at the end of a protracted courtship: she was twenty-seven by the time she stalked down the aisle on Dad's arm. I believe I felt her mortification more keenly than she did herself, to have reached this ripe old age before entering into the holy state of matrimony. Strange, how things change.

At the time of Zoë's wedding I was heavily pregnant with Kate, who spent most of the ceremony alternating between kicking viciously at my bladder and bearing down on it with agonising determination. Zoë had worn an ivory silk thing, which to my mind somehow contrived to shout its understated elegance to the world (with her figure, she certainly couldn't have got away with frills and froth), and Henry had simpered above a tie that didn't suit him.

I found the whole thing fatiguing and profoundly uncomfortable and exceptionally boring; I remembered also feeling disproportionate relief upon reaching the end of the service without Kate's having caused a disaster.

I'd been relieved, though, that I didn't have to play bridesmaid. Nowadays you see young women tittupping down the aisle eight months gone—and they're the brides, let alone the bridesmaids—but in those times it was more rigid, decorous—call it what you will. It wasn't entirely a bad thing, having notions of decorum.

At any rate, I wasn't expected to participate. I sat through the ceremony, breathing heavily and wishing passionately, desperately, that the baby would stop its demoniac activity. Steve beamed beside me. He was so proud: it was hilarious yet strangely moving. I couldn't have had more fuss made of me, more attention drawn to me, if I'd been anticipating a virgin birth. Which I certainly wasn't.

Zoë, entering connubial bliss, seemed largely indifferent. She was an extremely competent bride, avoiding most of the available nuptial excesses, the flimflam and the fairy floss.

I had actually pretended, at my wedding, to be a little more flustered than I really was, in order to present an image of coy feminine confusion calculated (if I had only realised it) to confirm unenlightened prejudices still clung to by the congregation. My blushing uncertainty enabled Steve to assume the manly protective profile for which he yearned. He actually referred to me in his speech as 'the little woman'. I don't think any element of self-parody entered into this nomenclature.

My sister, by contrast, adopted no girlish strategies, no circumlocutory fluffiness. She was wise enough, I suppose, to know she couldn't get away with it. Businesslike, sturdy, methodical, she superintended such challenges as table arrangements and flowers with military precision. A wedding was like a lesson: it had to be planned and programmed and rehearsed and, finally, got through with minimal disruption, discipline being maintained and the whole proving an edifying experience for all concerned. Henry came along for the ride: that was as much as he had to do with any of it. Zoë steered her way through it all with, so far as I could see, minimal consultation with him. A likely prevision of their marriage, I thought.

Henry was such a puzzle to me. He taught science at the

school where Zoë taught history. He still does. When Zoë first brought him home, I couldn't fathom him at all. Even in those days, when (I freely admit) many strange customs obtained, most men of Henry's age, which I suppose was his late twenties, didn't customarily wear three-piece suits.

I'd known Henry for over a year before I saw him in anything else. It made him look like an undertaker. He had a disconcerting habit of tilting his head back, appraising you through the lower half of his spectacles. Balding and bony, slightly stooped even then, a gold filling conspicuous in a front tooth, meticulous in his speech and careful in his movements, he seemed to me desiccated, ponderous and boring.

I recall teasing Zoë about him.

Blind as a bat, bald as an eagle
Henry isn't sexy; Henry isn't regal
Caught like flies in amber in his sober three-piece suit
Henry isn't clever and nor is Henry cute.

I know it wasn't nice of me. Zoë wasn't nice to me, either.

Anyway, she didn't see the joke.

My parents liked Henry. Well, they liked Steve, too, so it shows what their judgement in these matters was like. My mother thought Steve's blond, square good looks and his doglike adoration of me made him a delightful and endearing young man, and a suitor of eligibility *par excellence*. The irremediably comic element I detected in Henry was not visible to her.

'She can't want to *live* with him,' I remember saying, one evening after dinner. I think I was drying the dishes at the time.

'Why not?' My mother would have been wearing the bright pink rubber gloves that she always donned for this task, drawing them with elaborate care over her tiny hands. She was a slow and careful washer of dishes. It drove me mad, having to hang around while she scrubbed at specks minute as atoms and warily held spotless glasses up to the light.

'Oh, Lord, Mum. He's so frantically boring. He's such an old man. How could she even think of marrying him?' What I really meant was: *How could she think of going to bed with him?*

'He's a sensible man,' commented my mother. 'Have you heard the way he tries to tell jokes?'

'Delivering a good punchline isn't a mandatory skill for a husband.'

'No, but…'

'Actually,' said my mother, 'he has a good sense of humour. Very dry.'

I snorted and my mother frowned. 'He'll make her very happy.'

'They're not even engaged yet. Are they?'

'They will be,' said my mother with quiet certitude. 'They suit each other. You might find him unglamorous, Isabel, but he's a reliable, good-tempered man with a great capacity for loyalty. And he loves Zoë.'

I think I didn't care enough to argue the point. If Zoë wanted to wreck her future by attaching herself permanently to a tedious freak with bad teeth and bifocals, that was her funeral. I was getting on with my life—or that was how it seemed to me at the time. Amazing though it seems to me now, I was busy planning to marry Steve.

I'm not sure, now, why. It wasn't as if I was completely bluffed by the whole marriage scenario. I wanted my degree; I wanted my career. I wanted it all, I suppose. Well, why not? It was becoming evident that having it all might be possible: young women of my time, graduating in the early 1970s, were just starting to regard themselves as forerunners to a brave new world where injustice would never again be based on gender and where nothing would dare to intervene between oneself and the star one decided intrepidly to follow. Some of it has come true; a lot hasn't. In those days, there were no templates to follow, no blueprints to study. Not for careers, not for parenting, not for anything much. Mind you, I don't think you learn much about being a parent from anything but workplace training.

Being a grandparent, however, is different. I can't believe how dead easy it is, especially after all the times my own children ate me up alive and smacked their lips over me. It's so effortless, when Sophie wanders into my house in the late afternoon. 'Hi, Gandie,' she calls, and comes to give me a big hug and kiss. Never anything forced, never anything other than natural and affectionate and loving. It makes it so easy, to love back.

I must say, however, that the minuteness of her attention to the detail of my life is starting to wear thin. *No more wedding snaps*, I pray, silently. I've had my fill of staring down old aisles and those who people them.

But she takes a different tack, the next time. I'd almost prefer the wedding snaps.

'Look what I found, Gandie,' she says, rummaging in her bag. 'You'll never guess.'

I wouldn't have, either. It's a photograph, again; but this time it's not of a person but a portrait. It's a photograph of Max's portrait. The original—the portrait, I mean, not its subject—stands face to the wall, covered in brown paper, in my garage. It's a long time since I've taken it out and checked it for mould or rat nibbles or anything else.

The photograph is rather dog-eared and, since it is taken from a lower angle, presents an odd perspective on the painting. Max's head seems, somehow, further away than it ought to be, and his stance appears awkward. Max was never awkward.

'It's Max, isn't it?'

'Yes, honey. It's Max.'

'Did you paint it, Gandie?'

'Me? Goodness no, darling. I just mess around in water-colours, and all I do are sketches. This is a photo of a proper oil portrait.'

'Where is it now?'

'I don't know,' I lie.

'Did Max take it with him when he went away?'

'Yes,' I say, relieved to have so neatly packaged a solution ready to hand. 'Yes, he took it with him.'

'Who painted it?'

'Honey, where did you get this photograph?' I've never seen it before. I certainly didn't take it.

Sophie looks equivocal.

'I just found it,' she says, airily. She sees that I am looking hard at her and shifts slightly.

'Sophie?'

'I found it in one of Mum's drawers. I wasn't looking for it, or anything. Mum knew I was looking in her drawer. She was going to lend me some perfume and she told me to go and look for it in her drawer. And this was stuck at the bottom of it.'

'Does she know you've got it, Sophie?'

'Well. Not really, I guess. I thought I'd just put it back and, you know, everything would be cool. She wouldn't mind, I'm sure. I just wanted to show it to you, Gandie. Tell me about it, go on.'

I know I should be cross with her, but she can always wheedle me. And I love it when we share a secret from which Kate is excluded. I know this is mean and unworthy of me; I know Kate is her mother and she ought to be more open with her mother. But the fact is, I love it when Sophie says: 'This is just for us, Gandie, okay?'

But I don't want to talk to her about the portrait. I fudge it, the way I am fudging so many things with Sophie, these days.

'It was a present,' I say. 'It was for his birthday.' 'Which birthday? A special birthday?'

'Yes, it was his fiftieth birthday.' I am aware that to Sophie fifty must seem astonishingly old, momentously old. But that's what it was for: Max's fiftieth birthday.

We'd grown fond of a gallery in Richmond: one of the artists who exhibited there regularly had caught our eye. She did portraits in oils—rather fluid, elongated things, almost El Greco-ish or even Dobellian, their exaggerated perspectives delicate and witty, their hues gentle, the likenesses in the best of them magical, wondrous things that caught essential quirks and personalities as well as simply registering identities.

Her name was Hilary Jacoby and she was a funny, fey wisp of a woman, with pale puffball hair and hard green eyes that to your immense surprise you found looking right through you, into your innermost soul, just when you'd decided she was right off the planet.

I commissioned a portrait of Max for his fiftieth birthday; he promised to commission one of me for mine. We were going to hang them side by side in the lounge. 'There'll be a hundred years of life up there on our wall,' he said.

I thought of this when I turned fifty, but wasn't tempted to do anything about it. Why commission a portrait of yourself for yourself? I haven't heard of Hilary for years: she may not even be alive any more. She was only a little older then than I am now, but who knows what's happened to her.

There, at any rate, in this old and rather creased photograph of his portrait, is Max, elegant as always in a crisp, white, open-neck shirt, tailored grey pants, black shiny shoes. He's sitting back in a dark leather armchair; his long and beautiful hands lie, relaxed, on its armrests. Beside him is a small table and on the table is a photograph of me, sitting at my desk at Rain. On my desk is a photograph of Max's portrait, with its photograph of me inside it, and so on. It was something Hilary wasn't keen on, but Max persuaded her: he loved tricksy little things, puzzles that made you look twice and three times, and charmed you. Sophie doesn't fail to notice it, of course.

'Look, Gandie!' she exclaims. 'It's a trick, isn't it? It goes back, and back, and back. It's so clever!'

'Yes. It is clever.'

'Who thought of doing that? Was that you?'

'No, honey, that was Max. Max liked puzzles. Conundrums, riddles—anything like that.'

'He's got such a *nice* face,' says Sophie, studying the nice face closely.

'Yes.'

Sophie twines her arms about my neck. 'He just went away, didn't he, Gandie?' 'Yes, he did, honey.'

'Wouldn't you like to have him back?' she says, coaxingly, as if she were offering me an especially delicious chocolate.

'Oh, honey, it's all water under the bridge. When you're older you'll understand that. There's no point looking back, saying I wish, I wish.'

'Where's Max now, Gandie?'

'It sounds like one of those books, doesn't it?' I say with an effort, giving her a quick hug. 'Where's Wally? Where's Max now?'

'Yes, but don't put me off, Gandie.'

'I don't know, honey.'

'But he might come back?'

'I don't think so.'

'But he might, Gandie?'

'Sophie, darling, leave it. Max is dead, that's the truth of it. He's dead: he's not coming back. Let's not talk about it any more. And you make sure you pop that picture back in your mum's drawer, okay?'

'Yes, I will. Of course I will, Gandie. But listen, Gandie darling, you don't *know* he's dead, do you? Mum says he's still alive. Mum says he'll come back, one day.'

Bloody Kate, interfering again, I think in fury. And, suddenly, something snaps. She's twisted the terrible knife enough. I can't take this any more.

'I do know he's dead,' I say, tightly. 'I do know it.'

She cocks her head, sceptical, a little dismayed. 'Do you know it for absolute certain sure? I mean, have you visited his grave?'

'Yes.' I reach out and hold her hand. 'I have visited his grave. I do know he's dead. Sophie, you mustn't tell this to anyone. It's our secret, okay? You mustn't tell your mum, or your dad, or anyone. Can you keep an important secret, like this?'

Sophie's eyes grow wide as she absorbs this. 'But, Gandie, Mum would want to know, wouldn't she? Mum really liked Max; she says he was the best friend she ever had. Why don't you tell Mum?'

'I can't explain,' I say, aware that I am gripping her hand too hard and loosening my grasp. 'When you're older, I'll explain. I can't talk about it, Sophie. Not at present. When you're older, I'll tell Mum. I'll explain everything. But I can't do it now. Believe me, darling, you mustn't say anything to your mother.'

At last, puzzled and chastened by my disclosure, she settles down to her milk and apple and homework. She looks serene, but what is she thinking? What does she make of what I've told her? What will she do about it?

She sprawls at the kitchen table to work; I sit on the other side of the bench, in the living room, which opens out between the kitchen and the small, pretty back garden, with its ferns and roses and two young birch trees. This is what we usually do when Sophie does her homework. She's at the kitchen table; I'm in the living room drinking coffee and reading the newspaper, available to answer questions.

I often sneak a look at her around the side of the paper when she doesn't know I'm doing it. I like to watch her sweet face creased with concentration; I like to watch her chewing her hair and mumbling figures to herself and doodling on the side of the page.

Today, however, I use the paper to hide my face from her perceptive eyes. My hands, I notice, are trembling. Does she believe me? I wonder. I think she does. Will she tell her mother? I don't think she will: Sophie and I have shared secrets before, and she's been reliable. But this is different. It matters.

When she goes, I say, quite lightly: 'You won't forget, Sophie? It's our secret, darling. Just ours.' She nods solemnly, and leaves me on my own, with nothing to do but fret, and gnaw my fingernails.

I don't want to think about Max. I don't want to think about anything, really: I just want to calm myself down and return to a state of dreary neutrality, so that Sophie's interest in these matters loses its edge, so that I escape this awful sense of staring down the crevasse.

I know that the more emotional I get, the more her ready sympathies are stirred, and the more she wants to know and understand. I should be grateful, I suppose: how many children are obsessed with their grandmother's past?

In my determination not to think about Max or his fiftieth birthday, I find myself thinking about mine instead. It wasn't as we'd envisaged it when Max spoke of hanging our portraits together. I would have let it pass, frankly. The celebration of having spent half a century battling away at life is bound to be an ambiguous kind of occasion, after all; although I suppose survival pure and simple is probably something to celebrate.

Anyway, Kate and Zoë between them were determined not to let the day pass without some kind of family get-together, God save me. They even had a mild disagreement about where it should be held. Kate wanted it at her place so that, she said, the children could feel part of the festivities; Zoë thought it more appropriate (she actually put it like that) that she and Henry host the event. Ever since Max's departure from my life Zoë has treated me with a kind of scrupulously considerate and self-conscious benevolence that drives me stark raving mad.

'I don't see why we have to do anything at all,' I say. 'I've never been a party person: you both know that. It's just another birthday. Let's let it go.'

'Rubbish, Minky,' says Zoë. 'It's not just another birthday. I had a big fiftieth and I want you to have the same.'

'We're not kids, Zoë. I don't have to have a party because you had a party.'

'Of course you must have a party, Mum,' says Kate, beaming, misinterpreting my genuine pleading for a variety of specious attention-getting. She thinks I'm merely making a fuss so that I can then gracefully give in. Zoë knows better: I can tell that from the look in her eye, but all her native persistence is to the fore and, terrier-like, she's not going to let go till she gets her way and forces it on me as well.

'I don't like fuss,' I say.

'You used to like it,' says Zoë. 'Remember your sixteenth birthday? You had a huge party. I helped with that one, too.'

'Zoë, you mightn't have noticed this, but I'm not sixteen any more.'

Zoë laughs immoderately, as if I'd cracked rather a funny joke, and continues to discuss menus and methodologies with Kate.

The event was held at Zoë and Henry's. I could have told Kate this would happen: someone with her pliancy is at a disadvantage when dealing with resolve of Zoë's calibre. They actually went to a lot of trouble, or Zoë did, anyway: I don't suppose Henry had much to do with it.

It's a big house, in which they rattle around like a pair of dried peas. Sometimes they have students staying in one of the three spare bedrooms: they both involve themselves in their school's international program and a succession of Chinese and Malaysian and Vietnamese and Thai adolescents have come and gone through Zoë's militant domesticity and Henry's fussy over-organisation. They are always suckers for good causes, Zoë and Henry.

Sometimes, as I've said, I think our family is as dysfunctional as families get; other times I marvel, startled into unwilling admiration, at how well we manage, all of us, how we scrub up for the big occasion. We've improved, no doubt about it. This is partly because of Sophie, as I've said, but it's also because we ourselves try so damned hard. Assiduously we paper over the cracks, snip off the dangling telltale threads; and we front up, bright-eyed and bushy-tailed, to the big occasion.

We carry out all this feverish remedial activity only partly for the outsiders who will attend and for whom some sort of fiction needs to be maintained; principally it is all for our own benefit, to fool ourselves into a temporary acceptance of family unity and bonhomie.

Oh, the poses we adopt, the grins we artlessly flash at each other, the greetings and wishes and presents, the outward registering of all levels of pleasure between satisfaction and delight, the chattering and gossip and kindnesses with which we spuriously bless each other on such occasions! All of these are part of the same deluded plan we have concocted towards an ephemeral new reality that depends on our cooperation and whose success is measured by the extent to which we are able temporarily to forget old divisions, old quarrels, old hatreds.

There's a lot of energy involved, when you think about it. Duplicity always does eat up energy, I suppose, even when it's half-instinctive, as this is. Why do we put ourselves to the trouble? Is it a tribal, collective impulse, designed to ensure our survival by protecting us all from the awful truth about ourselves and each other? Or is it a more individual response, a deliberate and explicit resolution from each of us, grounded in pure self-trickery? Whichever, in my family we're all past masters, and our mastery came to the fore for my birthday.

All the family were there, of course, even Liam, who can't have been more than three at the time. Kate insisted on his presence. Sophie's excitement was touching: Zoë arranged for her to propose a toast and she made up a little nonsense rhyme for it. How did it go?

Swiftly Gandie's turning fifty
Gandie's always very thrifty
Will she be niftier, will she be thriftier
As she gets fitter and swiftly more fiftier?

Something like that, anyway.

Steve kissed my cheek in an unforeseen access of affection (unforeseen by him as well as by me, I imagine—or perhaps it was premeditated; perhaps he had to steel himself to it). Gavin told several Millie jokes. Kate beamed. Liam played with small cars in a corner. Henry fretted over the drinks. Dominic brooded darkly. Zoë bustled around capably and presided triumphant over all. I tolerated it as best I could. That is, we all behaved true to type. I trust some of us enjoyed it: I know I didn't, much, but then I don't suppose my enjoyment was the principal aim of the undertaking.

How fatiguing these celebrations are! How many of them one has to attend! At what point in my life will I be permitted to say: *No. No more.* How old will I have to be before my children and grandchildren will simply say that Gandie is a cantankerous old so-and-so and there's no point inviting her along?

One of the surreal things about resting in the bosom of my family on such occasions is that I can look around me and it is almost as if Max never happened. There is Steve. There is Dominic, with Paula or whoever. There is Kate, with her husband and children. There are Zoë and Henry. It is all too normal for words.

Ah, Max, Max. Where did you appear from? Why did you

come into my life at all? It wasn't so bad, as it was. Unremarkable, I grant you, but there are worse things than being unremarkable. Why did you storm my threshold, lay waste to my life, come prancing in with your glitter and your glamour? How did it all happen?

Part Two

Max entered my life as a hot knife enters butter. Without warning, without resistance. Suddenly, I was transformed, penetrated. Perhaps impaled would be a better word. There was no prevision, no sly astrologer's forecast. One moment I knew nothing of his existence; the next, there he was, in my studio at the office, saying, charmingly: 'Hello. My name's Max Knight. You're Isabel Weaving? You designed a house for a friend of mine.'

I had been working, as I always do, in the square patch of sun directly beneath the skylight, puzzling over the doors to a court-yard. As I blinked and looked up it seemed to me that the bright flicker surrounding him was no trick of the eye but a sexual dazzle, an aura of danger and appeal, a cross-hatching of faint glitter festooning him like a profane halo.

'Hello,' I said, squinting. 'Which house? Which friend?'

I don't do a lot of work on houses. Beatrice and I tend to concentrate on commercial and sometimes government develop-ments—buildings for small businesses, alterations to municipal offices, that sort of thing. Sometimes we'll do sets of villa units, if an up-market developer will give us enough land and not demand too much crowding on it: we're successful enough to be picky. But we don't do many houses. It's not that I don't enjoy them: it's just the way it's worked out. They don't on the whole come my way.

'Bianca Crawford,' he said. 'Ah, yes.'

The Crawfords were old friends of Steve's and they'd wanted an ultra-special beach house. They'd bought a block near Point Leo and driven us down to show it to me.

It was a great block: bush and ocean together. It whetted my appetite and I designed something for them at greatly reduced rates, partly because Steve wanted me to and I didn't have any objection, partly because the land set my blood racing: it was exposed on one side, sheltered on the other, on a rise, facing south-west into the bay. It offered fabulous sunsets and lots of challenges to do with wind and light and blending.

I finished up designing something flat and rambling, full of light and space, with small windows where you didn't expect them, vast sweeps of glass where you did. There were two court-yards where Bianca wrought wonders with native plants. She did the same in the main garden so that the house, in spite of being elevated, settled gently into its surroundings. Almost immediately, the whole thing looked as if it was meant to be there, had always been there.

It was more complex, and better, than your average beach house: they intended to retire there eventually and well before it was finished Bianca was starting to say she couldn't wait to get there permanently.

They called it Granada, because of some holiday they'd once spent in Spain. I have to say none of it looked very Spanish to me, but it was their house and they could have called it Patagonia or Upper Slaughter so far as I was concerned.

It had been a lot of fun and a great success, one of those projects where everything fell into place: the builder was snappy but meticulous and the Crawfords hadn't done any of the annoying things people who commission houses usually do, like endlessly changing their minds, or being cowardly about the drama the site offered. It had won one award and had been nominated for a couple more, and I'd been told it hadn't missed out by much. I'd thought at the time I could bear to do more of that sort of work, but it had been five or six years earlier and the business had hotted up and taken us in different directions.

And here was this stunning man, with his divine crinkly grin, wanting me to design another one like it.

It wasn't until much, much later that Bianca told me he wasn't really a friend at all. His silver Audi had pulled into the driveway one day when they were out on the terrace. He'd been all diffident charm: such a beautiful house; had admired it many times; could he possibly see inside; how imaginative; how striking; how understatedly gorgeous; who on earth had dreamt it up? They gave him a cup of tea and they chatted amiably and then he drove out of their lives and into mine.

It didn't matter: I took no notice. It had been cheeky of him, to claim acquaintance where none existed, but not a mortal sin after all. I taxed him with it and we laughed together about his nerve.

'I've bought a block,' he said, sitting down, all eagerness, passion reined in but peeking through, charisma blazing. 'I want a house like Granada on it. Can I show it to you? Will you do it for me?'

I always notice a man's eyes first. His eyes and his hands. Max had very black lashes and his eyes were grey and clear and smiling. His fingers were long and strong; his hands tanned and sinewy. He had beautiful oval fingernails, very clean.

Silly, to remember a man's fingernails.

His voice was wonderful. It was a cultured voice but not affected. Deep, with a burr to it that might have been Irish once, a long time ago. Sometimes I would listen to Max without hearing him properly because it was the tone and lilt and timbre of his voice that entranced me, not what the voice was actually saying.

When he had gone I waited five minutes or so, and then strolled into the little reception area off which our offices, Beatrice's and mine, gave. Dawn was on the telephone. Bea was there, rifling through a filing cabinet.

'Who was that?' she asked.

'A new client.'

'Where did he pop up from then?'

'Nowhere, really. He's a friend of the Crawfords. He wants me to do something like Granada for him.'

'Where?'

'Somewhere in Hawthorn.'

'He's got the land? In Hawthorn? Enough land for a place like Granada in Hawthorn?'

'I believe so. Roughly, anyway. He said it was a big block.'

Bea continued to flick through the files, her disapproval patent in the sharp jabbing of her fingers and the stiffness of her back.

'Did you meet him through the Crawfords?'

'I've only just met him.'

'You never knew him before he walked through the door then?'

'Never.'

'Izzie, why have you got that stupid smile on your face?' said Bea.

I hadn't known of it, but I got rid of it as fast as I could.

Dawn put the telephone down. 'You don't know him?' she asked.

'No. Never laid eyes on him till then. Why?'

'Well, I guess it was the way he walked in. He kind of looked at your door and said "Isabel in, is she?" and headed straight for it. Normally I would have given you warning, shown him in. But he seemed so confident, I thought he must be a friend.'

Max was always like that. He had an extraordinary capacity to get his bearings in a place, in a situation: he could walk into a room and know instantly what its layout was, who stood where, what strategic advantages it offered him, what traps lay in wait. He had a preternaturally keen nose for opportunity and a talent for judging when and how to sidle towards it.

'As if he owned the place,' snapped Bea. 'He looks like a con man, Izzie. Take care. Don't do anything till you get a hefty deposit.'

I thought she was jealous. I still think she was jealous.

They talk about love at first sight. Who can say? I don't suppose I really fell in love with Max during that very first meeting: it couldn't have lasted more than ten minutes, anyway. Who can say what it was or how it happened? Maybe I was having an active-pheromone day.

But the attraction was instant and I felt I'd never understood the word 'magnetic' before. It was as if my entire body were composed of iron filings that had snapped to attention: every skerrick of me was drawn to him, yearning at him, screaming for him.

Later that week I drove to meet him at the site. It was winter: one of those cold, still mornings with wisps of mist still hanging furtively, swollen black clouds above. It was indeed a large block—almost a double block—in what the real-estate agents are fond of calling a quiet leafy street in the heart of Hawthorn. You wouldn't have thought such a site could still exist in quite so built-up an area: it must have been worth a mint.

I wore my black leather boots and my scarlet coat. Normally, then as now, I wore quieter colours—olive, biscuit, tan, cream, and always lots of black; but I saw this coat and fell in love with it, as they say. You fall in love with coats, with men, with babies. I was very conscious, on this pewter morning, of how colourful I was, how I moved through the dulled landscape, a splash of geranium-red against the muted misty background.

It was the first time I noticed this very particular effect Max had on me, that he forced me to watch myself so that I was constantly aware of how I appeared to him: it was like having an internal video of me running in my brain. It was to be the same when we were in bed. I was always conscious of how I looked to him, especially in my nakedness. It was disconcerting at first, but then I grew accustomed to it: when Max was no longer in bed with me, it was not only him I missed but the curious new perspective I had acquired of myself: grainy slow-moving star of my own private cult movies.

But that day we were not naked, not yet. He was in grey: charcoal Italian jumper, grey tailored pants, good black shoes. His hair was silvering: it must have once—not so very long ago— have been jet black, as black as his eyelashes, as black as my hair.

I walked around the block, marvelling. There were two grand lemon-scented gums at the north-west corner, great white shafts thrusting through the ashen air, dissolving into their pale plumes of delicate long leaves at their extremities. They were as mighty as cathedral columns, as white as flour, as bones. You could smell their crisp fresh fragrance in the damp still air. I could see how the sun would glitter off them, as it glittered off the slanting windows I was already imagining.

'You'll keep these?' he asked, a shade anxiously.

I nodded. It would have been murderous to do anything else. Already I could see how I might use them: a half-frame to the entrance, great flagless masts off-centre from the main action. Granada had depended partly for its effect on asymmetrical angles and unpredictable planes, on nooks and sweeps and perspectives of sudden enchantment. I could do something very like that with this site, dissimilar though it was to Granada's ground. My fingers tingled with it.

The site was flat and scraped, unnaturally tidy in the way sites look when wreckers and backhoes have been through. Not much grass; no bush or shrubs. Only the two giant eucalypts. It had been prepared: it was ready for population.

'How did you come by this?' I asked. 'There must have been something here. You must have wrecked it?'

'It was a cottage. Not very big. I moved it and sold it. They sliced it down the middle and took it away on two of those huge trailer things, with *Wide Load* all over them. Quite a spectacle, in fact. Then I had people in to clean up. It's all ready to go. A blank page, for you to draw on.'

Judging by the houses in the rest of the street, it couldn't have been too small a cottage. If he had the resources to do that, I thought, to dispense with what must have been a pretty good house in so summary a way, he had the resources to build a fabulous home.

'You could have a pool,' I said. 'It's big enough. Do you want a pool?'

'Love a pool.'

'Or a tennis court?' But I wanted him to have a pool: I wanted the house to have water near it, water as part of its

89

thought patterns, just as Granada had.

'Don't play tennis.'

'Do you swim?'

'All the time.'

'That's settled, then.'

'Not bright blue,' he said.

'Sorry?'

'Not bright blue. The pool. Something subtler.'

In the event the pool had latte-coloured tiles, shot through with a darker shimmer, like raw silk. It was a gorgeous pool: it twinkled in the sun with a pale, exotic gleam. Inviting, coolly seductive.

The house sprang around me. Stairs flowed in shallow curves; doorways unfolded; space crystallised into shapes: my head hummed with the rhythms of it. Its colours danced: colours of salt and bark, leaf and foam. Rainwater and sunlight. Gravel and moss. The texture and grain of it all curtained me. I was practically orgasmic with it.

He was watching me. 'You can do something with it?'

'I can do something good with it. I can do something very good. What sort of a budget are we thinking?'

He shrugged. 'It's my dream house. The house of a lifetime. Of what's left of a lifetime, at any rate. No holds barred.' 'I have *carte blanche*, in effect?' I could hardly believe it.

'Absolutely.'

'No limits? You're seriously telling me I have no limits?'

'Not unreasonable ones.' He smiled. He had a crooked smile, a way of slightly crinkling his nose.

'It's incredible. It's what all architects long for.'

'Well, you've got it. I want to be in on the planning, mind you.'

'You will be. Oh, you will be.'

'And I don't want a mansion,' he said, glancing around at the surroundings, the old solid wealth on both sides. 'I don't want something that shouts or sticks out like a sore thumb. I want something like Granada: I want something that nestles in, that belongs, and settles itself into its surroundings, something that you have to look and look at to see how beautiful it is, something you keep discovering.'

I nodded. It was amazing, the feel the man had for all I held most dear. I would give him a house that sang, a symphony of a house, a house like no other in the world.

And then, without warning, the sky burst and it poured. It rained as if it hadn't rained for a hundred years and the sky had been saving it up all that time. Max had parked his car, his silver Audi, down the road a little way. We sprinted for it. We couldn't have been more than thirty metres away but we were pretty much soaked by the time we scrambled in, tumbling over each other in the back seat, laughing, breathless, wet hair in our faces, rivulets dribbling down our necks.

Of course he kissed me. Of course I kissed him back.

I can't even remember in what order things happened then. I'd fallen into the maelstrom, and there was no way out.

It didn't all happen suddenly, not all of it. I know that. I did try. I tried to withstand it, to pretend it hadn't happened, but finally that was impossible. It was six months from that day, that first visit to the site of Rain, before I slept with Max; it was a year before I left Steve. A delay like that shows something, doesn't it? I did try: for a while I tried hard. But there was no point. There was nothing I could do.

How can I describe that year? What can I say to give some idea of the change that came over me? It was not a change that I willed or welcomed. It was beyond my control. It was as if the molecules in my body quivered and melted and recast themselves in a new physical pattern.

I was a different person: that was what none of them could see. It was as if I had lived all my life in an invisible eggshell: my birth had been just one hatching; another was required. And as I broke through the eggshell I smelt different smells; I heard different sounds. I swear I saw different colours. It was like discovering that all your life you had lived in a vast deep shadow that was now withdrawn: suddenly you stepped into the sunlight. What were you meant to do? Creep back into the shadow again? Exchange the sweet fizz in your veins for the old sludge? Refuse to see the new colours? Turn your face away from it all?

My sister Zoë told me I had caused our mother's death by leaving Steve, by splitting the family.

'That would be in addition to the cancer, Zoë?' I said.

I felt guilty enough: why should I be made to feel worse? She understood no more than anyone: I was helpless. What was I meant to do? Look my only happiness, all my happiness, straight in the eye and refuse it? It was as if I could see my old life only through the wrong end of a telescope—as a series of tiny black figures on a horizon. Steve was the tiniest, and his distant cavortings interested me the least. I could not focus on him. I almost could not see him at all.

Zoë pursued me with biblical enthusiasm, squealing sin and retribution and hellfire, screaming wreckage and mayhem. I hadn't ever realised she felt so strongly about the religious side of things, nor that she was so fond of Steve, about whom she had always been somewhat condescending. 'Steevil the weevil', she'd called him, all those years ago when I became engaged to him and she had no fiancé. Now I reminded her of that and she told me I was being childish.

'Excuse me?' I said. 'I'm the childish one? You called him Steevil the weevil and I'm the childish one?'

'Don't trivialise this issue!' she yelled at me: this is one of the admonitions people grab at when they are at a loss. 'I don't know what's happened to you! You're infatuated, blinded! This man has changed you into somebody I don't know!'

And much more of the same, all emphatically punctuated. 'It's the sex,' she said to me one day, with a ferocity that approached real viciousness. 'I understand that, of course. It's just the sex. That'll fade away, sooner rather than later, and you'll look back and wonder what you ever saw in him.'

I didn't bother to reply, because it was such a foolish accusation. Sex on its own is terrific, but it doesn't finally matter as much as other things. Making love with Max was wonderful, but it was not for sex, nor for the glamour, that I fled to Max, curled in his embrace, hid under his protecting wings. It was for his kindness and gentleness, his ready responsiveness to me, his love and care. It was for his thoughtfulness and sympathy, his loyalty, his unending, unwavering support through everything we ever did together. I'd never had anything like it.

My family and Steve had always carped at me (*The trouble with you, Minky...*), criticised me (*Lovely, why can't you just...*), found fault (*Isabel, dear, couldn't you try a little harder...*). Nobody had ever simply loved and sustained me as Max did. This was what I found I couldn't adequately explain, what nobody would believe or comprehend.

Imagine you had lived your life within curtains, in silence, and one day someone had lifted the curtains and immediately shown you, let us say, a Rembrandt painting, played you a Mozart symphony. Imagine you had lived your life in snow and then discovered fire. Could you glimpse it all past the curtain's quiver, hear its echoes dying in the distance, and turn your back on it?

When we revisit the past, we are told, we inadvertently change it; we crystallise it anew, altering the chemical structure of our memories subtly but inevitably, definitively. Just by selecting words, casting our net into retrospective waters, we catch different fish. We try to reconstitute the flavour of the original experience and in that effort inevitably mislay something. I am making it sound as if it was all instant and perfect. It wasn't: I've said, I didn't leave Steve for over a year. And it wasn't all ecstatic either.

As I try now to connect these days, to construct the narrative faithfully, it is like trying to make a necklace out of different beads. It shouldn't look like a string of pearls when I've finished. Some of the beads do indeed have a fine soft bloom to them, like a pearl; others are jagged and crooked; some are delicate and flowery; others glisten with a dangerous obsidian polish.

Years later, when I had sold the house called Rain and was living on my own again—or, rather, with Borrow—Zoë asked me if I regretted any of it. She still couldn't understand that it was an irrelevant question. I had no choice in the matter. I was out of control.

It was like asking me if I regretted World War II, or the French Revolution. It wasn't up to me to regret, because it wasn't possible for me at the time to make choices other than those that imposed themselves upon me, those that became historical truth entirely without my connivance or intention. A storm can't choose to do other than it does. I was caught in the storm, at one with the hurricane.

I'd gone feral.

And it went sharply against the grain for me: that was the other thing everybody failed to appreciate. I'd never been a rebel. I'd had my faint resentments about life, my lingering suspicions about unfair treatment and inherent worth. I was utterly happy when I married Steve. I was unawakened and ignorant; but I was pretty happy, too.

I came out of an uneventful childhood, from loving parents, from the unknowing shadows of middle-class endeavour and the circumscriptions of middle-class satisfaction. I wanted a career, certainly; but I wanted a husband, too, and children, and all the domesticity that went with those aspirations. It never crossed my mind, when I married Steve, that I would want one day to unmarry him.

Divorced people were other people. People who had affairs were other people. People who fell newly in love, people for whom the world glittered like bushland freshly washed after rain, people who did wild and unpredictable things were other people.

Yet I had always sensed that there was something extra and dangerous in me, a capacity to do something radically unstable, threatening. Zoë didn't have it: Zoë marched militarily down the road of her life, not consenting to be distracted or delayed or to whiffle off on a sortie to the left or right. Steve didn't have it: Steve was wedded to comfort and habit and regularity as well as to me.

But I'd always feared and cherished the knowledge that there was inside me something bright and resilient and exotic—a great vivid tropical tree, perhaps, with glossy leaves and gaudy parrots flashing and gabbling in the thick branches—something that could explode and change the course of my life.

Sometimes I had felt it within me, this thing, pushing upwards like the blind nubby eyes of potatoes; but always I had firmly squashed it, because I had been frightened of what would happen if I let it go.

And now it had sprouted and was growing wild. It was still frightening, but it was something also to grin about, to relish. I had been so docile, always. All my life, even with Zoë, except when her demands became truly intolerable, I had been compliant, submissive—a good girl. I had always acted within the parameters of people's expectations of me. Pliant, tractable, biddable, docile, meek: I had been a veritable thesaurus of obedience. But now I was supine no longer. Now I was living my life for me.

Steve and I were savage with each other, over that year. At first he was deliberately obtuse: he refused to understand what I was saying. Before I said anything at all, I tried to let him find out. I left a trail of hints, a long string of unanswered questions that he had only to ask himself, or me, in order to discover how his life trembled on a precipitous brink. I left a packet of condoms in the bathroom. (Steve had had a vasectomy.) He didn't advert to them. I left a compromising note from Max on the floor of the bedroom: he obstinately refused to pick it up. Even when I wasn't seeing Max I was late home from work, with specious excuses. I never explained incoming telephone calls; I did my best to make the most innocent conversation sound mysterious, dangerous. Nothing worked. He had to have his nose rubbed in it before he could catch any scent, pick up any trail.

And when I eventually hurled it at him so he couldn't dodge it any more, I wasn't interested in rational discussion. I tried to provoke him, I think. I didn't know that was what I was doing, but I think that's how it worked. I was guilty, and I was infuriated by my guilt, and I wanted him to behave badly in order to justify my own behaviour. I wanted him to hit me, to bellow at me, to cast me out.

At the beginning, he would simply sit at the kitchen table and stare at me with bloodhound eyes. It drove me mad. It took him at least a month to work out that I really meant what I was telling him; and even after that it was a while before he lathered up a true rage.

But then we were off. It was hammer and tongs. We'd wait till the children were out of the way, but only barely, sometimes. I didn't care. The children were as distant and tiny to me as everyone else. I couldn't even look at Kate. I persuaded myself Dominic was too young to understand, that when he was older he would forgive me, see my side of it.

Dominic was ten. Plenty old enough to understand, as it turned out; and not of a forgiving disposition or an elastic perception.

'What's *wrong* with it?' Steve shouted bitterly at me one day. 'What's wrong with the bloody marriage? We've been married more than fifteen years, for Christ's sake, and you never complained before. What the fuck's wrong with it?'

In a way I could see what he meant. I hadn't complained; there'd been nothing, in a way, to complain about. And yet, when I looked back, I thought I had been endlessly forbearing. About the snoring, about lots of things.

The main thing, it seemed to me, that I had been long-suffering about, was the boredom. It had come home to me quite rapidly, after marrying Steve, that there were to be no fireworks in life. I'm not quite sure, now, what I expected of marriage, although I wanted it so badly. I do recall thinking that Steve was a comforting, steady presence—in a teddy- bearish kind of way—and I think I believed he would provide stability. I suppose I was right about that.

The thing is, you might want stability but kick against sheer immovability. Steve was great on routine. All-bran and sultanas for breakfast. The 8.10 from the local station, Monday to Friday. If he missed it, he still got to work on time; but missing it up-ended the day into Steve's version of really significant cataclysm. Saturday afternoon for gardening and listening to footy on the radio. The news at seven. Ringing his mum on Thursday nights. Sex on Friday nights, Sunday mornings.

It wasn't that I minded any of it in particular. It was fine, really. It was irritating, a lot of the time, but it was safe. He was so safe. He looked after me so much: he took such good care of me it drove me mad. He discovered I had a fear of spiders: he was all concern. He would hear me screech or see me go rigid and he would come running. 'I'll take care of it, lovely,' he would say. 'Just a little old spider, is it? I'll take care of that. Don't you worry about a thing.'

After dinner, at night, sometimes he would sit and beam at me foolishly. If I asked him why he was looking at me like that, he'd say: 'I'm just so happy to be with you, lovely. I'm such a lucky guy.' And that was comforting, and pleasant; and I became used to it, even if I did resist being called lovely the whole time.

Habit ensnared me, too. And it was better in the beginning, when we both had a routine: he'd go off to catch the 8.10 to the city; I'd hop into the Cortina and do the ten-minute drive to Bea's office. The business belonged entirely to Bea, in those days: I'd only just graduated when I started there. It was before she took me on as a partner; that came later.

*

And for two years or so, that was perfectly acceptable. But after I'd had Kate, it all changed. I'd decided to spend Kate's first two years at home. Steve and I had grappled earnestly with questions about motherhood and childcare, and we'd agreed I'd be a full-time mother for the first little while at least. We could afford it; and he'd be happier, he said, to think that his lovely was at home caring for the kids.

But then I found out about looking after children. I found out about the loneliness and the insecurity and the boredom and the worry, about the prison a tiny baby could build for you. I found out about being left alone in the house in the morning with a small child and the indescribable smell of damp toast crumbs.

It wasn't that Kate was a difficult baby. She was dead easy. Everyone kept telling me how lucky I was, pointing out how placid she was. She was sleeping through at nights within a couple of months. She was a cherub, a prodigy. Everybody said so, especially my mother. I asked her one day if she'd ever felt bored when she had Zoë and she looked at me as if I were a child molester, a monster.

Within six weeks I'd rung Bea. 'I can't stand it,' I said.

'What on earth do you mean?' asked Bea, in shocked tones.

I'd driven to the office the previous week, Kate in tow, and she and Dawn had carried on endlessly about Kate and what an unparalleled model of a baby she was.

'I mean, it's gorgeous, she's gorgeous, she's adorable, motherhood's terrific, I've never been so fulfilled. That's what everyone expects me to say and that's what I say; I say it to everybody. It's even true, in a way. Bea, don't be like everybody else, please don't. I can't stand it. Can I come back? You've got enough work, haven't you? You miss me, don't you? You haven't got anyone else yet, have you?'

Steve wasn't happy, but there wasn't a thing he could do about it and he was sensible enough to realise that. 'I just want you to be happy, lovely,' he said. 'You know that. So long as you're happy. It's just that we talked it through and I didn't think we'd be doing it this way; I thought we'd be doing it the way we talked about. You're not worried about the money, are you, Isabel? There's plenty of money. We don't need for you to work: you know that, don't you.'

He hated it, that I wasn't maternal enough to want to be with Kate every moment of every day. It embarrassed him in front of his mother, our friends. I pointed out to him that Kate didn't suffer from it: Kate was happy to be with anyone at all. The girls at the childcare centre adored her because she never gave them a moment's bother. He disliked that: he disliked thinking that Kate did perfectly well without me, but it was true.

During the terrible year of our gradual, creaking separation he recalled this, and accused me of never having really loved our children, never having really loved him. It wasn't true. I did love my children. I do love my children. I'd die for them. I had loved him—in so far as I had understood what love was all about, then. But it was over. Over, over, over. Max had flared into my life like a comet, beautiful, dangerous, fascinating. Nothing could ever be the same. Not love, not anything.

And in the meantime, while everyone shouted and harangued, we were planning the house, Max and I. Soon the permits had been obtained and we could start building. I've never known a project like it: everything went with miraculous smoothness. I thought it was a signifier of some divine approbation of our union, our love.

All the bits fell into place: there was none of the usual nonsense of trying to get the plumber to talk to the plasterer, or the bricklayer to tell the carpenter what he was going to do and when he was going to do it.

Then I found Max was liberally greasing the palms of almost everyone involved. At first I was annoyed: I confronted him over it. He was astonished. He thought I was ridiculously naïve, not to understand that this was how things were done; this was how you got things done. Then I thought it was funny. If he had so much money—which seemed to be the case—that he could do this without noticing it, so much that it simply didn't matter, why should I stop him? He enjoyed it, anyway: he enjoyed the comfort of largesse, of distributing ridiculous bribes.

There was a kind of wildness about it all, an intoxication. I was conscious that Dawn and Bea were watching me with harassed eyes as I came and went in the office. I didn't care.

'What does he do?' Bea asked me one day.

What does he do? I felt like replying. *He turns my blood to honey; he transforms me; he comes to me in a shimmering shower of nine-carat gold.*

I looked at her. 'Lots of things. Rather well, in fact.'

'What does he *do?*' Bea said, crossly. 'You know what I mean. Where does all the money come from? Tax evasion? Prostitution? Drugs? White slave traffic? Izzie, you don't know this man. You don't know where he comes from, who he is. You know nothing, nothing about him. What in Christ's name are you doing?'

I shrugged. Max was a businessman: that was all he had ever told me. I was quite incurious about his profession. I hadn't ever properly understood what Steve did in the bank, beyond putting on a suit and turning up to work every day. Why did it matter?

Still, after Bea started pestering me it did occur to me to ask Max where his apparently endless supply of cash actually came from.

'What do you do?' I said.

He burst out laughing. 'I wondered when you'd ask. They've been at you, haven't they? "What does he *do*?" they're saying to you. "Why don't you find out what he *does*?"'

Nobody could have been less troubled, more open, readier to find amusement in the interest people might express in his occupation.

'I consult,' he said. 'I develop. I invest. I keep fingers in lots of pies.'

'You're telling me not to bother my pretty head about it?'

'I'll tell you anything you want,' he replied, breezily. 'There's no single easy answer, that's all. I've got dozens of business interests, dozens of investments. I do all sorts of things, my darling Belle. I buy land and build things and then sell them as big packages. Then I buy more land and build more things. I own multi-storey car parks; I own rubbish tips. I own cranes.'

'Cranes?' I said, bizarre images of stalky long-beaked birds flapping through my mind. 'You run a rent-a-flock?'

'Industrial cranes,' he said, laughing. 'I lease them to builders, to large-scale developers. You've no idea how boring it all is,' he continued, diffident, modest, humorous, spreading his hands in that self-deprecatory, slightly puzzled gesture with which I was to grow so familiar, which indeed was to haunt me, years later. 'Lots of people pay me lots of money for all kinds of different things. Business advice, marketing advice, planning advice. It's all to do with bean-counting, really.'

I didn't actually care. It was just as well I didn't, for nothing much was clarified during our marriage. I was to discover, after we started to live together, that letters rarely came for Max.

'I use a post-office box,' he told me. 'More convenient, easier to keep tabs on.'

Much of his business seemed to be conducted in other people's offices or else in expensive restaurants. I met no colleagues, no associates. None of this bothered me in the slightest. This was all peripheral stuff, cloudy trivial filaments hanging inconsequentially around the solid gorgeous fabric of our relationship.

One day, when we were in my office, he used the telephone.

Halfway through the conversation—it was obviously about money, about shares, I recall, but I didn't try to follow it: I didn't want him to think I was inquisitive, and in any case it was impenetrable to me—he laughed, and started speaking in Italian. It seemed to me that he spoke with extraordinary speed and fluency: he sounded like a native.

'I didn't know you spoke Italian,' I said, later.

He glanced at me. 'I speak a few languages. Some better than others, some worse. It's helpful, for business.'

'Do you travel to those countries?'

'A bit.'

He did travel during the years we lived together, but not frequently. Once or twice to Bangkok; two or three times to Singapore. Indonesia, a couple of times. Maybe half-a-dozen trips to Sydney, the same to Perth.

He did spend a good deal of time on the telephone: his sleek, little study in Rain (mahogany desk, burgundy leather chairs) had separate telephone and fax lines; and that was when it was quite unusual for people to have such an arrangement at home. He did send and receive faxes, but unobtrusively, without fuss, and I think infrequently, too.

He didn't welcome anyone fiddling with his things, and

I soon learnt to leave his study alone, not to search through the papers on the desk, not to open the drawers. It didn't bother me. He was a reserved and private man: he had a right to keep his papers to himself if he wanted to.

Nor, I realise now, did I ever find out much about his life—his life, that is, before meeting me. He wasn't evasive; it just wasn't something we talked about. He had grown up in Sydney, the only child of patrician and distant parents. There had been a brief marriage, when he was still a very young man: his wife had died of a catastrophic and rapacious cancer within three years. Her name had been Caroline, and there had been no children. He looked faintly baffled when he spoke of this first marriage: when I said this to him he laughed, wryly.

'It's so long ago, Belle, that's all. It's as if it happened to some-body else. I swear I loved her: I adored her. But now I can't really recall what she looked like, to tell you the brutal truth.'

After her death he had travelled, lived for a while in Canada, for a while in London. It had been a rootless kind of existence, he said, dismissively. Comfortable enough, but finally without direc-tion, without substance.

On his return to Australia he had made Sydney his head-quarters, but he had always had a yen to live in Melbourne; and, after a windfall from some unusually successful enterprise, he had bought the land on which Rain was built with the intention of settling down for at least four or five years.

'And now I'm here for life,' he said, grinning at me. 'Well, for as long as you're here, anyway, my darling.'

He never avoided a question I put to him about his life. He never volunteered information, either. I didn't mind. As far as I was concerned, I'd emigrated to a brilliant new country: I didn't talk much about the old one, either. I suppose I assumed that, as we continued to live together, as we became more and more accustomed to each other, we would gradually learn more of each other's lives; our pasts would roll out slowly for each other's minute inspection, just as the years ahead would unfurl, like long, lush carpets, intricately patterned and richly interwoven, waiting to be trodden on.

But while Max and I worked on our house, our home, I was still living with Steve, and he and I were engaged in an intense and concentrated war. It was only by small degrees that he accepted the inevitability of the split. Towards the end there were awful nights when he wept—noisily, unattractively—and begged me to stay, begged me to give the marriage another go.

He offered me different domestic arrangements as a compromise; he said he would welcome Max at our house, that I could go and spend nights with him sometimes, that he would promise not to have sex with me for a year or more, that he would do anything, anything at all, if only I would stay with him.

All of it was impossible. He was desperate, mad. I'm not sure that it was me he cared about, so much as the life he had made, the life in which he was comfortable. I was up-ending his life, and he would never forgive me.

Eventually, however, he accepted it. And we started to talk about what would happen with the children.

'I'll take Dominic,' I say.

'Will you now?' replies Steve, rather unpleasantly.

'Yes. I will.'

'Not Kate?'

'It would be better if we split them,' I say. 'You know we talked about this: we don't want to have custody battles, that sort of thing. It's silly. The only people who profit are the lawyers: we both know that. I thought we'd agreed, it would be better to have one each. It isn't as if they're going to be broken up for good: they'll have plenty of time together. It isn't as if they're inseparable anyway, either: most of their time they spend apart.'

'I realise this. Why don't you take Kate? That's what I'm saying, Isabel. I'm not suggesting you take them both. I'll have them both, gladly, but I don't think that's what Kate wants. I'm suggesting you take Kate instead of Dominic.'

I stare at him. This is not an alternative I have considered. Why would I take Kate? Doesn't he understand? It's Dominic I want, my prince, my dark angel.

'But Dominic's mine,' I say, stupidly. 'We've always said that. Dominic's mine; Kate's yours.'

'Don't be so idiotic. We said that as a joke, a parody on ourselves if you like. The dark and the light. It doesn't work like that. You know it doesn't.'

'I can't take Kate.'

'Isabel, you can be so blind. Kate adores you. Dominic doesn't.'

'Dominic does love me.' With terror I feel the prickle behind my eyelids, tears approaching. It will never do, to start crying at this point. I have to be strong, to demonstrate that I can be strong.

'Of course he loves you,' says Steve, with that exaggeratedly patient manner I so resent. 'That's not what I said. You don't listen to what I say, Isabel: sometimes I think you've never listened to what I say. You'll break Kate's heart if you leave her.'

But I insist. Dominic will come with me. Kate will stay with her father, in whose mould she is cast and whose habits and predilections she understands and to a large extent shares.

I do not take Dominic's feelings into account. Why should I?

He is only little: he is ten. He is too young to know what he really wants. Of course he will do as he is told.

Dominic, of course, has never done as he is told. I find a quiet time to speak with him. I try to cuddle him (an ill-advised strategy), tell him how I love him, how happy we will be together. He refuses to listen.

'If you're leaving, well, okay then,' he says. 'Cool. You leave. I'm staying with Dad.'

I reason. I flatter. I schmooze.

'No,' says Dominic, regarding me with unfriendly eyes. Eyes like pebbles.

I represent to him how splendid life will be with me, with godlike Max, in our beautiful house, sharing our bliss.

Dominic measures me with his stern and pebbly eyes, and finds my dimensions lacking. 'No,' he says. And he will not be moved. Not then, not ever.

'I told you,' says Steve when I tell him. 'I told you, but you wouldn't listen. You never listen. What are you going to do about Kate then?'

'I'll think about it.'

'Well, don't think too long. She knows it's happening; she's worried sick. She's waiting for you to talk to her.'

But I talk to Max, first. I find this embarrassing, as in our previous discussions I have always assumed Dominic will be the child who joins us; I have assured Max of Dominic's virtues and painted vivid pictures of how he loves me and how he will love Max, how well we will all get on together, how beautifully our lives will mesh.

Max has met Dominic and has (I suspect) found him sulky and distant, but is too well-mannered to say so. Kate has played little part in our discussions. I find it hard to explain to Max that my beloved son doesn't wish to join us.

'He'll come for weekends and so on, I imagine?' says Max, consolingly.

'Well, yes, I suppose so,' I say, already hearing Dominic's flinty refusal.

'Well, then. There's no worry, is there?'

'No.'

And Max enchants Kate by bearing her off to various exotic shops where together they handle fabrics and inspect colours for the purpose of furnishing her bedroom: he even manages to educate her a little towards his own severe style of elegance, distracting her from the twee white four-poster and the ruffled pink curtains she at first covets. Kate has always had an unfortunate penchant for tinsel and frilly knickers.

It's rapidly clear that she adores him; at fifteen, ripe for crushes, deep in adolescence, she hatches a fully fledged worship of him. He's faintly amused, but flattered. I'm pleased, of course; and ironically it makes for greater harmony between us than she and I have ever enjoyed. But I miss Dominic's dark sardonic presence in my life.

I had little to do with Kate's bedroom, but I revelled in furnishing the rest of the house. For now we knew that we would live in this house together, that it would be not solely his but ours. We would sit on the patio during summer twilights; we would knock together dinners in the gleaming kitchen at the end of the day's work, we would dive into the pale beautiful pool. We were building not just a house but lives, furnishing not just rooms but years.

We would sleep together and make love in the glorious main

108

bedroom, so spacious and light; and waking, would together enjoy the view, framed by the lemon-scented gums we had so carefully preserved. Together we would gaze up through the vast clear shaft of the skylight Max had insisted upon, directly over the bed, inspecting the weather in the mornings, the moonlight at night.

Normally I had little to do with soft furnishings: Bea used an interior decorator on a casual basis and we called her in when clients didn't have the time or the nous to construct a heart for the body we had made them. I was asked for advice sometimes: Bianca had got me to talk her through Granada, and she had done a lot of what I'd suggested. But here I could run riot.

Not that Max was the sort of man to run riot. Nothing but the best, nothing over the top, was his rule. In one sense he was reckless: he loved lavish gestures and he could spend more extravagantly than anyone I'd ever come across, but he wasn't stupid and he didn't buy rubbish. His taste was immaculate.

We fleshed out the house's skeleton together, choosing the carpets and timbers, the tiles and the paint. We spent hours there, experimenting with colour and texture, holding up drapes, comparing ceramics and woodgrains. When we had these right, we moved to curtains and furniture, cushions and pictures, lampshades and ornaments and lights. It was one long, incredible spendfest.

I'd never known anyone who spent money like this. Nothing was too expensive for him. In the living room we chose lamps that spilt pools of brandy and whisky; cushions the colour of burnt toffee and a dark honey, like honey mixed with rust, to scatter over the fine milky leather of the acres of sofa stretching in a soft crescent around the fireplace. I felt drunk every time I walked in there, intoxicated by the room's simple magnificence, the beauty

109

of colour and sweep, stone and glass.

One evening I went there after work (it was before we were living together, and we used to meet there for an hour or so at the end of the day, for our daily charge, our shot of ecstasy). Max was standing before the fireplace (its façade a streaked amber stone) rolling something over in his hands. As I entered, he turned and held it out to me.

It was a sculpture, about the size of a grapefruit. It was round and smooth and startlingly heavy, a deep polished cream, marbled with the amber of the hearthstone. One's hands curved around it with gratitude for its cold smoothness, its satisfying weight and density. Its centre was carved into a hollow, crossed over with swathes of the stone, passing and weaving in heavy ribbons that intersected and dissolved back into the substance of the stone.

It was like a highly stylised version of one of those Chinese puzzle spheres that nest within each other, except that there was only one of it. I weighed it and turned it and stroked it: I didn't want to put it down. I cradled it in my hands.

'Where did you get it?'

'That gallery in Richmond,' he said. 'The one on the corner, you know. It had those woodcuts you liked. Isn't it exquisite?'

'It's perfect. What sort of stone is it?'

'Don't know. I thought it might be onyx or something of the kind, but I think it's too grainy, too heavy. The gallery bloke didn't know.'

'It's meteor stone,' I said. 'It came flashing down to earth, just for us. It's our meteor.'

'It is, too,' he said, hugging me.

*

On the day I finally left Steve, he wept inconsolably. I took little—only clothes, and a few books. He ought to have been pleased, that I left him with everything, that I didn't force him to a division of property. I wanted nothing. He could have the house; he could have the car, the shares. None of it meant anything to me.

Max bought me a new car. He bought me a Fred Williams painting and a crisp, glittering diamond ring.

Zoë spat bitter things into my ear. Bea wrung her hands.

My mother cried.

'You're just being bought,' she sobbed.

I didn't say that if Max had wanted to buy me he could have managed the transaction a lot more cheaply.

I did keep on trying to explain to them, to my family and my friends. But they none of them wanted to know. Even my mother, who was at the time so ill, even she—knowing death approached, knowing that within the year she would leave us—was harsh to me after I'd moved in with Max.

'Thank God your father's not alive, Isabel,' she said. 'He was so fond of Steve. We all are.'

'Well, I'm not. It seems to me I'm the one who counts, here.'

She shook her head. 'Of course you're still fond of him,' she said, impatiently, just as if I were still ten, a child who needed reminding of common sense. 'This is some kind of mad aberration. You'll grow out of it. You'll regret this, Isabel: you mark my words. You'll regret it.'

She astounded me. I had thought Max would fascinate away her prejudices in five minutes. She was usually susceptible to personable men, and I'd expected Max's sheer good looks and fluent charm to knock her over, if not immediately, at least in time. She remained conspicuously unaffected; and her obduracy was reflected by almost everyone I knew. Kate was the only person to respond with warmth to him.

Everyone seemed to assume that I had been bewitched by his glamour, by the sheen and gloss of him. Of course he was glamorous; of course he was sexy; but his glamour and his sexual charge weren't all there was to love about him, and it enraged me that nobody seemed able to see this.

Everyone apparently assumed the man I had fallen for was nothing more than a silver-haired debonair stud, who had seduced me and bemused me with wealth and sophistication and flair. Was I so shallow? Did they think me so easily enamoured, so ripe for cheap enchantment?

His gifts were amazing. No less amazing was the manner in which he delivered them. If Steve gave a present, it was heralded and trumpeted from afar. It seemed Max's gifts slid sideways from his pocket, like those of some captivating and talented conjuror.

'The start of your investment portfolio,' he said, kissing me as he gave me the ring. It had not just one diamond but three, set elegantly on a simple band of white gold.

I'd never known generosity like it, nor extravagance. It was dizzying, intoxicating. He would bring things home for us, for Kate and me—a bikini for me, a pair of sandals for her, a silk wall-hanging, a Mixmaster, a silver cocktail shaker, theatre tickets, a Swedish glass vase, pewter candelabra. I had to tell him to stop.

'You'll be coming home with frankincense and myrrh next,' I said. 'It's all getting ridiculous.'

He laughed at me, but did as I asked. He could see my worry about Kate: her world had been turned on its head and this giddy shower of presents was doing nothing to restore a sense of reality to her life.

*

112

So we all settled down, more or less. I continued to work in the partnership with Bea; Kate continued to go to school; Max continued to pursue his mysterious financial occupations.

Little by little, we made Rain the house we wanted it to be. We added pictures, ornaments, rugs. The pool was constructed and we admired its pale brilliance; Max employed the most expensive landscape gardener in Melbourne to encircle it in bright gardens and a tempting, shaded patio.

Summer came and we swam daily. I swam, too, though I'd never been much of a swimmer or a sun-worshipper; but I joined Max in relishing the whole experience: the clean cool splash of the water as we dived in, the ice-clinking drinks he made for us as we lounged on the long cedar chairs, the slow twilights.

It was rather like entering the heady ambience of an exotic travelogue, like seeing ourselves up on a wide and colourful screen across which privileged people, glistening like olives, gambolled expensively.

And during the short, warm summer nights we tumbled into bed and made love, Max's long lean fingers travelling across my body sensitively, imaginatively, always with a planned and steady vision of my pleasure, of our pleasure. Sometimes it was intense and direct and shattering; at other times, a slow journey towards the concentrated passion of our delight. He laughed at me; he said I had never been awakened before.

It was true. I came to Max a virgin in everything relating to sex except its actual prosaic progenitive happening. I didn't know about foreplay or afterplay. I didn't know about play. I didn't know about teasing, or timing, or waiting, or holding out, or submitting, or frenzy or peace or anything.

I had never understood the theatre of sex, its drama, the frisson preceding it or the harmony concluding it. Nobody had ever done these things with me before, and I was left astonished and breathless and disbelieving and grateful. All my life I'd been frigid, but nobody had told me; nobody had explained it to me. I'd mistaken the tepid enthusiasm Steve had sometimes managed to arouse in me for the real thing. And suddenly I had arrived in a new life, a life in which I was as new, as freshly awakened and untouched, as everything around me.

For a little while at least, life proceeded in this unbroken golden string of days, this peaceful meandering, isolated from the rest of the world. I remember we moved into Rain in December, just before Christmas. I remember it so clearly because Christmas was our goal, and we made it with only a few days to spare.

After Christmas, I recall it as if the months stretched out endlessly in the hedonistic vein I have described. It can only have been a matter of three or four weeks, however: we were all on holiday during January and it was January that gave us this magical spell. Then the spell was broken: there came a telephone call from Zoë, who had assiduously ignored me since I had left Steve.

'It's Mum,' she said, without preamble. 'Yes?'

'She's dying.'

'We've been told that many times these last two years.'

I was suspicious. Zoë had already made a number of claims on me by invoking our dying mother. I loved her, too; I cared that she was dying, of course I did. But I was resentful of all the emotional blackmail Zoë had already tried, and I was wary of sudden claims of impending death. It was also true that we had been on a more-or-less permanent alert, she and I, like people on a platform expecting a train that never comes.

Five years earlier, the doctors had told us our mother had a maximum of three years to go; two years ago, that death was imminent. Yet she continued. My father, a big strong man who looked as if he would last forever, had died many years before with no warning and astonishing speed. Frail and small as she was, the more murderously the cancer raced through her body, the more stubbornly my mother clung to life. When this happens, people say admiringly of the ill person that he or she is a real fighter.

I'd never thought of my mother as a fighter. Where I was concerned, her mode of fighting seemed to be to burst into tears and tell me I was wrecking her life, which I didn't really count as fighting so much as underhanded and manipulative tactics designed to wear me down through the unwelcome accumulation of guilt. They were successful tactics, too, in so far as guilt was certainly generated. But I had vowed that I wouldn't change my life because of them. And I dreaded deathbed demands, weighted with all the unfair burdens of guilt and love and expectation.

'I don't know what's wrong with you,' said Zoë, crossly. 'Of course she's dying. We know that. We know that, yet you haven't visited her since before Christmas.'

'Firstly, we know that she's dying, but not that it's about to happen. Secondly, when my family's treating me like a bloody leper, why should I feel as if I have to visit them daily?'

'She's in hospital.'

'She's been in hospital before.'

'This time it's different.'

'You said that last time.'

'Well,' said Zoë. 'Ignore me, then. Take no notice. Go ahead and do exactly as you please. Just don't blame me when I ring you to tell you she's dead. When I ring and tell you our mother's passed away, don't tell me you couldn't help it. Okay?'

That is the kind of vicious stab at which Zoë has always excelled.

When I visit the hospital (which I do the following day), I can see that Zoë is in fact right. There is a different look about my mother, a new look of being dragged down, rubbed away. Somehow her features seem blurrier, her face sunken. She lies in the narrow metal bed, apparatus snaking around her, up her nose, down her side. She looks tiny and apathetic. I bend over to kiss her and she turns her cheek, with slight impatience, as if to repel the caress. I feel hurt.

'How are you?' I say, searching around for a chair that isn't piled high with books and Kleenex boxes and bedjackets. (Does anyone in the world apart from my mother still wear bedjackets? I wonder.)

'How do I look?'

I know as well as the next person that to ask a dying person how she is mightn't sound smart. But you have to say something, don't you? It's a formal expression designed to communicate interest and concern. It's a way of saying: *Here I am, and I care about you, and I'm not sure how to negotiate all of this. So I'm asking you how you are. I know it's a dumb question, but you're meant to answer it politely.* If I know this, why doesn't she?

I've brought some red roses, which I lay on the tray straddling her bed. I know that she loves red roses, and I've gone to some trouble to get these.

'You'll need to get a vase,' she says, petulantly. 'The nurses say they haven't got time to be arranging flowers.'

'Thank you for the beautiful flowers, Isabel,' I murmur

116

to myself, looking about for a vase. I know it's rude of me, bad-tempered, but the provocation is great. A spasm passes over my mother's face; I'm not sure whether she's in sudden pain or whether she's heard my resentful muttering. Heaven knows, when I actually want her to hear things, she's always too deaf.

Why are there never any empty vases in hospital rooms?

'There's a room down the corridor,' says my mother.

I glance out the door. The corridor stretches endlessly on both sides.

'Which side?'

'How would I know which side? Have I ever been there? Do I look as if I can jump out of bed and go wandering down the corridor?'

I grab the flowers, stomp out of the room and mooch down the corridor. I can't find anything that looks remotely like a room where vases might live. Nobody shows any sign of wanting to help me.

God, I hate hospitals.

Predictably, the vase room when I eventually discover it is down the other end from the direction I've been travelling. As is always the case, none of the vases is the right size for my roses.

I take my time arranging them, in a vast receptacle clearly meant to accommodate small trees, and hope that by the time I get back someone else will be visiting my mother, so that I won't have to talk to her and can leave early. This makes me feel ignoble and selfish and therefore even guiltier.

When I return, I'm still the only visitor. I plonk the vase on the shelf, displace some jetsam from a chair, and sit down.

'It's too *big*,' she whispers, in evident anguish. I decide to ignore this.

'It's not such a bad room,' I say. 'You've got quite a good view.'

'Have I? It's a pity I can't sit high enough to see it, then.'

'At least you've got a room to yourself.'

'I get lonely.'

She and I both know perfectly well that, if some poor unfortunate were to be sharing the room with her, her complaints would lift the roof. So I disregard this play for sympathy and try another tack.

'Is the food good?'

'I can't taste it.'

'Why's that?'

'It's the medication. It makes everything taste like cardboard.'

'That's a pity,' I say, vaguely. Conversation lapses. I gaze out the window (she's right, in fact; she can't see it, and that's a shame: it's a pretty view, of big, old oaks and smart, cosy terrace houses) and wonder if grumpiness is an automatic by- product of the dying process.

'So you're living with him, then?' says my mother.

I'm startled. 'Sorry?'

'With him. With that man. You're living with him.'

'Max. His name is Max. Yes. I'm living with Max.'

She folds her lips and another spasm jumps over her face. 'Steve visited me this morning,' she says.

'Why tell me?'

'He's a good man, Isabel. I hope you don't live to regret what you've done to him. I hope you don't live to regret what you've done to your little family.'

'What you mean is you're damn sure I will and you'll be pleased if I do.'

My mother closes her eyes and turns her head. 'You never would be told. You never would be told anything, would you? You always had to do it all your own way, didn't you? You always were a wilful, artful child. A cold, uncaring child, you were.'

For someone who's dying, she spits the words out with extraordinary clarity and energy. Clearly, she doesn't mind that they hurt me, that they're unfair.

It's not long before I leave, feeling under all the circumstances that my visit hasn't been a great success. As I bend to kiss her I see a tear slipping down her papery old skin. This is clearly not something I can do anything about and I beat a rapid retreat, sighing in relief as I escape the hospital and find safety in the sunny day outside.

Zoë rings me that night.

'Did you have to upset her like that?' she asks, furiously.

'Excuse me?'

'Can't you ever just be nice to her? She's dying. How many times do I have to tell you that?'

'I didn't do a thing to her.'

'She was crying when I came in.'

'So it has to be my fault?'

'It was your fault. She told me it was your fault.'

'What did I do?'

'You snapped at her. She said you bit her head off.'

'*I* bit *her* head off? She didn't happen to mention some of the remarks she made to me?'

'She's dying, Isabel.'

'I have that message, actually. Loud and clear. I don't see that dying gives you the right to say whatever you feel like saying. She always was a tactless cow and dying isn't improving her.'

I don't really mean to say anything like this: of course I don't; but by this stage I'm seriously upset and I simply don't see why everything is always and inevitably my fault.

'What a bitch you are,' says Zoë. 'She's in the most terrible pain. Why should she be thinking about your feelings?'

'It'd certainly be a change for anyone to do that.'

'Isabel, don't you ever think of anyone but yourself?'

I slam the phone down. Most conversations with my family are finishing with the slammed phone these days.

The next few weeks are not much fun. Our holiday mood, abruptly shattered, returns only to mock us with its memory. Kate goes with Steve to visit her grandmother and creeps around the house with a stricken look for days afterward, glancing at me reproachfully every so often when she thinks I'm not looking.

Everyone in the world is against me. Except for Max. Max is delicate and considerate; he brings me bunches of flowers and small gifts; he drops gentle kisses on my head; he makes tender love to me until I tremble with the tense joy of it. He takes me out to dinner. He obviously thinks I endure a lot from my family, and puts himself out to compensate for this. We all go back to work. Well, I go back to work. Max says he goes back to work, but it's hard to tell the difference, so far as I can see. Kate spends hours in her bedroom and says she's reading texts in preparation for the new school year. Maybe she is.

I go twice more to visit my mother. The first time Zoë is there, too, and monopolises the conversation to such an extent that I might just as well not be there.

The second time, she's asleep. My relief is overpowering. I sit quietly, so if Zoë pesters me I can say I stayed for a decent time; and, after a little while, I find myself observing my mother's face.

I hadn't realised how old she has become—how old the cancer has made her. I do a couple of sums in my head and confirm that in fact she's only sixty-three. It's terrible, that she should look so old, that her face should have collapsed and that her bare arms are so skinny and crêpelike.

I remember when my father died, but that was a heart attack and it came out of the blue. Better to do that, I think: better to take everyone by surprise; far better than this apparently endless degeneration, this cruel, slow, deteriorative process that eats one up so. I've never watched anyone dying like this, bit by bit. Little by little.

Will I die like this? Will a cancer eat me like this, and will Max loyally visit me when I lie in hospital? Will he bring me roses? Will I snap at him and tell him to find a proper vase? Will Dominic visit me? Will Dominic sit by my bed and express penitence?

Perhaps Steve will come, and tell me he now appreciates the depth of his deficiencies, his perfidy, and comprehends finally why I had to leave him, why I had to escape from the hell our marriage had turned into.

I'm tired and depressed, and these are affecting pictures. I become aware that I'm crying and rummage in my bag for a tissue.

It's at this point that the door opens and Zoë enters. Her belligerence on seeing me immediately dissolves when she realises that I am weeping: she drops to her knees beside me and envelops me in a hug, a massive hug, a benevolent, loving, forgiving, big-sisterly hug.

'Oh, Minky!' she says. 'Oh, Minky, dearest Minky!'

So I am reinstated—temporarily, anyway—in Zoë's good books, and we have a nice cry together. It doesn't seem necessary to explain to her exactly why I'm crying; and I'm not sure that I could do this in any case. Perhaps it really is my mother I'm grieving for. In fact, I'm sure it is. Sorrow works on us in complex ways, after all; and my mother's weakness, the corrosion of her body, its gradual decline, the knowledge that the end is on its inexorable way—these have all powerfully distressed me. Possibly I've even been rather brave, to withstand my grief so steadfastly thus far.

In any case, Zoë's mollification is for the moment complete. We mop up our tears and sit silently for another ten minutes. My mother half wakes then, but she's blurry and confused, and seems not to know with any certainty who we are, and soon drops off again. Softly we tiptoe out, and part in mutual sisterly amicability.

Zoë rings me the next day, and tells me our mother is dead. I know it sounds absurd, but it comes as a shock. I hadn't expected it so soon. For so long we had been reminded—frequently by my mother herself—that her end was approaching, momentous and inescapable, that it was hard to realise that the cataclysm was no longer imminent. Suddenly, swiftly, it had happened, and she had gone.

Zoë made most of the funeral arrangements: she consulted me about various details and indeed I accompanied her to the undertaker, but it was clear that she was in her organisational element and I was definitely superfluous. I didn't mind.

I couldn't think of worse things to do than choosing a coffin, deciding what sorts of flowers to decorate the coffin with, working out what music to play. Zoë enjoyed all of it and it obviously gave her solace. I let her fly solo. It was an efficient funeral and I was grateful to her for managing it so competently.

The goodwill between Zoë and me did not last, and it was not long before she returned to the same accusations and the same blistering diatribes. I figured in these alternately as Jezebel and Jill the Ripper, and either way they became tedious.

I was having enough difficulty in coping with my mother's death. It wasn't that I missed her. It was that I didn't. I was depressed and upset, but not because I had lost a loved and loving mother. I suppose she did love me, and I suppose I did love her, but it was hard somehow to recover that love, to recall it fully and experience it again as part of what people like to call the grieving process.

I kept pushing away the knowledge of her death; I kept thinking that I would deal with it later, when I could accustom myself to it and think about it properly. But when I tried to think about it properly, I found I couldn't.

Questions of death, questions of life. How they torment us. Dominic as a child was fascinated by the bad banksia men and adopted the term 'deadybones' until it drove us mad. He made it the subject of one of his rhymes, along with his old teddy bear Fred.

Ned the Red shot Fred the Ted
in the head
as he lay in bed.
Beddy-byes, Teddy dies;
Teddy bones all deadybones.
Ready, steady, Teddy, go!

He would chant it again and again, capering and spinning like a dervish, shouting the last line in explosive glee, grinning evilly.

'Do you ever worry about Dominic?' Steve asked me once, tentatively, after one of these performances.

'No,' I lied.

'You don't find that teddy rhyme of his…well, a little disquieting? He's only six, after all.' Steve scratched his head, regarding me with ill-concealed anxiety.

'No,' I said, calmly, though I agreed with Steve, deep down.

It *was* disquieting. But, now, as I look back, I think it might have taught him to understand death, not to fear it, to live with it. I couldn't live with it, not at any rate with my mother's death. Perhaps one needs to be a touch disquieting to survive. Perhaps being disquieting is something to be fostered.

I actually tried to make myself cry, by hauling out all of the best memories I had of my mother. I remembered, for instance, the time Zoë had bossed me about the garden. I suppose I was about five, which would have made her ten. I think we had been given a children's gardening set; or perhaps it was only Zoë's. There was a little, wooden-handled rake, I recall, its prongs painted red, and a blue spade. Somewhere there is a photograph of Zoë holding these items, smirking.

Our father had dug us a space in the backyard so that we could plant our own flowerbed. He went to a good deal of trouble: the bed was kidney-shaped and beautifully edged. I can't remember now what the cause of the quarrel was, but perhaps we wanted different flowers, or perhaps Zoë regarded me as slave labour and forced me into too much digging and raking.

At any rate, it all ended in tears and I recall my mother sweeping me, sobbing, into her arms and bearing me off. It is this feeling of being suddenly swooped upon and borne off, a shred of dandelion upon a great maternal gust, rescued, safe, that principally stays with me.

As I clung to my mother, startled by her action but relishing it, I can remember a gush of emotion for her, a kind of grateful daughterly access of affection, which I now tried unsuccessfully to re-create.

Recollection of other, similar incidents was equally unavailing: I didn't understand why. One loves one's parents: of course one does. One is sad when they die. Isn't one?

I wanted to grieve; I wanted to mourn. I wanted to deserve the kindness and mute concern, the slightly deferential consideration people like Bea and Dawn were extending to me. The discovery that I couldn't plunge myself into these processes made me abstracted and bad-tempered. I tried to explain this to Max.

'I don't feel it as I think I ought to.'

'Is there an "ought" about how you feel grief?' he asked.

'Possibly not, but even I feel there's something unsatisfactory about my response.'

'Why?'

'Well.' My brain was sluggish.

It was late, time to go to bed. We were sitting in the living room, on the milky leather lounge suite with its long curves that were somehow both sumptuous and pristine. I picked up the meteor stone from the coffee table and rolled it from one palm to another, absent-mindedly relishing its coolness and density, its clean spherical perfection.

'It's so hard to know how to put it, Max. I expect to feel sorrow, and I look inside myself for the place where the sorrow ought to be, where it's kept, so to speak, and I can't find it there.'

'What do you find instead?'

'A kind of blankness, to tell you the truth. Almost an emptiness.'

'Mightn't that be an aspect of sorrow?'

'I don't know? Might it?'

'Tell me, my beautiful Belle, why does it worry you so?'

'Because I worry that I'm a monster,' I said, hearing my voice break. 'Because I worry that if I can't properly register grief, I can't properly register love, I can't love. She was my mother, for God's sake: why can't I feel her death more, like Zoë does, like Kate does? Even Dominic is more upset than I am, Max. I ought to be inconsolable; I ought to be bursting into tears; I ought to be devastated, and I'm just not.'

He came and sat beside me, and held my face in his hands. 'Do you love me?'

'You know I do.'

He kissed me, warmly, tenderly. 'You are the most loving, most caring, kindest, dearest woman in the world. I adore you. You mustn't do this to yourself.'

That seemed to terminate the conversation. We went to bed. We didn't make love that night, but we lay like spoons, me fitting into the contours of his lean body, him holding me. I fell asleep like this.

He brought me such peace, such confidence.

He brought more than that, too. He came home one day, perhaps a month after my mother's death, with a large white box. He set it on the kitchen bench and looked at me with his beguiling crooked smile.

It had been a rough day at work: I was peeling potatoes, I think, and drinking wine, and trying to overcome the dragging depression that continued to tug me downwards, some days.

'Where's Katie?' he asked. They often attached the suffix to each other's names. She was Katie; he was Maxie. I don't know why.

'In her room,' I said, eyeing the box and feeling a faint thud of disappointment that it evidently wasn't for me.

He called Kate and she came running down the stairs.

'Now,' he said, in a considering way. 'What are we going to do, here?'

A faint scuffle came from the box and Kate's face lit up. 'A pet!' she cried. 'Maxie, have you bought me a pet?'

'Well, now,' he said, stroking his chin.

Max loved these situations. He was never happier than when he was opening his wallet and throwing hundred-dollar bills around. Partly this was a matter of pure generosity; partly it was a case of an innate love of splendour, of luxury, of abundant surprise and lavish gesture.

'Well, now,' he said, pulling a comical face. 'There's a bit of a problem.'

Kate and I laughed and he grinned back at us.

'The thing is, you see, I have a present and I'm not sure who it's for.'

'Show it to us,' crowed Kate. 'If you show it to us we'll work out who it's for.'

'Ah, no,' he said. 'It wouldn't work, you see. You'll both want it.'

He was teasing Kate, but his eyes sought mine and smiled in the manner of someone who was sharing a superb and immense secret with the only person who mattered. He could always do this to me; he could always make me feel that everyone else in the world was peripheral: I was the core and the heart and the centre of everything for him.

Kate's excitement was becoming uncontrollable, and he started to lift the box's lid, only to pause and say anxiously: 'You'll have to share it, mind. You'll both have to share it. You'll have to borrow it from each other.'

And there he was, Borrow, a golden Labrador puppy with impeccable lineage and huge floppy paws and a heart-melting smile. He scrambled out of the box and into Kate's plump and eager arms, wagging his tail and whimpering with enthusiasm and wriggling and licking her face while she issued rapturous little screams.

Borrow was to become so integral a part of our lives that it was hard to believe we had not always had him. Noble and stupid, he treated Max and Kate with all the adulation his giant heart could muster, which was considerable. They were his favourites; me he tolerated.

And yet he has finished up, happily enough, with me and with neither of his heroes; it is with me that his days will amble to what I hope will be a benign and pain-free end. Old and venerable now, with white whiskers, increasingly cloudy eyes and a gammy hip, he limps after me and good-naturedly pretends he doesn't remember the dark side of me. Do dogs remember? I am sure Borrow does.

It wasn't only the dog that arrived in my life with such panache, such bold munificence. Addicted as he was to the grand entrance, the dispensation of gifts, Max kept on spoiling himself and me. He walked in the door one evening with a large, flat, silver box, an extravagant crimson ribbon jauntily tied on top of it. I eyed it inquisitively.

'I bought you a wedding dress,' he said, all crinkly grin, presenting it to me.

It was so like Max. No preliminaries, no questions. There was no question, of course. No proposal. We were head over heels, still; then and always. We both understood that we were partners forever, that we couldn't live without each other.

'Who am I marrying?' I asked, undoing the box. 'When?'

He laughed.

It was a floaty, fine thing: layers of shimmer, lilac and aquamarine, crystal and snow. It had drifted right out of the silky expensive-smelling pages of *Vogue* into my delighted arms. The material was so delicate you could have passed the entire dress through a wedding ring. He had bought shoes, too: fragile jewelled sandals, with soft leather soles and sleek gleaming straps.

He was extraordinary like that: how many men are there in the world who could walk into a dress shop or a shoe shop and choose so unerringly, with such imagination and confidence? He always knew sizes and colours; he understood my preferences and my style and everything about me.

'They're not my colours,' I said, marvelling, letting the fineness of it slip through my fingers, like bright shadows of silk, almost no substance to it.

'They're not the colours you usually wear,' said Max, dropping a kiss on the back of my neck. 'It doesn't mean they're not your colours.'

'It'll make me look sallow.'

He snorted. 'Try it on and see.' I did. I didn't look sallow.

'I thought a beach wedding,' he said, while I twirled in front of the mirror, craning to see different views, liking them all. 'Twilight.'

'When?'

'Whenever you say.'

I tried to describe all this to Zoë. I made a real effort.

'I couldn't bear it,' she said.

'Couldn't bear what?'

'Such an overbearing attitude. I don't know what's happened to you, Minky: once upon a time you wouldn't have put up with being pushed around like this.'

'He's not pushing me around,' I snapped. 'He doesn't push me around.'

'I couldn't bear it. It's not natural, for a man to act that way. How is it he knows so much about women's clothes? You ask him that.'

'You're just jealous.'

She laughed, nastily. 'Jealous? Of you and your con man? Don't be silly.'

'I'd be jealous,' I said, spite getting the better of me. 'If I was married to Henry, I'd be jealous of just about every other woman on the face of the earth.'

She gave me a wounded look. 'Anyway, those colours don't suit you.'

Well, it's no wonder I didn't invite her to the wedding, which happened about four weeks afterwards, just as he'd said, on a fine, still evening, on a beach down on the Peninsula, near Point Leo, at twilight.

I got Bianca Crawford and her husband to be witnesses; no one else came. I didn't want anybody else. Bianca was about the only one of my acquaintances not to resist Max. We had coffee once, and I told her about how unfair everybody was, and she laughed and leant forward and tapped my cheek. Bianca was half-Italian and when she felt like it she would become very European.

'Don't you worry about it, *cara*. You go and live your own life. Don't you give a damn about any of them, old killjoys.'

'You like him, don't you, Bianca?'

She rolled her eyes. 'Like? Like? I fancy him, my dear, and so do they, if they were only honest. Oh, but he is a dangerous man, you mark my words, Isabel. *E uomo molto pericoloso, cara*. Believe me. You take care with your Max.'

I laughed, knowing how safe Max in fact was. I could see why she called him *pericoloso*: it had to do with the sharp edge of his sexuality, the vertiginous quality of it, the physical frisson he generated, the quiet sizzle of his mere presence. But he wasn't really dangerous at all. I'd never felt safer with anyone in my life.

So Bianca was delighted to be invited. She used up a roll of film with languishing shots of us standing in our finery on the flat white sand, gazing together at the sunset, walking hand in hand into the golden beyond, kissing against a tangerine sky. She sent us copies later and Max said they looked like ads for Jim Beam and coke.

Max had a friend who was a celebrant. She was a plump, motherly lady who wore a rather lovely, black tailored pant suit and read a beautiful service; and she kissed me afterwards with, it seemed to me, real feeling and affection.

We drove to a swanky hotel in Portsea and got tipsy over dinner and made love several times in a gorgeous suite with a four-poster bed. It was so romantic I almost didn't feel married. That's a laugh, now.

I kept my name. Weaving is my own name, not Steve's. At the time of our marriage, it was unusual for a woman to retain her maiden name, but Steve's surname is Bell. Even so rigid a conservative as my mother could see that I didn't want to be called Isabel Bell. Steve's mother wasn't so sympathetic, but her name was Marjorie, so the problem hadn't presented itself for her. And by now, of course, I had a professional name—not a huge one, but in certain circles well known enough for me to want to keep it.

Bea was as difficult about it as everybody else. I told her I'd be away on the Monday (married on Saturday: two days' honeymoon didn't seem unreasonable to me). She asked why and I told her. She sniffed disapprovingly.

'Oh, Christ, Bea!' I said. 'You're my oldest friend as well as my partner. Don't you go and put me in the doghouse, too.'

'It's not a matter of putting you in the doghouse. It's a matter of seeing you stuff up your life, your husband's life, your kids' lives.'

'Steve's not my husband any more. The divorce is through. I haven't stuffed up anyone's life. I'm just living my own.'

'Izzie,' she said, stretching out her hand. 'Izzie, just living your own life isn't possible. You know that. Everything we do touches on other people, on other people's lives. You *know* that. It's so awful to watch. I just find it infinitely depressing to see you permanently infatuated with that—that—*gigolo*.'

I shrugged and turned away. I was so wounded and so angry that I couldn't trust myself to say anything.

It hurt a lot, of course, that everyone was so harsh to me, so determined to judge me, not to understand. Sometimes I felt oppressed by the malice they all seemed suddenly to be sprouting, by the burble and hiss of spite. At first, as I've said, I tried to explain. To Bea, to Zoë. I could no longer explain to my mother, since she was dead, but she hadn't wanted to understand, any more than they did.

But I was happy; I was incredibly, wildly happy: that was what they couldn't understand, how essential that happiness had become to me. Happiness bubbled through my blood: I felt I had little neon glows flickering like Christmas lights through my veins. When I walked down the street, when I went to the shops, it seemed to me everyone must notice and admire my incandescence.

*

132

Yet, although I was so happy, it was at this time that the Lost Dream started. This is not something I can explain. I woke one night next to Max, perhaps two hours after making love, in a cold sweat, weeping.

I had never before woken from a dream, from sleep, with actual tears sliding down my face. The dream had begun as it always has done, subsequently, with a stroll through bushland, walking through the dull silver gleam and tangy air of eucalypts. I am content: it is warm; I am secure; the bush is beautiful, restful. Magpies chortle; rosellas dart and chatter.

But the air turns colder and the path more winding and the trees more swarming, pushing their way over the path. I walk on, knowing I have to get to the end of the path, knowing I have to reach a certain point. But it is colder and darker all the time. I panic; I try to turn back, but the seething trees block my way. And I cry *cooee*.

It is what we were taught to do as children, if we walked or played in the bush—at regular intervals, to stop and shout *cooee*. It is what Australian children have always been taught to do. Well, that is the myth, anyway. Most Australian children these days are brought up in the synthetic environment of the suburbs: they may see a gum tree in a park occasionally but they wouldn't know real bush if they fell over it.

But there are old legends of the bush, old legends of the children who were lost in it—some whose bodies were never found. The bush scoops a wandering child into its heart quicker than you would believe. So, if you are lost, you cry *cooee*. And back, strong and sweet, comes the answering *cooee* of father or brother or friend. If you remain within cooee, we are told, you will never be lost.

And now I call *cooee, cooee*—but I have gone beyond cooee;

there is nobody to hear me; nothing around me but the teeming, muttering bush that could contain anything, anything at all.

I feel rather than hear a low vibration emanating from the crowding leaves, which quiver above me, sage-green, pale silver, thin as paper, thin as skin. I am so cold I can hardly breathe. The wild cackle of kookaburras explodes in my ears.

My heart's in a flurry; it's like a lunatic, plump pigeon hurling itself against the cage of my ribs, heavy, panic- stricken.

Cooee, I cry, and again, in accelerating desperation. *Cooee*. No one answers; no one is there to answer; I am alone in the world. Fear possesses me utterly. I wake, weeping.

Max was not generally speaking a patient man, not perhaps somebody who readily sympathised with psychic ailments and traumas of the imagination; but he was always tender with me after this dream. He used to call it the Lost Dream, capitalising it somehow, as if to acknowledge its searing power over me, its horror. I still have the dream sometimes; and now it doubly sears me: when I wake from it, sweating and shaking, I miss his hard arms around me, his murmur in my ear, his long, kind fingers stroking my neck, soothing me.

I miss him so. I miss his kind-heartedness, his gentleness, his generosity.

How they disparaged him, my friends and relations! They insisted—in direct contradiction to all my evidence—that he was dubious and underhanded. Crooked, grubby.

'What have you put your name to?' Bea asked me one day at work.

'What do you mean?'

'Have you signed papers for him? Have you stood surety for

him, or anything like that?'

'You're referring to Max?'

'Come on, Izzie: you know I am.'

'I haven't, but there's no reason why I shouldn't, and if he asks me to I certainly will.'

'Listen, love,' said Bea, sitting down on the chair in front of my desk where Max had sat when I had first met him. 'Izzie, just don't sign anything, okay?'

'You all drive me mad,' I said, furiously. 'Completely mad. He's a lovely, lovely man, and I'm the luckiest woman in the world to be married to him, and you all carry on as if he were a serial killer.'

'It's up to you, Isabel. I'm telling you. Don't sign anything.'

'Why shouldn't I? Why do you all behave as if there must be some deep, shameful secret attached to him? I'm telling you, he's the most straightforward, transparent, honest man I've ever known. Leave me alone, Bea.'

Bea did her heavy sigh and trudged out.

'Sign these, ma Belle, my sweetheart,' said Max one night not long after this conversation, brandishing a sheaf of papers and dropping a kiss on my forehead.

'What are they?'

'A surprise, my love. A small surprise for the belle of my heart.'

I unfolded the papers. 'Can I look at them?'

Max burst out laughing. 'Is it likely I'd ask you to sign anything without looking at it?'

I leafed slowly through them. They were legal papers, title papers.

'Max,' I said. 'Max, what are you doing?'

'I'm giving you Rain.'

I couldn't believe it. 'What do you mean?'

'Look, we're married now, aren't we? We should share things. All my worldly goods, and all that.'

'But this isn't sharing. This is giving.'

'I love you, Bella. I love giving things to you.'

'Max, this is ridiculous.'

He spread his hands. 'You're going to beat the truth out of me,' he said, shaking his head mournfully. 'The fact is, I'm only doing it as a tax break.'

'Max. Darling Max. Please be serious.'

'Well, it seems a shame to be serious when I don't have to, but I'll do my best for a little while. Bella, my love, this is our house; we live in it together, but it's all in my name, and you had so much input into it that it's absurd for you not to own it. Rain is your invention, my darling. Your creation.'

'We did it together.'

'Yes, but you were the guiding spirit, the inspiration, the genius of it all. You know you were. This is only a logical extension of that fact. The other thing, my sweetheart, if I'm going to be perfectly honest, is that it actually is a good tax move for me. My accountant tells me I ought to cut down on my assets. He's advised me on this one. I always take my accountant's advice.'

'But you can't just give something away like that, can you? Aren't there tax penalties to gifts, too?'

'Arthur says to trust him,' said Max, grinning. 'As I always do. He'll manage it all for me. But in the meantime we need you to sign these. Don't do it now, but read through them so you're sure you understand what's going on, and tomorrow, if you can take an hour or so off, we'll wander down to Arthur's solicitor and talk about it so you understand it all and we'll make it all legal.'

He was set on this, fixed on the course he had described. I tried to dissuade him, at first. I was uncomfortable about accepting so enormous a present. But Max could be stubborn, when he wanted something badly enough, and it became apparent that this was something he wanted. We signed the papers; the title was handed to me. Rain became mine.

I told Bea, after it had happened, of this transaction. I must say I told her with triumph, with a strong flavour of *I told you so* mixed with *How could you say those things*. She was nonplussed, though she tried not to show it.

'Well, good,' she said, staring at me across her desk. 'Good. I'm pleased for you, Izzie.'

'So you were wrong. Aren't you going to admit you were wrong, Bea?'

'Nothing's proven about my rightness or wrongness. Not yet.'

She was unrelenting. I didn't care—or not much, anyway. I had Max to comfort me. Max, and Rain. I'd never owned property before. When Steve and I married the house had been in his name. I'd never questioned that, though now I find it hard to believe that I could have been quite so pliant, so yielding to the master's voice.

I wandered through Rain now, familiarising myself to the curiousness of possessing it. I ran my hand along the jarrah banister and gazed out the study window, feeling a kind of new richness—a material, selfish richness, which complemented my inner and less selfish spiritual richness. *All this is mine*, I said to myself, in active and questioning wonderment at the strangeness of it.

Max never mentioned it. It had been done; the gift had been given, and that was the end of the matter so far as he was concerned. We lived in the house together as if it belonged to us together, without reference to who its actual owner was.

Sometimes I would wake before Max did, and I would lie there studying him, not just his face, but the contours of his body. He was a lean man, tanned and sinewy, strong and incisive in his movements. His presence dominated: it was impossible to be in a room where Max was and not know he was there; and somehow this innate and effortless habit of authority made him seem all the more vulnerable when he was asleep. Sometimes he would lie on his back, one arm flung up so that the inner arm was exposed. I found its whiteness, its susceptibility, intensely moving. He had curiously pointed elbows. Is it ridiculous to swoon at a man's elbows? I dare say.

I was obsessed by him, infatuated with him. I freely admit it. But it wasn't merely obsession or infatuation. It was a dense, profound and lasting love. Luminous and expansive, it had invaded every particle of me. He was the love of my life.

The supposed love of Kate's life, Gavin, hove onto the horizon when Kate was, I suppose, eighteen and studying not very hard at a fine arts course. Fine arts was the kind of woolly thing she *would* be interested in. He was a postgraduate, studying for his doctorate, which in Kate's eyes, I suppose, invested him with some *cachet*. He was unimpressive from the start: tall, gangly, he would come to pick Kate up and (because she was never ready) would be trapped in conversation with Max and me.

Max was especially good at this kind of encounter: easy and fluent in his behaviour and his language, he was adept at the kind of genial bonhomie that comes in so useful in potentially strained situations. But Max never really succeeded with Gavin.

He had a quick stuttery laugh, did Gavin; and nervous feet

and hands; and he was too long; there was too much of him to occupy any given space, and he was uncomfortably aware of this. He was like a giant fifteen-year-old: he'd never properly matured, never got past the gawky self-conscious stage. If he'd had any physical coordination worth talking about he would have been great at basketball; but he hadn't. His head seemed to bob around in a manner disconcertingly separate from his angular shoulders. He had no social grace whatsoever. I found him painful to be with.

I couldn't understand what the attraction was. Kate had had boyfriends before, and to a man they had manifested more appeal than Gavin. But the liaison persisted and she appeared to enjoy it. Summer was coming on, when Gavin first appeared, and the pair of them spent much time in the pool at Rain.

Kate had always been shy about being seen in bathers, but for some reason (God only knows what) the company of Gavin seemed to confer on her a new aura of physical and sexual confidence: to my astonishment, she bought an expensive turquoise bikini, and freely let herself be observed in it.

Kate has always been plump, and pink and white, too, which are not promising coordinates for bikini wearers. But somehow, on her, it worked. Her body was firm and well- proportioned; she moved gracefully; the bikini was well-cut; and, although she did not tan beyond the palest café-au-lait, her fairness lent her a nymphlike aspect that was quite fetching.

A new Kate emerged, languorous and quietly confident, one whom I shouldn't have been surprised to find swimming naked in the pool on moonlit evenings, pearly and dripping in the silver air, the silver water. Gavin frolicked awkwardly around her, lanky and adoring. Max liked him more than I did.

'He's not stupid,' he insisted.

I raised my eyebrows.

'He's not. Look, you can't be stupid and be writing a PhD on Rousseau.'

'I've known a fair few stupid people who had PhDs.'

'Believe me, he's not one. And he's very sincere.'

'I'd prefer another quality, I think. Sincerity is such a dispensable virtue.'

'He's genuinely in love with her.'

I shrugged. But I didn't spend much time thinking about Gavin, because I didn't expect him to become a fixture in my life. I realised, of course, that they were sleeping together: when he started sheepishly to appear for breakfast, it was not a difficult conclusion to reach. I didn't think much about it, except to register a vague incredulity: it seemed to me going to bed with Gavin would be like going to bed with an extremely large daddy-long-legs.

Around this time, the business—mine and Bea's—started to expand. Bea and I had always managed quite happily, just the two of us; after struggling for a while, we made a small name for ourselves and hummed along very nicely for several years. Suddenly, it seemed, we were making more of a name, and people wanted more of us.

We had seen a gap in the market and had developed a good line in adapting old houses—especially terrace houses—for offices: streamlined, modern offices that nevertheless retained the spirit (and what people like to call the ambience) of the original houses, with their cool, high ceilings and narrow stairwells and elaborate cornices. It seemed our fame had spread. Bea one day had an invitation to quote on a row of old terraces in Sydney.

'It's worth a fortune to us,' she said, leafing through the photographs the developer had sent her. 'Look at this, Izzie—and this. They're great little houses, and it's the Rocks; it's very central. Such good publicity.'

I picked up the photos and agreed. The houses looked as if they were run down, but so far as you could tell they were still solid and well worth the effort and expense required for the conversion.

It was a question of who would go. We hadn't had much interstate work, but when we did it was usually Bea who went: she liked the buzz of it; and she had a brother in Sydney she liked to catch up with. This time, however, it didn't suit her.

She looked hopefully at me. 'I don't suppose...?'

'I don't mind,' I said, musing. 'It does look interesting, and it would be a shame to miss out. A shame not to even try, at any rate.'

In fact I was tempted by the prospect. Steve had always disliked it when I travelled on business: arrangements had to be made for the children and, furthermore, my absence reminded him that he was not the sole provider, the great white hunter, to which condition he aspired.

By agreeing to undertake the task, I was able to demonstrate to Bea that I was now in a more independent and mature relationship, that I could carry my professional share of responsibilities, that Max was not going to jump up and down in a petulant fit because I was away for a few days. Also, to tell the truth, I thought that I should like to show Max that I, too, had pressing business interests; I, too, had a professional life whose demands I was required to meet, able to meet. I hadn't been in Sydney for years and the opportunity was beguiling.

*

141

So I spent five days in Sydney—and, apart from missing Max, I enjoyed myself thoroughly. Even missing Max had its advantages: I knew that the absence was short, with a defined conclusion and an inevitable joyful reunion, which would be made the more rapturous because of the sting caused by the separation. I anticipated the reunion with such sharpness, such keen-edged imagination, that I could almost relish the period preceding it in the thought of what was to follow.

Bea found other things for me to do—contacts to follow up, an exhibition to attend—and I worked hard for three days and turned into a tourist for the last two days of the week. I travelled on ferries and enjoyed the breezes and the views from the deck; I wandered around the Opera House; I shopped in Double Bay; I had cocktails at night before dinner. It was all consistent with the kind of easy, well-heeled, prosperous existence to which Max had introduced me; and, charmed, I found that I was able to create and savour it myself even when he was not there to share it with me.

I told him this on the phone on the last night of my visit, and heard his deep delighted chuckle.

'What you've taught me!' I said. 'I've turned into a regular lotus-eater.'

'Do you good. I've never known anyone who deserved to eat lotuses more than you do. I'm pleased I've shown you how to have a good time, even if you're having it without me.'

'It's a talent to be fostered, I'm finding.'

'And you're fostering it.'

'I certainly am.'

'Good for you, my darling Bella.'

That night I was unusually wakeful. I switched impatiently from one channel to another on the TV in the opulent hotel to which I had treated myself. (Bea had said the practice could sustain three stars; I stretched it to five.) I raided the minibar. I ate peanuts and tried a can of rum and coke, which I didn't usually drink and didn't much enjoy.

I went through the papers I had collected over the last few days and sorted them into order for Bea. I lingered over some of my sketches. The terraces had been less enticing than I'd expected: something could be done with them, certainly, but their fundamental dinginess was a matter of construction and siting rather than neglect, and possible remedies brought their own difficulties. I didn't think we should take it on, even apart from the travel that was going to be involved in the project.

Although I knew I was going to see him the next day, I missed Max with a nearly unbearable pang. I could not calm my restlessness and the night stretched ahead of me black and bleak. I stared out the window and saw that Darling Harbour, several floors below, was bright with lights and busy with people—people strolling, chatting, dining at the pavement cafés. Small brilliant boats, which I presumed were water taxis, bobbed and slid across the dark water.

As is the way with these modern glossy hotels, I couldn't open the window, which meant I couldn't hear anything. It gave the scene a bizarrely unreal and distant quality, as if I were watching it on television with the mute button on. The lights strung along the waterside were like jewels: it sounds clichéd to say so, but they had the prismatic glint, the twinkle and the lure of jewels.

On impulse I grabbed a jacket and went on down. It felt as if I were doing something immensely daring, something slightly dangerous and even risqué. Steve would certainly have been horrified (*No, no, lovely*, I could hear him saying. *You can't go down there on your own. You just hang on a tick and I'll pop on some shoes and come with you*); Max would have been puzzled that I even thought twice about it.

It was a mild night, only a flick of cool breeze coming off the water. People were everywhere. It had looked crowded and jolly from my bedroom window: being in the middle of it was at once more and less cheerful than I'd imagined: the buzz of conversation and laughter was intoxicating; but I was alone inside all the merriment, and felt conspicuous and isolated. I sat at a waterside café and ordered a brandy.

The alcohol bit into my veins and I started to relax. The café had a guitarist, a dark young man strumming a guitar. Something about him reminded me of Dominic: not so much his dark good looks, I think, as an expression in his eye, a tilt to his head. I found myself staring at him, pondering almost abstractly the set of his shoulders, the concentration of his closed lips. I was looking at him but I was thinking of Dominic, and was embarrassed to register a few seconds late that he was gazing back at me. I felt colour rush up my throat to my face, smiled apologetically, and transferred my attention to the pavement, the water, the boats.

Five minutes later I became aware that the young guitarist was standing by my table.

'You permit?' he asked. His voice was soft and rich, accented. Spanish? I wasn't sure.

Confused, I nodded, and he sat next to me, carefully propping his guitar on the ground beside him.

'I think I have not seen you before,' he commented, with one of the most rare and charming smiles I have ever seen. 'You are tourist? Not local?'

'I'm from Melbourne,' I said.

I could be your mother, I thought.

I was flattered by his attentiveness, his concentration on me. Something like this hadn't happened to me before. When I'd been young and a likely candidate, I'd been too carefully sheltered. And marriage to Steve had done nothing to loosen the shackles.

I was flustered, but there was something exhilarating, something fascinating, about the situation: here I was, with a son almost as old as this beautiful young man with the warm adoring eyes; and here was he, with his appreciative gaze and his ravishing smile, paying court to me.

A waiter brought him coffee.

'Holiday?'

'Work, mainly,' I said, wondering if this luscious creature was indeed picking me up and concluding that he probably was.

'You are here for much longer?'

'I go home tomorrow.'

He nodded, sipped his coffee. 'You liked my music?'

It was all feeling more and more surreal.

'You play superbly,' I said, politely.

He sipped his coffee again and turned his glorious brown eyes on me.

'I can play for you. Just for you. You will enjoy.'

I started to demur.

He flashed his excellent teeth again.

'I am not so expensive,' he said.

Suddenly I understood what was happening, saw how naïve I'd been.

'No,' I said. 'No. Sorry, but no.'

He lifted his gracefully arched brows, looking more than ever like Dominic. His eyes widened. Bedroom eyes, gigolo's eyes.

'Please go,' I said.

He shrugged and went.

Two minutes later, I left, too. They charged me for his coffee, but I didn't have the confidence or presence of mind to argue the toss. I felt a fool, an absolute fool. Here I had been, preening myself on how attractive I was, how desirable I must be. Nothing but a fool, a middle-aged old chook deluding herself.

I strode back to the hotel (how different from the way I had sauntered out), let myself into my room with shaking hands. The telephone was ringing.

'My beautiful Bella,' said Max's voice in my ear. 'Just ringing to say goodnight, my darling. Together again tomorrow. I didn't wake you, did I?'

'I was in the shower,' I said.

'Sleep well, Bella, my love. I love you.'

'I love you, too. I really do, Max. I really do love you. You know that, don't you?'

He sounded slightly surprised. 'You know it, too, my love.'

'Yes,' I said. 'Yes. You sleep well, too.'

But it was a long time before I slept. The incident had deeply upset me, and I wasn't sure quite why. Partly, of course, I simply felt foolish. There I was, forty-one, silly enough to think that a boy making calf's eyes at me was smitten. I'd been a different sort of target, and it had taken me too long to realise it.

I think it was also a question of the things Bea and Zoë had said about Max, the way they had both so contemptuously called him a gigolo, the way their contempt had washed not only over Max for being a gigolo but also over me for my evident readiness to succumb to a gigolo. *Gigolo*, I kept repeating to myself. What an awful word it was, redolent of sleaze and self-interest and corruption.

Max was at the airport to pick me up the next morning. I'd never been more pleased to see him. I felt as if I'd sailed back into harbour, as if I was rocking safely again, lapped, unharmed after a close shave out on the open waters. I didn't tell him what had happened with the young guitarist. There was no reason why I should, of course; still, it felt odd to keep something from Max, to whom I told everything, in whom I confided as I had never confided in anyone before.

Doubly glad to be back home, I nestled into Rain, consciously luxuriating in its beauty and comfort, letting its surfaces and textures, its angles of light and its slanting shadows, soothe me. It was easy to be soothed.

During the day I worked with Bea: the business was booming and, although we didn't pick up on the Sydney terraces, more and more work was coming our way, and we were doing it well and enjoying it. Bea started to speak about employing a third architect. I didn't mind much one way or the other, so long as it was somebody who could be trusted with the name we were building for attention to detail, smooth, unfussy plans, flowing space, subtle planes and clever use of light.

There was plenty of work and I worked hard, but at the end of the day I went home to Max and enjoyed the life I had created for myself. I rang Dominic regularly: he didn't want to talk to me, but that would come in time.

When I look back on this period, I think it was the happiest time of my life. I had descended a little from the dizzy heights of my first wild infatuation with Max: that had been intensely happy, it is true; but it had also been accompanied by much trauma. Now, as we headed into our fourth year together, our life had settled and established itself: we were comfortable together in ways that were essentially domestic, undramatic, snug.

Our snugness was shared by Gavin, who turned up more and more frequently. We got to a stage in which we no longer noticed his presence at breakfast: it seemed as regular and predictable as Kate's own and I poured his orange juice without thinking about it.

It was no surprise when they appeared one night, silly and giggly and high as kites, interrupting our pre-dinner Scotch and announcing their engagement with all the erupting excitement of five-year-olds on their way to a circus. They declared that they intended to marry soon, soon!

I was conscious of a vague, undefined disappointment, but I tried not to show it and I certainly didn't make any attempt to dissuade them. Gavin didn't light up any candles for me, but I wasn't Kate, and in fact when I thought about it I found it impossible to imagine Kate marrying someone I might have liked.

Gavin was at least relatively inoffensive: he didn't put my teeth on edge more than three or four times a day. He did seem genuinely in love with Kate; he was working as a part- time tutor and seemed quite likely to turn into an academic (heaven knew there wasn't much else I could imagine him doing), so there was some prospect of his being able to support a family.

We all drank champagne and hugged and kissed and said how wonderful, and part of me half meant it. I knew Kate was very young, but so had I been when I'd married for the first time. If mothers chose their daughters' partners, after all, the world wouldn't work any better than it does now.

I suppose it was two or three weeks later—and a week or two before the wedding—that I came across Kate throwing up in the toilet.

'Is there anything you think you ought to tell me?' I asked, when she'd got herself cleaned up. We were in the kitchen and she was sipping the peppermint tea I'd made her. Peppermint tea had helped me through the early stages of both pregnancies, and it seemed to be doing the trick for Kate, too: she still looked peaky, but her colour was starting to return, and so was her composure.

She smiled her fey smile and cradled her mug in her hands.

'Well. Yes, I guess so.'

'You're pregnant?'

'I suppose so, Mum. Are you cross?'

'I'm not cross, no. I didn't think you and Gavin had been playing Scrabble up there in your room all night. But do you *know*, Kate? Have you done the tests?'

'Oh, yes,' said Kate, smiling again. 'It all seems pretty clear. The right colour and everything, you know. The blue line.'

This was incomprehensible to me. There hadn't been a blue line in my day.

'But have you seen a doctor?'

'Not yet. I will do. I've got an appointment.'

'Is that why you wanted to marry so quickly, Kate?'

'Not really. I mean, it isn't like it used to be, is it? Nobody really minds these days, do they? I guess we just couldn't see any point in waiting.'

'And Gavin knows?'

'Well, yes, Mum,' said Kate, looking slightly hurt. 'Of course he does. He's terribly thrilled.'

'Kate,' I said, very earnestly. 'Kate, you know you don't have to get married, if you don't want to. I don't want you to feel trapped.'

She looked astonished. 'Why would I feel trapped?'

'Well, only that if you thought—because of this, I mean because of being pregnant—that you had to get married, I'm only saying, you don't have to.'

'But, Mum. That's what I've been saying. I don't feel I have to get married. I *want* to get married.'

'To Gavin?'

'Of course to Gavin. There's no other candidate, is there?' said Kate, laughing.

'If you're sure,' I said.

'Of course I'm sure.'

'I just want you to be happy, Kate.'

'I'm going to be happy.'

'Okay. That's fine, then.' I stood. I was running late for work. She put up her arms to me. 'Aren't you pleased, Mum?'

I embraced her, somewhat awkwardly, murmuring reassurance.

Was I pleased? I wasn't sure. I thought about it as I drove to work. I should have guessed, of course: Kate and Gavin were no more competent to supervise their own contraception than the guinea pigs Kate had kept when she was eight. I wasn't sure if I was pleased, to tell the truth. I was only forty-one. I wasn't at all sure that I was ready to be a grandmother.

To my relief, Kate didn't want a big wedding. I'd had some misgivings about this: two years before, she'd been bridesmaid for one of her cousins on Steve's side of the family. Sarah had gone right over the top on the tulle and the glitter. The bridesmaids had frothed down the aisle like a trio of big white cappuccinos, preceding the large and twinkling pavlova of Sarah in her wedding dress. Kate had been very taken by it all, and I confidently expected a replay in her decisions about her own marriage. It didn't eventuate, however. Whether it was the lingering morning

150

sickness, or consideration for her father's budget, she requested and got something a lot smaller, a lot quieter.

After the wedding, she settled into domestic contentment with the dreadful Gavin, rather as if all her dreams had been fulfilled and this was all she wanted of life. To be pregnant and not quite barefoot.

Well, I suppose I wasn't too far from that, when I married Steve.

They settled into a nasty little house with cheap second-hand furniture Steve helped them to buy; Steve also gave them some old things, things he and I had bought when we were first married. I contributed the nursery furniture, which was neither second-hand nor cheap. I must say, Kate was most appreciative.

She painted the nursery herself, and got me to help her put up a wallpaper frieze with elves and hedgehogs and whatnot scampering over it. We bought a walnut cradle with white lacy sheets, and a gleaming white cot, and a sumptuous navy pram with a suspension that would lull any baby to sleep. I started to dawdle in babywear shops, feeling a maternalism to which I was unaccustomed, and bought the odd growsuit and fluffy toy. It was all rather pleasant.

Towards the end of Kate's pregnancy, late on a Sunday afternoon during which she and Gavin had visited us, I came across Max standing absorbed in thought, chin in hand, in the back garden.

'A penny for them,' I said, snuggling into his side and kissing his cheek.

'Do you still want the pool?'

I was taken aback. 'It's you who wants the pool, not me. I don't mind one way or the other.'

'It's a beautiful pool,' he said, thoughtfully.

'You've always said so.'

'I'm just thinking. There's not much of a garden, is there? Not around this side. The pool takes it all up. We're going to have a grandchild. Well, I know it'll be your grandchild, but I think of it as ours. I'm just thinking, wouldn't we rather have a garden for the little tyke to run around in?'

'I don't know. Wouldn't you miss it?'

'I'm not sure.' He rubbed his chin. 'I'm not sure I wouldn't rather have a bigger garden, you know. Couple of rose beds, perhaps? A herb patch? Maybe a winding path, a big tree or two? Bit of a lawn?'

'I don't mind,' I said.

And it was true: I didn't. Max could do this sometimes: we'd been through it with Rain's sunroom, which at first he'd loved. After a year, he found there was too much lemon in it, and eventually, once he'd worked up steam, the room was completely repainted and refurnished. Suddenly, what had been perfectly adequate turned out to be misguided, a foolish error, unsatisfactory from the start.

So I wasn't surprised that he wanted a garden, and I wasn't surprised when, in the next couple of days, he started to contact landscapers and pool demolishers. Max had never been a procrastinator.

He devoted immense effort to the planning, and, instead of returning to the swanky landscape gardener he'd originally employed for Rain, held endless discussions with Jack, of Jack's Landscape Solutions, recommended by some business acquaintance. Jack was a fatherly man with a ginger beard, which he had the habit of twirling, deep in thought.

Together they pored over diagrams and garden books. Max went out to nurseries and examined their stock, engaging in intense conversations with the nursery staff about anticipated heights and growth habits and conditions and colours and heaven only knows what else. What Max did, he did thoroughly.

And then Sophie was born.

It is impossible adequately to describe how Sophie's new presence, her existence as a new person, affected me. Everything was more fun. I fizzed more; I laughed more. Making love was better than ever; I embarked on an extravagant series of kitchen explorations, buying new equipment, cooking new things, trying new flavours. I attacked the front garden, which it seemed to me needed a lift, and planted dozens of seedlings, most of which died within a week because I forgot to water them. Max came across me humming one day: I was ironing, and I hate ironing. He laughed at me.

'You're worse than Pollyanna. It's like living with Julie Andrews: suddenly the hills are alive.'

I was startled. I knew I felt different, but I hadn't realised I'd shown it so clearly.

'You are utterly transparent, my love,' he said, kissing the back of my neck. 'That tiny little mite has transformed your life completely, and there's no point in denying it.'

Well, I didn't want to deny it. Something melted inside me every time I picked her up, every time I saw her. And relations between Kate and me were so good, too: after a lifetime of tension, we were finally doing the mother–daughter thing.

I started to work part-time, turning up maybe three days a week if they were lucky. Bea complained loudly, and I laughed and said I was learning how to be a granny and she'd have to get used to it.

I drove over frequently and helped Kate to bathe Sophie: peacefully we marvelled together at her perfection, stroking her cheeks, kissing her tummy, cuddling her, giggling like a couple of schoolgirls.

It seemed to me that Kate liked me more than she ever had before. I certainly liked her. She was deft and gentle with Sophie, and sweet. She was willing to defer to me, to ask my advice. 'What should I do here?' she would ask. 'How should I handle this, or that? Did I do this, when I was a baby?' And so on.

New harmonies established themselves, crept into our conversations, our modes of discussion. We conferred over what name I could be called. Nanna? Grandma? Gran? We settled on Gandie because it was a bit different, and I liked its rhythm, its slow movement.

We would sit together quietly as Kate breastfed. I took to knitting small things in fleecy white or soft pink wool, on fragile metal needles that clicked companionably through our amicable chat, our compatible silence. We were there together, hanging over her cradle, when she smiled her first smile. 'You can't say *that's* wind!' Kate cried in triumph, and we hugged. We actually hugged.

Picture postcard, we were. No, better: high art. I see us in retrospect, heads bent, sitting in the slanting sunshine of a rustic Dutch interior. Tendrils of hair, shimmering in the faint and dusty light, escape from our starched white caps. Blue hyacinths make a statement in an earthenware vase; a solid curvaceous milk jug squats on the wooden table. The baby kicks and coos. There's probably a damsel playing a dulcimer in a courtyard out the back.

Well, it happened. It was brief, I grant you; but it happened.

*

When Sophie was about three months old and we were engaged in one of these idyllic scenes, Kate said one day: 'Families are so important, aren't they, Mum.'

'Mmmm,' I say, with some wariness. I am conscious of being vulnerable in this kind of discussion.

'And ritual's important, too, I think. Don't you?'

'Possibly,' I say. I have no idea where this is heading.

'Dad asked me the other day if we were going to have her christened.'

'Ah,' I say. Religion has never meant much to me. It seems clear to me that if there is a God up there he's just as baffled by everything as I am, and he's therefore not much use to me. I was faintly surprised, after we were married, to discover that Steve had C-of-E leanings. Not that they ever made much difference to anything.

'And are you?' I ask.

'No, I don't think so,' says Kate, reflectively, detaching Sophie from her nipple and lifting her to her shoulder. 'There you go, my precious, see how you feel after that little lot. I talked about it with Gavin. He doesn't really mind: he'll do whatever I want, he says.'

That'd be right, I think. Hopeless.

'And I don't really want the full christening deal. You know? It seems hypocritical, somehow. I mean, we never go to church, and I really don't want all the trappings and so forth. But we agreed we wanted something. Just something to sort of celebrate Sophie, and her arrival into the world, and how perfect she is. To welcome her formally, I suppose. She's had enough, I think. Can you take her for a moment, Mum?'

I receive Sophie into my arms. She gives me a bleary grin and my insides liquefy into warm honey. It keeps happening, the

155

miracle of holding her and feeling myself melt with the wondrous beauty of it, the beauty of her.

Kate is doing up her bra. 'So I thought, perhaps, let's have a kind of reception.'

'A reception?'

'Well, yes. I mean literally. A receiving of her, into the family. You know? Just like a party, really.'

I don't know, at all, but I'm feeling soppy these days and I'm prepared to agree to pretty much anything Kate suggests. Within reason.

'Of course,' she goes on, thoughtfully, 'it would mean you and Dad would be here together. Would that be uncomfortable for you, do you think?'

It will be exceedingly uncomfortable, of course. As I've explained, Steve and I didn't split up with the kind of cold-fish amity other couples seem to achieve on occasion. We were bitter and hot and hurt; we shouted and screamed; we wounded each other with express calculation. We never actually hit each other, but we came close. Well, I did, anyway. And now we avoid each other with resolute circumspection.

But I have thought about all of this. Steve and I are grand-parents, now, and perhaps it is time to face up to our joint obligations. Grandchildren are different. There will be birth-days, Christmases, school sports, school concerts. There will be ballet performances and netball matches and tennis finals and maybe eisteddfods and piano competitions. Trophy presenta-tions, prize-givings, all the trappings that accompany clear public evidence of excellence. (Not that I'm necessarily expecting these, you understand; but they might happen all the same.) There will be graduations and debuts. And then there will be more weddings. So if I can manage to be grown up about all of this,

Steve can, too.

'That's fine,' I say, casually. 'Max will have to be invited, of course.'

Kate nods. 'Max is part of the family, too,' she says, seriously.

I am pleased she says this. I tell him about it, later, that evening, when we're having a whisky in the light stone courtyard leading in from Rain's well-equipped kitchen—silvery granite-topped benches, best-quality Swedish appliances, capacious and ingenious cupboards in pale mountain ash.

He tinkles the ice in his glass, gazing down at it and saying nothing. I think I can tell, however, from his faint crinkly smile, that he's glad Kate has said this, that he interprets it as her cementing his relationship with Sophie, with her family.

So Kate's reception proceeds. She chats about it a lot: it fills her mind. Invitations are sent out for a Sunday afternoon. We are each to bring a gift: not a physical, wrapped gift (though I intend to bring one of those, too: I have bought a glorious snowy crochet wrap which will, I realise, be of strictly limited use but drapes superbly and seems to me to establish my gravitas as a grandmother), but a metaphoric gift, a spiritual gift, which requires each of us to nominate the essential quality that in an ideal world we would pass on to a baby aspiring to the best of everything. In short, we are to be fairy godmothers.

I give much thought to what I will propose as my gift to Sophie. I am not blind to the possibilities this occasion offers for Steve and me to insert vengeful blades sleekly between each other's ribs, but I am determined to rise above this, to demonstrate my large-mindedness, my benign serenity. Should Steve meanly come up with some quality such as fidelity, I am prepared to look mildly hurt and to forgo my corresponding opportunity. Forewarned, I smugly believe myself forearmed.

Max is interested in what he sees as Kate's ingenuity and engages to think seriously about his own gift, but for some reason we do not discuss our intentions.

Before we leave for the reception, I glance out the back door and see that the wattle is in vibrant bloom. Yellow has always seemed to me to be Sophie's natural colour, and even at that stage of her life its radiance carried its own appropriateness for her special glow, her sunlit essence, her goldenness. I rush out with secateurs and mutilate the young trees, carving out great swathes of vivid flowers, which deposit themselves all over the fine leather of Max's back seat on the way over. Ever since then, whenever I see the electric lemon fuzz of early cootamundra blossom, I remember Sophie's fairy godmother party.

I realise when we get there that the wattle has been a mistake: Kate exclaims over its beauty but is clearly at a loss when trying to find a suitable vase, and it makes the devil of a mess of her carpet while she struggles with it. Never mind: it gives us a way to get through the awkwardness of Steve, who has already arrived and has obviously decided to behave well. He nods at me, shakes Max's hand mournfully, and mutters something which may not be gracious but at least is not provocative.

So we're all sitting around and dandling Sophie and covering awkward gaps with exclamations over her beauty and intelligence. Then, at a sign from Kate, the hapless Gavin shambles over to the fireplace and looks about him with myopic satisfaction.

'Thank you all for coming,' he says, and meanders on for some time about Sophie, and Kate, and how happy he is to be married to Kate, and the importance of families.

We sit on the cheap, velveteen lounge suite and listen to him with more or less pleased looks on our faces. Kate is on my right, I recall; holding Sophie and watching Gavin with approval. Dominic is beyond her, tight, tense, closed in. (Dominic was about fifteen. He still had the slim fawnlike look of prepubescence; when he wore bathers you could see the delicate angular projections of his shoulder blades, jutting out as if his skeletal structure hid wings that were trying to bud through the bones. His chest and arms hadn't filled out. His voice was just breaking and his skin still had a childish sheen to it. He was so beautiful he made you weep.) Steve is beyond Dominic; his shoulders are hunched and he stares at the carpet.

And on the other side of the room—in the old armchairs Steve has given Kate, the armchairs he and I bought when we were first married—sit Zoë and Henry. I hadn't expected Zoë and Henry to be here and I'm not sure why they are: I'd thought it was only the immediate family; but I'm determined to be good-tempered about everything today. Max is next to me (I've made sure of that), on the other side of me from Kate. I see Steve glancing at him, every now and then. Sophie is making gurgling noises, bless her.

Gavin comes, with slow humour and elephantine tread, to the end of his speech. He beams at us all and then says, with no particular emphasis: 'And my gift to my daughter is charm.' And he goes and sits down.

Kate breaks in to protest. 'You have to say why,' she cries, dissolving into laughter.

We have all been instructed thus. It is not enough simply to give: we must speak to our gifts, describing the manner in which we wish them to manifest themselves and the reasons for our choice. Gavin has, of course, forgotten this. Smiling ineffectually, he lumbers to his feet again and considers.

'I haven't got it,' he says. 'Charm, I mean. I've never had it.' Some people make ineffectual demurring noises. (I don't.) 'No, I haven't,' he continues. 'I know I haven't. I've always wanted it. I've always been—how would you put it—*beguiled* by charming people. They make you want to be with them; they make you want their good opinion; they make you want to do things for them. People who have that—they've got the battle won. That's what I want for my little girl. If she's got that, I reckon everything else will follow.'

Kate applauds and the rest of us, unsure about whether we are meant to join in, clap in a piecemeal kind of way as Gavin, blushing and ungainly, sits down again and tries to look as if he has some marginal capacity for self-possession. Later on, as we have a quiet drink in the courtyard at Rain, Max will say to me that he found this speech touching.

'Touching?' I say, mystified.

Max regards me in what seems a slightly odd way. 'You really don't like Gavin, do you?'

Briefly, I investigate my emotions.

'I don't like him or dislike him. I don't know what she sees in him. But I don't specially dislike him. It's just that he irritates me. How can she go to bed with him, Max? He's like a long, thin puppet, a clown puppet; his head bobs around as if his neck's on a spring; he's so gangly and bumbly and he always looks so damn worried.'

'But you don't dislike him,' says Max, laughing.

'No. He drives me mad, but I don't dislike him.'

'It was a very honest speech,' says Max.

Anyway, whether Gavin was touching or not, we now move on to our next contributor, skulking palely in the corner.

'Dad!' calls Kate, who is the self-elected emcee for this

160

occasion. 'Your turn.'

Steve has actually written out a speech, which he drags from a back pocket and self-consciously unfolds. 'I have thought a good deal about this,' he reads, flat and hurried. 'I have found it a difficult task.'

I school my features to look earnest: it will not do to snigger.

'It is a new thing for me to have a granddaughter,' continues Steve. 'I find I am quite surprised by it. It seems to me only the other day that Kate was still a little child herself and I do not know where the years have gone. But here we are, and suddenly here is Sophie, who is now a part of our family.'

Steve pauses and takes a deep breath; a light sweat gleams on his upper lip. I am puzzled. Grace and sophistication are not attributes of Steve's: I realise this; indeed, no one knows it better than I, but he can normally exhibit a kind of bluff self-possession that serves him better than this awful rehearsed floundering. Suddenly I wonder if he is as disconcerted by my presence—and, of course, by Max's—as I am by his. I suppose it's possible.

'I have thought a lot about Kate's request and I have tried to come up with something that is appropriate for me to give Sophie as her gift from me,' Steve goes on, so clearly uncomfortable and embarrassed that these sensations are communicated to us all like a rabid infection.

'Of course I understand that whatever I come up with it will only be my wish for Sophie and not actually a real gift, no matter how much I would like it to be. Still, it is important to wish for the right thing. And so I have decided to wish for Sophie not beauty or wealth or talent but something else that I think is more important. I am wishing her resilience. You don't ever know what life will bring you, and whatever it does bring you, you have to try to bounce back from. This is something all of us know from different experiences, in different ways.'

He pauses and glances around, in a dissatisfied, unfocused way. 'So,' he finishes, lamely. 'So. That is my wish for Sophie.'

Again, as he sits down, the patchy applause dribbles around, Kate clapping over-enthusiastically and the rest of us still not sure about joining in. It's a bit like a school prize-giving where none of the students like each other very much. I'm relieved. Resilience is okay, as Steve's wish. Fidelity I would have had trouble with.

'Max!' Kate declares. 'Your turn.'

Max stands, with the graceful diffidence he's so good at. He's not at all nervous, unlike his predecessors, but he's not going to err on the side of over-confidence either. Oh God, he speaks so well, and I am so proud of him! He says, with his own gorgeous quiet understated charm, how glad he is to be here, how much he appreciates everyone's forbearance and warmth and how good it is to feel part of a family.

He goes on: 'I've never been part of a family—or at least, not for so long that I almost can't remember it. I'd been on my own for a long time, before I met Isabel. Frankly, I'd expected always to be on my own. And it's such a privilege, such an honour, to be accepted among you all.'

He pauses, and glances around with that candid and somehow vulnerable look of his, the one that always slays me.

'Like all of you, I've thought a lot about what I'd like to bequeath to this bewitching scrap of humanity here. And I thought perhaps at first I'd focus on this element of her life: her centredness in a family, the way she nestles in the heart of her family. It's an extended family, I grant you, and my member-ship of it is a surprising part of it, I know. But it's a group of related people who all—whatever else they do or don't share—do share a profound and confident wish that Sophie's life will be the best life that it can possibly be, that we can possibly help to make it.

'And so it seemed to me that it would be redundant to wish Sophie a strong and embracing family. She already has that. It encircles her and protects her; it provides her with all the support and love and sustenance she needs. And so the best gift I can give Sophie is a spirit of adventure, a spirit that will tempt her away from the safety and comfort and shelter of her family into the excitement and challenge of the unknown. A spirit that will lead her to test herself, to find how limitless her limits are, to leap into space and fly.'

Max actually goes over to Kate, and leans over her to kiss the top of Sophie's head. It's quite a theatrical thing to do, and I think a brave one. We all clap him (I am a little too enthusiastic, but really, I am so proud of him), and Kate turns to Dominic.

Dominic is unfazed, of course. He has notes—three or four small squares of paper—and holds them carefully, periodically shuffling the front one to the back as he speaks. He has prepared so well that he knows which notes are on which piece of paper.

'So much,' he says, glancing around in a rather peremptory way, as if to make sure he has our attention. 'So much one would like to offer to Sophie. So much one would like to have oneself, that somehow one doesn't have. I suspect we will all offer Sophie something that shines the more brightly for us because it isn't in our own possession.'

Shines the more brightly! Ah, what an orator. What a future this kid has! How articulate, for fifteen! I recall Steve telling me (in one of our stilted antagonistic sessions during which we consult about the children) that Dominic is in the debating club at school. Even the president of it, perhaps. I must find out.

'I am no exception,' continues Dominic. 'I'd like Sophie to

163

have something I've always wanted. Try as I might, it's always eluded me.' He pauses.

There is something I can't quite read about him. He's speaking so eloquently, so lucidly: he's mixing it so impressively with the adults; you'd expect him to be enjoying himself. Dominic's used to occupying the limelight in a variety of contexts and normally he adopts its sheen with aplomb. Not so today. There's something missing. He's not relishing any of this.

'What I wish for Sophie...'

There is an awful second or two during which he seems to look into the middle distance and gulp slightly, and forget what he's saying. Just as I'm becoming nervous, however, he gains control and returns to us.

'I'd like Sophie to believe in herself,' says Dominic, to my utter astonishment.

Was there ever a child, I think, born with greater self-belief than Dominic?

'I'd like her to be deeply confident within herself. Not stupidly arrogant, not up herself. I'm not talking ego; I'm not talking conceit. Just a realistic and abiding self-belief. I reckon that'll see her through more than anything else.'

I am so thunderstruck by this assertion and its implications that I miss a beat or two of Kate's mild and inconsequential connecting remarks and the next thing I know Zoë has bounced up.

'It's been a very interesting exercise,' says Zoë. 'I'd like to thank Kate for the opportunity to think through some of the questions that her request inevitably generated. In thinking about what we would wish to give Sophie, as Dominic has so intelligently pointed out, we have all thought about what we ourselves would like to possess. And that naturally leads to a reappraisal of our own lives. Henry and I'—she ducks her head towards Henry in an acknowledgement—'have spent many hours discussing the matter. It's been most instructive.'

She smiles at us all, in a pleased way, as if we should be especially grateful for the chance at self-instruction.

'What to wish for?' proceeds Zoë, clearly enjoying herself. 'Kate didn't make it clear whether she wanted our gifts to be *qualities*, that is, an integral part of Sophie, or *conditions*, things like money, extrinsic to Sophie but available to her. So it was, for instance, open to any of us to choose great wealth, or immunity from disease. These would be good gifts. Instead, all of us so far have concentrated on qualities. This is what Henry and I decided, too, though of course I mustn't pre-empt Henry's choices in this matter.'

I suppose this is how Zoë talks when she gives a class. It's rapid, crisp, articulate, assertive. She feels no doubt, no diffidence. The outlines are clear; the colours are bright. We sit there, listening like obedient schoolchildren.

'I think the reason we have all instinctively focused on qualities is that we implicitly acknowledge our own roles in our destinies. It would be possible to wish for Sophie, say, happiness, but happiness is something we achieve ourselves, not something that can be handed around on a plate. If Sophie is to be happy— and I certainly hope she will be—she must win that happiness herself. Nobody can give it to her.'

I'm trying not to look bored, but it's getting harder by the moment. It's just like Zoë, to turn all of this from a family celebration into a purely didactic occasion in which she can herself play a leading part and make a lot of unfounded assumptions about life and how other people live it. I recognise in her comments a barbed reference to my own circumstances, and hear her voice as it has sounded forth on other occasions, earnestly telling me that I am the master of my fate, the captain of my soul, and so on.

Zoë smiles, holding her hands clasped in front of her. She looks as if she is about to announce the winner of the under-twelve hurdles.

'I wish Sophie a love of learning,' she says. 'Through learning Sophie can become whatever she wishes. She can discover great opportunities and she can make the most of those opportunities. In some ways I feel this was an entirely predictable choice for me to make—exactly what you would expect of a tunnel-visioned, obstinate, old-fashioned, chalk-'n'-talk teacher.'

She laughs, slightly, as if she thinks this description of herself will seem inadequate to her audience. 'But there it is. Sophie, I wish you a fine education, and I wish you the capacity to make the most of it.'

Zoë looks as if she will go on for a long time in exhortation and explication, but fortunately Kate breaks in with delighted exclamations. She turns then to Henry.

I am to be last, then. How am I to read this, I wonder? Does the last person speak more weightily, or am I something of a post-script to the proceedings?

All I can think of, for a few moments, as I try to concentrate on Henry, is how very much I have always disliked him. Then his words arrest this train of thought. He's been saying something about the specialness of the occasion, the bright promise of a new life, and so forth.

Then he says, in his finicky way, pronouncing all his words carefully in that over-particular manner he appears for some reason to cultivate: 'None of this would matter, of course'—(I'm not sure what it is that wouldn't matter)—'if we only focus on those attributes, those characteristics, that in fact we do see as important, as significant.'

That's Henry all over. Never settle for one word if two will do the trick. Zoë always maintains he is a wonderful teacher. 'Inspirational,' says Zoë, with bull-like force, so you don't feel like contradicting her. 'Simply inspirational. He has them hanging on his every word.' I don't believe it, though.

'Indeed,' says Henry, beaming around, 'as *necessary*. However, let us not forget, in the daily striving, the competition, the conflict that constitute our lives, that other elements, other characteristics, characteristics that have nothing to do with competition, are still an integral part of our beings. In the great competitions that life sets us, enters us for, if I may put it that way, there are still other aspects of our personalities that are just as important, although they are not attuned to winning, to victory. One of these is the capacity to love.'

Shit, I think.

'It is this capacity to love—to love and to accept love—that stands us in such good stead in the significant relationships of our lives. Without it, we are unable to give or to receive the affection that in old-fashioned terms used to be called loving-kindness, that provides the links for all our friendships, the cement for our families, the single thing that holds us all together.'

The fact is that Henry has stolen my thunder. My gift to Sophie was going to be the capacity to love. And, in fact, the capacity to be loved, which he seems to have cottoned on to also. In the midst of my irritation and confusion, I am astounded that Henry's desiccated soul is capable of formulating these concepts. Goodness knows where he's got them from.

But what am I going to say? It's nearly my turn. While Henry rabbits on about love and its importance or significance or whatever, I'm thinking as hard as I can. I've got my little speech all prepared. I've known what I'm going to say: I haven't got notes because I don't need them; unlike Steve, I'm perfectly capable of making a simple statement without rustling my way through several sheets of A4. But the simple statement I was going to make suddenly isn't available to me any more. So far as I can tell, Henry's taken pretty much an identical line, and left me high and dry.

And how am I going to look? Everyone else has gone to a lot of trouble; everyone's thought about Kate's request and made an effort to meet it. So have I, of course, but it's not going to look like that. I, who love Sophie best of all: I'm going to be the one who looks inadequate, ill-prepared, uncaring. It's not fair.

I'm thinking so hard that I don't realise Henry has come to an end and everybody is looking at me.

'Earth to Isabel,' says Gavin. 'Earth to Isabel.'

I can never see why this is supposed to be such a witty thing to say, nor why people say it to me. Steve used it all the time and it drove me insane. *I am listening*, I felt like saying to him. *I'm listening, but you're not saying anything.*

'Sorry,' I say. 'The thing is...' The thing is, of course, that I don't want to say what the thing is. I don't want to admit that Henry and I jumped on the same tram. I'm not quite sure why this is. Well, perhaps I am. I can't stand Henry and don't wish to be bracketed with him. What I wanted for Sophie was special, and Henry's gone and spoilt it. I decide to improvise.

'I've been sitting here, listening to you all,' I start. I look around and smile winningly. Well, I try to. I don't want any of them thinking I'm a bad grandmother. So many of them think I'm a bad mother. Wrongly, wrongly; but it's what they think.

'And it's been fascinating, seeing what you've all chosen.'

By mistake I look at Dominic, and find his gaze on me, stern and brimming with judgement and perhaps slightly baffled, too, as if he's wondering what I've done to deserve being there at all. He's wearing that awful, fastidious, unforgiving look he gets. I turn my eyes from him.

I look around this group of people most of whom I do not love, although they are through genetic and legal ties the closest people to me in all the world. I see Max's concern, Kate's puzzlement, Zoë's irritation, Dominic's antagonism. I see Gavin's embarrassment, Steve's unease and Henry's disdain. I see Sophie, burbling away, quietly sociable, on her mother's knee.

And suddenly it comes to me. So many of these people have combined to thwart and frustrate me over the years; so many of them have militated against my happiness in different ways. I know what I want for my granddaughter, growing up amongst them.

'I wish this for Sophie,' I say, firmly and steadily. 'I want her to have a mind of her own. I want her to think for herself, to grow in strength and independence of character, not to be frightened to trust her own judgement, and to act as she sees fit, as she thinks best.'

Everybody looks relieved that I've actually thought of something to say and have said it, even if they don't much like the thing itself. Kate gives me one of her big gooey smiles.

'What about you, Kate?' asks Dominic. 'Don't you have a gift for Sophie?'

Kate gives him a gooey smile, too.

'I do,' she says, as if this were a matter for particular congratulation.

She pauses, apparently gathering her thoughts. God knows, it shouldn't take her long.

'I want to thank you all. Each and every one of you has

given Sophie something truly worth having, something she'll be grateful to you for to the end of her days. I'm going to make a little book for her, with pictures in it, and I'm going to include all her gifts in it, all the wishes you've made for her and the presents you've given her. It will mean she can look back to this day and see how lucky she is to be at the centre of such a loving family, such a good and thoughtful and generous family.'

It seems as if she really thinks we have verifiably given Sophie the things of which we spoke, rather than simply speaking of them. Kate has always dwelt in her own special version of la-la land. Would that it were so easy! Would that I could have organised for Dominic to have a loving heart, for Kate to have some brains!

'My own gift might seem an odd one,' says Kate. 'I guess it isn't obvious, straightaway, as something you'd choose to give a child. But it just seems to me so important, I can't tell you. I'm not even sure what to call it. It's got to do, I suppose, with catching the wave, knowing the right time. That makes it sound like opportunism, jumping on the bandwagon sort of thing, but I don't mean it as purely an opportunistic thing. It's more like—well, catching the wave's the best way I can put it, I think. Seeing when something is the right time for something and trusting yourself to act on it.'

'Don't die wondering,' says Gavin, helpfully. 'That's it,' she agrees. 'Don't die wondering.'

And on this note we disperse, drink, eat, chat, more or less awkwardly. I've been quite nervous about this occasion, as it represents the first time, really, that Steve and I have consented to meet each other as part of the family. It doesn't go too badly. We manage to have a conversation, or at least to be in the same conversing group, and neither of us positively scratches the other's eyes out. It has to be a good sign.

Max isn't a chatty man, but he's a bit quiet even for him in the car on the way home. It isn't until later, when we're sipping whisky in Rain's peaceful courtyard, that he refers to the afternoon, making his comment about Gavin. Then, to my surprise, he congratulates me on my family.

'You have to be joking,' I say.

'No, why?'

'My family! Actually, love, I don't usually regard them as grounds for congratulation.'

'I know. But you'd have to admit they all came up looking pretty good today.'

'Did they?' I consider it. 'In what way, would you say?'

'Well, they'd all thought about it, hadn't they? They'd all tried hard.'

'I did, too. I'd practised endlessly, what I was going to say. But then Henry pretty much said it for me, so I had to think about something else.'

'Ah. I wondered what prompted the stage fright. You did well, Bella: that was a good present you gave her, especially if you thought of it at short notice.'

Max stretches out and contemplatively swirls the liquor and ice around in his glass.

'Yours was pretty good, too.'

'I hope it will stand her in good stead,' he says, seriously. 'It's a dangerous thing to wish on someone, a sense of adventure.'

'It hasn't done you any harm.'

'No. Maybe not.' He smiles and leans over to me, strokes my arm, makes me tingle. 'It didn't stop me from meeting you, anyway. That's been my biggest adventure.'

There's a brief pause, spent in mutual smug contemplation.

It's one of the nice things about being one half of a happy couple, that you can do this sort of thing.

After a little while, I say: 'I was surprised by what Dominic said, though.'

'What bit of it?'

'The bit about lacking self-confidence. I would have said it was one of the principal things Dominic absolutely doesn't lack.'

'Truly?'

'You surely don't think Dominic an unconfident person?'

'Well,' says Max, 'I haven't been given the opportunity to get to know Dominic very much at all. But I've never thought of him as particularly confident.'

I am baffled by this, and say so.

'He didn't seem very confident today, though. Did he?'

'Perhaps not, but I've seen Dominic in that sort of situation before—one, I mean, where he has to speak more or less publicly—and he always carries it off just fine.'

'I thought he was feeling very exposed,' says Max. 'I thought he was being forced to reveal more of himself than he wanted to. I suppose all of us were, but I think Dominic in particular found it uncomfortable, an invasion of privacy. He had to draw the curtain aside, didn't he? He had to let people in. He didn't like it.'

I mull this over.

'But he's not unconfident,' I say, eventually. 'He's not an unconfident person.'

Max shrugs. 'You know him far better than I do, Bella, obviously. But I've never thought of Dominic as very confident. Confident people don't need to put up the barriers Dominic puts up.'

I'm genuinely puzzled by this. I see what Max means, but it doesn't square with how I think of Dominic. To me, he always seems as swift and strong and confident as an otter, a tiger, a hawk. How can Max think he isn't?

'Don't worry about it,' says Max with a slight smile. 'You look so anxious, Bella. There's nothing to worry about.'

I let it go, but it returns to niggle at me. Dominic: unconfident?

He certainly doesn't seem unconfident the next time I see him, which happens to be at his school's speech night. He picks up several prizes, makes a cogent contribution to a kind of mini-debate they offer as part of the evening's entertainment, and generally seems as untroubled as ever by attention. I mention this to Max (who doesn't come, as he thinks it tactless to inflict himself on Dominic at these occasions) when I return home. He nods, cheerily.

'It's only that you said he was unconfident,' I say.

'I'm probably wrong.'

'But he seemed so much on top of everything, Max. I wish you could have seen him.'

I am bubbling over with undisguised pride: it's pleasant to have produced a child who so conspicuously achieves high standards in everything he attempts. A number of Dominic's teachers have made admiring remarks about him during the evening. Dominic himself, doubtless borne along and uplifted by his success, has even attained a degree of civility to me.

Max pours my drink and hands it to me.

'I believe you, my darling Bella,' he says, with his charming grin. 'No question.'

I lean back, kick off my shoes, relax. 'You know what I was thinking? I was thinking, heavens, if Kate can have a child like Sophie, imagine what Dominic's children will be like.'

Max looks puzzled.

'Well,' I say, suddenly realising that I'm not sounding kind. I like to sound kind, for Max. 'What I mean is, I know Kate's lovely, and of course we love her very much, but in terms of beauty and brain power...well. You know what I mean.'

'Kate's intelligent,' says Max, with a hint of shortness. 'Kate's got a lot of perception, a lot of insight.'

'Yes. Of course I agree.' (I don't.) 'But...'

'Look,' says Max, 'I know Sophie's the most brilliant child ever to exist, but she isn't very old yet, Bella darling. Don't count too much on her intelligence and beauty, will you?'

I shrug. Somewhere, dimly, I intuit a degree of what one might almost call displeasure in Max's responses. But it's been a good night, and I don't want to dig too deep, or to enmesh myself in a tricky argument. Happily, I concede to his caution.

Soon, we go to bed and make love; and making love is as glorious and radiant as it always is. There seems no limit to our luck, our felicity, the extraordinary generosity of the providence that watches silently over us.

Part Three

So I moved into a new phase. If not a genuine fairy godmother, certainly a devoted grandmother.

Not long after Kate's little celebration for Sophie, Max and I went over to their house one afternoon. Max didn't usually come with me on these occasions. He derived great enjoyment, he said, from my new status, and he delighted in my pleasure with a tender and attentive mirth that moved me deeply; but he didn't find it necessary always to be there, hanging onto my sleeve. He was a very sensitive man, Max, and highly attuned to female responsiveness, feminine priorities.

He handled Sophie deftly enough himself—surprising, in a man who had never had children—but he preferred to see me holding her, to chuckle at my raptness and to encourage my captivation. He said that he thought it good for me to spend time with Kate, to strengthen my relationship with her at what he called a very special time—which it was—rather than insisting on being there all the time himself.

But on this day he drove me over, and stayed twenty minutes or so before going on to a business appointment—one of those mysterious business appointments into the mists of which he disappeared, debonair and unassuming, one of the appointments about which information was never forthcoming. Not that I sought such information, then or ever.

The previous day the demolition of the pool had commenced. A small swarm of men had arrived at an early hour and made themselves at home in our back garden. We'd already drained the pool. Jackhammers had noisily shattered the pale tiles and trucks had deposited neat slagheaps of filler earth around its perimeter. Before we left for Kate's, I remember, we conducted a brief inspection of the back. The cavity in the ground gaped roughly as if a bomb had dropped in it: it was hard to believe we had lounged around it, dived so hedonistically into it. It all looked awful, but Max was pleased that the work had finally started.

'You won't know it,' he said. 'Going to be brilliant. Instant garden. Nothing like it.'

Kate's cleaning lady was there, when we arrived. We had given her twelve months' worth of cleaning lady, Max and I, when Sophie was born: I remembered so clearly Kate's own infancy and the difficulty I had found in ordering the most trivial components of one's life in a halfway efficient manner. (Not that Kate hadn't managed pretty well. She took to motherhood, I must say, better than I had.) She was a nice lady, Charmian: she had badly dyed, tight auburn curls and a hard-bitten, scrappy, sinewy look about her, but she was soft as butter inside, and *gooed* and *gaaed* around Sophie as much as any of us did. She cleaned the bathroom a treat: I remember that.

Max had gone. Kate was on the phone to some friend who had rung. I was playing with Sophie. Charmian had just finished vacuuming and came into the living room. She tickled Sophie under the chin.

'Goodbye, my precious,' she said. 'I'll see you again next week, I expect.'

Sophie was lying on my lap. She cooed and waved her fists about.

'You can certainly see the likeness to her grandfather,' observed Charmian.

'Sorry?' I said. I didn't think Sophie resembled Steve in the slightest.

'Even at this age, you can see the nose, I reckon. And the way her eyes are set. But specially the mouth. Your husband's a very good-looking man, isn't he? Striking. She'll be the same, I shouldn't wonder.'

I went to explain, laughingly, that she had it wrong, that Max was my husband but not Kate's father, and as I did so I glanced down at Sophie on my knees and the words—as the phrase has it—died on my lips. Died quite dead, all quite deadybones, as Dominic would once have said.

Sophie lay on her back, beaming up at us, and as I looked at her she gave a delighted little clucking noise and crinkled her nose.

I had seen that nose-crinkle before.

'You hadn't seen it?' asked Charmian, misunderstanding my silence. 'Likenesses are strange, I always think. Families often don't notice them: it takes an outsider to see what's right before your eyes. Funny things, genes. See you later.'

I said something. Charmian left. I continued to sit, Sophie beaming up at me.

I suppose I was slow. It didn't all fall into place immediately. Right in front of me it had certainly been, but that didn't mean I comprehended it rapidly. Comprehension was a tall order, at that moment.

But as I sat there, some of the pieces started to fall into place. I recalled Kate's new maturity, her unselfconscious indolence and her adolescent glamour, the new charge of sexuality flickering through her. I recalled the bikini, the hours around the pool. I recalled, quite specifically, the satiny way her skin shone when she climbed out of the pool. I recalled my week in Sydney.

It's always the oldest stories in the world that make least sense when they happen to you.

And this one made no sense at all. For against my memories of these things, against my enforced new interpretation of absences and silences, of laughter and glances, of intonation and gesture, stood all my experience of Max, all the experience of our love and my trust. My absolute trust.

It was not within the range of likelihood that Max had cold-bloodedly, deliberately deceived me. The understanding that we shared simply transcended that possibility. Max's kindness, his loyalty and generosity and openness and sweet nature—all his qualities came crowding into my head. It was not possible that this man had betrayed me. Not with the icy intention of betrayal. Not knowingly, not as a plan.

Yet betrayed I was. I gave my little finger to Sophie and she grabbed it, chuckling with that uncomplicated, entirely unmanipulative delight that makes babies such a joy. I drew it away gently and she pulled it back and stuck it in her mouth. She chuckled again, crinkling her nose.

At this point, Kate entered. She took one look at me and nodded, quite calmly.

'You've seen it, haven't you?' she said, rather as if we were discussing a television program.

I couldn't say anything.

She bent over and took Sophie. 'I knew you'd see it soon,' she said, matter-of-factly. 'It's time for her sleep. I'll put her down. I'll be back in a moment.'

When she returned she sat opposite me and regarded me levelly.

'Well,' she said. 'I understand it's a shock for you. Do you want to talk about it?'

I tried to speak and couldn't. I tried again. I stood up. I didn't want to be sitting down. She stood, too, and put her hand out as if she meant to comfort me. I winced away.

'Talk. What good will talking do?' In my own ears my voice sounded vicious, its bitterness spraying uncontrollably.

She said nothing. She interlaced her fingers and looked down at them, as if she were considering some conundrum they posed.

'Why?' I asked. 'Why did you do it?'

'You're blaming me?'

'You can ask that?'

'Why assume it's my fault?'

I stared at her. 'You're telling me he raped you?'

'Good God, no.'

'Then you must have seduced him.'

She actually laughed. 'Mum, can't you imagine making love outside rape or seduction? I was in love with him. I am in love with him.'

'What the fuck do you mean?'

She flinched, at the word, I suppose. I thought it was rich of her to take exception to my language when she'd just seduced my husband.

'I've been in love with Max for a long time. Since I was sixteen or so, I think. You're not the only person who's allowed to fall in love, Mum.'

I raised my hand to hit her, but she stepped back, alarm on her face.

'I only slept with him once,' she said. 'You saw Max and

181

you fell hopelessly in love with him and you decided you had to have him. I saw Max and I fell hopelessly in love with him and I slept with him once. It's all I asked. I knew I couldn't have him, not permanently. But why shouldn't I make love with him, just once?'

'Why shouldn't you? My God, you can say to me, why shouldn't you?'

'Well, why would it matter, just once? The opportunity came. I didn't think it would matter, just once.'

'You caught the wave. I wondered what you'd meant, at your precious reception.'

She nodded. 'I caught the wave,' she said, simply.

'You're obscene. What about Gavin?'

'What about him?'

'You've cheated on him.'

'I don't think so,' said Kate, with maddening placidity. 'I don't think it's cheating on him. I wasn't married to him then, anyway. Such concern for Gavin, Mum. You surprise me.'

'You knew you were pregnant to Max when you married Gavin?'

'I knew I was pregnant.'

'Does Gavin know?'

'I'm not sure. Sometimes I think he does; sometimes I think he doesn't.'

'Aren't you afraid I'll tell him?'

'It's hardly in your best interests,' said Kate, composedly.

'You're pretty bloody cool about it all.'

'I've had time to think about it. You'll be cooler, too, when you've had a bit of time.'

'I don't think so.'

'Mum, let's leave it for the moment. It's been a big shock for you. In a little while, I'll talk about it as much as you want.'

'What makes you think I want to talk about it at all?'

'It has to be dealt with,' said my daughter. 'It's happened, that's all. It's something that's happened, and we can't make it unhappen. We just have to deal with it; we have to find the best way to deal with it.'

I started towards the door. Something was thudding in my head, behind my eyes. I seemed to have lost peripheral vision, but I could see where the door was and I headed for it.

'Don't forget your bag,' said Kate, holding it out to me.

I snatched it, but something else occurred to me. 'Who knows?'

'I don't know.'

'Who have you told?'

'Nobody.'

'Have you and Max discussed it?'

'Not a word.'

'That's absurd. You can't expect me to believe it.'

'It's true, though.'

'You expect me to believe Max doesn't know?'

'Of course he knows,' said Kate, patiently. 'He can't help knowing. But so far we haven't talked about it. I don't think anyone else has noticed. I knew you would. I'm not at all sure Dad will notice, or Dominic. I'm not sure about Gavin. I don't think it's the sort of thing men necessarily do notice. Especially if they're not expecting it.'

I shook my head and fled, helpless in the fury and shock and disbelief that throbbed through me, possessing me outright.

I caught the bus home. It was just as well Max had taken the car: I was in no fit state to drive. As it was I missed my stop and had to walk back to Rain. Images played themselves before my eyes: the young satiny sheen of Kate's skin; Kate's hair, its brightness and softness; Kate's clear blue eyes, her pretty hands, the new confidence displaying itself in her stance, her languor, her suave new sexuality. Max's hands, Max's lean body, Max's hands, his hands, his hands. His hands that caressed me; his hands that brought me such delight; his long, fine, strong, beautiful hands.

He had not arrived home. I went into the lounge. I couldn't sit down. I walked up and down, up and down. I poured myself a brandy. And another.

When he came home, he looked at me just once and a kind of defeat came over his face, a resignation.

'You know. You've seen it, haven't you?'

'How could you?' I said. 'How could you?'

He shrugged, wearily, and went to pour himself a drink. 'I don't know how it happened, Bella. It was when you were in Sydney.'

'I'd worked that out, thank you.'

'We missed you, Kate and I.'

'Indeed?'

'Well, I know it sounds fatuous. But we did. We missed you. Kate said, let's do something special. So I went and got a crayfish. We had crayfish and a bottle of wine for dinner. Then we jumped into the pool.'

'And?'

'I can't explain it, Bella. These things happen. We'd had a glass too many. It was a hot night.'

'I bet.'

'It's partly why I wanted to get rid of the pool. It kept reminding me.'

'I'm sure.'

Max took a swig of his whisky and placed his glass on the shelf above the fireplace, next to the photograph of us holding hands, standing on the white sands at Point Leo, half silhouetted against the darkly golden sunset. He looked down, and then up. He partially spread his hands and then let them fall, in that puzzled, self-deprecatory movement so characteristic of him. His face was sad, drawn.

He stood there, by the fireplace, one foot on its chunky hearth of slate with its streaks of amber and gold. I was by then sitting on the creamy leather sofa, leaning forward towards the coffee table, where we kept the beautiful object we had christened the meteor stone. I think I was clenching and unclenching my fists. I remember looking down and seeing my hands resembling claws—slight, powerless, little claws. They talk about seeing things through a red haze. I don't recall the redness, but I certainly had a haze hanging thick over my eyes.

I picked up the meteor stone and threw it at him. It struck him on the left temple.

Max looked at me, for a moment, through clear and perplexed eyes. His right hand jerked up, slightly, towards me, and then fell, loose—as if it no longer belonged to him—to his side.

Without a sound, without even swaying, without trying to save himself or break his fall, he toppled. He fell the way a tree falls, heavy and straight. As he crashed onto the floor his head struck the hearth's rich slate, which we had chosen together.

I don't remember what I did next. I think I just sat there. Next thing I found myself crouched by him. I called his name. I shook him. I tried to feel his pulse, to detect his breath; I put my head to his chest to try to discern his heartbeat; I screamed at him.

But there was no doubt about it. He was dead. All quite deadybones.

Borrow came loping over and set up a shrill keening that vibrated through my skull. I hit him hard over his aristocratic nose and he stopped abruptly, with a look of astonishment. I'd never hit him before.

Sometimes even now Borrow looks at me slantwise, his expression revealing his belief that I am someone not to be trusted, someone who at any moment might run amok, throwing, striking, killing. Perhaps I am. Well, obviously I am.

I felt guiltier, at that moment, about hitting Borrow than about killing Max. Borrow's pain was real and graspable; Max's death wasn't.

I sat on the floor, next to my love, the love of my life, he who had fathered my daughter's daughter, my granddaughter, my stepdaughter. Borrow lay on the other side of him, head between paws, his eyes dolefully fixed on me.

I don't know how long I sat there. Max's eyes were open. I thought they might hold an expression of bewilderment, or recrimination, or hurt; but they just looked dead. Fishy, really.

Finally I leant over and closed the lids, as gently as I could, and was startled by the slight but palpable fleshy resistance they offered. At some stage I went and poured myself another brandy. My hands were shaking. I remember watching my hand shake as it tipped the bottle over the glass. The brandy went all over the benchtop. Scrupulously I wiped it up. Max hated mess.

I went back into the lounge. I sat on one of the deep leather armchairs and let my body sink into its resilient softness and rested my head against one of the honey-rust silk cushions and sipped my brandy while Max's portrait, so lovingly commissioned, so triumphantly hung, gazed enigmatically down at me.

I suppose there were all sorts of options open to me, but I didn't consider many of them. It never occurred to me, for instance, to ring the police, or an ambulance, or to say there had been an accident. Of course I would have rung an ambulance if there had been the slightest chance of his still being alive. (It was amazing, how dead he was: I didn't know you could die as fast, as decisively, as that.)

It never occurred to me to ring either of my children, or my sister. Funnily enough, I did think of ringing Steve. There was something ineffably consoling at that moment about the thought of Steve—stocky, slow, practical, careful. *I'll take care of it, lovely*, he would say. *Just a little old corpse, is it? I'll take care of that. Don't you worry about a thing.* A pity, really, that a phone call to Steve was out of the question.

It didn't occur to me either to go out, to come back a few hours later, to find the body and raise the alarm. Well, that would have been a daft thing to do, anyway. Someone would have cottoned on. Some balding, unnecessary neighbour, behind his curtains, straight out of a 1940s Hollywood crime movie, would have noticed, would have blabbed to the good- looking detective in his soigné hat and knee-length coat.

It was clear to me that I would be seen as culpable—that indeed in some sort of technical sense I was culpable—and that I had to dissemble in order to save my own skin. It was a question of how best this deception could be managed, not of whether I would indulge in it. I could not bear it, that I might have murdered Max. I could not bear to have people saying I had murdered Max. I had to slip through the sudden giant padlock I had fastened on my life.

I did think of disappearing. I had enough money in the bank. I had a passport; I had credit cards. I could lock the house and go and catch a plane somewhere. Anywhere. But it seemed too difficult, too unwieldy, too outlandish somehow. And it required decision and purpose, and a capacity to deal with complex activity, and these were things of which I was then incapable.

I watched Max. I didn't know much about rigor mortis. I supposed it would set in soon. I looked at the indentation in his fragile skull, at the darkness beneath it, the livid pool that had formed under the skin of his temple, near the roots of his thick and silvery hair. No blood had been shed. It was astonishing, that there was no blood. I thought it was good, a bloodless death: it would be easier to clean up. The pale oatmeal carpet was unblemished: it bore no trace of death.

I contemplated the fact that Max would never again make love with me—nor, for that matter, with anybody else; not my daughter, not anybody. I thought of the cruel extraordinariness of time: approximately twelve hours ago I had arisen, a wife, a grandmother, a fulfilled and happy woman, singing in the shower, eating muesli for breakfast, brushing my teeth carefully afterwards to extract the little pieces of nuts and grains. And now, I was a widow, a murderess; my granddaughter was also my stepdaughter. The transformation had been breathtaking. I was astray in the awful bafflement of it all.

I can see now, of course, that I was in shock. But at the time it seemed to me I was functioning with commendable lucidity, that the cogs were all spinning and connecting to each other with at least usual efficiency, that indeed I had somehow achieved a singular purity of vision.

I breathed silently while death and guilt and anger and fear and other great nameless things swirled around me, while possible new, murky futures unfolded like dark, narrow paths on all sides, while Borrow uneasily snuffled and my lover gradually cooled and stiffened.

After a while—it could have been twenty minutes; it could

have been hours—I set down my glass of brandy, which under the circumstances I had managed to stretch out pretty well. I walked over to Max's corpse. I squatted beside him and I stroked his hair.

His head was very cold.

I didn't know what to do. I felt in his jacket pocket and took out his wallet. It was an old wallet, but good quality: it was a soft, dark leather, with claret-coloured silk lining. I'd never looked at it closely before: Max didn't appreciate people messing with his belongings; and I wouldn't normally have dreamt of examining his wallet or his desk or his papers or anything else belonging to him.

I opened it and found my picture inside. It was a nasty shock, considering everything. There I was, grinning insouciantly up at me. There were a number of credit cards and what appeared to be a huge amount of cash. I counted it, quietly and methodically, pleased in a way to have something to do. There were thirty-five crisp, neat hundred-dollar notes, and a medley of smaller denominations as well. It was a very orderly wallet.

Steve used to stuff everything in his wallet: bits of paper, addresses, cards, advertising blurb, receipts. Max had been so meticulous about everything. I was amazed that he carried so much cash around. He was never short of cash, of course, but three thousand dollars plus seemed excessive. I was cross, in fact: it wasn't only excessive but careless. Anything might have happened to him, carrying as much as that around with him.

But I had no time or energy to think about it: I replaced the notes carefully and took the wallet upstairs, and put it on the table beside our bed, on Max's side, next to the novel he had been reading, a murder mystery by P.D. James.

Only a night or two ago he had asked lazily, as he closed the book and turned the bedside lamp off, why women wrote the best murder mysteries. I'd told him it was because we had the most devious minds, and he'd laughed and pulled me towards him and…Well, there was no point in thinking about that.

I went back downstairs, stepping heavily on the carpeted treads. Max's body was still there, exactly where I had left it. It seemed odd, somehow: I had so competently extinguished his spirit, it seemed as if his body should also have evaporated, vanishing into the air with a wreath of white smoke. Yet here it lay, stubbornly corporeal, dead but otherwise fit and svelte, as Max always was, requiring disposal.

And suddenly it was so easy, to see how the disposal was going to work. It was as if there was a divine dispensation, looking down benignly, knowing all along this was going to happen, having arranged for me in advance the perfect—the brilliant—solution. Its timeliness was breathtaking. How frequently during the course of my life, after all, would I need to dispose of a body? It was nothing short of phenomenal.

I was going to have to move him. I tugged at his ankle, experimentally. Nothing happened except that Borrow started whimpering again. I tugged again. Nothing.

He was a dead weight, of course.

'Shut up,' I said, fiercely, to the dog. He shot me a resentful leer and dropped his head between his paws again. I stood and pondered.

We had a trolley in the garage. We'd got it for moving furniture around when we were setting up in the house. Feeling gratitude for my forethought in providing direct access between house and garage, I padded into the garage with its chilly concrete floor and disentangled the trolley from the garden tools. I knocked a spade and it clanged against the Audi's silver bonnet as it fell. No dent. Not that it mattered, of course: Max was past fretting over the duco. Carefully I steered the trolley into the lounge.

It was a good trolley, with triple wheels and strong webbing that you could use to stabilise large items such as refrigerators. We'd paid a bit extra for a reliable article: always thoughtful consumers, we had eschewed the cheaper varieties, which looked as if they'd buckle under anything with real bulk or weight. I laid the trolley on its back and, after a number of ham-handed attempts, rolled Max onto it.

I deduced from the chill inflexibility of his limbs that rigor mortis was setting in; but if anything this made the process easier. I buckled the webbing straps tightly and experimentally raised the trolley handles. It was surprisingly easy to manoeuvre. Borrow looked on, lifting his lip slightly as if to demonstrate his contempt for the proceedings. I didn't blame him.

I went out to the switches by the back door and made sure that all the outside sensor lights were turned off. I was proud of my composure: I was thinking of everything. Softly I opened the door and wheeled Max out into the night. The neighbours' lights were off. I stood a moment, to allow my eyes to accustom themselves to the silver-shot darkness of the moonlight. Borrow loped to one of the wattles and absent-mindedly urinated against its trunk.

I rolled Max over to the gaping mass of clay and broken tile where the glossy pale pool had sparkled in sunlight, its water transparent against the latte ceramic sheen of its tiles. I undid the webbing buckles and tipped him in. It was hard: he was very heavy and for a moment I thought I wasn't going to be able to gain sufficient leverage. It was a relief when he toppled.

My eyes were more used to the moonlight now: I could see

the dim outline of his body, sprawled where once he had dived with easy grace, his olive skin glistening in the water, his silver hair plastered to his skull.

I rolled the trolley back to the shed and brought out the spade. I noticed the wheelbarrow was full of weeds and grass clippings, so I also wheeled that out and tipped it into the great cavity. There were prunings, too, from the jasmine Max had trimmed back at the weekend. It all went in there. I slipped and slid down the edge of the slope, cutting my hand on a bit of tile.

Borrow lay in his sphinx position at the edge of the hole, concealing his confusion by asserting disengagement from my disreputable actions. I scrabbled and scraped, doglike, at the bottom of the hole, under the naked, callous moon, covering up the dreadful thing I had created. Please, God, I thought, don't let the neighbours wake up and look out. Please, God, make the neighbours keep on sleeping.

It was hard work, and I had to try to be quiet, too, which made it harder. When I thought I had done enough, I climbed up. I cleaned the spade on the grass, replaced it, and went back inside. Blood dripped on the kitchen floor from the wound to my hand. I wiped it up very carefully and wrapped a tea towel around the gash. I would bandage it properly later, I thought. I went back into the lounge and inspected it. So odd, I thought again, that there was no blood—or, rather, that the only blood was mine. The room was blank and peaceful, volunteering no information about the violence that had so recently ruptured it.

I examined the hearthstone, to see whether there were tell-tale hairs, whether some vestigial evidence clung to it. I could see nothing, but I wiped it down anyway, using the clean part of the tea towel. I took Max's half-empty whisky glass and rinsed it in the kitchen.

I returned to the lounge and gazed around. I noticed the meteor stone, where it had rolled away into the corner of the room. I picked it up and scrutinised it closely. Even on this, the murder weapon, I could see no incriminating evidence—no smear of congealing blood, no tuft of hair, no scrape or abrasion on its smooth surface to betray what it had done, what I had done. I dabbed at it with the tea towel, but it didn't need cleaning. It was clean as a whistle already.

I replaced it on the table, where it belonged. But it vexed me there. Its character had changed: it now looked squat and evil, as if it harboured of its own volition an unpleasant secret that it might speak aloud bluntly to some stranger entering the room. Formerly it had symbolised the happiness and harmony of our union; now its presence mocked and corrupted that memory. Also, it was evidence.

I took it outside and chucked it, too, into the large cubic hole in the garden where our beautiful pool had nestled. I heard the crack and thud of its landing.

I showered. I bandaged my hand. I rinsed the blood-stained tea towel. I went to bed. I lay awake in bed, staring at the ceiling, at the walls, at the blankness all around me. After a while I started to shake uncontrollably. I remember I was relieved by this: it demonstrated to me that I had retained some shred of humanity, that I was not a monster.

And then the tears came. I wept for hours. Borrow crawled up from his mat onto the bed, which he was not allowed to do, and I grabbed him very tight and shook and sobbed until the morning.

Then I slept, for an hour or two. I had a mad painful dream in which Max was forcing me to think of a rhyme for the word *corpse*, and I woke up mumbling *borps, morps, porps, dorps.*

Forceps. Forceps is the closest I can get, Max. And Max loomed impossibly high and dark above me, clenching his fists and threatening me, shouting at me (as he had never shouted in life) that *forceps* wasn't good enough, that I had to think of a proper rhyme.

And then I got up and I showered again, for a long time, and I started to face up to a new kind of life.

I didn't see anyone for a couple of days, except for the contractor who turned up to topple the slagheaps of filler earth into the fractured shell of the pool. This did not happen the day immediately after I killed Max, but the following morning. He came very early, when it was still half-dark, and buzzed around in the grey air in his bright little bobcat, trundling like a bulbous orange beetle across the garden.

I glanced out at him from time to time, my chest and throat tight, a hammering inside my head, wondering how he could possibly cross and recross the garden so frequently, so blithely unaware of what lay beneath him. The beetle's throbbing rumble stopped at one point, and I peered out to see what was happening.

The contractor was standing by the void of the pool, looking meditatively across it. He was having a smoko. I could see the bluish trail of the cigarette fading into the morning air. Inhale, exhale; inhale, exhale. He looked down at the corner where Max lay, and my heart thudded harder. He threw in his stub. He sighed and stretched and flexed his arms, and ambled back into his machine. He continued to empty quantities of dirt into the space where the pool had been, and departed.

The next day Jack, of Jack's Landscape Solutions, arrived to check out the site, twirling his beard and promising graders and rollers and ready-made turf and rose bushes and instant flower-beds, all of which duly eventuated over the following couple of weeks without my doing anything to prompt it. Max had organised it all, of course, with his usual precision, his reliable attention to detail.

It looked terrific when it was all complete. Jack was disappointed that Max wasn't around to see the finished product; I apologised and said he was on an unexpected business trip.

I rang work and said I had a stomach bug and wouldn't be there for a few days. I didn't answer the telephone: I didn't even listen to the messages on the answering machine. I didn't go out, except to empty the letterbox after dark. I didn't bother to open the letters: I just didn't want to leave the letterbox looking untended.

Borrow was cross, because he wanted a walk. It wasn't until the fourth day that he got one. I slunk out in my sunglasses and ran immediately into one of the neighbours, out doing the edges of his lawn. He waved jauntily and I waved back.

I can't remember much about those days. I was in shock, or denial, or limbo. Wherever. Certainly, I was somewhere I'd never been before. Max's brutal quenching had engulfed me with such thoroughness, such rapidity, that I could do nothing but crouch and hide. I didn't even cry very much, after that first night. The tears welled up sometimes, but as the days passed it was as if the reservoir within was drying up, its bed hard and eroded and cracked. A drought inside.

I thought a lot—but to no great purpose—about death. I found it hard to credit that Max was really dead; I found it even harder to believe I was responsible. I dreamt the Lost Dream again and again at night, waking in sweat, trembling, turning to the embrace that no longer held me, the arms that were no longer there.

I thought about murder. Surely it hadn't really been murder? I hadn't meant it, after all. *Let's call it manslaughter*, I said to myself. It sounded so much better. And I thought about punishments. The state no longer sanctioned capital punishment. If I was discovered, exposed, I wouldn't actually die. I wouldn't be hanged. This was quite a consoling thought. But what would happen? Would I be jailed? And for how long?

What did you wear in jail? I wondered. Some sort of uniform, I supposed. I hoped it wouldn't be yellow. Or pink.

Then again, perhaps it was murder. Perhaps I was a murderer. A murderess. Perhaps intention didn't have anything to do with it. In any case, who could say what I had intended? It was only my word to say I hadn't meant it. People might not believe me. People probably wouldn't.

I went around in circles, dreary and lonely and frightened.

On perhaps the fourth evening the doorbell rang. Dominic stood there.

'Honey! Dominic!' I said, brightly.

He stared at me. I opened the security door to let him in. His gait was curious, not his usual light, elastic tread, rather shambling, rather as if he were sleepwalking.

'What is it?'

I was alarmed. I thought perhaps something had happened to Steve. Had Steve died? Was Dominic coming to tell me that Steve had died? Had both my husbands died together? At a level that I can't possibly explain I thought this sublimely amusing, if it were the case. I prepared myself to restrain laughter.

'Dominic,' I repeated. 'What is it? How did you get here?' And then I saw the bicycle, leaning against the wall behind him.

'You rode here?' I asked, stupidly. 'It's miles, Dominic. It's miles from Dad's place to here. How long did it take you?'

I noticed then that he didn't look well. His skin had a chalky colour and his eyes seemed huge charcoal blobs, Boyd eyes. He reminded me of the black-crayon stick people he used to draw as a child: dangly, puppetlike, white triangular faces with vast eyes like lumps of coal. A different Dominic from the suave young man at Kate's party for Sophie, from the prizewinner at speech night.

'You cow,' he said. 'You bitch.'

I was dumbfounded. How did he know? How could he possibly know what I had done? He didn't even like Max, I thought. Why is he so angry, when he didn't even like Max? I couldn't think of anything to say.

'You just don't care, do you? You couldn't give a fuck about me.'

Him? Care about him? What the hell did *he* have to do with it?

He laughed. 'You don't even know, do you? You don't even remember.'

I did remember, then. It trickled back into my consciousness. I'd been supposed to meet him at an appointment and take him home. I'd forgotten. Could that possibly be what this was about? *Dominic*, I felt like saying, *Dominic, get your priorities straight. A man has died here, and you're fussing about a dental appointment?*

'You're so fucking self-absorbed.'

'Dominic,' I said. *Dominic, apple of my eye, light of my life, stay and support of my feeble old age.* At least, I didn't say all of that, but I thought it, and I hoped it was strongly implied in my gaze.

'You were supposed to be there. You were supposed to take

197

me home. I waited for an *hour* after, and you didn't show up. How could you forget me like that?'

'I'm sorry. I know, I know, you had a dentist's appointment, didn't you?'

'I had a *wisdom tooth* pulled out,' screamed Dominic. 'It hurt like hell. It went wrong. He couldn't get at it. You were supposed to be there. There was no one to take me home. It was bloody dark by the time I realised you weren't ever coming. I was bleeding. I was bleeding and it was dark and you didn't *come*.'

'I'm sorry. I haven't been well, honey. I'm sorry. Things haven't been good.'

'I'm supposed to feel sorry for you? Things haven't been good? Things haven't been fucking good for me, either, but you haven't bothered to enquire, have you?'

I was aghast but fascinated. I'd never seen Dominic like this. I'd seen him sarcastic and scornful and bitter and wry, but I'd never seen him flamingly angry, like this. To my astonishment I saw that he was weeping. Tears seeped from his large, black eyes and made sparkling snail-tracks down his cheeks. I didn't think I'd ever seen Dominic weep before—at any rate, not since he was a toddler.

He was fifteen. He was behaving like Kate, who sobbed over trivia and came out in awful pink stains and blotches. I'd forgotten about picking him up from the dentist, for Christ's sake, and he was crying. I couldn't understand it. *Pull yourself together*, I felt like saying. *Dominic, if you want something to cry about, contemplate the fact that your mother's a murderer. You want to weep, boy? I'll give you something to weep about.*

'Honey, I'm really sorry, truly I am, but I don't see why it's so important. I overlooked it. I'm sorry if it was uncomfortable for you. I'm sorry, but I didn't mean to do it. Next time I'll be there.'

'Next time isn't the *point*,' he said, suddenly sounding immensely tired, even bored. 'Whether you meant to do it isn't the point. Being sorry isn't the point. The point is that you didn't come when you were supposed to. The point is that you forgot.'

'It's not my fault. It's truly not my fault, Dominic. I couldn't help it.'

'That's what you always say,' he threw at me, belligerence returning.

'You've got no idea how much I've had on my mind. I've been having a really bad time, Dominic.' I heard my voice waver. I wasn't putting it on to impress him: it was genuinely wavering, all on its own. 'Max has left me, Dominic.'

And as I said it, I nearly believed it. It was what I'd decided on. Just to say, well, we quarrelled. He left. I'd tried to think my way through what happened after that, but it was hard. I couldn't quite work it out. But it would be enough, as a first step. And here I was, taking the first step. The lie slipped from my lips smoothly and easily.

For a moment he didn't say anything. He just looked at me, his eyes wet and burning. And then he made a funny, small sound, something like a cough, half sob, half laugh. 'You know what it feels like, then, don't you?'

I found I couldn't say anything. The manifest unfairness, the sheer cruelty of it, kicked me too sharply. And then he turned and left, wheeling the bike down the front steps, mounting it in a swift, fluid movement, riding off with decision and crispness.

Absalom, Absalom.

Oh, my son, Dominic. My son, my son, Dominic.

But it forced me back into the land of the living, Dominic's visit.

I started to pick up pieces. I had to. I listened to the answering machine. I opened the letters, and paid the bills. I turned up to work again. I cleaned the house, top to bottom, scrubbing obsessively; I hired a gardener; I took Borrow to the vet to get his shots. I took him for a few extra walks, too. I thought about going to see Kate, who had left two messages on the answering machine, the second one gratifyingly desperate. I thought about Sophie. I thought a lot about Sophie.

I gathered a number of Max's clothes, laying them out carefully on the bed and working out what he would need if he were to go away for an extended holiday. I packed his elegant, charcoal suitcase with changes of underwear and hankies and socks, and spare shoes and an umbrella and a jacket in case it rained.

I checked his overnight bag and cast an eye over his deodorant and toothpaste and shampoo. Max was fussy about his shampoo: he didn't like using the sort hotels give you. His gleaming black wetpack was kept fully packed: it was his habit to keep it always ready for use, so everything was in pretty good order. I replaced the toothpaste with a fresh tube, just to be sure; and I included his blood-pressure medication and his vitamin tablets.

I put the cases in the boot of my car and drove into Spencer Street Station one Friday afternoon. It was busy; there were people streaming everywhere. I felt extraordinarily conspicuous, but calm common sense (which I could dimly perceive somewhere in the distance near the horizon) told me nobody was paying me any attention. I hired a luggage locker and left the cases in it. The ticket they gave me said that if I didn't claim my property within two weeks it would be confiscated and eventually disposed of. I tore up the ticket and the printout of the lock combination and threw them out in a street bin. Then I drove home.

He'd gone away. We'd quarrelled and he'd gone away. He'd

walked out of the house carrying his suitcase, all packed, all ready to go. He'd gone away and I didn't know where he'd gone. He must have deposited the case in the locker himself: it was nothing to do with me. He'd put the case in the locker and gone off to do something else and never came back. He'd met with an accident. Or perhaps there had been foul play. Perhaps he had been murdered. Why would anyone murder Max? I don't know, officer.

I looked around our bathroom and threw out Max's toothbrush and his comb, and his aftershave and a few nondescript tubes and suchlike. A minimalist in these matters, he had left little for me to do. I'd packed his favourite razor.

Max's wallet was lying by the side of the bed, where I had put it after he died. I hadn't known what to do with it. I'd taken and used some of the cash, but most of it was still there. I put the wallet back, inside his bedside drawer. I saw that there were three or four letters in there—opened envelopes, anyway, with papers in them, in a careful pile at the back corner of the drawer. I picked them up and turned them over. I noticed they had someone else's name on them, not Max's. I didn't care. I didn't want to know. I felt like an insect, splattered against the windscreen of the great truck Life. Later, I thought, I'd look at them later. Right then I didn't have the strength.

'When is later?' Dominic used to ask, when he was a child, waiting for some treat. 'When is later, Mummy?' And we made up a nonsense rhyme about it, which he would chant endlessly.

Later, later, alligator,
Put him on a merchant freighter,
Feed him salt and fried potater, Shoot him 'cos he is a traitor.

Dominic would come back, I thought. He would be sorry, and he would come back. I would be calm and peaceful, when he did: I would utter no recriminations, no blame.

Max wouldn't come back, but I was the only person who knew that.

I went to see Kate. By then it had been, I think, six days since I'd seen her. It was the longest I'd been away from them since Sophie's birth. As I rang her doorbell I remembered that I had meant to telephone first. It had slipped my mind. I noted that, and thought that I'd have to be careful: it didn't matter so much this time, but now I couldn't afford for things to slip my mind.

I'd thought so much about this. Not so much about the visit, as what it betokened. I'd had to try to work through all of it, to work through what I was prepared to do, what I wasn't prepared to give up.

The single thing, the factor that mattered, the consideration that towered above all other considerations, was Sophie. I was worried that I wouldn't feel the same way about Sophie: I'd been wondering how it would be, now that I knew her genesis, now that I knew she was no longer just my granddaughter, no longer the daughter of Gavin and Kate. But I'd felt something new and precious enter my life when I held Sophie for the first time, and I wasn't willing to relinquish that, not without at least trying.

So far as Kate was concerned, I'd had to think my way through the morass I was trapped in. To my surprise, I didn't hate her. At first I had; at first, my hatred had swamped me. Now, however, I'd calmed down. I won't say I was looking forward to seeing her, but I was concentrating on thinking of her as Sophie's mother. Not my daughter, not Max's lover. Just the mother of this child who mattered so much.

Kate answered the door holding Sophie. Her shirt was crumpled: it had been hastily pulled down and I could tell she had been feeding the baby. She didn't look surprised to see me. She just held the door open and stepped back.

'Hello,' I said.

'Hello.'

'You're feeding? I'm sorry to interrupt,' I said, formally.

'I've just finished. Do you want to hold her?'

She held Sophie towards me and I took her. She was sleepy and cuddled into me. All the rich warmth flooded back into my veins; I felt the same mesmeric joy, the same startling physical bliss at the contact with her. I was enormously relieved. It was just the same: an entirely involuntary, entirely inevitable response. I held her and the miracle of her impressed itself on me, just as it had the first time I'd held her. I was simply filled with love for her.

I knew I was doing the right thing; I knew that no matter how this hurt me, it was something I had to do, for my own survival. The connection with Sophie was something I couldn't jeopardise, couldn't bear even to think of losing.

Kate was adjusting her bra strap, watching me. 'Coffee?'

'I'd like a coffee,' I said. 'Is she ready for a sleep?'

'She probably needs a burp. Do you want to hold her for a while?'

I followed Kate into the kitchen and put Sophie up on my shoulder, rubbing her small solid back, smelling the clean, milky smell of her. Kate put the kettle on and got together mugs and sugar and so forth.

We sat down at the kitchen table, facing each other. 'What are you going to do?' asked Kate, stirring her coffee.

'I'm not going to do anything. I'm never going to talk about this again, Kate. It's all over, it's all in the past. It didn't happen.'

'It did happen, though,' said Kate, with a hardihood I hadn't expected. 'It did happen, and we both know it did happen. How are you going to cope with that?'

'That's my business.'

'As she grows older, as likenesses develop—as likenesses *may* develop—how are you going to feel?'

'I'll be all right. It's not her fault.'

Sophie gave a contented burp.

'Of course it isn't her *fault*,' observed Kate, with the shadow of a smile. 'We know that. But it's not a matter of fault, is it? Not, I mean, so far as she's concerned. She is who she is, and it may not be her fault, but she still is that person.'

'I don't want to talk about it any more. I've said that. That's it.'

Kate sipped her coffee, rubbed her chin. 'I'd like to explain. I'd like to explain how it happened.'

'I don't want to listen.' I heard my voice rising and tried to take the edge off it. 'I don't want to know anything. I never want to talk about it again.'

She chewed her lip.

'There's one thing I have to tell you,' I said. 'Max has left me.'

She looked at me narrowly and nodded, almost as if she had expected this. 'Will he come back?'

'No, I don't think so.'

'You quarrelled?'

'It's not your business what happened.'

'I suppose you're right.'

I turned slightly so that she could see Sophie's face over my shoulder. 'Is she asleep?'

Kate nodded again. 'Fast asleep. I'll put her down.'

When she came back, she sat opposite me.

'There's one thing I have to say,' she said. 'I want you to know it. I heard what you said: I understand you don't want to talk about it. But this is something I have to tell you. I have to. You always said Max was the love of your life. Well, he was the love of my life, too. I adored him. I'll never love anyone else, not like that.'

'You've got a husband,' I said, furiously. 'What about your husband?'

'What about yours?' snapped Kate. I wasn't used to Kate biting back. 'What about yours? You had a husband, too, when you met Max. Gavin is a darling. I love Gavin dearly. I'm going to be a good wife to Gavin. But there'll never be anyone else but Max, for me. I've given him up. I know he's yours.

'I'm just saying, so you know—all right?—it wasn't a whim; it wasn't something I did idly, without thinking about it. It mattered to me more than anything else in the world has ever mattered. It was that important. I didn't mean to hurt you. I didn't mean you ever to know. It was the most important thing in the world, for me. I just want you to know that.'

Her voice was starting to shake. I couldn't bear any of this. Why was this necessary? Why did I have to know anything? For Sophie's sake, I was going to try to forgive her, or at least to pretend that none of it had happened: wasn't that enough? Wasn't that more than she had any right to expect?

She stopped, and we sat there in silence.

'I'm not patching this up for you,' I said. I knew it would hurt her. I wanted to hurt her. 'I'm patching it up for her. For Sophie. You don't matter.'

Kate winced slightly. 'Oh,' she said, with a dry bitterness I'd never heard in her voice before. 'You didn't have to say that,

Mum. I know I don't matter. I've never mattered, have I?'

I was enraged by this idiotic grandstanding. I was worked very thin by this stage, like pastry that you roll, and roll again, trying to make it stretch, and it starts to tatter at the edges and to spread into faint withering patches that eventually split and gape. I was stretched so far I couldn't possibly stretch any further; I couldn't cover any more space. She had no right to say such things. What right had *she* to be bitter?

'That's a stupid and hurtful thing to say,' I shouted. 'Haven't you hurt me enough without attacking me like that?' I wanted to hit her; I wanted to hit her very hard. 'It's not fair,' I cried into her startled face. 'I haven't deserved this from you.'

I felt the surge of anger within me as a surge of blood; my head was full of it, dizzy with it. If I had had a knife, I think at that moment I would have lurched at her and plunged it into her.

Well, perhaps I would; perhaps I wouldn't. There's something about the imagined meeting between flesh and blade that's very disconcerting. But if I'd had a gun, I would have shot her. I would have shot her as much for the shocked and wounded look she turned on me, as for what she'd said, what she'd done.

'Never mind, Mum,' she said, quietly. 'So long as we do it, patch it up, I mean, so long as that happens, it doesn't matter why we're doing it, does it? If it's for Sophie, okay, it's for Sophie.'

I didn't stay long. I was shaking. I was afraid of what I might say, what I might do, if I stayed. I drank my coffee (it was awful coffee: Kate's always made bad coffee) and left.

I paused at the door, I remember, and looked at her. 'Tell the others, will you? I don't want to have to talk about it to anyone.'

'Okay,' she said.

I took another step and then I paused again and turned. 'I mean, tell them that Max and I have split up. I don't mean tell anybody anything else.'

'Am I likely to?'

'I don't know if you're likely to or not. But I'm telling you, nobody's to know.'

Kate swallowed. 'Mum, believe me, I've told nobody. I'm not going to tell anybody.'

'Promise?'

She nodded and then said in a dry, croaky voice: 'I promise.'

And then I left.

I don't recollect a lot of that time very clearly. Perhaps my subconscious has ensured that I don't. I got up; I went to work; I came home from work. Borrow stopped regarding me reproachfully: at least, I thought he did.

I made sure I saw Sophie two or three times a week. I babysat whenever I could. I must say, Gavin and Kate had it made with me: I was every young parent's dream grandmother, even if I had killed the baby's father. Sometimes, when Kate was tired, I even spent the night with them and walked around with Sophie through the wee small hours. She wasn't a good sleeper, in her first year. My infatuation with her grew and prospered. I outgrew an obsessive early propensity to trace Max's lean elegance in her tiny, chiselled features.

Fortunately, the likeness was intermittent, fleeting: it depended more on expression and angle than anything else, and seemed to me moreover to diminish with time, although that was a hard thing to judge. It did not take long for Sophie to acquire a presence and personality that were all hers and had nothing to do with her progenitors—although people often said (they say it still) that in her dark, quick slenderness, her neat limbs and fine bones, she took after me. These days, I look at Sophie and think about her and speak with her and hug her and love her without even thinking of Max.

Well, perhaps not entirely. But almost.

One evening, quite early in the piece, Zoë visited. Kate had told her Max and I had split up. I knew I'd told her to tell everyone, but then I wished she hadn't. There she was, my sister, when I opened the door, arms extended, replete with coo and drivel.

'Minky!' she cried. 'Minky, darling!' She enfolded me in her capable embrace. I stepped backwards, but it was impossible to evade. Zoë in full flight is simply something that can't be evaded. In she came, glancing around her, absorbing every detail even as she surrounded me with her crisp perfume and her unctuous readiness to comfort and support. She wanted me to throw myself upon her breast. *Come home, Minky,* she wanted to say. *All is forgiven.*

Well, I wasn't going to do that, and if she had learnt anything at all about me during the forty-two-odd years we'd known each other by then, she wouldn't have expected it. She wanted me to weep on her bosom because my love had left me; she wanted me to admit my sins and tell her how right she'd been and how sorry I was. She wanted me to pour it all out to her, open my heart, weep. She wanted to know every last, sordid detail. She was disappointed. *He's gone for good?* she wanted to ask me. *Never to return? Never mind, darling, you're better off without him.*

I wasn't better off, and I wasn't going to pretend I was. Not then, not ever.

In fact, one of the major irritations of this time and the following few months was the way in which people treated me:

full of sober consolation, a reverential and pitying circumspection as if Max had died. Which he had, of course, but they didn't know that. What had happened to me was much worse, much more traumatic, than a mere death: it seemed to me I deserved far more sympathy than anybody was prepared to give me; and it exasperated me that I could explain this to nobody, could weep truthfully on nobody's shoulder.

When I told Bea, she was just as pleased as Zoë was, but she handled it with more tact. (Zoë and tact have always been strangers to each other.) I told Bea that Max and I had split. She nodded non-committally, her eyes on my face.

'Are you all right, Izzie?'

'Yes.'

'Do you want to talk about it?'

'No.'

'Okay,' she said. 'Thanks for telling me. Any time you want a cup of tea, or something stronger for that matter, let me know.'

And that was that. I dare say she jumped up and did cartwheels when I'd left her office, but at least she didn't make her delight evident. Nor did she display Zoë's itch to find out exactly what had transpired. Zoë never did like it when I had secrets from her.

When you have secrets in a family, after a while you start to wonder who knows them. Who knows, who guesses, who hasn't a clue? Sometimes, when our family gets together on one of those appalling occasions—birthdays, Christmas, whatever—I glance around the room; I briefly study their faces. Who knows the identity of Sophie's father? Does Zoë? Does Gavin speculate? Dominic? Steve? No, surely not Steve. Has anyone else detected

Max's finely drawn mouth in Sophie's exquisite lips, his long, slender hands in her small, neat fingers? Who knows?

I found I became edgy on my own in Rain. I developed the habit of keeping the radio on at all times, so I never walked into silence. I still do that, even now. I can't bear a silent house. I hated sleeping in the capacious bed, in the vast acreage of the main bedroom, under the skylight, the heavy square sky always falling into my eyes, into my head. I depended on Borrow a lot. Once, I remember, he had to spend a night at the vet's for some minor operation. With the comfort of his presence withdrawn, I hardly slept.

I'd never been a nervous person, and I didn't believe in ghosts. Well, I didn't think I did. But solitude didn't suit me any more; and Rain, which had been a comfortable house for two or three of us, became ridiculously large. I thought of selling: this was one step I could take without legal complications, since Max had given the place to me. But it was all too hard and required too much energy, too much thought and action. In any case, I loved Rain; it had housed my happiest days. I tried not to think of what lay in the garden, under the smart, new flowerbeds. I procrastinated.

One night, about four months after Max's death, a light knock came at the front door. It was slightly later than I would normally have expected Foxtel or Jehovah's Witnesses, and I opened up cautiously, wishing I'd locked the security door. A small and unremarkable man was standing there. He was balding and his hands were in his pockets. He wore a striped shirt and a dingy bomber jacket; his face was lined, ratlike and attentive.

'Can I have a word with Matty?' he said. His voice had the

hint of a soft lilt to it. Irish?

'Matty?' I said. 'I'm afraid you have the wrong house.'

He shook his head cheerfully. 'The fool I am. It's Max I'm after.'

'Max?' My mouth was dry. Silly of me, not to be more prepared, when it happened. I had known moments like this would come; I'd rehearsed them. 'I'm sorry,' I said. 'Max isn't here.'

'When will he be back?'

'No. What I mean is, Max doesn't live here any more.' It sounded absurd, when I said it, like a pop song.

His eyes widened slightly. 'Then it's a forwarding address I'm after.'

'He didn't give me one.'

'I find that hard to believe.'

'Sorry,' I said, starting to shut the door.

In a quick and supple movement the little man prevented me from doing so, and suddenly, instead of being outside the door looking in at me, he was inside the door, next to me, his hand closed hard on my wrist.

Borrow was just behind me, having ambled after me to see who was at the door. He barked once, uncertainly.

'Good dog,' said the bald-headed man, leaning over and scratching him behind the ear. Borrow wagged his tail and slobbered cheerfully over the man's hand, glancing at me smugly. 'You'll forgive me. I'll take a quick look around.'

My heart was pounding so hard I could hear it in my ears. 'You can't do that. Get out.'

He was already halfway up the stairs. Borrow watched him amiably.

'I'll call the police.' My voice sounded quavery and foolish.

'You can if you like,' he said, laughing. 'I'll be gone in two minutes, and it'll take them forty to come, minimum. So no harm done. But Matty mightn't like it.'

'There is no Matty,' I called after him. I followed him up the stairs.

He was a quick mover: he'd already looked in the ensuite. He had returned to the bedroom and was inspecting Max's wardrobe, which was pretty well non-existent: most of what I hadn't packed in the suitcase I'd taken by then to the Salvos.

He turned to me. He looked oddly at a loss. 'What happened? He's gone. I can tell he's gone. Where did he go?'

'I don't know,' I said.

We stood there and eyed each other.

'I'll be on my way,' he said, eventually. 'But I'll be back. When you hear from Matty, you tell him Colin wants to speak with him. Okay?'

And he was down the stairs and out the front door. I followed him to the landing and called after him, but he'd gone. I looked out the window and saw him get into a nondescript dark blue hatchback and drive off.

I sat down on the bed. My heart's hammering had taken over my body, and I concentrated unsuccessfully on diminishing its force. My legs felt weak. It had happened so quickly. Well, nothing had happened, really, but what might happen? What might not happen, next time? Was I to be perpetually constrained by my guilt from taking action whenever I was threatened? I seemed to visualise a future as in a series of oblique mirrors, a conga line of endless bald-headed little men bursting into my house whenever they felt like it, charging up my stairs, searching my bathroom cupboard and my wardrobe, peering under my bed, through my drawers.

And what did he mean by *Matty*?

I stood up and my legs felt so wobbly that I sat down again, speedily. Eventually I lurched downstairs, gripping the rail, settling both feet firmly on each tread before attempting the next. I reached the kitchen safely, poured myself a slug of brandy in one of Max's elegant Swedish tumblers.

I sat in the kitchen and sipped it until I felt its fire enter me and strengthen me. I'm turning into an old soak, I thought. Off to the brandy bottle every time something goes wrong. It was true: I had been drinking too much. It always seems more, and worse, when you do it on your own; but it does help so.

Then I grabbed the keys and locked the security doors, front and back. Borrow accompanied me, full of benign importance.

'You weren't any bloody use,' I said to him, bitterly. 'Call yourself a watchdog?'

He wagged his tail happily and licked my hand.

I went back upstairs. I sat on the bed and opened the drawer in Max's bedside table, where I had kept his wallet, where I had noticed the envelopes. They were still there, four of them, the addresses all handwritten but all in different writing. The address was the same for all: a post-office box in North Ringwood.

Why North Ringwood, God help us? We lived in leafy Hawthorn: why drive out to the godforsaken edge of the city to collect your mail?

Two envelopes were addressed to Max Knight. One was addressed to Martin Ritter. The last was addressed to Matthew Templar. They were all neatly slit open at the top. Max always used a rather evil-looking letter-opener with a sharp curved blade, like a miniature silver scimitar. It was still in the drawer.

I sat and looked at them. Some ancient schoolgirl memory awoke in my brain. I went downstairs, carrying the envelopes gingerly, and found the old German dictionary.

It was as I had remembered, or half-remembered. 'Ritter' was German for 'knight'.

Hadn't the Templars been crusaders? Knights? Max Knight. Martin Ritter. Matthew Templar. Max Knight. Martin Knight. Matthew Knight.

Oh, Max, Max. If that was your name, which it seems it wasn't. What a wag you were. It would almost have been funny, if it hadn't been so frightening.

I turned the envelopes over in my hands. There was little point now in being prissy about Max's privacy. I opened them one at a time, taking care to keep the contents of each next to its envelope.

Inside the two envelopes addressed to Max Knight there were two cheques, one for twenty thousand dollars and one for thirty-two thousand dollars. They were made out to Max and stamped non-negotiable. The signatures were the same, but illegible.

Inside the envelope addressed to Martin Ritter there were four photographs—black and white, roughly cut at the edges— of the kind you take in passport photo booths. Each was of an Asian girl, head and shoulders. None looked older than fifteen or so. A name was written in black ink, in delicate careful handwriting, on the back of each. There was May, Susie, Kylie and Lindy Lou. All were pretty and smiling. Susie's expression was a trifle forced, but the rest of them beamed at the camera like true professionals. A folded piece of flimsy paper—like old-fashioned airmail paper—was also in the envelope. On it, in Max's unmistakeable spiky writing, was written: *SQ 277, 14.50, 15/7.*

In the envelope addressed to Matthew Templar there was some stiff yellow paper with a number typed on it, apparently by an old-fashioned typewriter. At first I thought it might be a telephone number, but it had too many digits. Fourteen digits. It could have been the number of a bank account.

I sat and regarded these things and heard Bea's voice in my head. *What does he do? Where does all the money come from? Tax evasion? Prostitution? Drugs? White slave traffic?* I heard the despairing pitch of her voice. *You know nothing, nothing about him. What in Christ's name are you doing?*—I looked at the paper with Max's writing on it. *SQ?* Flight prefix, Singapore Airlines? Yes, I was sure of it. I'd picked Max up at the airport from Singapore Airlines flights. *14.50* that would be the time. *15/7*—date.

I looked at Lindy Lou and Kylie. I found I didn't want to know anything about them. I didn't like the expression in Kylie's eyes. I fingered the cheques. One of them, I noticed, was from a German bank, although the envelope had been locally posted. I realised I didn't even know what bank Max was with. I'd seen him use ATMs, from time to time, but I'd never seen him walk into a bank.

I went back upstairs and replaced the envelopes in the drawer. I took out the wallet. I'd looked at it briefly, before, but it was time for an exhaustive search.

There was still a thousand dollars, more or less, inside, in crisp hundred-dollar notes. I'd used a lot of the money by this stage: I'd regarded it as a kind of informal banking arrangement, one that hadn't required me to find an ATM or a friendly teller. (People still used tellers, sometimes, in those days; and some of them were friendly.) I hadn't used the credit cards, nor examined the rest of the wallet's compartments. Now, I turned it inside out.

There were five credit cards, one of which was AMEX and the others different versions of Visa and MasterCard. All were gold, or platinum, or whatever signified a VIP cardholder in some way. All bore Max's name except the Visa. That belonged to Matthew Templar.

There was a driving licence. I examined this carefully. It was made out in the name of Maximilian Knight. His date of birth was 4 August, which was when we'd always celebrated his birthday. His age here was consonant with what he'd told me. He'd been fifty-two when he died. I turned it over in my hands, feeling it, weighing it, squinting at it.

I retrieved my own driving licence from my purse and compared the two. If Max's licence had been forged, the forger had been talented. Reliable. Well, Max liked having reliable people working for him. He'd often told me that. When Rain was being built, he'd been angered by unreliability and tardiness. If somebody told him something was going to happen, it had to happen.

It was ridiculous, I thought crossly to myself. Why should I expect Max's driving licence to be forged?

Max Knight. Martin Ritter. Matthew Templar.

I went back to the wallet. His Medicare card. His private health insurance card. Both apparently in order, the name of Maximilian Knight embossed on the plastic.

There was the photograph of me, of course.

There were two receipts. One was for petrol, the other for the dinner we'd eaten at a local restaurant the week before he'd died.

What would happen to the credit cards, I wondered. To the accounts, I mean. Did he use them? Where would the bills be sent? To North Ringwood? They didn't come to Rain, I was sure of that. All the household bills—electricity, telephone, and so forth—came to the house, as well as the MasterCard we shared, but none of these. What would happen when they were not paid?

How much was owing on them? Did the banks have Rain's address?

There was nothing else in the wallet. Bare and neat, it gave nothing away.

I wondered if I should go out to the post-office box at North Ringwood and investigate it. What illicit and unwelcome mail might be accumulating behind its small, bland exterior? Would I need to provide identification? I'd never used a post-office box.

What had the little man meant when he said Matty wouldn't like it if I were to call the police? Who had I been living with? Who was this man I had married?

It came to me that post-office boxes were small and black and mounted in rows on walls outside post offices. I'd seen people unlocking them and walking away. You walked up; you unlocked your box; you walked away. Nobody stopped you; nobody asked for ID or anything else. You just turned up.

With a key. You turned up with a key.

I'd put Max's keys in the suitcase in the station locker. I hadn't anticipated needing them. I'd glanced quickly at them: I'd seen the house keys and the car keys, of which naturally I had duplicates. There must have been other keys: the post- office-box key, for example; perhaps the key to a place of business; perhaps the key to a house where Kylie and her friends lived.

I'd never seen Max with other keys, only the bunch I now regretted disposing of. I looked quickly through the other drawers in the bedside table, but there was nothing there apart from a couple of prescriptions, a nail file, a calculator, the vicious little curving letter-opener, a packet of mints: the sorts of innocent items any man might have in his bedside table.

Max had a study, too, of course. I had taken some delight in creating it. It had smoke-grey carpet, burgundy leather chairs, a magnificent mahogany desk, framed Chinese prints on the walls. The furnishings were all dark and sumptuous, but the room itself was bright and light-filled because I had designed it with two huge north-facing windows that looked down over the pool. Where the pool had once been.

Max had always joked that it was the only design fault the house had, that his study window lured him away from his study.

He hadn't spent a great deal of time here. Maybe two or three hours a week. He had always kept it fastidiously tidy—never with piles of papers lying around, never any mess. I'd hardly been in it, since he'd died.

I came in now, looked on the desk, in the desk drawers. Bills, a birthday card I'd given him. Pens, paper. His Mont Blanc fountain pen. The kind of bits and pieces you expect to find in a desk. A folder with some papers in it. House insurance. Car registration. Max had remarkably few papers, all things considered. I was amazed by how little there was.

What on earth had he done with all the paraphernalia of his life, the endless forms and identification papers, the letters and bills and receipts, the shifty bits of paper that flutter through life around us, mapping our lives, exposing our histories, defining our limits, recording our tiniest transactions? If he owned shares or stocks, if he conducted mysterious business through consultancies, if he made money, surely there must be paper trails somewhere, trails that I or the tax man or anyone else could follow?

My own desk, downstairs in a study-cum-sitting room where I very occasionally worked and which we called the studio, was crammed with such extraneous material.

No cheque book, no bank book. No passport. And no keys.

There was a filing cabinet, though. A handsome, shining,

black two-drawer filing cabinet. Of course. That was where everything was. But it, too, was locked.

So many keys, I suddenly needed! So many keys, where I had thought none existed. So many locked doors dividing me from the things I needed to know.

There was nothing I could do about the box at North Ringwood—or, at any rate, nothing I could see at that point. But the filing cabinet belonged to me; it was in my house and I had some kind of power over it, control in a zone where control was spinning away from me.

I rang a locksmith the next morning and it took him approximately two and a half minutes to open the filing cabinet. He was a middle-aged chap with grey stubble over his chin, a bag full of tools and a mouth full of chat. I said as languidly as I could manage that I'd lost the keys, such a bore, just couldn't find them.

'Ah, it's a bugger, isn't it?' he said, settling down to work. 'You lock something up all safe and sound and you pop away the key in a nice safe place and the next moment you can't remember what you've done with it. A real bugger. And there'll be something in here you need as a matter of urgency, I suppose? There always is.'

'Just some papers. They're not really urgent, only that I do need them, sooner or later, and I thought I might as well get it all done before there's any urgency.'

I don't know why it is that whenever I lie I rattle on compulsively, adding trivial details which seem to me to lend conviction to an increasingly threadbare story.

'Well, you know,' he said, 'now that you've called me and tackled the problem head on, you'll probably find those keys tomorrow.' He seemed to take a lot of pleasure in his forecast.

'It always happens,' he said, grinning. 'And you'll be saying to yourself, my goodness me, why did I bother to go and get that

219

bugger of a locksmith, when all along the keys were right here? That's what you'll be saying to yourself.'

All the while he was working, it seemed to me, his beady eyes were glancing around the room, noting its contents, memorising the layout. I wondered if I were becoming clinically paranoiac.

'Here we go,' he said, easing the lock out. 'Not a hard one, this one. Here we go, nice and easy. See, I haven't had to do much damage at all: I can pop in a new lock for you and you'll never know anything happened. Good as new.'

He rolled the top drawer out. Apart from a half-dozen or so suspension files, it was completely empty. He glanced at me. 'Nothing in this one.'

'They're all in the bottom one,' I said, off-handedly.

He paused. 'Will I pull it out for you, then?'

'Yes, of course,' I said, because it seemed foolish to say anything else; I thought it would seem suspicious to prevaricate, to demand privacy. The worst that could happen was that the lower drawer, too, would be empty.

He pushed the top drawer back in and opened the lower one. I heard the intake of his breath. I glanced down and saw the revolver lying at the bottom of the drawer.

I couldn't think of anything to say. Nor could he.

'That's what you expected?' he asked, finally.

'It's my husband's gun,' I said, reflecting that this at least was certainly true. 'I didn't realise he'd put it in here. He's away at the present. He's on a business trip.'

'He's got a licence?'

'Well, of course. He shoots with a local club.'

Amazing, how rapidly one could invent things.

Both of us were staring at the evil-looking thing.

'It's a Smith and Wesson,' he observed.

'Yes.'

'The sort James Bond uses. Isn't it?'

'I have no idea,' I said. In fact I didn't think it was. Steve was crazy about James Bond and some of it had rubbed off on me: I seemed to remember that James Bond customarily carried a Walther. But I wasn't about to engage in a debate on such matters.

'Is it loaded?'

'I don't know. No. No, I shouldn't think so.'

'Well then. I'll put this new lock in for you, will I?'

'Thank you,' I said, coolly.

When he left, he asked me for an amount I found surprising. It's not unusual, of course, for tradesmen to do this: what's unusual is for them to charge you something you think a fair amount; but it really did seem exorbitant.

It occurred to me I was being blackmailed, that he felt he could freely ask a ridiculous sum because he sensed something dodgy going on. He was right, of course. I paid him without query. I suppose it was cowardly of me, and perhaps stupid, but I so overwhelmingly wanted him out of the house, I probably would have paid him three times as much just to get rid of him.

When he had gone, I returned to the study and took out the gun. I weighed it in my hand. It wasn't bulky, but was still surprisingly heavy. I had always thought revolvers like that tucked neatly in a pocket or holster, that you wouldn't really be aware of their presence about your person until you were in need of them. This was so heavy, you couldn't possibly forget it. I examined it carefully, and wondered suddenly if it had Max's fingerprints on it, if my own fingerprints had just obliterated his. I knew so little about guns that I did not even know whether it was loaded or not.

It is a strange and frightening experience to handle a gun. The sight of a gun is so recognisable: it is familiar to us from movies and television, from gangster fiction and war documentaries; it is a part of our culture, a common pattern on the wallpaper of our lives.

Yet actually to hold one, to consider it and balance it, to stretch out your arm and point it as if you were truly threatening someone—these are foreign and bizarre actions, as alien to the comfort of our souls as anything can be. The object exerts an uncanny fascination, so that touching or stroking or gripping it forces you to recognise that it is so much more than a mere object, so replete with its potential and with the menace deriving from its function. It's unlike anything else. Its function is unmistakable and singular, and it cannot be contemplated without reference to that function.

I could not accommodate the gun to the texture of ordinary life. I felt like a character who had landed in the wrong movie. I'd been looking all my life for something along the lines of *The Princess Bride*, and instead I'd found myself deep in the latest Tarantino release. I returned the revolver to its drawer and, a deep and unfamiliar disquiet in my heart, locked the cabinet with the shiny, new key the locksmith had provided.

That evening I sat down with Borrow and a brandy and reviewed my situation.

It was plain enough, I suppose, if unpalatable. I was a widow. I was a widow of means, but it appeared to me that any of my means might be stripped from me at any point. My own income was adequate but not magnificent. Max's bequest was huge, but Max's bequest appeared to be not just a house but a house on sand. Pretty wobbly sand, too.

My marriage had been to a man I had never known. I had

loved this man more dearly than I had ever loved anyone in my life, more (I was convinced) than I would ever love anyone again. Yet he had betrayed me monstrously and it seemed reasonable to assume or at least to speculate that his wealth had been accumulated by unorthodox and possibly illegal methods. If this were so, I supposed I might, as the inheritor of his possessions, face criminal charges. I might be convicted of aiding and abetting. I might in fact have aided and abetted, without realising I had done so.

And he was dead. Nobody knew this but I. Nobody else knew I was a widow. And, given the circumstances of his death, that gave me some protection.

Where did this leave me? Was I in danger? It seemed preposterous to regard myself as in danger of any kind, but I had lost my toehold on the tectonic plates of my life: they were slipping and sliding and could finish up anywhere. The gaps they left in the wake of their eruptions were alarming already, and seemed to be widening speedily. I was going to fall down one of those crevices any day now.

It was like inventing a whole new landscape and inserting myself in it. It was something of a desert, this landscape, with many thorn trees and a good deal of hot sand and not much in the way of oases.

So I had to find my way out of it. But it was hard to make my mind move. Normally I am a quick thinker, I believe: but now, stymied and shocked as I was, trying to devise strategies was slow going. I tried to force myself into a logical train of thought, imagining outcome, calculating consequence and risk.

All I could really think of was that I had known one fine, glimmering light, one unrepeatable moment of apparent perfection, one dazzling flame of passion and—yes, purity—and that I had permanently quenched it. Yet the darkness I inhabited was not my fault. It was the fault of those who had betrayed me. The dazzling flame had been treacherous.

Well, then, it must be my responsibility to discover the sunlight again. It wouldn't ever again have the brilliance that had drenched me with Max's coming, but surely I could ferret my way through the gloom that had descended; surely I could find a point from which I could start to try to refashion my life.

When Steve was trying to work something out, he used a thing he proudly called his Thought Strategy: he had been taught it at some staff development seminar or other.

SWAT. Strengths, weaknesses…

I ran into a brick wall here. Strengths, I muttered to myself. Strengths, weaknesses. Borrow whimpered quietly in his sleep. I stared at the wall.

I had it. Not SWAT but SWOT. Strengths, weaknesses, opportunities, threats.

What were my strengths? Off-hand, I could bring none to mind. Weaknesses there were aplenty. Ditto threats. Opportunities? Concentrate, concentrate. I felt my mind slipping off track. I had another brandy.

Well, if I had a strength it had to be financial stability. I had enough money. On the other hand, of course, I had now to suppose that Max's ways of making money might have been at least open to question, in which case I might have my money taken off me. Since I had been married to Max, I wondered, might I be liable for his debts? It was surely likely. What had Max done, exactly? Photographs of young women were not in themselves incriminating items. They might have been models, actresses, applicants for respectable jobs. Because a mysterious man called Colin burst into the house, it didn't follow that Max had been involved in illegal activities. Was I being ridiculous?

But there was the question of the name—the three names. And now there was the revolver, black and deadly in its dark drawer. And, the more I thought, the more it seemed to me I had been unforgivably stupid.

Max had never answered a straight question on the origins of his improbable wealth. I'd never asked him one. I couldn't get Bea's voice out of my head. *Tax evasion? Prostitution? Drugs? White slave traffic?* I recalled his fabulous largesse, his evidently limitless funds, his casual teasing whose function was finally always evasion. I recalled the business trips whose purpose and outcome remained cloudy. Well, murky rather than cloudy, one had to say.

But we had known each other intimately, hadn't we? We had been transparent to each other, hadn't we? There was no point in dwelling on any of that. What I had to do was focus on what I had to do.

It seemed to me that the first thing was to sell Rain. Some little time previously, the thought would have dismayed me, struck a dead chill into the roots of my soul. But I couldn't bear Rain any longer. That man Colin had invaded with such ease, such neat, irritating panache; and there would be more invaders, I was sure. I could lock them out only for a brief spell: they would find their way in and would torment me. It was up to me to evade them, to make it impossible for them to up-end my life.

And Max lay outside, under the smooth turf and flowerbeds of Rain's brand-new back garden, under the rubble of the cool and gleaming pool I had designed for him. No, I didn't want to stay.

Well, Max had given me Rain. The title was in my bank: nothing mysterious or evasive about it, thank Christ. It belonged to me outright, and there should be no difficulty in selling it. I would call an agent the next day. Max had invested enough in the house: property was booming and probably the investment would prove to have ripened speedily.

What next?

I hadn't changed my name, of course. If people wanted to find me, it would be Isabel Weaving they would have to find, not Isabel Knight. Nor Isabel Ritter, Templar, whatever. At first this seemed rather a strength, but, as I thought my way through it further, I didn't think it mattered much. If Max had mixed with the sort of pals who were likely to seek me out and (for instance) gun me down, they presumably had kept tabs on me enough to know my name and my whereabouts.

Yet why would anyone want to harm me? If they thought Max had absconded with funds; if they thought I knew Max's whereabouts...Or, to put a different spin on it, if they thought Max had absconded but that I had access to the funds. Then I might well be a person of considerable interest to them.

Surely, however, nobody would guess the truth? Nobody would guess what had really happened to Max. Would they? The truth was so unlikely, so extraordinary and implausible, nobody could possibly guess it.

This was a strength, I thought, not a threat. If it were an opportunity of some kind, I couldn't see how.

Then I thought of the revolver. My first instinct had been to creep out at dead of night (an evocative phrase, that) and hurl it into the nearest deep-flowing river. Perhaps, however, I should keep it as protection? Yet surely that was laughable: I, who had never fired a gun in my life, to use the thing for safety. I'd be more likely to shoot myself in the foot. Or the neck. And if I didn't manage to kill myself, I'd surely kill someone else. That would make me a double murderer. On the way to serial status, in fact.

So. I'd sell Rain. I'd get rid of the gun.

I was starting to feel mildly better. Until now I'd been like a one-finned fish, swimming in circles and sinking to boot. If I could regain control—or at least the illusion of control—over my life, I might regain something more than control: I might feel that sanity and peace were possible again. For some time, now, they hadn't looked like accessible options.

The sooner I acted, the sooner I would be able to disentangle myself from a scenario whose ramifications were becoming alarming.

I rang three agents the next morning and chose the one I thought the sharpest and least scrupulous. You could see from the glitter in his eyes how much he wanted the property, how far he'd go to get it and to sell it for a top price. He wouldn't even have to lie. He didn't know about the back garden and what lay in it.

'I want to move fast,' I said, and he nodded ecstatically.

The house was clean already, but I got cleaners in. I got gardeners in, too, and I rented a huge skip and spent two or three days manically tossing out as much as I could.

I spent five solid days driving around looking at units and houses nearer to Kate and Gavin and eventually found one I liked enough to imagine myself living there. I put a deposit on it and told my agent that I wanted Rain sold within a month. As it turned out he managed it in ten days.

Then there was the gun to dispose of. It was easy, in fact. I took Borrow for a long walk, one night. It was dark and chilly; I wore a parka. In its deep left pocket was the gun, with a heavy axehead (I'd found it in the garage; I don't know where it came from), swathed tightly together in an old rag. It knocked against my thigh as I walked.

Borrow was excited: for some reason he loves walking at

night and at first he tended to caper slightly, puppylike, displaying his pleasure in the unexpected treat. It was a long walk, though—nearly two miles, down to the river—and he settled eventually, padding beside me contentedly.

When we arrived at the bridge, I threw the awful package over. It splashed, but nobody was there to hear it. Cars spurted back and forth; a tram rumbled past. No other pedestrians were around. It was so dark that I couldn't see down into the water. I turned and headed home, faintly surprised that it had been so easy. A criminal life appeared less demanding than I had always believed.

Then there was the car. The silver Audi, his pride and joy, which had stayed in the garage since his death. It was the third silver Audi he'd had since I'd known him, his third pride and joy.

For Max, a new car had been like a new suit—perhaps even a new shirt. He had liked the luxury of new cars but the reliability of what he knew, the comfort of what he was accustomed to. He'd been happy with a silver Audi (well, why wouldn't he have been?) and that was what he'd continued to buy. I imagine the salesmen at the Audi dealer knew him well.

I couldn't throw the car in the river. The registration papers were in the folder in Max's study. It was Max's, not mine. I couldn't sell it. I didn't want to drive it.

If Colin came back, if anyone else came, could I give away the car, use it as a bribe? No: that wasn't a good idea. It was too much: it would make them suspicious. More suspicious. I imagined the scene: Colin sliding into the house again, refusing to go until I told him where Max was. Or Matty. Or Martin. Whoever. *I don't know*, I'd say. *I don't know, but here: take his very expensive car. Will that do?*

No. That wouldn't look good.

I had keys, of course: each of us had owned a set of keys, although I had my own car and had rarely driven the Audi. I should have got rid of it somehow at the very beginning, I thought. I hadn't been thinking properly, not to do that. But then, of course, nobody knew that I hadn't. Nobody had seen inside the garage. The natural thing for Max to do would be to drive away in his car, and I could still make it look as if that's what had happened.

So I drove the car out the next Friday evening, when the shops were open late, and headed for somewhere a long way away. I'd decided a big shopping centre would be best.

I'd gone through the glove box and removed anything that would provide easy identification. Not that it would matter in the long run, of course; the registration would identify the car and its owner. But I figured the more time I gave myself the better it would be.

I parked the beautiful silver thing in a multi-storey car park in a shopping centre on the city fringe. I'd never been there before, and I didn't plan to return. I lowered a back window a tiny bit, placed the key in the glove box, patted the Audi on its sleek and bulbous bonnet and caught a bus back into the city.

So that was the end of the car, I thought. For the time being, at least.

These decisions, these actions, gave me a new sense of control, a sense that I had some sort of power over what was happening to my life. Until now I had felt perilously like one of the crude cartoon characters in the computer games of the time—dashing hither and yon, avoiding random assaults from traffic, buckets of water, arrows and boulders. Dominic had a game like that: he was remarkably good at it. With Dominic at the joystick the round-headed man had a genuine chance. I didn't know how much chance I had: I seemed to live with a permanently breath-less feeling that a boulder was about to drop on me and shatter me.

Part Four

And the boulder did drop, one day. The sharp-eyed real-estate agent had sold Rain, but I was still living there. I was about to leave: I think the move was scheduled for two or three days distant, and I had started to congratulate myself on evading the buckets of water and the arrows. Colin had never reappeared. Nobody else had descended on me. It seemed I was safe.

I was drinking black coffee before going to work, glancing around me at the denuded, too-clean kitchen and wondering how I would adapt again to an ordinary, little kitchen—without a long sweep of polished granite bench, without dozens of smooth capacious cupboards, without a vast walk-in pantry—when the knock rattled the front door. A purposeful, deliberate knock, a knock that meant business.

This time, it was a policeman. I knew he was a policeman because he was in uniform. I thought I would have preferred a gangster.

He was a middle-aged, thickset man with short spatulate fingers and pale eyes. He didn't look friendly. He flashed his ID at me. I tried to look nonchalant and slightly surprised. I raised my eyebrows in what I hoped was an approximation of a kind of lazy detachment, and unlocked and opened the security door. I always kept it locked, now.

'Frank Pritchard,' he said. 'Inspector Frank Pritchard. Mrs Knight? Mrs Isabel Knight?'

'I don't use that name,' I said.

'You're married to Maximilian Knight?'

'Yes,' I said, with a *so-what-if-I-am?* inflection. 'But my name is Weaving.'

'Could I have ten minutes of your time, Ms Weaving?'

There wasn't much point in saying no. And I was impressed by the carefully enunciated 'Ms'. Most policemen, I felt, wouldn't have been up to it: they would have messed around with Mrs and Miss and finished up mumbling something that could have been anything.

I led him into the lounge and saw him glancing around with what struck me as disproportionate interest. I gestured vaguely at the sweep of cream leather and he sat down. Some people felt overpowered by all the leather and perched on the edge of the seats. Inspector Pritchard wasn't. He sat firmly foursquare, and gave me his full and undivided attention. I reciprocated.

'Mr Knight's not in?' he said.

'Mr Knight hasn't been in for some time.'

'He no longer lives here, ma'am?'

'That's correct.'

'Might I ask on what date he moved from this residence?'

He really did talk like that. And he really did have a notebook, too, and a pencil.

'I don't remember the exact date,' I lied. 'It must be six or seven months ago.'

'You're not expecting him back?'

'I'm not.'

'Do you have a forwarding address?'

'I don't.'

'A contact number?'

'No, I don't. Look, what's this all about?' I injected mild irritation into my voice.

'We're conducting an investigation,' said Inspector Pritchard, examining the end of his pencil.

'Into what?'

'Into the whereabouts and activities of Mr Knight.'

'I know nothing about either.'

'Forgive me, ma'am, but if you're married to Mr Knight I think you must have some knowledge of Mr Knight's activities.'

'I don't regard myself as married to him any more.'

'Do you mind explaining that to me, ma'am? Are you divorced?'

'Separated.'

'Since what date, may I ask?'

'I'm not sure that it's any of your business.'

'You'll let me be the judge of that, perhaps.'

'Well, perhaps I won't,' I said, thinking that perhaps it was time I started to show a bit of temper. He wasn't being rude or unpleasant, but he had control and he wasn't about to relinquish it. But if I was too subservient, if I tried to mollify him, wouldn't that make him think I was hiding something? On the other hand, I didn't want to get him offside.

'You'd be well advised to cooperate, ma'am.'

Nowadays it's quite common to call women *ma'am*. Those infuriating people who ring you up and want your money call you *ma'am*; so do people behind counters, and ticket inspectors, parking officials, people like that. In those days it wasn't so usual. It made me feel uncomfortable, as if he was jeering at me up his navy serge sleeve.

'I don't understand,' I said, assuming the tone of someone who was trying to be reasonable against mounting odds. 'I don't see why you're conducting an investigation. Why won't you tell me? If my husband had done something wrong, something criminal, don't you think I'd know about it?'

'Yes. Yes, I'm thinking you would know about it. So why don't you tell me what you do know, Ms Weaving?'

'Like what?'

'Like what does your husband do?'

I stared at him. Anxiety sprang a level or two and bloomed into panic.

'What is it, ma'am?'

'I'm wondering if I should get a lawyer.'

'If you want to get in a lawyer, Ms Weaving, you're entitled to. At any point. But I'm only asking about Mr Knight's occupation, after all. I'm laying no charges. I'm not thinking I'm going to arrest you. I'm not even necessarily thinking I'm going to arrest Mr Knight, when I find him. I'm not thinking of laying charges, at present. I'm gathering information, you see. It's a friendly chat. You'd be ill-advised, I'm thinking, to call in a lawyer on the basis of me asking you for a friendly chat.'

'Well,' I said, uncertainly.

He waited.

'What do you want to know?'

'Principally, I want to know how I can contact Mr Knight.'

'I can't tell you that.'

'No idea at all, ma'am?'

'Honestly. None.'

'No leads, no possibilities, no friends he might be staying with?'

I shook my head. 'I just don't know. I swear I'm telling you the truth. My husband—my ex-husband I think of him as—didn't have many friends. I didn't know them, anyway.'

'How long were you married, ma'am?'

'Nearly five years.'

'You were married for five years and you don't know any of his friends?'

'Well, I didn't. It may sound odd. But he was a solitary sort of man.'

'Business associates?'

'I never met them.'

'What does he do, ma'am?'

'He had…business interests,' I said, desperately. 'He owned things and he rented them out and he bought things and sold them. He was a consultant. He advised people about investments and…and things like that.'

'Ma'am, are you aware that you're speaking in the past tense?'

'It *is* past, for me,' I said, kicking myself. 'I suppose he still does all of those things, but I don't have anything to do with him any longer, so I think of it all in the past tense.'

'When did you divorce Mr Knight, ma'am?'

'I'm not divorced. We're separated. I told you that.'

'Are you expecting a divorce?'

It was a funny question, when you thought about it. Not that I was grinning.

'Yes. I suppose so. I don't know.'

'So how did he come to leave?'

'We had a quarrel.'

'A quarrel.'

'That's what I said, yes. It was a very significant quarrel. We'd been unhappy for some time,' I said, improvising frenetically. 'It was just…the last straw.'

237

'And he left?'

'Yes, he left.'

'He just walked out the door?'

'No. He packed. He packed lots of things. And he left.'

'And you've heard nothing since?'

'Nothing at all.'

'Forgive me, ma'am,' he said, with a sudden unexpected gentleness, 'but that's hardly likely, is it? I'm thinking, a man isn't going to walk out of your life as quickly and easily as that, is he? There must be things you have in common, things that needed to be worked out between you both. Money, financial arrangements, so forth.'

'We had separate financial arrangements.' I could feel sweat condensing and crawling down the back of my neck, down my spine. 'There was nothing to work out.'

'Your house?'

'The house is mine.'

'You don't find it odd, that you haven't heard from him?'

'I didn't expect to hear from him.'

'Such a final break,' he said, marvelling. 'Such a quick, final break.'

'I told you, the marriage had been going wrong for some time. It was just the final thing. The final disaster.'

'And what caused the final…er…disaster?'

'I don't have to tell you that.'

'You don't,' he agreed, almost paternally. 'So, when you didn't hear from him, you weren't surprised?'

'Not at all.'

'You hadn't thought there might be a reconciliation?'

'It was clear that there wasn't going to be a reconciliation.'

'And he didn't forget anything?'

'Forget?'

'When he packed. He didn't forget anything, and come back for it later.'

'No.'

'An expert packer,' said Inspector Pritchard, admiringly. 'Me, now, I always forget something when I pack. Specially if I'm in a hurry.'

I said nothing.

'And none of your family's heard from him?'

'No. So far as I know.'

'Mail?'

'I believe he had a post-office box for business mail.'

'So he did.' The inspector nodded, as if he approved of this arrangement. 'And it didn't occur to you to worry about him? When he walked so completely out of your life, I mean?'

'Why should I worry?'

'Why, indeed?' he agreed. 'You wouldn't have thought, for instance, of reporting him as a missing person?'

'Why should I do that?'

'Such an absolutely total disappearance? And you never thought he might have met with foul play?'

'No. Why should he?'

The inspector shook his head in apparent perplexity and looked down at his notebook, in which he had, from time to time, made tidy and apparently leisurely notes.

'You've sold the house, Ms Weaving?' Of course, he would have seen the real-estate board out the front, with its flamboyant *SOLD* sign.

'Yes. It was mine. I told you. The house was mine to sell.' I knew I was sounding defensive.

'Ah. And you're moving elsewhere?'

'I am, yes.'

'May I have that address, ma'am?'

I told him. He gave me his card and suggested I might like to ring him if I remembered anything else.

Not bloody likely, I thought.

'Lovely place,' he said, looking around as I showed him out.

'Yes.'

'Cost you a pang or two to move, I should think?'

'I guess.'

'Built it yourself, I understand?'

'Yes,' I said, wondering how he knew that. He smiled at me as if he knew what I was thinking. He paused at the door.

Go, I was thinking. I was suffused by fear and fury. Just go.

'You'll be in touch, then. You'll be in touch if you think of anything. Or if you hear from Mr Knight, of course?'

'Yes,' I said, stopping myself from saying: *But I won't hear from him.*

After he had gone, I tried to stop the sweat and the trembling. I sat down and closed my eyes and breathed deeply.

I should have been better prepared. What a fool I was, not to have thought my way through it all. Of course, people didn't separate like that, not with that kind of suddenness, that abrupt and volcanic rupture. People didn't just walk out of a five-year marriage and not return, not like that. Both the inspector and I knew that. I should have thought my way through the story more carefully, should have negotiated its twists and turns and sharp treacherous corners with more prudence, more care.

But he couldn't prove anything. Nobody could prove anything. Not unless they dug up the back garden. Max had packed and left. He'd walked out of the house. He'd driven his car away. Maybe he'd met with foul play after that. How would

I know? I'd have no way of knowing. Anything could have happened. All I had to do was remember that I didn't know anything, that I had no way of knowing anything.

Only the day after I'd moved, there he was at my new front door.

'Nice little place, ma'am,' he said.

'Yes.'

'A bit different from your last home, though.'

'Yes.'

He stood there, gazing at me. He wasn't going away.

'Would you like to come in?' I said.

'I'm thinking I'd like five minutes of your time, ma'am. If that's convenient.'

'It's not.'

He grinned. Ponderously he came in. We sat on the new furniture (flowered Sanderson linen) in the living room. The cream leather suite had no chance of fitting into this house, and I'd sold it to the new owners of Rain, so it would stay where it belonged. I'd chosen the Sanderson because it was so unlike anything at Rain: time for something completely different, I'd thought.

'A different style of place altogether,' he observed.

'Yes.'

He shifted, looked at his fingers. 'The fact is, ma'am, I don't know how to raise this matter with you.'

I tried to give him a look that was stony without being overtly hostile. Neutral, I thought. Be neutral.

'What's it connected with?' I asked.

'Well. It's connected with your marriage.'

'My marriage?'

'Your marriage to Mr Knight.'

'In what way, connected?'

'Well, when did you marry Mr Knight, ma'am?'

I gave him the date.

'And where?'

On the beach, I told him. 'Down Point Leo way.'

'I see. And you'd have the certificate?'

'Of course I do.'

'Would you be able to lay your hand on it?'

I wondered where the hell I'd put it.

'If I was still in Rain—in my old house—I'd know where it was. I'm not sure, here. I've only just moved; you know that.' I gestured around the room at the cardboard cartons, the piles of books, the mess. 'Honestly, I don't know if I can find it. It's here somewhere. It'll take me a while to get everything sorted out.'

'Ah.'

'Why do you want to see it? What's it going to prove?'

'Ma'am,' said Inspector Pritchard, 'since you've broken up and all, and since you don't expect to hear from Mr Knight again, perhaps this won't matter to you. But it does seem to us as if no legal wedding ceremony took place.'

'No legal ceremony? But I've got the proof. I've got the photographs; I've got the certificate.'

'It seems as if the ceremony may not have been all you thought it.'

I couldn't understand what he was talking about. 'Look, I was there; I was the damn bride. What on earth do you mean, it may not have been all I thought it? I thought it was a wedding. It *was* a wedding.'

So he explained it to me.

Maximilian Knight, he said, had a wife in the US and

another in Perth. He had married the wife in the US under another name (Pritchard didn't say what) some twenty years ago. He hadn't divorced her. He'd come back to Australia, about twelve years ago, and he'd married the wife in Perth. He'd been Martin Ritter then. She'd been Mrs Martin Ritter. (For reasons I would find it impossible to explain, I was obscurely grateful that she hadn't been Mrs Max Knight.) He hadn't divorced her, either. Not that you could divorce someone when you weren't legally married to her, of course.

'You'll have to tell me again,' I said. 'I'm not taking any of this in.'

'You don't look well, ma'am,' he said. I think he was really concerned. It was small wonder if I'd gone grey. I felt nauseous. I needed a drink, but I didn't want to have one while he was there.

He told me again. It didn't sound any better the second time around.

'It can't be true,' I said. 'It can't be true. Why should I believe you? How do you know all of this?'

He explained that, too. They'd been looking into Mr Knight. They hadn't been entirely satisfied about some of the activities Mr Knight had engaged in. There were questions, for instance, about Mr Knight's bank accounts, about his travel. There were questions about Mr Knight's name, about his history, about his intentions. Questions hung thickly all around Mr Knight.

'Two wives. Two previous wives. You must be mistaken. You *must* be mistaken. He told me he was married once. But she died. She died of cancer.'

He wasn't willing to admit any mistake. 'Were there children?'

He wasn't sure.

I went to the carton that contained photographs. I was after

243

the photograph of our wedding, the sunset, the beach, the deep mellow light, the photograph beside which Max had stood when I killed him. I found it at the bottom and drew it out. I hadn't been going to display it.

'Look,' I said. 'Look. This is when we got married.'

Seriously, soberly, he examined it.

'It's a wedding, isn't it? See?'

'I can see that it looks like a wedding, ma'am. I don't dispute that. I don't dispute that the event took place. I'm only saying, it wasn't legal.'

'But I have the certificate. There was a celebrant.'

'What was his name?'

'It was a her, a woman. I've got a photo of her somewhere, too. Everything was signed, witnessed.'

'I'm sure it was. But what I'm saying, ma'am, is that the ceremony wasn't legal. It was a con job, I'm afraid.'

'A con job?'

'You don't have to take my word for it. Go to the registry office. Births, deaths and marriages. It's in Collins Street, in the city. You go down there and you ask for a copy of the marriage certificate. They won't have it.'

'But why?' I asked, stricken. 'Why? It makes no sense. Why should he go through a charade like that?'

I think I'd forgotten at this stage that Pritchard was a policeman, that he was lined up on the enemy front.

'He couldn't marry you. He already had a wife. He already had two wives.'

'But he could have divorced them. He *must* have divorced them.'

'I imagine the difficulties related to his name.'

'His name?'

'Ma'am,' said Pritchard in a burst of what seemed very like true candour. 'You have to understand, that wasn't Mr Knight's real name, Maximilian Knight.'

'It was on his driver's licence,' I said, as if that proved something.

'Forged.'

'It didn't look forged.'

'Good forgeries don't look forged, that's the thing about them. Or maybe the papers he used for it were forged. See, for a long time we were interested in the activities of Martin Ritter. We were asked by our colleagues in the US to look into Mr Ritter. Mr Ritter was hard to track. And then, when we did find him, suddenly he wasn't around. Gone. Disappeared. Phut. So we had to start all over again. It took us quite some time to work out that Mr Ritter and Mr Knight were the same person. Then there was Malcolm Baron.'

'Baron?' I was reeling.

'Yes. Malcolm Baron.' He eyed me. 'So you knew about Martin Ritter, but not about Malcolm Baron?'

'I found an envelope,' I said, slowly. 'I found an envelope addressed to Martin Ritter. It didn't make sense. But, no, I've never heard of Malcolm Baron.'

I wondered briefly if I should mention Matthew Templar, but decided against it.

'Do you still have that envelope, ma'am?'

'No.' That was true, in fact. I'd burnt it. I'd burnt the pictures of May and Susie, Kylie and Lindy Lou.

'What was in the envelope?' he asked.

They talk about people watching like a hawk. Inspector Pritchard's eye's were entirely hawklike. Hooded, sharp, bright. Quite at odds with his fubsy and unremarkable face.

'Nothing,' I said. And then, seized with a curiosity so sharp it bit into me, I asked: 'What was his real name? Do you know?'

Pritchard shrugged. 'We don't know. I'm almost inclined to say Mr Knight himself didn't know. There have been so many, you see.'

'What did he do?'

'You mean, what crimes did he commit? You don't know?'

'How could I know? There was always plenty of money. Heaps of money.'

'I imagine there was,' he said, dryly.

'He told me—well, I told you what he told me. Consultancies, investment, properties. But you're saying there were illegal activities.'

'We don't know the full extent. We suspect him of involvement in a number of illegal activities.'

'Yes, but what *sort* of illegal activities? Are you saying he was a criminal? Is a criminal?'

'I was hoping you could tell me some of those activities yourself, ma'am.'

'Did he do drugs?' I ask, baldly.

Pritchard's eyes never left my face. 'We don't think he did drugs himself, ma'am. We think he may have sold them, though: yes. Not a user. A dealer.'

He would give me no more information. Well, I had enough to cope with, I suppose. Before he left, looking at me narrowly, he said: 'I didn't expect you to be so distressed, Ms Weaving.'

'Didn't expect me to be distressed that I wasn't really married to a man I regarded as my husband for five years?'

'No. By your own account, you didn't much care for him, by the end. You weren't much distressed, when he left. You were getting on with your life quite nicely, ma'am, according to you.

246

Marriage had been going downhill for some time, you said. Inevitable outcome. So no, I didn't expect you to care so much.'

'You overestimated me, I'm afraid. What I told you was true. It wasn't good. It had all been going downhill. But...but...'

To my immense relief, I felt the sobs coming. I let my voice shake; let the tears roll down. I'd felt frozen, until then. It was starting to come home to me, now. I didn't have to act at all.

'It's been such a shock,' I managed to say. Well, that was certainly true.

After he left (he couldn't cope with tears, which was a useful thing to know, or might have been, if I'd been able to summon them at will), I felt as if the shock would never dissipate, that it would continue to reverberate through me all my days, a little continuous tremor that would never die down. *Two wives*, I kept saying to myself. *Two wives. At* least *two wives.* Bea's voice returned again and again. *What does he do? Where does all the money come from? Tax evasion? Prostitution? Drugs? White slave traffic? You know nothing, nothing about him. What in Christ's name are you doing?*

What in Christ's name had I done?

I continued to unpack, stacking, tidying, folding, ordering, emptying, filling, smoothing, dusting, arranging, making hundreds of trivial decisions. Methodically I flattened the cardboard cartons as I took out all the household things, all the pots and pans and glasses and plates, the photographs and vases and books and pictures.

I'd thrown a lot out, but a lot remained. Kate offered to help, but I didn't accept: I wanted to sift through everything myself, to know exactly where everything was. It was part of the business of wresting back control over my life.

Now, as I sorted through all the flotsam, all the bits and pieces that turned out to be so much less important than I'd once thought, I kept thinking: *He'd been married twice before. He'd been married twice before.*

What were they like, these wives of Max? Had they been like me? Physical attractions, sexual attractions, are supposed to remain consistent to type. Had they been dark and quick and slight? For some reason I found myself imagining them as statuesque blondes. I didn't want them to be like me. I understood none of it. I knew he had loved me; I knew this just as surely as I knew I had loved him. *What were you doing?* I screamed at him inside my head. *What were you thinking? How could you let this happen to me?*

The fact that he had engaged in criminal pursuits (as Frank Pritchard would have put it) troubled me far less than did the previous marriages. I felt a little ashamed when I realised this was the case; still, it was so. Lindy Lou and Kylie and the rest of them had given me a nasty shock, but their presence in Max's life seemed to me a professional matter, as it were. I had absorbed the shock of their appearance. They were extraneous; they had not invaded his emotional life—or even, I thought, his sexual life. They posed no threat; they remained at a psychic distance from him and from me. I supposed he had made money out of them. Well, that was different from falling in love with them. It was the wives who bothered me.

Over the next six months or so, Frank Pritchard and I got to be on first-name terms. He dropped in rather a lot, after the visit in which he first told me about Max's wives.

Sometimes he had a cup of coffee. Sometimes he asked me questions: during the first couple of visits, he pressed me quite hard. I thought he was trying to exploit my new knowledge of Max's previous marriages: he was hoping my hurt and resentment would lead me to betray Max. I continued steadfast in my denial of knowledge of Max's activities or whereabouts, and gradually he came to believe me, or so I started tentatively to believe.

He let information slip, from time to time. Heroin, he said. Prostitution of minors. He said a number of pretty unpleasant things, which included embezzlement and fraud, but those two were probably the worst.

I thought of us as locked in deadly (albeit extremely civilised) battle, but sometimes we had quite pleasant chats. I didn't exactly relax with him, but I had to concentrate on not letting my guard down, which I was sure was his aim. I grew to know his knock—that businesslike knock on my door, which never failed to jolt my heart. The hardest thing was to open the door to him looking untroubled.

Once, Kate dropped by with Sophie while he was there. Unfortunately, he was in uniform at the time (sometimes he was, sometimes not). Her eyes popped when she saw him. I had to introduce them, to explain that Kate was my daughter. Frank's eyes flickered over her in the manner that had become so familiar to me. Taking everything in. He did the same to Sophie, but in a cursory way. I had one moment of sharp anxiety, in case he saw the likeness; but then I realised that Frank had never met Max, knew him only through photographs.

Sophie was just starting to walk then, I recall, and when Kate put her down her attempts to wobble around took centre stage in the way that young children can instantly manage.

Frank made a couple of admiring comments; there was some desultory small talk about toddlers. He started to leave, but stopped at the door, in that infuriating way he had of pretending (I was sure it was a pretence) that something had just occurred to him.

'I don't suppose you've seen your stepfather recently?' he asked.

Flummoxed, Kate shook her head.

'Or heard from him?'

'No,' she said, all at sea. 'Absolutely not.'

He fumbled in his inner pocket, brought out a card, gave it to her. 'In case you do.'

Kate rounded on me when he had left. 'What the hell was all that about?'

I was silently cursing Frank. I'd really wanted to get through all of this without having the rest of the family know anything about it, and I'd thought I was going to succeed.

'He sometimes comes by,' I said, tiredly. 'It seems there are things about Max's business affairs that they think aren't quite right.'

'Why don't they ask Max, then?'

'They can't find him.'

'Well, you know where he is, don't you?'

'No.'

She looked at me sideways. She knew she was on forbidden territory, that I didn't want to talk about Max, that she wasn't allowed to. But she didn't stop.

'What sort of things aren't in order?'

'I don't know. I think there's a couple of tax queries, things like that,' I lied.

Kate lunged at Sophie, who was heading for a low table with breakables on it. 'You wouldn't have a policeman asking about tax stuff, would you?'

'I don't know.'

'Well, but you wouldn't,' she persisted. 'You'd have someone from the tax office, not a policeman. Sophie, love, come here to Mummy and leave that alone. You wouldn't, Mum.'

'I don't know about that,' I said, heading Sophie off at another pass. Sophie was very enterprising and surprisingly quick on her feet for one so unstable.

'But listen—'

'I'm not talking about it.'

'For God's sake!' she said, in exasperation, whether aimed at me or at Sophie it was hard to say.

Sophie fell over and started to cry. I picked her up and comforted her, but she wanted her mother. I passed her over, with a prick of envy.

Kate cuddled her. 'Just tell me this,' she said. 'Do you honestly not know where he is?'

'I don't have to tell you anything,' I said, just in case she hadn't got the point. 'But no, I don't. And I don't want to. And that's all I'm saying.'

She wasn't satisfied; she wanted to go on talking. But I wouldn't, and she knew it. She gave in. Kate always gives in, eventually. She's got no spine.

Quite soon after that—a week or so, I think, Frank contacted me and asked me to go down to the local station with him. Some property had been recovered, he said. Property of Mr Knight's. He'd like it if I could identify it for him.

I thought it must be the car, and it was.

It was sad. Somebody had beaten the heart out of Max's beautiful Audi. It was on the back of a tow truck in the car park behind the station: it wasn't even driveable. The luxurious soft leather seats had been slashed; the windows were broken; the boot lid had been wrenched off; someone had lit a fire in the back seat.

I'd thought, after I'd driven it that last time, perhaps I ought to have worn gloves; perhaps they'd powder it or swab it or do whatever they do to get fingerprints off it and they'd be able to tell I'd been the last one to drive it. I needn't have worried. It would have been as difficult as trying to get fingerprints off a prickly pear.

Poor battered, blackened, ravaged Audi. Max would have wept. The registration plates were gone, but the police had traced it through the engine number, Frank said. Was it Max's, did I think?

I shrugged. 'How can I tell?' I asked, walking around the poor devastated thing. 'If the engine number is right, I guess it must be. But there's no way I can tell. There was a scratch on the duco at the back, I remember, that he was going to have fixed. But there's not much point in looking for a scratch on that now, is there?'

'And Mr Knight drove this when he left?'

'Yes.'

'And you've not seen it since?'

'No.'

'Well,' he said, looking dissatisfied.

I didn't think he'd wanted me to identify it. What was the point? They had the engine number. That was enough. The car had been in Max's name: I'd seen the papers. What use was there in asking me to identify something that was nine-tenths destroyed and unrecognisable anyway? He wanted me to be upset; he wanted me to show emotion. I wasn't going to.

'Does it concern you?' he asked, abruptly.

'Seeing the car like this? Of course.'

'But don't you worry, now, about what's happened to Mr Knight? He was fond of this car, wasn't he?'

'Yes, he was.'

'So he wouldn't have been responsible for this damage himself?'

'Good heavens, no.'

'Then what do you think has happened to him, ma'am? Aren't you concerned about that? Where do you think he is?'

'Frank, we've been through this so many times. Given what you've told me, I imagine he's in Rio de Janeiro chatting up the local talent.'

'He would have just ditched the car?'

'No, he wouldn't. He would have been careful with it. He would have left it somewhere it would have been safe. It must have been stolen.'

'He didn't report it.'

'Well, you're always telling me he had good reason not to go anywhere near the police. Anyway, he probably doesn't know the car's been stolen. He's probably left the country.'

'We have no record of his doing so,' said Frank.

'How many thousands of people fly in and out of Australia every week?'

'Not so many that we can't keep track of some of them,' he insisted, stubbornly. 'Mr Knight hasn't left the country.'

'You can't be sure,' I said. And, of course, he couldn't.

After this episode, Frank stopped coming for a while. It's as if it was his last fling, his last attempt to prise out of me all he can.

I think he thought seeing the devastated Audi might make me crack. Having failed, I think he's given up. I even think he might finally accept that I know nothing more than I say I do. I almost stop listening for the knock on the door.

But it comes again. It comes one night, quite late. I've decided to have a drink. I've actually decided this quite early in the evening, and by the time Frank knocks at the door I'm right into it. Perhaps I'm on the fourth brandy? And the brandies have got bigger and less diluted on the way through the evening.

'Hello, Frank,' I say, opening the door. Then I hiccup. The hiccup wafts in the air between us before drifting, gently and featherlike, to the floor, where it rests. Frank's eyes—grave, even troubled—regard it there before he looks straight at me.

'Hello, Isabel,' he says. 'I hope it's not too late. I was driving by and saw your light on.'

'No, not a bit,' I say, foggily, waving him in. I'm almost pleased to see him. It gets lonely, drinking on your own. I tell him this, and press a brandy on him, fortuitously refilling my own glass in the process. I'm a little surprised that he accepts, as I had a notion that cops are not meant to drink on duty, but I guess Frank's on top of what he's doing. Perhaps he's not on duty? It's all a bit fuzzy and I can't quite focus on anything as I know I should be doing.

We sit at the kitchen table and observe each other silently for a period. I know what he's thinking. He's thinking he's found me sozzled. He's thinking I'm cornered; he's thinking he can extract from me anything he likes. His eyes are bright with anticipation of my errors, my contradictions, my admissions.

Fat chance, Frank, I think. But I think it a bit blearily. My mind isn't crisp enough; I know this. It might not be equal to my stubborn determination to give nothing away. Silently I double my resolve and, with an immense effort, concentrate.

Well, sozzled I may be, and cornered, too; but I am buoyed by the competition of the situation (he's a very competitive person, Frank, but so am I) and by the knowledge that a ratlike cunning is budding deep within me. I can keep Frank out there on the perimeter, where he belongs. I can stop Frank from hopping the fence, stalking closer to me, closer to the truth. I have to stop Frank.

The thing is, he can see I'm a little under the weather. It's written all over his face, his excitement that he's finally caught me with my guard well down. And if I can keep one step ahead of him, if I can manage not to give anything away this time of all times, perhaps I'll convince him at last.

I smile at Frank. I try to make it a winning smile, and hope I don't look merely predatory. Or drunk.

'So,' I say, trying to cross my legs and almost getting there. It's a good thing Frank can't see under the table, I think. Or perhaps he can?

Frank's equal to this ploy. 'So,' he says, smiling.

There's a pause.

'Don't you ever go home?' I try.

'On my way.'

'Doesn't your wife get cross with you when you're so late home?'

'No wife.'

This is something I've often wondered about Frank. Somehow, to me he has always looked married, and I'm mildly surprised that he isn't. I'm sure he's not gay.

'Can we talk about Max?' he says.

I'm even more surprised by this. Frank is usually rather more subtle in his approach: he'll stalk around for a while before he pounces. Furthermore, he's always referred to Max as Mr Knight, a careful formality I've occasionally found bizarre. It turns out

Frank wants me to tell him about Max and me, about how we met, about what he was like.

'I've never met him, remember,' he says. 'I'd like to get a feel for the man.'

So I tell him. It's an expurgated version, certainly; but I answer all his questions (*yes, we met at my office: he wanted an architect to design his house; no, I didn't meet many of his friends; no, we didn't travel together much; yes, he did give me my dog*). And so on.

While I am steadily answering his cruel questions, managing what I think is a halfway decent impersonation of a woman who doesn't give much of a damn any more, Frank leans over and scratches Borrow's chin on the exact place he loves it. I am really irritated by this, and try not to show it.

All in all, it's my finest hour, I think. It is so hard, presenting these details of everything that has mattered most, dazzled brightest, in my life, without breaking down; but I do.

Once or twice, affected I suppose by the alcohol, I am almost tempted to say to hell with it all and tell Frank everything. I'm so sick of him persecuting me in his courteous, obstinate way; and he's a nice man; surely he'd understand. It'd be such a relief, to tell somebody all about it.

But I manage to retrieve myself from this idiocy. I remain polite, slightly distant, slightly puzzled by his interest, by the way it's all turned out. I don't think I give anything away at all.

When he leaves, after half an hour or so, I sit quietly and gaze into space. I haven't heard his car drive off, and he's tried this trick on me once before. And, sure enough, there he is, at the door again, having (he says) forgotten one small question, his eyes positively ablaze with pale fire at the possibility of catching me out somehow. But lo! I am calm, unflustered. I answer the inconsequential remaining question; he goes; I hear the car leave.

In fact the strain of it all has pretty much exhausted me. But it turns out to be worth it. Frank doesn't come again. He's given up. It takes me a long time to be sure of this, and even when I am practically sure I still continue to listen for that knock, the resolute knock that signifies Frank's return.

Sometimes I wake during the night, suddenly persuaded I have heard it, the knock that presages investigation, conviction, punishment. My heart thumps as I lie in bed, listening as if my life depended on it, which perhaps it does.

Sometimes I get up and pad barefoot out to the slanted window through which I can see the front porch. There's never anybody there. Gradually, slowly, I start to believe I might have satisfied Frank; he might not return. I can get on with my life.

Well, I can almost get on with my life. Before I can properly do so, there's something I have to sort out. I do some homework. I look up addresses. I fly to Perth and hire a car.

It's a fine sunny day, and the ritzier bits of Perth unfold before me, wide streets and bright gardens. I find the address I'm looking for, the only M. Ritter. Immediately I know I've hit paydirt. There's an old silver Audi in the drive.

The woman who opens the door isn't statuesque, but she is blonde. That ash-streaked, expensive blonde that goes so well with a lustrous golden tan, which she has. She's on the plump side, but she's pretty. She's in jeans and a T-shirt, but they're classy jeans and a designer T-shirt, and her thin, gold leather sandals are just gorgeous: I feel like asking her where she bought them. Her expression is unfriendly.

After a second or two I realise I am staring at her mutely, drinking in every detail of her appearance.

'I'm sorry,' I say. 'I'm really sorry. Please, can I talk to you. Just for a few minutes?'

I'm stupid, of course: such an important meeting, and I've rehearsed nothing, prepared nothing. It's not like me. I've been so consumed with it all, so consumed with the thought that I'll perhaps actually be meeting one of the wives, that I'm not ready: I haven't got my act together.

'My name's Weaving. But that won't mean anything to you. I was married to Max Knight.'

Her eyes widen and harden. She starts to close the door.

'Please. Please. I'm from Melbourne. I won't ever bother you again. I'm going home tomorrow. I came over here just to meet you. Please. I only want ten minutes. Then I'll go and you'll never see me again.'

'What do you want to ask me?' Her voice is cold.

'I only want to ask you some questions. Please. I lived with him for five years. There are things I don't understand. I thought if we talked we might both understand more about it, about him.'

She hesitates. Then she steps back, nods. 'Ten minutes.' We sit opposite each other in a remarkably pleasant room, all sun and chintzy wicker chairs and big extravagant pot plants and glass-topped tables. I don't like wicker furniture very much, and I don't like pot plants very much, but she's put it all together (at least I suppose it was she who put it together) so that it looks summery and airy and fresh.

'My name's Isabel,' I say.

'I'm Meryl.'

'Thank you for seeing me.'

A long pause settles between us. We examine each other. I dare say it's an unusually frank appraisal between two women who have never before met each other, but we need it. I certainly do, anyway.

My initial impression is reinforced: this is a classy lady. She has that costly sheen of preservation about her that only really chic, really wealthy people get. She's chubby but it's fit chub, firm and gym-toned flesh. Her eyes are bright. She has terrific teeth.

'How did you find me?' she asks.

'A policeman.'

'Cops are pigs,' she says, with a vigour that surprises me.

'At least, he didn't tell me how to find you, but he told me Max had married in Perth when he was calling himself Martin Ritter. So I looked up Ritters in the phone book. There aren't many. It wasn't hard.'

'He left you, too?' she asks, abruptly.

'Yes.'

'How long ago?'

'Nearly a year.'

'Did you know it was going to happen? Did he give you any warning?'

'No,' I say, reflecting that this would have been a difficult thing for Max to have managed.

'Me neither. One day he just went away. He left a letter. Did he leave you a letter?'

'No.'

She raises her eyebrows. 'Unusual. He usually leaves a letter.'

'Usually?'

'Well, he did with me, and apparently he did with my predecessors.'

'Your predecessors?'

'Didn't you know? He's a serial bigamist, dear.'

'I knew there was one other wife.'

'A whole trail of them, probably. I know of three.' She looks at me. 'Four, now.'

'Are the others in America?'

'Yes. Well, two of them are. God knows how many others exist, or where they all are.'

More than two other wives, I think.

'Meryl,' I say, experimenting with her name. 'How did he make his money?'

She smiles, thinly. 'You don't know?'

I shake my head. I've got a pretty good idea, or at least I think I have, but I want to hear it from her.

'Three ways, mainly. He imports prostitutes from Asian countries, and he launders money. But principally it's drugs.'

Tax evasion? Prostitution? Drugs? White slave traffic? What an irony, I think. I must make sure Bea never finds out she was right after all.

'Drugs?'

'As I understand it, heroin. I believe he dabbles in boutique stuff, too, from time to time. But the basis is heroin—at least, it was then, and I assume it's the same now. That's where most of the money came from. Honestly, didn't you know?'

'He told me he was a consultant of sorts.'

'So he is. A consultant on whores and heroin. He has other interests, too, of course—legit ones, to give him a cover. I believe he does a nice line in hiring out heavy industrial machinery. But most of it's prostitution and drugs. You must have suspected something? Did he throw money around?'

'Yes. But I didn't want to think about it. I didn't want to think anything was wrong.'

'I was a bit like that, too,' she says. 'Common sense was telling me something was wrong. Nobody has as much money as that: I knew that. But I didn't want to face up to it, either.'

I realise her eyes are on my ring.

'That's a fabulous diamond,' she says. She holds up her hand and waves it at me. The diamond ring on her middle finger glitters. Its design is similar to mine.

'Tell me,' she says. 'Did he give you a Fred Williams?'

I can only nod.

'I sold mine. I didn't like it. And I thought a painting might be repossessed. I wanted the hard cash. I advise you to sell yours, too.'

This is an even more surreal conversation than I expected it to be.

'What did he say in his letter? If you don't mind my asking.'

She sighs. 'He said he loved me, we'd had a great time, he was an adventurer at heart, sorry not to live up to what I'd have liked him to be, ta-ta. Classic stuff. The cops turned up about a week after he'd left. He always manages to keep one step ahead of them, apparently. They weren't very nice about it.'

I stare at her. I don't know what I expected, but it wasn't this. Probably it should have been, but it wasn't.

'Look,' she says. 'I know it's hard. Try to see the bright side. He's probably left you pretty well off?'

I nod.

'Well, take my advice, get rid of stuff like paintings. I did; I converted practically everything into cash. Except the diamond ring and the car. I liked the car, and I kept it. It still runs okay, though it's really old now. But that's a precaution: you probably don't need to worry. Martin has excellent accountants. The cops made lots of threats, but they never actually took anything away. Martin never seems to leave a paper trail. Except when everything's kosher, of course, and then he leaves a really clear one. He enjoys that.'

261

Every time she calls Max *Martin* it's a surprisingly intimate irritation, as if someone were stroking a feather across my face. I try to ignore it. 'How long were you married?' I ask.

'Well, of course, we weren't married. You weren't either, I take it?'

'No. Not as it turns out.'

'We were together around four years.'

I sit there, running through it all in my mind. It's so much to take in. Meryl looks at me with something rather like compassion. She actually leans over and pats my hand.

'Listen to me,' she says. 'It gets better. Really, it's only just happened to you, hasn't it? He's a bastard, and I know he's a bastard, but at least he leaves people better off than he finds them, in a material sense, anyway. I mean, I'll never have to work again. I bet you won't either.'

I stare at her. I'm overcome—well, nearly overcome—by a desire to sink my face into that plump, fit bosom and tell her everything. Everything. I come very close. She misinterprets my expression (which must be an odd one) and pats my hand again, almost in a motherly way.

Then she starts blurting things out. 'I've thought an awful lot about Martin,' she says. 'I think he just has different needs from most people. He *is* an adventurer. I mean, I know it's no excuse. I'm not trying to make excuses for him. But I've tried to understand what happened to us. I just think he can't help it. Honestly, I thought we were so happy. I believed we were so happy. I certainly was. I've never been so happy before, and I do believe he was, too, for a while.

'And he's very generous—he wants to give, all the time; he wants to shower you with stuff: you must have had that, too. Jewellery, clothes, all kinds of things. He loves doing that. He loves coming in and being Father Christmas, being a good fellow, and spreading good cheer and all the rest of it.

'Mind you, it's partly because he's guilty, because he's totally unable to be faithful. So he cheats, then he heaps presents on you because he feels guilty. But finally he gets bored. I mean, it's partly keeping ahead of the cops, and he has to do that, because I reckon they've got enough to put him away for a thousand years if they ever caught him. The drugs alone—I mean, hell.

'But it isn't only that: he just wants to keep moving on. The woman isn't born who can keep on satisfying him. He needs to be an impostor; he needs to have mystery and adventure and all the rest of it. You'll never find him, you know. He sheds everything—name, identity, everything. He's probably not even in Australia by now. He's got friends who make him a whole new set of papers and off he goes again.

'And listen, love, you're well rid of him. I know you love him, and I know you miss him, but you think about how he makes his money, and you ask yourself if you really want to profit from that. Do you know any heroin addicts? Well, I do, and let me tell you, it's not good, to be making your money out of poor lost souls like that. I've sometimes thought, if I had any principles, any real principles, I'd give it all away to a refuge and go and do work for addicts. But I guess I haven't got principles. Sometimes I think it's soiled money, I don't want any of it. But look, it's money, and it's there, and all the harm's been done already. So I keep it, and I live a comfortable life. And, after all, why shouldn't I? I suffered enough, when he left me. I deserve something.' She pauses. 'Heavens, I don't usually let go like that. I wasn't going to talk to you at all.'

'Why not?' I ask, almost humbly.

'I thought you might be a cop.'

'Me?' I start to laugh. It's funny: you can't get away from it. Imagine thinking I'm a cop.

She smiles. She really has got excellent teeth.

'That's better,' she says, encouragingly. 'Look at me. I've lived through it. I've got my life together. You can do it, too. It's amazing: at the time you think you'll never recover, but you do: believe me. You do. Are the cops pestering you?'

'Yes. A bit. There's one cop. He comes around a lot.'

She nods, recognising the scenario. 'That'll keep going for a while, probably. But look, Martin really is clever. They tried so hard to pin stuff onto me, but they never managed to. He didn't leave anything that connected me with anything he'd done. He will have done the same with you. He tied up all the ends: really, he was so careful. They made lots of threats; they hung around. Then they got bored and they moved on, went to nobble someone who was easier game. These days, I never hear from them. That'll happen to you, too, mark my words.'

I suppose it will; but of course I didn't give Max time to tie up all the ends. The impulse to confide has evaporated, now, and I'm in no danger of telling her anything else. There's one thing I want to ask, though.

'Was he unfaithful to you?' I enquire, trying to make it sound as if this is a normal question to ask someone you've just met. Heaven knows why I'm worried: the rest of the conversation hasn't exactly been normal.

'Oh, God, yes. All the time. He can't help it, you see. I just didn't realise.' She looks at me narrowly. 'You poor darling. You're still in love with him, aren't you?'

I nod. There doesn't seem a lot left to say. We actually kiss goodbye, after a brief and embarrassed hesitation.

'Did you have children?' I ask her at the door.

She shakes her head; her peachy face suddenly sags, slightly. 'I'm infertile,' she says, simply. 'And you? Did you have children?'

'Not with Max. From my first marriage, yes.'

'Hang onto them. Kids are worth more than men, any day.'

I suppose she's right. I think about this, on the way home, on the plane. I think about Meryl, and about Max, and about Martin. I see what she means, about his being an adventurer, about his liking to move on, to shed old identities and don new ones like coats.

It's like an old fairytale, in a way: the swineherd who's really a prince (or vice versa, come to that); the impostor who competes in arcane games and wins them, who appears from nowhere, whose real identity isn't known till the end of the story, who changes his shape, pushes his luck, inveigles his way into bed with the princess.

Well, Max was a good inveigler. And adventuring was the gift he gave Sophie: that makes more sense, now. I think, too, of what Meryl has told me about the drugs, the heroin. I still have such trouble thinking of this.

All the evidence to the contrary notwithstanding, I cannot think of Max as anything but kind. I remember the photographs of Kylie and her friends; still I cannot imagine Max as malevolent or even uncaring. I know he betrayed me and lied to me, but in fact he didn't leave me; I don't believe he would have left me. Really, my only reservation, the only big black cross against his name, is his sin with Kate.

And I blame Kate for that.

I stare out the window at the apparently endless red desert beneath, and wonder what will come next.

*

As it happens, to my surprise and relief, nothing much does come next.

Gradually, very gradually, I start to relax. There's a long period during which nothing really happens to disturb the even tenor of the way I've grittily carved out for myself. I don't mind this: a patch of boredom is hardly unwelcome. I go to work. I cut back to part-time.

Sophie grows; Liam is born and grows. We all get older. Dominic goes to university, leaves university, becomes a solicitor, makes a lot of money, has a succession of sophisticated untalkative girlfriends who all look down their noses at me.

Steve, rather to my surprise, fails to find a new partner. Even after Dominic leaves home to set up the first in a succession of glossy bachelor pads, Steve remains in the old family home. It's far too big for him on his own, but he says he likes it, likes pottering around.

He and I mellow, a little, towards each other, or at any rate we pretend we do. Zoë and Henry continue to live energetic lives devoted to teaching, good causes and annoying as many of the family as they can. We all continue to turn up at the obligatory family gatherings.

I turn fifty. I notice silver strands in my hair and an unattractively crêpey look to my neck. The years roll past. Suddenly, Sophie is twelve. *Twelve!* we all say to each other. *Fancy our Sophie being twelve!* as if we hadn't all known that this would happen, as if she hadn't had an eleventh birthday the previous year.

The Lost Dream continues to return from time to time, always painful, always dislocating, always forcing home Max's physical absence. Slowly it worsens. The bush is darker, the muttering louder, the path longer. The leaves still quiver above me, thin and sharp, but now they transform themselves into a thousand pale, silver knives: I know that if they drop they will split my flesh.

I drink, perhaps, a little more than I should, from time to time. At first, I listen always for the knock that will herald my exposure and the retribution that it seems to me, in my more depressed phases, might in the end be inevitable. But curiously, miraculously, he doesn't come. Gradually, I forget about Frank—or, at least, let him sink to the back of my mind.

It's hard to distinguish between days, weeks, months. At the beginning of these grey, flat years—in which Sophie is the only bright, distinctive feature, Sophie's voice the only voice to touch a responsive chord in me, Sophie's milestones the only events that matter—I still think about Max a lot.

I try not to think about him, of course, and by dint of keeping busy, and still working most days, and making monstrous efforts, I do in fact manage to disengage my life from Max's over-whelming absence, during the daytime at any rate. It's in the long, lonely evenings, during the sleepless nights, that Max's ghost and I chase each other wearily around the bleak arena of my memories. By the time Sophie is twelve, this happens less frequently.

The drinking, on the other hand, probably happens more frequently. I can't help it. It makes such a difference, to sit down with a brandy at the end of the day, to feel its warmth and vitality seeping through your tired, stringy veins. I always remember the night I nearly came to grief with Frank, when I nearly told him too much, because of that same inner glow; and I'm usually careful not to risk that. If I know people are coming, I don't touch it.

But people don't come very often.

*

And then, one night, Kate rings.

'Mum,' she says. 'Sophie and I thought we might come and see you. Now. Is that all right?'

It is around eight o'clock and there is a television program I was planning to watch. I pause. Something in Kate's voice—some tight, stretched quality that wasn't at all characteristic of her—alerts me to an incipient drama, a crisis of some kind.

'Right now?'

'Is that okay? You're not going out?'

'No. Kate, what—?'

'We'll be there soon,' she says, and hangs up.

They come in, hand in hand. Kate looks tense. Sophie has a tiny, nervous smile playing around her lips as if she deserves praise but doesn't expect it.

'Mum, Sophie's done something,' says Kate. 'It may not matter and it may matter: I don't know. But I thought she ought to come and tell you what she's done.'

'It can't be so bad,' I say, consolingly, not having the faintest clue what she's talking about. We all sit down.

'I had a visitor yesterday,' says Kate. 'His name is Frank Pritchard. I think I met him once, ages and ages ago, here. He was visiting you and he asked me to get in touch with him if I knew anything about Max. I've never forgotten it because I thought it was so weird. He asked me a number of questions. I think you need to know about this, Mum.'

If they wanted my attention, they've got it.

'Tell Gandie what you've been doing,' says Kate, turning to Sophie.

'I went to the police,' says Sophie.

It's so astonishing, so out of the blue, I can't begin to understand. At first I think I've misheard. It takes a while to fall into place.

268

'What for, honey?'

'I was trying to get Max back. I was trying to get him back for you, Gandie, because I knew you wanted him back.'

I can't say anything. All I can do is stare at Sophie in dismay. God only knows what I look like.

'Tell her everything,' says Kate. 'Tell it to her, the way you told it to me.'

Uncertainly, Sophie unveils the horror. It appears that she has been deeply moved by my suffering. For some time it has been apparent to her that I am, God help me, still *very much in love* with the absent Max. It turns out that Max has exercised more fascination over Sophie than either Kate or I had supposed.

She has always thought he has a lovely face. She has always thought how cool it would be if he were to return from whatever mysterious corner of the earth he inhabits, solitary and depressed, longing to return to Gandie. She has always thought he must be still *very much in love* with me, and that our reconciliation would be only a matter of his realising that, yes, in fact, I still care for him. This realisation would inevitably then lead to a reunion and to subsequent endless felicity for us both.

By the time we get to this point Sophie is starting to understand that this initiative of hers isn't going down well. Her smile is fading. She pauses and looks at Kate, who tells her to go on.

So. For some time Sophie has harboured this dream that it will be she—and only she—who plays the leading part in reuniting the riven pair, but she hasn't in fact seen how this can be accomplished.

And then she happens to watch a program on television about missing persons. This program makes it blessedly clear that the police are the right people to approach. For how can the police do anything constructive about tracing a missing person if they do not know that the said person is indeed missing? And I have told Sophie quite plainly—haven't I?—that Max is to all intents and purposes a missing person and that I have never instigated a search for him.

So she sallies forth, our Sophie, to the local cop shop. At first, nobody will take much notice: they treat her as if she's a little girl. Not wise, to put Sophie off like this. So she insists, and she gets a toe in the door, and eventually a junior cop—a constable, she thinks—takes her statement.

And, says Sophie, with a faint intonation of triumph, when she says the name of Max Knight, the constable sits up and starts to take an interest.

And, quite quickly really, only a week or so later, she's talking to this very nice man whose name is Mr Pritchard. He's very interested in what she has to say. Very sympathetic. At this point Sophie halts her narrative and shoots a scared glance at me. She's mostly been looking at the floor, until now.

What she sees in my face obviously doesn't reassure her. Her voice trails off and her gaze reverts to the floor.

'What in Christ's name did you tell Pritchard?' I ask. To my own ears my voice sounds harsh, croaky. Kate glances at me, startled.

It's not hard, to see how it's gone. Frank has clearly been on the ball, has enticed Sophie to chatter away artlessly about her beloved grandmother and her grandmother's perplexing missing spouse. I can imagine it so clearly: Sophie burbling away about the love story she has imagined with such enthusiasm, Frank nodding, smiling, encouraging. A query here, a prompt there. He's a personable-enough man, Frank: he wouldn't have had trouble enlisting Sophie's confidence.

Does her dear old grandmother think Max is dead? he asks.

Well, says Sophie; she's so sad about him: she thinks he'll never come back. Of course, he might be dead. But what if he isn't? she asks. What if the cops could find him, and present him to Gandie. Wouldn't she be surprised?

Well, she certainly would.

Christ, Christ, what have I told Sophie? I pull my brains apart trying to reconstruct our conversations.

And Sophie proceeds to remind me, falteringly: she visited me again, and we talked about Max again, the time she showed me the photo she found in her mother's drawer, and this time—*this* time—I told her—didn't I?—that Max was dead. Truly dead. In fact, so dead is Max that he lies in a grave I've visited.

Kate's eyes are on me.

And by this time, of course, Sophie has got the cops looking for a missing person, so she feels a bit guilty to have put them to all this trouble. She thinks she'd better head them off. So she goes back and she tells Pritchard. She tells Pritchard that Max is dead. She tells Pritchard that Gandie knows where Max is buried.

She is starting to snivel.

'Sophie,' I say, and I still don't recognise my voice. 'That was a secret. That was our secret. I told you not to tell anyone.'

Sophie responds that I really only told her not to tell her mother. And anyway, she figured I wouldn't want the police wasting their time.

Kate's eyes are wide and hard, and full of consternation and judgement.

'You're not cross, are you, Gandie?' says Sophie in a small voice.

'Jesus Christ,' I say, in this voice that isn't mine, that is coming from somewhere outside me. 'Jesus Christ, Sophie. You little cow. What have you done?'

Sophie flinches, shrinks into herself.

And suddenly Kate is up and at me. 'She meant well,' she cries, flailing her arms around ineffectually. 'She meant nothing but good. She did it out of love for you.'

I'm so livid, I can't think of anything to say.

'Don't be angry with her. She didn't mean to do anything wrong.'

'Sophie,' I say. 'Sophie, next time just…just…'

But of course this is an idiotic thing to say, since there won't be a next time. The damage is all done. Sophie glances up at me, her lips quivering. I stare at her and for the first time in my life I find myself regarding my granddaughter without love.

All I can think of is that she has stirred up old muck, long-ago sludge, from the bottom of my pond, that she has muddied the water that I had come to think of as clear and safe. I am no longer safe.

For so many years, I have worked patiently and carefully, constructing protection, devising masks and invisible cloaks and hideaways and shields and God knows what, all designed to maintain my security, and now, on a childish whim, on an ignorant and foolish caprice, she has jeopardised all my travail.

I can't bear it.

Sophie has now gone perfectly white and is staring at the floor. Kate is starting to cry. Trust Kate. She stands, wiping her nose.

'We'll go now, Mum,' she says. 'I wanted Sophie to tell you herself what she'd done and she's done that. I know this has been a shock to you, but I think she's been very brave, don't you?'

'Brave,' I say, hoarse with the absolute horror of it all. 'Brave. My God.'

Kate yanks Sophie to her feet.

'I'm sorry, Gandie.'

'Get out,' I shout. 'Just get out.'

They do. Kate pauses in the doorway.

'Are you at home tomorrow morning?' she asks.

'Why?'

I'm not trying to sound encouraging.

'We need to talk. I'll be over.'

And she is. We sit in my little kitchen and look at each other over the teapot.

'Mum,' says Kate. 'Please. You must tell me what happened to Max.'

'I don't know what you mean.'

'That man Sophie was put onto, that Pritchard man who visited me: he's the one I once found at your place, isn't he?'

I try to put her off, but she cuts over me.

'I know he's the same man. Don't snow me. It's important. You know it's important. Mum, we have to talk about this. Has that man been in touch with you? Since Sophie spoke to him, I mean.'

'No.'

'When did you last see him?'

'Years ago.'

'Do you think he'll come again?'

I try to laugh dryly, but it comes out as an odd rasping sort of noise.

'I should think so. After what Sophie's told him.'

'I don't understand any of this, Mum. Tell me about Max. Tell me what happened to him.'

'Nothing happened to him. We split.'

'But something did happen,' says Kate. 'You told Sophie he was dead. You told Sophie you'd seen his grave. You have to tell me. Pritchard's questioned me once already, and I'm sure he'll try again.'

'What did he ask you?'

'When I stopped living with you and Max. What my relationship was with him. Things like that.'

'What did you say?'

'What could I say? I told him. That is, I told him I stopped living with you when I got married; I told him Max and I got on fine. But it seems to me, Mum, there are things I don't know, and I need to know them if I'm to give the right answers.'

I say nothing.

'Anyway,' says Kate, 'I know something's happened to Max.'

'How can you be so sure? You don't know anything. You can't.'

'Yes, I can. I do know.'

'Why?'

'He's never contacted me,' says Kate, quietly. 'It's been twelve years since Sophie was born and he's never contacted me. I know he would have.'

'You know no such thing.'

'Yes, I do.'

We eye each other.

'Listen,' says Kate. 'The way I see it is this. You and Max quarrelled about me, and Sophie, and you split up. Then Max disappeared, and someone reported it, all those years ago, and that man Pritchard was looking for him. And now he's looking for him again.

'Aren't you surprised by how much interest they're taking in Sophie's story, Mum? She's just a kid. They wouldn't be taking this sort of interest if they didn't think something was seriously wrong. And that wasn't true, what you told me, was it? About

Max's business affairs, I mean? They weren't looking for him because of tax stuff, were they?'

'No. No, it wasn't tax. They were very interested in finding Max, and not because they thought he was just missing. There were big problems, Kate. Big problems.'

'Tell me,' she says.

Well. She's supposed to be an adult. She might as well know some of it, anyway. I tell her about the photos of Kylie and Lindy Lou, and about their obvious interpretation.

'I don't know what you're talking about,' says Kate, tears springing to her eyes. 'Max was a good man. He was a good man, a kind man. He wouldn't do something like that.'

I shrug.

'Perhaps they were children he was sponsoring. Third-world children, through one of those charity programs,' says Kate, desperately.

I tell her about the gun. I have to say I'm getting a perverse pleasure out of all this. My illusions were splintered to smithereens twelve years ago: why should hers be intact?

'A gun?' she whispers, her eyes wide.

'And then there was the heroin trading,' I say, brutally.

Kate can't say anything. She's looking at me in total horror. 'A drug dealer,' she murmurs to herself, as if I'm not there. 'Max is a *drug dealer*?'

I consider telling her about the wives, about Meryl, about the serial bigamy, but I don't. Is this due to some vestigial pride, I wonder? If I tell her Max was a born philanderer, it'll make her feel worse, but it'll also diminish my own relationship with him. I don't want to do that. I don't want to tell her that the soppy photographs taken after the ceremony on the beach signify nothing, nothing at all, that we were never married.

I can't bear to tell her that.

No, I can't bear that. But an odd thing is happening to me nevertheless. After all these years of silence, all these years when the only person I've ever discussed Max with has been Frank (if you don't count Meryl), it's as if there's a melt within me. I can practically feel the ice crack, the snow soften, the chill streams start to flow. And perhaps Kate knows already. Perhaps she's guessed what happened anyway.

But she is in deep shock. She certainly hadn't guessed anything of what had generated Max's copious funds.

'How long have you known all this?' she asks.

'All the time. Since then. Well, some of it only appeared gradually. Say, ten years.'

She shakes her head. 'Are you *sure* it's all true? Are you quite, quite sure there hasn't been some awful mistake?'

'Quite sure.'

Kate mulls it over.

'So where is he?' she asks, suddenly. 'Tell me, Mum.'

And the melt takes over. I tell her about that evening. I tell her about the meteor stone.

'It wasn't my fault,' I say. 'I didn't mean it to happen. It was an accident.'

Kate's eyes are fixed on my face as if there's some invisible mechanism hooking them there.

'You killed him?' Her voice is so faint, I can hardly hear it.

'I didn't mean to. It just happened. It wasn't my fault.'

'You threw the stone at him.'

There is that, of course. In simple terms, in terms of cause and effect, I suppose this is true.

'But I didn't mean to. I didn't mean it to happen.'

Kate's body contracts into itself, winces away from me.

Her eyes have doubled in size.

'Why are you looking at me like that?' I ask her.

'You can ask me that?'

'Kate, I've told you, it was a terrible accident. It must have been one chance in a thousand, one chance in a million even, that the stone would hit him like that, that he would fall like that. It wasn't something I meant to happen.'

'I left you with my baby. I let you look after my baby, and you had Max's blood on your hands.'

This is a foolishly melodramatic and unhelpful way of looking at things, besides being extremely hurtful, and I tell her just that. She doesn't seem to be listening.

'I knew something happened. I knew something must have happened. But this—but this! How can I bear it?'

Her hands are twisting, each kneading the other. Tears run down her cheeks. She makes a little moaning sound.

'Did you not guess at all?' I ask, curious. I've always wondered if someone had guessed. Someone in the family, I mean.

She shakes her head. She's still moaning in that slight, ineffectual way. 'How could I?' she asks. 'How could anyone imagine such a thing?'

'Kate,' I say, urgently, speared by a sudden and dreadful anxiety. 'You mustn't breathe a word.'

'Am I likely to? Am I likely to tell anyone this? Oh, my God.'

She's shaking, and rocking backwards and forwards.

I find myself wondering whether it's really so very bad. Of course (well, of *course*) I know murder's a bad thing. And I can see it must be a jolt for her. But it really was more a case of manslaughter than murder (this argument has over the years acquired amplified persuasive value, for me). And it isn't as if I meant to do it. It isn't as if it wasn't an accident. I suppose I've become over time so used to having killed Max, so used to the knowledge of my having killed him, that the act's moral edge has blunted somewhat for me. I can't help feeling Kate is slightly overreacting.

'What did you do with him?'

'What did I do?' I don't immediately understand what she means. I've just told her, haven't I? I killed him.

'With the…with the body?'

'It was when the swimming pool was being filled in,' I say, watching her to see how she'll take it. 'Remember? It was all dug out.'

'So…?'

'So I took the body out to the garden, at the back, and I hid it at the bottom of the hole where the pool had been. Among the rubble. Before they filled it in.'

'You carried it out? The body? You were able to carry it?'

'I used the furniture trolley.'

This circumstantial anecdote is almost too much for her.

'So Max—Max is buried in the back garden at Rain?'

'Yes.'

There is a long, long pause while she absorbs this.

'And now?' she says, finally. 'Will anything happen because of what Sophie did?'

'I would imagine so. I would imagine Pritchard will turn up again. At first he was just pestering me because he thought I knew where Max was; he thought I'd lead him to Max. But now he'll be smelling a rat. Oh, he'll be back: don't you worry. He'll be back. Everything was all right, Kate. I had everything all sorted, until Sophie went and wrecked it all.'

'Everything was all right? You murdered Max, and you're telling me everything was all right?'

278

'I didn't murder him,' I hiss at her. 'I keep telling you: it was an accident.'

She shakes her head again. Her eyes are fixed on some point on the floor, and she's hugging herself in a strange way. She doesn't stay for long, which I suppose is not surprising.

'I need to get used to this,' she says, her voice breaking. 'You've got to give me time.' She scurries out the door, dabbing her eyes, giving me a nervous sidelong glance as she goes, as if she thinks I'll take a swipe at her on the way. It's not out of the question.

Well, she was the one who wanted it. She was the one who wanted to come around and have a comprehensive talk about everything. It was her fault, anyway. Well, you could argue that it was her fault. None of it would have happened if she'd stayed out of my husband's bed.

And she's offered no sympathy at all. Nothing like: *Oh, Mum, how awful it must have been for you. Living with that, all these years.* Nothing like that.

I pull myself back, at that point. It might be a little much, to expect Kate to be sympathetic right away. It's been a shock for her, I can see that.

Still. Haven't I been brave, and lonely, too? Aren't I to be pitied?

For a couple of days, nothing happens. I worry about Sophie, but I'm still so angry with her that I think it's better to let the whole thing die down, to wait until I can be calmer about it, to wait until…Until what?

I realise that I've frightened her; I realise, too, that she did, as Kate says, mean well. I resolve to fix things up between us. But not yet. I can't do it yet.

All I can think of is the knock on the door.

It takes three days. And then, in the evening, it comes, and there he is.

'My God,' I say, trying to sound spontaneous and cheerful and innocent. 'Inspector Pritchard, as I live and breathe. Where have you sprung from, Frank?'

I've been thinking, thinking, thinking about this.

He grins, a bit foolishly. I've always thought Frank's foolish grin is a deliberate ploy. It's a good one. He indicates his shoulder and the stuff on it in a gesture which at first I don't understand.

'Superintendent, actually.'

'Wow,' I say, hoping it doesn't sound perfunctory.

And then, when we've got past the civilities and I'm pouring a cup of tea, he says: 'You're probably surprised to see me again?'

'Well. Not entirely. I think you've been talking to my daughter and my granddaughter, haven't you?'

I say this with the utmost composure. The stream of tea from the teapot's spout doesn't so much as quiver.

'Well,' says Frank. 'Your granddaughter's been talking to me.'

'She's such a romantic,' I say, brightly, offering Scotch fingers.

Frank is watching me. He's not going to make it easy. 'A romantic?'

'Goodness, yes. Couldn't you tell?'

'I'm not sure. She seemed a truthful child to me.'

He still has that rather ponderous way of speaking; still surveys his flat fingertips while he chooses his words. But then he looks up, and his eyes search me.

I try to look intelligent and unconcernedly interested.

Alert, not anxious.

'It seems Mr Knight is dead?'

'Ah,' I say, shaking my head in a manner that implies a world of unspoken stories, unexplored explanations.

'So Mr Knight's not dead?' asks Frank, politely.

'You're going to think this is a bit weird, Frank. I'm almost embarrassed to tell you.'

He chuckles, reassuringly. I almost expect him to lean over and pat my knee, so fatherly is he.

'Try me,' he says. 'You wouldn't believe the number of weird things I've heard in my time.'

'Well, Frank. Sophie's very romantic.'

'You said that, yes.'

'Kate and I—Kate's Sophie's mother, remember: you once met her here—Kate and I have been a bit worried, you see. Sophie has this tendency to fantasise, and lately she's been getting a bit fixated on Max.'

'Fixated?' says Frank, interested.

'Yes. Well, that might not be quite the right word. But for some reason she's been looking at old photographs, and poring over them, and it seems she's created quite a little story for herself, out of Max.'

'A story. Well, well. Kids!'

I take heart from this. 'Of course, Max was a handsome man.'

'A very handsome man,' says Frank, generously.

'And a bit of an adventurer, I suppose.'

'Indeed.' Frank's tone is dry.

'Well, from her point of view, I mean. Of course, she doesn't know the things you've told me. I can't tell her those. But it does seem as if she's been—well, romanticising him. Daydreaming. And Kate and I were both a bit worried about it.'

'Kate knows about her stepfather's—er—adventuring tendencies?'

Oh, nice one, Frank, I think.

'Oh, yes. Of course, I've told Kate what he was really like. What he was really doing.'

'Of course.'

'Anyway. So I thought, perhaps best to give the whole thing a smart knock on the head. Sophie had been carrying on, saying how he might come back, saying how she was sure we still loved each other. You know what teenage girls are like?'

'My word, yes,' says Frank.

'So—I suppose it sounds a bit silly, but honestly we were getting quite concerned—I told her he was dead. Just to put it all to rest, get it all out of her mind. And of course, it might well be true by now anyway.'

'And the grave…?'

'The grave?'

'Your granddaughter—nice little girl, isn't she?—she said you'd visited the grave.'

'Well. That was a bit of extra information designed to… um…make it all a bit more convincing.'

'Corroborative detail, intended to give artistic verisimilitude to an otherwise bald and unconvincing narrative?' suggests Frank, helpfully.

I'm not sure where Frank is coming from, with this. It rings a bell, but for the moment I can't quite place it and decide to ignore it.

'I guess so. The point is, we needed to find some strategy to divert her, to stop her carrying on. So we thought the best thing to do was just to say, well, he's gone.'

'Good thinking.' Then Frank pauses, apparently puzzled. 'Then why would you have told Sophie not to tell her mother? If you and she had cooked this up between you?'

It's my turn to look puzzled, concealing my anger and panic

as best I can. Why in God's name did Sophie have to pass on this sort of minutiae?

'I told her it was our secret, certainly. But not to tell Kate? No. Sophie's obviously got confused on that one.'

'Ah,' says Frank, pensive now. 'Such a smart-seeming kid, too.'

I try not to glare at him. 'Well, that's how it happened.' It does sound a bit lame.

Frank nods affably. 'And what do you think?'

I'm at a loss. Think? What am I supposed to be thinking?

'What I mean is, do you think Mr Knight really is dead?'

'Well, I guess we have to accept that it's certainly possible.'

'When we last spoke, you didn't think he was dead. In fact, you were sure he wasn't.'

'Years have passed, Frank.'

'During which something has happened to change your mind? I can accept that, but I'd like to know what.' His tone alters. 'Or perhaps you weren't telling the truth earlier? Perhaps you knew then that he was dead? Perhaps that's something you've known all along?'

This is suddenly more confrontational than I'm expecting. I keep my voice low, reasonable.

'Frank, it was years ago. I knew nothing then and I know nothing now. But, as time goes by—well, we have to think it's more likely, don't we?'

He is silent, and I think perhaps it's time to bring the battle right up to him.

'Frank,' I say, hurt. 'All those years ago, when you came to see me, when I kept telling you I didn't know where Max was and you wouldn't believe me—did you think then I'd had some-thing to do with his disappearing like that?' I pause, then I think it's safe, perhaps advisable, to say the unsayable, to approach the unapproachable. 'Did you think I'd *killed* Max?'

'Well, no, actually. We didn't think he was dead, you see. We were thinking, he's gone to ground, and sooner or later he'll pop his head up above the parapets, and then we'll nab him. But he never has, you see. And there was a rather large amount of money he could have got his hands on, without too much trouble at all, and he didn't. And there hasn't been one reliable sighting, here or overseas. Also, some items came to light.'

'Items?'

'Items from a suitcase.'

I'd always wondered about that suitcase. I do the baffled look.

'By the time we got to it, it had been gone through pretty thoroughly and I imagine some of the contents had gone missing. But a few remained, and one of them had Mr Knight's name on it. A medication, it was. But what it looked like to us, you see, was that Mr Knight was still manufacturing his own disappearance, perhaps with a little bit of help from you, not that he *actually* had disappeared.

'But it didn't make sense, you see. We had it from you that Mr Knight had taken his car, so we couldn't see what he'd be doing leaving a suitcase in a railway station locker. It didn't add up, not really. So at that stage, no, all I thought was that you knew where he was and you weren't talking. I wasn't even sure of that. We had nothing to go on. But I did notice, and I did make a note at the time, that you tended to talk of Mr Knight as if he were in the past. He *was*, not he *is*. He *did*, not he *does*. And I'm puzzled, Mrs Knight. Ms Weaving.'

'Isabel. You used to call me Isabel, Frank.'

'Isabel. I'm puzzled, Isabel. You see, I tend to believe that Mr

Knight is dead. I tend now to believe that he was dead even when we were looking for him, twelve or so years ago. And now— yes, now I think you knew he was dead. I'm not sure what was happening to you back then. I don't know whether you'd been blackmailed or bribed or bullied. Or none of the above. But I'd certainly like you to tell me.'

I stare at him with absolute blankness. It seems to me my responses here are really important. He's flying a kite, I can see that. He's doing his old thing of trying to unsettle me, catching me off guard. I don't want to give him even the faintest sniff of anything untoward.

It doesn't matter what he thinks or suspects or wonders about. What matters is that I don't open the door to him, that I don't open it even a crack, even a skerrick, that he remains entirely ignorant of all the goodies I'm hiding, the veritable treasure chest of what he would call relevant material. He can suspect and wonder all he likes, so long as he isn't certain, so long as he doesn't *know*.

On the whole, I don't think I handle it badly. I'm shocked and astonished and, yes, hurt; but mainly I'm just tired. It all happened so long ago.

'For Christ's sake, Frank. You're really scraping the bottom of the barrel, aren't you?' I say this wearily, heavily aware of his eyes resting on my face (they're small eyes, rather too close together: my mother would have said he wasn't to be trusted), affability forgotten, the bloodhound gene taking over, his body fairly trembling with alertness and suspicion and mistrust. I maintain my fatigue, my incredulity.

I've never been so pleased, to see the back of him. When he finally goes I'm limp with exhaustion and damp with sweat. I'd thought it was all over. I'd thought he'd lost interest, that I'd fought him off, that I could relax. But I'm right back in it again now. Thanks to Sophie, I can't stop worrying, not yet.

The knock—the final knock, I mean, the knock that tells me it's all over, red rover—is still out there somewhere, waiting to happen. It's like the iceberg, bobbing around in the Atlantic (well, really big icebergs probably don't bob; they probably just mooch along, heavy and full of destiny), patiently expecting the Titanic to happen. And then: *Wham!*

The next time I see Kate, I draw her aside.

'Pritchard's been,' I say.

'And?'

'And what?'

'Does he know?'

'He doesn't know. Not yet.'

'But he suspects? Because of Sophie, he suspects?'

'God knows what he suspects,' I say. 'He certainly thinks something odd has been happening.'

Kate looks unhappy, as well she might. I don't suppose anyone really wants their mother convicted of murder.

I couldn't bear to stay at home: I was too edgy. I went to a couple of movies, but that was hopeless as a strategy for self-distraction. I couldn't have told you what they were about, not even two minutes after I'd walked out of the cinema.

So I went to work. The arrangement I had with Bea was that I would work two days a week. She gave me a narrow look, one morning.

'This is the fourth time you've turned up this week, Izzie.'

'So?'

'The practice can't afford to pay you extra, you know that.'

This was manifestly untrue, in fact. Bea was making so much money she didn't know what to do with it all. I didn't care, though.

'I'm restless,' I said. 'You don't have to pay me. I'm happy to put in a few extra hours. That new job's got a couple of tricksy bits. I'm just ironing them out.'

She raised her eyebrows.

I wandered into my office and worked, sitting under the same skylight where I had sat when I first saw Max—how long ago? Nearly twenty years.

I doodled at my sketches for our latest project, a vast old mansion in the hills that someone with more money than sense wanted to convert into a health resort. I wanted to tell him to knock it all down and start from scratch. He was set on old-world charm and what he called art-deco flair. The place wasn't remotely influenced by art deco, and I'd tried to explain that to him, too, but eventually I'd given up: when a client doesn't want to hear something, it's no use telling them.

Inspiration wouldn't come. It was a huge, leaden manor with cold corridors, small windows, tiny attics and antiquated plumbing. Nothing would save it. I was running behind schedule on it, and starting to loathe the whole project. Bea agreed with me that it was hopeless, but pointed out that it was worth a heap to us. The incentive didn't seem enough, somehow.

There's a knock on my door. *Not here*, I think, suddenly panicking.

But it's only Kate.

'Hi,' she says, cheerily, presumably for Dawn's benefit. 'I was passing.'

'Hi,' I say.

She comes in, closes the door behind her, sits down. 'I was going to ring. Then I thought, might they be tapping your line?'

'I can't imagine they are,' I say, although in fact I have privately canvassed this possibility and concluded it is highly likely. 'Anyway, you could have rung my mobile.' I'd often thought how Max would have loved mobile phones—their convenience, their glitziness, their whizzbangery.

'They tap mobiles, too.'

'How do you know?'

'They do,' said Kate, definitively. 'Anyway, it doesn't matter if they are or they aren't: I just thought, we have to talk.'

'I don't see why.'

'Mum, I've got an idea.'

These are not words to fill me with confidence, not from Kate, but it's clear I'm not going to be able to stop her.

'I've been thinking,' she says. She has an odd look on her face. 'I've got a plan.'

And she tells me what it is.

'What I thought is this. I'll go to see Superintendent Pritchard.'

I stare at her. She's leaping right into the lion's mouth?

'It's a natural thing to do. I'm Sophie's mother, after all. I'm the mother of the child who has been telling him things, asking him to do things. We've talked already. I'll ring him up. I'll say I want to see him, want to talk some more.'

'But why?' I ask, dazed.

'You'll see.' She pauses, thinks. 'You may not like what I'm going to do. But it's the only thing I can see to do. I think it might work, so please, Mum, just consider it. Okay?'

I look at her, mutely. My mistrust is profound. First Sophie meddles in my affairs; now Kate. What in God's name is she hatching?

'So,' she says. 'I go to see Pritchard. I'll be rather cool, you know. I'll say, he should have contacted me earlier about Sophie. I'll say, I could have saved him a lot of trouble. Sophie is an emotional child and she's got a bee in her bonnet. I'll say, she's got the wrong end of the stick, and if he acts on anything she said, he'll find himself in trouble. Up the creek without a paddle. Chasing mares' teeth.'

'Mares' nests,' I say, automatically. 'Hens' teeth; mares' nests.' The thought of Kate thinking she can threaten Pritchard is making me physically ill, the bile rising in my throat.

'Whatever. So then he'll ask why. So I'll say, I don't really understand what his interest in my stepfather was, and you won't tell me. And he'll say, why not? And I'll say, there were reasons why you won't talk to me about Max. And he'll say, what are those reasons.' She pauses.

'Yes,' I say, swallowing. 'Go on.'

'So I'll tell him. I'll say, the reason my mother and Max split up was that Max was having an affair with me. And I'll say, he kept on having it. I'll say Max went to Sydney after you and he split up—I thought Sydney would be a good place to have him live, because it's so big, so crowded, you couldn't possibly prove someone hadn't been in Sydney—but I'll say he came down, every so often, to see me. I'll say this went on for around two years.

'And then I'll say he went overseas. I'll say, I've had postcards from Prague and Mexico. I thought Prague and Mexico would be good because they're a long way away and a long way apart. I'll say I last heard from Max maybe two, three years ago. And I'll say I don't have the postcards any more, because I didn't want my husband to see them.'

Kate pauses. She's twisting her fingers, knitting them unconsciously into the old game of church and steeple that she and I used to play together when she was tiny. *Open the doors and let out the people*, I nearly say.

'Do you see what I'm doing, Mum? It'll all work, you see. It'll explain for him why you never told him why Max left, because of course you didn't want to admit that he'd slept with your daughter. And it explains why Max left, too. And it makes him think Max kept on being alive long after he left you.'

She muses for a moment. 'And, the thing is, I think I can make him believe me. There'll be enough truth in the lies I'll be telling for me to pretend to myself it is real, that everything I'm saying has really happened. In point of fact, and you might as well know this, all I'll be doing is telling him a story I've told myself. When Max and you split up, I thought Max would come to see me. I was sure he would. I didn't think in a million years he'd go away without somehow coming to see me. Because he knew about Sophie, of course he did. Max wasn't stupid: Max would have taken one look at Sophie and he would have known. And we needed to talk about it, and I know we would have talked about it. But he never came.

'Now, of course, I know why not. But then I didn't know, I just thought, where's he gone? I thought, sooner or later, he's bound to come. And I kept imagining I'd open the door and there he'd be, and then, because, you know, you and he had broken up, we could...well. We could get together again. Just for a little while. And I kept imagining that he'd gone somewhere not very far away, and that he'd turn up. And everything would be the way it had been, could be. Well, that was the story I told myself. So if I tell this to Pritchard, I'll only be telling him what I wanted to happen, what I'd talked myself into believing was going to happen.' She breaks off, tiredly.

I sit in a trance and watch her hands. *Here's the church; here's the steeple.*

'I don't know what to say,' I eventually manage. But the rage flickering within me is going to tell me what to say, very soon.

290

I feel it grow. I let it grow.

'I think it might work, Mum. It might make you safe. I want it to make you safe.'

'You think he'll believe you?' I snap.

'I don't know. Yes, I think so. I think I can be very believable.'

'Kate,' I say, the tsunami inside me swelling, overflowing, rushing out of control. 'Kate, this would be the most...the most half-baked, idiotic, perverse, *stupid* thing to do. Can you not see that?'

She looks at me, sideways, clearly surprised. 'It'll prove Max was alive, after he was really dead. Why will that be stupid?'

'There is no reason in the world for Frank to believe any of this half-cocked crap. Can't you see? All he will think is that you and I are conspiring. All he will think is that I've been foolish enough to set you onto him, to spin him a story to make him believe Max is still alive. Can't you see how transparent it is, how ridiculous?'

She simply stares at me.

'You're a fool,' I say. 'Thank Christ you haven't done anything.' A dreadful suspicion smites me. 'You haven't, have you? You haven't done anything? You haven't spoken to him again?'

'No.' She has a blank look.

Can she really not comprehend? What right does she have to break the secret, the secret of her and Max, the secret she told me she'd never tell? Can she really think Frank will be such an idiot as to fall for a story like this, that she can maintain a defence against all his art and skill, his little levers and screws, his delicate chiselling and his slow, relentless assaults? And how dare she lay claim to Max? How dare she imply that his interest in her could have been anything other than a passing aberration?

291

'Thank God for that, anyway,' I snarl.

'But I want to save you, Mum. You're in danger, and I want to save you.'

'If I want to be saved, I'll let you know, thank you very much.'

'Is that all you can say?' Kate's voice breaks. 'Is that all you can say to me? I've planned this all for you. You mightn't like what I've thought of, but it might make you safe. I'm telling you, I'll perjure myself for you. I'll do anything for you. I only want to try to help you.'

'For God's sake, Kate,' I say. 'Fuck off, will you? Just fuck off. And mind your own business, you and Sophie both. Just stop meddling. Leave me alone.'

Tears stream down her cheeks. 'Ever since I can remember,' she sobs. 'Ever since—oh, God, what does it matter? I've always wanted...'

She can't go on, and it looks as if I won't ever know what it is she always wanted. My anger against her balloons. I cannot bear the thought that she could even consider telling Frank about her and Max, about her and Max in bed together. I can't bear to imagine Frank sitting at my kitchen table, his eyes meeting mine, the knowledge of Kate and Max, of what Kate and Max did, shared between us. The thought of Frank's sympathy, his genial commiseration, is intolerable.

Kate's sobs increase, multiply. People will hear. Dawn will hear, and anyone else who's around. I remember that Bea has an important meeting with clients in her office this afternoon. I look at Kate helplessly. I go over to her, pat her shoulder. I find my hand grasped with a ferocious strength. She pulls me down to her and hugs me wildly, hysterically. It's very uncomfortable, and I try gently to disengage myself. Irritated beyond enduring, I make soothing noises, glancing at the door and hoping Bea can't hear. Dawn probably can, out in reception.

'I'm so sorry.' She weeps into my shoulder. 'I'm so sorry, to get it all wrong.'

Gradually, she quietens. She looks terrible. I'm still livid with her, but I suppose I can try to get over it. I pat her some more, trying to quash my fury and despair. What more can she expect of me?

She grabs my box of tissues and blows her nose noisily, several times. She stands, regards me with an unreadable look on her face.

'I love you so much, Mum,' she says. And is gone.

Part Five

The telephone rings just after three o'clock in the morning. My heart leaps from its normal position and rattles against my throat as I reach out of bed for the handset. I expect Frank, Frank ringing me in the middle of the night, ready to catch me adrift, to trap me. Instead, I hear Henry. 'Isabel?'

'Henry,' I mumble, blurrily cross as I surface from sleep. Here I am, badly frightened, thinking everything is over, that Frank is ringing me to say he knows it all, no use going on, and it's only Henry. What the hell is he ringing for?

His voice shakes. 'I've got bad news, dear.'

Henry's never called me dear in his life. Suddenly I'm bolt awake.

'It's Zoë.' He stops, choking.

'Yes, Henry,' I say, keeping my voice steady. An accident, I think. She's hurt, that's all. A car accident, maybe. She can't be dead. Not Zoë, not my sturdy, vigorous sister. 'Tell me, Henry. Tell me.'

'Dead.'

'How?' I ask, transfixed.

'Heart attack. Acute myocardial infarction.' It's so Henry, to add that.

'But *how*? I don't understand. Was she ill? Was there no warning? What happened? What in God's name happened?'

'It was out of the blue.' He sounds apologetic, as if he has been uncharacteristically careless. 'No warning. None at all.'

'When, Henry? Where? Where are you ringing from?'

'I'm at home.'

I picture him, alone in his study, in his big, faded, brown corduroy chair.

'What happened?'

'I don't know,' Henry says, suddenly sounding old and exhausted and confused, and with odd pauses. 'I don't know, Isabel. We went to...bed as usual. She got up, went to...the bathroom. I heard her cry out. She was...on the floor.'

And that was it. She had lost consciousness even before he'd reached her. He rang the ambulance. He said they had arrived rapidly—not more than five minutes. But she was dead.

It is strange that Henry and I should have this bond, this powerful link of finding our spouses dead on the floor. It's different for him, of course: he didn't put her there. Well, I presume he didn't. I briefly contemplate the possibility of explaining the irony to him, but decide against it. He's not going to appreciate this.

My mind's in overdrive. I don't know why this happens to me, why this feverishness grips me in a crisis, why it crowds out my grief, my shock. Already I'm thinking, when will the funeral be? Has he told anyone else yet? Ought I to go over? I'm even wondering what I'll wear to the funeral. My brain's manufacturing thoughts to prevent it from thinking the things it doesn't want to confront. That must be what's happening. I try to concentrate.

'Would you like me to come over, Henry?'

'No,' he says, to my huge relief. 'No, there's no point.'

'Are you all right?'

He says he is. We exchange a couple of bleak remarks, promise to be in touch the next day, hang up.

It's so hard to imagine a world without Zoë. I lie in bed and think about it. I can't sleep, so I get up and make myself a cup of tea. For once, I don't feel like a drink: I'm not sure why not. Borrow pads after me and regards me sorrowfully.

I try to cry. I actually do squeeze out a tear or two. What am I feeling? It's hard to say. I'm surprised, certainly. I recall Zoë's stocky figure, her positive stride, her firm, strong voice, her annoying way of articulating words very clearly in case the person to whom she was speaking was mildly retarded. Well, that's how it sounded. She didn't look like a candidate for a heart attack. What has Henry been thinking of? How has he allowed this to happen?

I manage not to ask him these questions when he rings me the following day. I still feel stunned, trapped in the ice in some frozen hinterland where the full realisation of Zoë's death is withheld from me. Soon I will comprehend it and cope with it.

'We're all getting together to talk about the funeral, Isabel,' says Henry, sounding weary. 'Would you like to come over?'

Who's *we*, I wonder? Henry's an only child; he and Zoë are childless; all our parents are dead. I suppose Zoë had friends who want a say in it all. I don't like Zoë's friends, most of whom are authoritarian women who have spent their lives bellowing in classrooms, and Henry doesn't sound as if he especially wants me there anyway. I excuse myself and ask him to keep me in touch.

'You don't want to speak?' he asks, surprise inflecting his voice.

'At the funeral? God, no.'

'Are you sure, Isabel?'

I tell him I am sure.

I hate funerals. In fact I remember once saying this to Zoë, who replied sarcastically that there was nothing special about me; nobody actually enjoyed funerals.

I think she was wrong. I think some people do enjoy funerals. They remind us, after all, that we're still alive, a condition not applicable to the person at the centre of the occasion. I've been to lots of funerals now, and I've often observed a kind of avid relief rampant in the congregation, an ungodly solace perhaps derived from outliving the deceased and perhaps from finally being able to speak frankly of him or her with impunity.

When we marry we take on other people's families, their births and deaths and traumas, their scandals and skeletons. This is a fact that certainly hadn't revealed itself to me when I skipped so smugly down the aisle to Steve, awaiting me with a goofy look on his square face.

It started to become clear when we'd been married only a year or so. An elderly aunt of his died and I discovered to my alarm that Steve and his entire family confidently expected my attendance at her farewell. I'd never been to a funeral. It sounds silly: I was twenty-one, after all. I suppose I had remained unusually untouched by death. Two grandparents had died during my childhood, but nobody had expected me to go to their funerals. I didn't think funerals were my business. I panicked at the thought of this one.

'I didn't even know her,' I said to Steve. 'I only ever met her once. Why do I have to go?'

He had that pained expression I was starting even then to

resent so sharply.

'She was my aunt, lovely. Of course we have to go. We both have to go.'

'But I didn't *know* her,' I wailed, despairing of making him see reason. 'Can't you say I've got morning sickness?' Already I was pregnant with Kate. 'It wouldn't be a lie.'

I was not certain why my response was so negative. Normally I did what Steve asked me to do: I regarded docility as one of the wifely panoply of virtues to which I aspired. But this time my alarm was disproportionate: I passionately did not want to be a strand of the tapestry of this dead woman's life; I did not want to be caught up in a grief that was none of my business, a loss that I had never felt.

'It wouldn't be true either,' said Steve. 'You're over the morning sickness, lovely: you know you are.'

I could not withstand his obduracy. So he hauled me off to his Aunt Bessie's funeral, where, ironically, I did indeed feel nauseous, although this was (as he pointed out) probably because of the heat of the day and the closeness inside the church, rather than because of my pregnancy. I hated it all but I was morbidly fascinated by it, too.

And I understand now what I didn't then, that in marrying him I assumed for him (as he did for me) afflictions and encumbrances such as illnesses and deaths and funerals, that marriages entail families and joining in what families do. When we marry, we share lives; we learn customs; we adopt relations; we inherit deaths.

Except marriage to Max, of course—or at least what passed for marriage to Max. Max had no family: no mother to terrorise me (as Steve's had), no father to glance appreciatively up my legs and down my cleavage (as Steve's had), no sister to patronise me (as Steve's had). No family at all.

*

And so I go to my sister's funeral. It is a typical Melbourne day—cool, bleak, grey, with the occasional perverse flash of sunshine disrupting the dismal threat of drizzle.

I sit in the funeral chapel, front pew (membership of the deceased's family offers me these privileges), and gaze at the coffin, which undertakers always insist in calling a casket. (I note that these undertakers wear brass badges on their lapels that identify them as *bereavement consultants*, whatever that might mean.)

The coffin is bright and smart and snazzy and rather too ornate, its decorated brass handles gleaming and its dark mahogany veneer polished to the clean, brilliant gloss of a new mirror. She would have thought it tacky: Zoë had taste, after all, and she wouldn't have liked the tawdry dazzle of the brass, the fussy curlicues on the handles, the insufficiently solid look the whole thing somehow has. It is so narrow, it is hard to believe Zoë's robust figure is contained within.

The taped music is Vivaldi, and seems too sprightly for the occasion. I don't think Zoë had any particular affection for (or indeed knowledge of) Vivaldi, and presume this choice is Henry's flight of fancy. Zoë was a Mahler person, a Wagner person. The Valkyries might have farewelled her, or the Meistersingers, not Vivaldi.

Henry is out in the foyer, looking solemn and burdened, thanking people for coming. Who knows? Probably he does indeed feel burdened; perhaps he is genuinely grateful.

I remember the last time I sat in a church for a ceremony at which Zoë was a central participant. It was her wedding, some thirty years ago. A little more than thirty years. Well, I hadn't much enjoyed that, either.

302

I find myself glancing around, every so often, to the back of the church. I pretend to myself that I'm doing this out of interest in who will attend. But it's Frank who's on my mind, Frank's shadow I expect to see lurking at the back, sliding behind the door, treading up the aisle in that measured, weighty way he has.

The Vivaldi finishes and the service begins. It is quiet and unexceptional. Henry (always technically proficient, as becomes a science teacher) speaks with the accompaniment of a powerpoint screening that shows photographs of Zoë at various stages of her life. Zoë as a baby, toddler, schoolgirl, teenager, debutante, graduate, bride, daughter, sister, wife, aunt, teacher. All the roles of her life, neatly clipped out and presented. I am in some of them, especially the early ones. I feel oddly uncomfortable about this, and find myself thinking that Henry should have asked me if I minded. I don't like it, being on show in this way: it's one thing in a family living room or a photograph album, quite another in a funeral chapel with a coffin next to one.

Here we are, Zoë and me, neatly attired in our school uniform, our hair freshly combed, standing awkwardly together, holding hands (a thing we never normally did, as I recall). Here we are sitting on our father's knee, too old to be doing so comfortably, displaying forced grins. Here is Zoë in a long dress, going to her first ball. Here she is marrying Henry in his silly tie, looking for once as if she mildly likes him. Here she is being aunty, holding Kate as a newborn. There she is, in her coffin; here I am, in my pew. It is bothersome.

My thoughts stray as Henry speaks. I cannot believe Zoë has died: I am cross with her for doing so. She is—was—only five years older than I am, and it seems to me she had no business relinquishing her spirit so easily, with so little warning to the rest of us, so little fight.

I know they say the grief issuing from bereavement takes you inexorably through several stages, of which anger is one. This isn't like that, though: it isn't profound, burning anger, but exasperation, much as I might feel if we were playing Scrabble and I knew she wasn't trying. It worries me that I cannot tap any deeper feeling than this for my sister. I have not grieved for Zoë, any more than I grieved for my mother. Can it be that I do not feel grief? Surely I loved her. She was crabby and annoying and difficult, but surely I did love her?

Why can't I *feel*?

Henry is saying something about Zoë always having wanted children of her own, about her being a fond aunt, about the fondness deriving partially from her own dashed hopes, her profound disappointment at her own barrenness.

I don't think this is true. I don't think Zoë wanted children at all; and Henry certainly didn't: it would have up-ended their neat lives, their organised lists, their careful careers, their complex diaries, their tidy house.

She never forgot the children's birthdays, I'll give her that. But she was perfectly happy, it seems to me, to remain an aunt, to forgo all the messiness and indignity and turmoil of motherhood, retaining an arm's-length intimacy, a burdenless responsibility, an affectionate distance.

I am annoyed by Henry's easy assumption that Zoë's child-lessness was cause for sorrow or sympathy, and I stop listening for a while.

I try to put Frank out of my mind, but it's an effort. He's starting to hover in the pew directly behind me, his flat capable fingers about to descend vice-like on my shoulder.

Deliberately I turn to repel him and find myself gazing into the reproachful eyes of a mousy-looking woman I've never seen before in my life, who presumably is an ex-colleague, or an ex-student, or somehow a beneficiary of my sister's efficient and intrusive habits. I turn back again.

I can never go to a funeral without visualising my own. I don't know if everybody does this: I suppose it's egotistical and perhaps irreverent. But I can't help it. While Henry speaks, reading in his finicky tones from a piece of paper that he has obviously prepared with meticulous care on his computer, I can't help reflecting that there will be no husband to speak at my funeral.

Not that husbands or wives usually do speak, anyway; Henry has already made reference to this and said that he feels this is something he needs to do; he feels for some reason I cannot understand that he will not have bidden Zoë goodbye unless he does so formally, publicly. He looks tired, but his voice doesn't shake and he seems to have himself well under control.

I never did think they were very fond of each other. I wouldn't want a husband who could get up and say a few pernickety, dry-eyed words about me when I died.

But if Steve won't speak at my funeral—and Max certainly can't—who will? Who will be left? Will Kate say anything? Will Dominic? Will they care? What will they say? I steal a look at Dominic, sitting in the front pew on the other side of the chapel, next to his sister. He is on his own: Paula hasn't come. Steve has: he is sitting in the same pew as Kate, further down. Sophie is there, in her school uniform, on Kate's other side. Kate told me she wanted to come; so did Liam, but she sent Liam to school as usual, because she thought he wasn't old enough. She's probably right.

Well, Sophie's twelve. She's old enough to know people die; people go away for good. She is sniffling quietly into a tissue. She knows I'm here, but hasn't looked over at me. She's still upset with

305

me after our last meeting.

Kate is upset, too, but she and I have achieved our precarious semi-reconciliation. I can tell nothing from Dominic's expression. Is this something he felt he had to come to? It meant time away from the office, after all, time stolen from the all-important things he has to do that crowd in on him and prevent him from having a proper lunch. He is soberly suited, eyes cast down. Was he impelled by a sense of propriety? Did he care much about Zoë? Does he care much about anybody?

Just as I look across, I see Kate lean towards him, whispering something; he leans back, nods, smiles. He puts his hand on Kate's for a second.

Let's replay that.

He puts his hand on Kate's hand. I feel the shock of it quiver through me. This is Dominic: Dominic the isolate, the ascetic, the austere loner; Dominic who hates to be touched, who doesn't kiss, doesn't hug, doesn't do any of those vaguely social things people expect of one. And here he is, touching his sister. Unbidden, evidently in compassion and—well, yes, love.

Why are they all sitting over there, anyway? Why are they sitting with their father? I'm more bereaved than he is: she was my sister, after all. Steve didn't even like Zoë very much.

I can't recall the last time Dominic willingly touched me, let me touch him. Probably during his toilet training.

I find myself thinking about the apparent closeness with his sister that Dominic has just manifested. Will she talk with him, I wonder, uneasily. Will she tell him any of the things she now knows? Dominic is a lawyer. Not a criminal lawyer, but a lawyer just the same. He probably has strong views about people who kill people, whether they do so inadvertently or not.

Suddenly I feel immensely vulnerable because of Kate's

knowledge. I wish I'd never told her anything. I don't think she'd deliberately betray me: it's not that she's untrustworthy in that way. But she's such a fool, such a hopeless idiot, she might easily say something to incriminate me without meaning to.

There goes that shadow again, behind me, Frank's shadow, the quick blurred movement of Frank's hand about to grip my shoulder. For a moment, I tense.

Will Kate come and visit me if I go to prison? Probably, I think. Will Dominic? Much less certain, I imagine.

Perhaps, though, Dominic might be nicer to me. If I went to prison, I mean. Surely he'd be a bit sorry for me?

My attention is drawn momentarily by something Henry is saying about Zoë being warm and generous, somebody young people could easily relate to, somebody her pupils readily confided in. I'd as soon confide in a death adder, I think; and then I feel ashamed of myself.

Seriously, what will happen at my funeral? Will anybody even come? Will anybody bother? What music will they choose? I don't want Vivaldi. But what do I want? And how will they know what I want?

Now Henry is saying something about Kate.

And, suddenly, Kate is standing, going pink and blotchy around the cheeks, as might have been expected, holding a piece of paper in her hand. She is making her way to the microphone.

Nobody told me Kate was going to speak. Henry asked me if I wanted to; he didn't say a word about Kate doing so. I didn't want to. I don't know most of these people: they are Zoë's friends, Zoë's professional acquaintances, Zoë's ex-students.

I've met some of them, but they have nothing to do with me. Why should I open my heart to them and speak to them about my dead sister? I don't know what I'd say, in any case. I don't know what's in my heart: it's closed, even to me.

But Henry mentioned nothing about Kate speaking. What on earth will she say? Kate and Zoë weren't a bit close. Is she going to make a fool of herself? She hates doing things like this: Steve and I used to have terrible trouble with her whenever some kind of performance was demanded of her at school. There's nothing Kate hates more than standing up in front of a crowd of people.

And it's really very crowded, not just full but spilling over, and mainly with people I've never seen in my life. Ex-students? I can't think of a teacher whose funeral I would willingly have gone to, but I imagine they are ex-students: they're mainly pretty young. Why on earth is Kate doing this? Why is she exposing herself like this?

When Henry said *we* like that, did he mean him and Kate and Steve and Dominic?

Well, Kate got on reasonably well with her, I know. Zoë made an effort: she was not acerbic with Kate as she was with me. She did not positively hound Kate, or criticise her, or flay her. But surely they weren't close.

Kate looks dreadful. The pink blotches make her resemble a plague carrier; she's been crying and the flesh around her eyes is soft and swollen; she's ill at ease, shifting from one foot to the other. I feel a trifle cross with Henry. Why is he forcing her to go through this?

Kate starts to speak. 'My aunt Zoë was a very special person,' she informs her audience, in faltering tones.

Well. Here's originality.

'Dominic and I always used to like it when we were little and Aunt Zoë visited,' Kate confides to the chapel at large.

It's another of the irritating things she does: *Aunt* Zoë; *Uncle*

Henry. It infantilises her. They were always taught to call their relatives by their Christian names, none of this circuitous aunting and uncling. Sophie and Liam call their uncle plain *Dominic*. Well, Sophie does. I can't recall what Liam says, in fact. And I certainly don't recall my children jumping up and down for joy when Zoë happened to drop by, which she did infrequently.

Kate continues, feet shuffling, blotches flaring, looking as if she's about to fall over. 'Whenever Aunt Zoë came, she'd always talk to us as if we were real people.'

And when did anyone not, I wonder?

'What I mean is, she wouldn't talk to us as if we were kids. She wouldn't talk down to us. And she'd tell us what she thought. She wouldn't be soft on us. I remember once I didn't do well at school in something, and everyone else was inclined to say, oh, well, never mind, and Aunt Zoë said to me: "Kate, you can do better than that. What went wrong?" And I had to think about it, and I had to come up with what I thought went wrong, and she said: "Well, next time, you'll know what to do, won't you?" And I did.

'Dominic and I used to think she would be the most fabulous teacher, and I can see'—she looks up, smiling faintly—'I can see, from the numbers of you here today who must have been her students, you all must remember her as the most inspiring teacher imaginable. She was always very honest, that's what I valued most about Aunt Zoë.

'She was very direct, and she told you exactly what she thought, and you always knew you could trust her. And she knew we trusted her, and we knew she loved us. I hope she knew that we loved her. Goodbye, Aunty Zoë. We'll always remember you, and we'll always love you.'

Kate sniffles once more, casts a desperate apologetic look at

Henry, and goes to sit down again while an approving kind of sugary murmur creeps across the chapel.

I remain still. I become aware that I am sitting stiffly, my muscles at full stretch, and it occurs to me that my face may look stiff, too. I arrange it in order to minimise its stiffness, its amazement, its pure steaming rage at my daughter's soppy sentimentalising, her distortions, her craven fibs.

Zoë may well have felt affection, to some extent, for my children, but she had no capacity to interact with them—or with other people's children—spontaneously. This is something I recognise since I, too, suffer from it; but I did better than she did, with my own children anyway. I suppose she may have been a spectacularly good teacher of adolescents (though I must say I doubt it); but she did not have the gift for speaking with small children; she was unable to address them save through a bracing interrogative style under which Kate (little as she seems to recall it) positively wilted. Her directness wasn't because she was honest; it was because she was undiplomatic and insensitive.

Steve and I used to joke about it. *Your bloody sergeant major of a sister*, he used to call her. Involuntarily I glance over in Steve's direction and see that he is nodding and smiling encouragingly at Kate, who is still dabbing at her eyes.

Yes, indeed: I remember Stalinist cross-examinations like that which Kate has just described so winningly: *Well, Minky, why did you do that? You can do better than that, Minky. What went wrong? How can you do better next time?* On it would roll, deadly as a puffball fish, inescapable as a guided missile. Caught in her sights, one could only shuffle in agony. And, invariably, to finish, in a despairing wail, as if you were the most moronic person on the face of the earth: *What were you thinking, Minky?*

But none of this had anything to do with self-improvement,

310

with doing better next time, with strengthening oneself or one's relationship with Zoë. It was only to pander to her ego, to foster in Zoë the entirely erroneous impression that she was necessary to one's development. It didn't issue from love or warmth. It issued from a paranoid need to dominate, to intimidate, to prove how indispensable she was, in short to bully.

I feel like jumping up and shouting all this to the assembled snivelling congregation. Then I see to my horror that Dominic is approaching the lectern. What the hell is he going to say?

He doesn't say much, as it turns out; but what he does say is to the point. Dominic has, as I know, a gift for this sort of thing. He doesn't allow himself to be overcome by Kate's brand of sentimentalism; he speaks crisply, without fuss.

How handsome he is!

He tells a couple of mildly funny stories; subtly he intimates that it would be foolish to deny that Zoë could be a difficult person. Well, a bit of a character, anyway. I start to relax.

Then he says: 'Zoë was a remarkable aunt, and a no less remarkable sister. It is not possible to conclude this tribute to her, to her energy and compassion and her sheer zest for life, without referring to her relationship with my mother, to whom she was devoted.'

My rage is swelling again. Why is Dominic doing this to me?

'For Zoë,' he continues, 'Isabel's welfare was always paramount. When Isabel was born, Zoë's delight knew no bounds. Zoë would have done anything at all for her little sister. She adored her as a baby, a toddler, a child and as a woman. Nowhere did Zoë's exceptional generosity of spirit show itself more clearly than in her love for my mother, who wishes to join with us in this tribute to her greatly beloved big sister.'

I glare at Dominic, who pretends that he does not notice, and will not meet my eyes. He says one or two more things, to which I do not listen, and steps down.

How dare he? I am thinking, the question pounding through my head with the force of an elephant stampede. I am so furious that I can sense the urgent particular throb of the blood in my temples. I am so furious that I could strangle Dominic.

Why should he have done this? Why impose upon me a wish I do not feel, a love I do not acknowledge, an obligation I deny? And, if he was going to say anything of the kind, why should he have made it sound as if the generosity was all on her side? It wasn't easy to be loved by Zoë, to be perpetually battered by her powerful zeal and her strident self-righteousness. What about *my* generosity of spirit? Why doesn't that rate a mention?

I am only dimly aware of the rest of the service, but sooner than I expect I find to my relief that it is over and the front pews are dispersing.

I am surprised, when I turn around, to see how full the church now is. Again I think I see Frank at the far corner of my peripheral vision; it turns out to be some innocent person with no great resemblance to Frank on any count. We all file out into the uncertain weather, where a few cold drops are starting to fall, and two or three people whom I distantly remember approach me and say trite and hypocritical things about what a shock it is and how much we are all going to miss Zoë.

Speak for yourself, I feel like saying, but do not. I excuse myself as soon as I decently can, and look for Dominic; but he is caught up with other groups and I can dimly sense by now that it's not going to be a good idea to stalk up to him and demand an immediate explanation.

A private cremation follows the service. I consider absenting myself, but in the end I decide to be generous and I go. Kate (who hasn't asked my advice on this matter) brings Sophie, who is too young for such a thing, and I am infuriated by her insensitivity.

I buttonhole Dominic at the end of it, as we trail towards our cars.

'Why did you say that?' I ask. 'About me, about me wanting to join in the tribute.'

He looks down at me. It's annoying, that he's so much taller than I am.

'I did ring you about it,' he says, sounding bored. 'You weren't home, or at any rate you didn't answer, and I thought I could surely assume you'd want one of us to say something. Henry said you didn't want to speak. I presumed you were too distraught to do so.' (He draws out the word 'distraught', accentuates it, makes of it an insult.)

It is probably true that he rang. I often ignore the telephone, especially if I've been drinking. But it is no excuse.

'I gave you no permission to say anything on my behalf.'

'Isabel, I'm trying to explain that it wasn't up to you. Henry wanted you to be included. He knew Zoë would have wanted you included, somehow, and so it was important that this was in fact achieved. Kate and I discussed it. The most significant thing appeared to us to be that Henry have the sort of ceremony he wanted, the sort he thought Zoë would want. That's all there is to it.'

'You should have asked me.'

He shrugs and starts to move away. 'I'm sorry you should feel like that. I must say, I don't see what the fuss is about.'

So cold, so formal! If only he had put his arm around my shoulder, given me a squeeze, said: *Hey, Mum, c'mon.* If only he would come halfway to meet me, only condescend to give the faintest impression—just sometimes—that he cares about me. I'd melt in a moment. I'd be so loving.

I turn on my heel and stride to my car. It's hard to stride in the black patent high heels I'm wearing, but I manage it pretty well. Out of the corner of my eye I catch the expression on his face as I move away. It's quite blank.

It's that blankness, I think, that finally pierces my armour, triggers the reaction I turn out (to my surprise) to have been suppressing all along.

As I drive home I think about Dominic's blank face, about Dominic's refusal ever to engage with me, to talk with me, to love me. It comes to me that the blankness will last forever, that it will never be replaced by concern or responsiveness or even friendliness. My only son will stare blankly at my face for the rest of his life. He will never love me. I discover that tears are slipping down my face, slowly at first and then faster and wetter and heavier until I can scarcely see the road, the traffic.

By the time I get home my face is smeared with mascara and snot and my sobs are out of control, causing me to shake violently. Somehow I park my car and I stumble inside my house where I weep and weep and weep. I weep for my son, for the relationship I will never have with him. I weep for my love, who lies dead because I killed him. I weep for my sister, whose absence I suddenly feel like a cavernous and painful rupture in my heart. I weep for my lostness, for my aloneness, for the final disappearance of hope from my wilted life.

Later that evening I sit alone, sipping my brandy. I wonder wearily what Frank is doing; in some sense I realise that I am waiting for Frank, that now I am always waiting for Frank. I feel exhausted, depressed, betrayed beyond all bearing.

Who has betrayed me? I don't know, but I am sure it is the sourness of betrayal on my tongue, the flat acrid taste of the disappointment betrayal brings, a taste like wine gone bad.

I also feel guilty. It is my fault that Max has never had a funeral, never been farewelled, celebrated, squabbled over. Max has had no decorous grave, no purifying flame, no sober headstone. Nobody has played Vivaldi for him; nobody has shown photographs of his childhood to an appreciative and tearful congregation; nobody has delivered a eulogy. There he lies, or what's left of him, in a hole of rubble. Does he know, I wonder? Does he care?

As always, the brandy helps. It dulls the edge of the pain. I know it dulls the edge of thought, too, but there is nobody now to care whether my thoughts are muddled or not. Its consoling warmth is miraculous; miraculous, too, the steadiness and ease with which it seeps through my body. It comforts and pillows me; it insulates me from my own loneliness.

And still I am listening for the knock on the door, the knock of a man who will tell me that he knows what I am guilty of, a man who will neither compromise nor negotiate, who will arrest me and deprive me of everything.

Perhaps Borrow will die before I have to desert him. He is an old dog. He creaks; he totters, a little, especially on the left rear leg, where he had the operation a few years ago. His eyes are clouded. He'll die, soon: he'll die, selfishly, and leave me all alone.

And Sophie will grow and become different, and—perhaps, probably, certainly—love me less. Already I have alienated her. For God's sake, I think, I've snapped at her *once*—after years of love and devotion and gentleness and constancy. But that one lapse was enough: already, her disengagement has clearly started.

As we both grow older, I suppose I shall have to try to retrieve the relationship. I'm not certain that's possible. I'm still angry with her. I have the right to be angry with her. As she grows into adulthood, as she becomes a mother herself, it seems inevitable that we will drift from each other. It requires so much energy to remain close with people, to have quarrels with them and forgive them and reconcile with them.

Maintaining relationships is like maintaining cars: you have to keep servicing them, repairing parts, mending tyres, polishing and replacing and tightening. Not enough people care about their relationship with me. Not enough people love me, or love me enough. Nobody wants to polish up the screws, the nuts, the bolts. Nobody cares about making sure the components are tight enough, making sure everything's in working condition.

Maintaining bodies is problematic, too, of course. My own body is starting to give way. I'm only in my mid-fifties, but I can feel it through me, the grim loosening, the start of the slow vicious collapse. I grow old. Nothing is left for me but growing older. I'll mutter, when I'm old, like a witch, and my great-grand-children will be frightened of me, especially if I'm in prison. And it's quite likely that that's where I'll be.

I'll grow hairs on my chin. My body will weaken and creak, its bones slowly corroding, disintegrating until they snap like celery, and my mind will fray and crumble like old lace. And then I will be dead, too. All quite deadybones.

Surely, surely, I have deserved better than this. Haven't I?